RETURN TO CANYON CREEK

BOOK
THREE

JOHN LAYNE

Return to Canyon Creek
A Luxton Danner Western, book three
© 2025 John Layne

Second Edition 2025

eBook ISBN:	978-1-956856-60-6
Paperback ISBN:	978-1-956856-61-3

Library of Congress Control Number: 2024925952

Published by *thewordverve* (www.thewordverve.com)
Canton, GA

Cover and print interior design by Robin Krauss
www.bookformatters.com
eBook design by thewordverve

— For my mother, Rita —

CHAPTER 1

Saturday 6, July 1878

GILFORD KNOX – CIRCLE X RANCH

Gilford Knox read over the letter he received from his father. Dated June 1, 1878, the message outlined the ongoing negotiations between several railroad companies that planned expansion across the western frontier, including Texas. A highly respected and wealthy businessman in Washington, DC, Horace Knox was privy to most of Washington's politics and business. Bankrolling his son and sending him to North Texas ahead of the western railroad expansion was a well-conceived plan that was about to take shape.

A trained military man with a striking command presence, Gilford Knox had never married, not wanting the distractions a wife and children brought with them. He carefully studied the Texas Range map, always impeccably dressed in a suit and a fine silver bolo tie. His successful purchase of the KC Ranch from Sam Coleman was an excellent start to his plans, but he needed the parcels that Coleman sold off before the KC purchase. According to his father's communication, the Texas and Pacific Railway Company had bought Southern Pacific and completed a rail line to Fort Worth. There were rumors that the Texas and Pacific were negotiating with the International and

Great Northern Company to connect rail lines north of Oneida near Canyon Creek, then proceed west. If those rumors were true, Knox needed all three ranches that Coleman had sold.

Knox further examined the topography of the North Texas panhandle region. The easiest path to completion would run right through the land currently owned by Virgil Robertson, Carl Kincaid, and Dale Morgan. Following the trail further north, Knox figured the territory between Canyon Creek and the town of Thornton would also significantly increase in value, even if not directly used to extend the railway. Knox leaned back in his wingback bull-hide chair and gazed out the front window of his office. He smiled at the revelation that his purchase of the KC Ranch was better than he and his father imagined. Now, Canyon Creek needed to expand. It needed to become a town that everyone knew. That would easily convince the railroad companies to purchase his property and establish a railhead at Canyon Creek. He had already begun purchasing businesses in Canyon Creek and accelerated the building of his new companies. Convincing the ranchers would take a different approach—a far more forceful one. Knox lit a cigar. The thick purple smoke billowed from the fiery end, forming a cloud. He stepped onto the front porch and saw one of his wranglers working a horse in a nearby round pen. He whistled, drawing the attention of the wrangler.

"Yes, sir, Mr. Knox," the wrangler called to his boss.

"Find Colbert and tell him I want to see him right away," Knox demanded before returning to his office.

Knox thought about his three primary adversaries. Virgil Robertson would be the easiest to push out. He was nothing more than a farmer and had to worry about a wife and three daughters. Kincaid would be a more formidable opponent. He was younger and had a gunslinger for a foreman. Dale Morgan wouldn't be a pushover either. He didn't know Morgan very well but knew he would put up more of a fight than Robertson. He'd save Morgan for last unless something unexpected changed his plans. The pounding of boot heels on the plank-wood floor disrupted Knox's thoughts. He set his cigar on the lip of a large glass ashtray and waited for his top gunhand.

"You called for me, sir?" Erwin Colbert asked before removing his hat and standing at attention in front of the boss's desk.

Erwin Colbert was a tall, sinewy man with long, black, greasy hair and an uneven gunpowder burn on the right side of his ruddy face, thanks to a prior misfire from his rifle as a cheap hired gun and cattle rustler.

"Yes. I've decided to up the ante for the Robertson, Kincaid, and Morgan land. I'll need it sooner than later. They've all refused the previous offers I've made. It's time to tell them they would be better off somewhere else. You know what I mean, Colbert?"

Colbert smiled, showing what few tobacco-stained teeth he had left in his mouth. He instinctively reached down and grasped the handle of his pistol.

"I believe I do, sir."

"We'll start with the Robertsons. Take a couple of men over there tomorrow night and run their herd off. Scatter 'em as best you can. Run a few over to our pasture. Just harassment right now. I don't want any killing yet. That'll bring the law around, and I don't need that kind of a problem."

"What about Kincaid and Morgan? You want us to hit all three at the same time?" Colbert asked.

"We'll wait a bit for them. They'll be more of a challenge. We'll probably have to kill them both if they don't agree to sell. Robertson first, then we'll take on Kincaid and his foreman,

Cox. I need to learn more about Morgan before moving on to his place. After he sees what happens to Robertson and Kincaid, he may be more open to selling."

"Yes, sir," Colbert answered, then began to turn and leave.

"Colbert, take a couple of unrecognizable new men. And make sure you're not recognized. I want this to look like rustlers," Knox ordered.

"Yes, sir. You can count on me."

Knox retrieved his cigar and puffed while he scanned the map again. He committed most of the map to memory, but he wanted to take note of the rivers and creeks. After a few seconds, he rolled the map into a tight cylinder and placed it under his desk.

Well, Virgil Robertson, we're about to see what you're made of. Knox rolled the fat cigar between his fingers.

CHAPTER 2

Sunday, 7 July 1878

VIRGIL ROBERTSON & SHELLEY ROBERTSON – ROBERTSON RANCH

The four riders leaned back in their saddles, scanning the crowded pasture below. The full moon's burnt-orange hue, propped behind the riders, confirmed another sweltering day would follow a night of nefarious exploits. At half past midnight, the oppressive heat already took its toll on horse and man. Each mount billowed snorts of opposition while beads of sweat stung the riders' eyes and cracked lips. The men impatiently waited for the last light in the Robertson ranch house to flicker out. On an illicit mission to run off Virgil Robertson's herd, the rustlers received orders that this was a harassment raid; thus, there'd be no killing. For now, the boss wanted the four hundred acres of pasture and its water access, not dead neighbors. After another impatient twenty minutes, the flame of the last lantern faded into darkness.

Erwin Colbert, an unsavory saddle tramp and hired gun, waved to his three cohorts before spurring his horse down the shallow incline toward the 450 or so bullocks milling about in Robertson's main pasture. The orders were simple: wait until the ranch house was dark, quickly scatter the herd in as many directions as possible, then hightail it out of there before any of the Robertsons started shooting.

Colbert headed around the right flank of the herd while the others took positions on the left and middle of the stoic group. Once in place, Colbert drew his pistol. *Crack!* A single shot began the chaos, followed by yips and yells from the four brigands. *Crack! Crack! Crack!* All four rustlers fired into the night's dense humid air, sending their horses into a charging force. The gunfire echoes sent cattle thundering in every direction, reminiscent of ants fleeing their jolted nest. Colbert kept his right flank of cattle pushing toward the west while the others moved the rest outward into the moonlit night. *Crack! Crack!* More gunfire sent the stampede rolling off the Robertson land.

Virgil Robertson rolled out of bed, clutching his Colt pistol. Dashing through the house with bare feet and a tattered nightshirt, he crashed headfirst through the front door, his .45 poised and ready for action. The heat-soaked auburn moon wasn't lighting up the pasture with its customary bright light, limiting his vision. All he saw were shadows of his remaining herd and a couple of riders on horseback disappearing over the north ridge. He eased the hammer back down on his pistol and slumped onto the weather-beaten top step of the porch.

Shelley Robertson rushed through the front door behind her father, cocked Winchester in hand. The eldest of three daughters, twenty-three-year-old Shelley was a crack shot with both rifle and pistol, not afraid to use either. Clad in a long white nightshirt that danced against her slender ankles, she took a seat next to her father, propped the Winchester against her right leg, and looked out toward the barren pasture. "You know who's responsible for this," she sneered through clenched teeth.

"We don't know for sure," her father half-heartedly answered, sounding out of breath and defeated.

"The hell we don't!" Shelley shouted, her voice echoing off the barn into the still night air.

"Michelle Robertson! Don't you use that kind of language in this house!" her mother bellowed from the doorway, much to the delight of Shelley's two younger sisters giggling at their mother's feet in their wrinkled white nightshirts dulled from too many washboard visits. "You two get back to bed! Nothing left here to see!" Madeleine Robertson called down at her young daughters. Both girls obediently hurried back to their room without a word.

"Maybe we can find a few in the morning," Shelley offered as encouragement to her father, keeping her sights on the north ridgeline.

Virgil patted his daughter's knee and nodded. "Maybe," he said before slowly standing and returning to the house for what would be a futile attempt at getting some desperately needed sleep.

Shelley didn't move, and her father knew better than to order or suggest she return to bed. His eldest daughter had become a fine woman who had taken it upon herself to be the son he never had. She was a better shot than most men and could ride and rope with the best wranglers around. Choosing a close-fit bib shirt, riding pants, and vest instead of the print dresses and prairie skirts ladies of her age preferred, she hadn't yet found a young man willing to take on such a woman. At twenty-three, when most women were married and had children, she remained with her parents, working hard to make her father's modest ranch a success. At 300 acres, they had quickly built a nice-size herd in the year since her father purchased it with the proceeds of his small sugar cane farm in Louisiana. Now, because of its water source on Coldwater Creek, it had become precious to the more prominent surrounding ranchers, particularly Gilford Knox and his 4,500-acre Circle X Ranch bordering on their western edge.

Having purchased Sam Coleman's KC spread a year earlier, the wealthy, ambitious Knox had been pursuing the purchase of nearby land with intimidation and strong-arm tactics available to men with wealth and the power that comes with it. Employing rowdy cowboys to work his herds and gunfighters to protect his assets, Knox had successfully pushed many of the nearby landholders out with so-called offers they couldn't refuse or amounts of money poor men wouldn't turn down. Virgil Robertson and Carl Kincaid were two stubborn holdouts. Kincaid's 400 acres abutted Robertson's on the north side. Their properties bordered Coldwater Creek on the east. Relying heavily on the season's rains, it delivered water to the surrounding grassland and the large cattle herds. Although no one could legally blame Knox for the recent rustling of the smaller ranchers' herds, Shelley and a few others around Canyon Creek believed Knox was behind the harassment.

The first-born Robertson daughter laid her Winchester across her lap and leaned forward, closing her eyes. The night had become eerily quiet after the unwanted guests had fled. She listened hard, hoping to catch the sound of a lonesome cow's call. Nothing. Not a cow, owl, or coyote. Just the faint buzzing of a passing insect flushed from its nighttime grass den. She opened her eyes and stared at the Winchester. *You'd better hope I don't find out it was you, Gilford Knox.* And she surrendered to the need for sleep. After all, it would be a busy day when she woke in a few hours.

CHAPTER 3

Sunday, 7 July 1878

VIRGIL ROBERTSON & SHELLEY ROBERTSON – KINCAID RANCH

A bright yellow sun replaced the solemn moon's glow and ignited an onslaught of sweltering heat despite the early morning hour. Virgil and Shelley were already in the saddle, making their way toward Carl Kincaid's ranch, looking for remnants of last night's raid. Virgil hoped his spooked animals would flee to the nearest herd, then settle down. Although Gilford Knox's land spread all around Robertson's and Kincaid's ranches, Kincaid's place was the closest. Retrieving his cattle from Kincaid was no problem, but if Shelley was right, and he believed she was, encroaching onto Knox's property would be far more precarious. Thus far, they'd quickly rounded up fourteen head that hadn't entirely made it off the pasture. After pushing those back toward the house, father and daughter moved quickly onto Kincaid land, where they had checked dozens of cows, all burned with the Kincaid brand. Up ahead, a lone rider, tall in the saddle, was heading their way at a steady trot.

"Dad, looks like Mr. Cox is coming to talk," Shelley announced to her preoccupied father.

Clay Cox had been with Carl Kincaid since the end of the war. In his late forties, with close-cropped gray hair, a narrow face, and a muscular build, he was known to be as good with a gun as he was managing cattle. He shared Shelley's belief that Knox was behind the raids and rustling that had plagued Canyon Creek's small ranchers for the past few months.

"Good mornin', Virgil, Shelley. What y'all doin' over this way so early?" Cox asked in his Deep South pleasant manner as he reined his horse to a stop.

"Morning, Clay," Virgil greeted his neighbor's top hand.

"That damned Knox ran off our herd last night!" Shelley exclaimed.

"Shelley, please," her father begged, taking his hat off and mopping a dirty red bandana on his tired face already gleaming with sweat.

Cox's face darkened, his eyes narrowing above a sharp frown centered amid a whisker-clad square jaw.

"What happened?"

"Some riders showed up around half past midnight shootin' and hollerin'. Put the herd into a stampede. By the time I got out there, they were running all over the place."

"Get a look at any of them?" Cox asked, leaning forward on his saddle horn.

"Didn't have to, Mr. Cox. It was Knox's men. I'm sure of it," Shelley said between a tight-lipped expression.

"Now, Shelley, we don't know that fer certain," Virgil offered.

"Why is it, then, that Knox never complains about his herd being run off?" Shelley asked.

"Shelley has a point, Virgil. I'm inclined to agree with her. Knox has the most to lose, yet he doesn't seem bothered much, outside spoutin' off in town once in a while. I reckon that's just for show," Cox offered.

"I know, I know. I reckon I just don't want to believe it. With Knox's power, we really could use him on our side," Virgil explained.

"It's that power that separates him from the rest of us," Cox said, glancing west toward the Circle X.

"That foreman of his, Erwin Colbert, is nothing but an outlaw. Everybody knows it," Shelley continued.

Cox gave a faint grin and nodded. "He does have a bit of a reputation. I know he was part of a land war further south. Rumor is that's why Knox hired him."

"Maybe we should hire a gun of our own then," Virgil said.

"I don't need no one gunning for me!" Shelley declared, slapping her Colt Lightning.

"Ain't no cows or land worth you gettin' killed for Shelley!"

"Your paw is right, Shelley. Knox has a dozen or so men, all professionals. None of them give a damn about anything but earning their pay."

"I've kept back a little money. Think I'll ride over and talk to Carl and see if he's willing to hire a few guards," Virgil said.

"Go on ahead, Virgil. I'll join Shelley, round up any of your strays that mingled with the herd, and drive them back to yer place."

Virgil nodded, then snapped his reins and headed toward the Kincaid house.

Cox and Shelley watched him for a moment before Cox spoke up. "I've never seen your father look so defeated," Cox said in a deep voice.

"Nope. He was a confident man when he was farming sugar cane back home. He probably should've never left, but he and Ma agreed to come to Texas and give ranching a try. They figured there was more money in cattle, so he invested in that."

"Yep, more money and more risk. Just like a Louisiana gambler," Cox answered with a chuckle.

Shelley smiled. She dug the soles of her boots into the stirrups and sat straight up.

"We gonna chat all morning or look for our stock?" she asked with a laugh.

"Yes, ma'am! Let's go!" Cox shouted, tapping his spurs and heading toward the herd assembled down in the bottom pasture.

⬥

Virgil pulled up on the reins and stopped at the expansive front porch of Kincaid's massive log house. Filling a full half acre with rotund beams supporting lesser-sized timbers, it was home to Carl, his wife Anne, and two young sons. It was one of the finest places in Randall County. Virgil dismounted and tethered his horse to the hitching post. Before his boot hit the first step, Kincaid stepped through the front screen door. His six-foot-two muscled frame cast a younger look than his forty-seven years, mainly since his bald head had already shed what gray hair he had in his younger years. The touch of gray on his unshaven face lent a clue. "Hello, Virgil. What brings you out this morning?"

"Good morning, Carl. Me and Shelley have been out looking for my herd that got run off last night."

After their cordial handshake, Kincaid rubbed a worn, calloused hand over his unshaven chin and looked at Virgil. "Again? What the hell happened this time?" Kincaid asked, waving Virgil toward a couple of pine ladderback rocking chairs on the porch.

"They got almost all of them this time, Carl. They ran them off just past midnight. It was quick. By the time I got out there, they were headin' over the ridge. It looked to be four or five rustlers. I didn't see who they were. I found a few cows left in the south pasture. I figure the rest of the herd is scattered all over yours and Knox's land."

"Well, you know you're welcome to gather any from my place, but going onto Knox land may not be too smart."

"I know, thank you. Clay and Shelley are already out lookin' to cut ours out of your herd. Both Shelley and Clay think Knox is behind these raids. I tend to agree, I guess. I figured he had enough land, but I hear different. You?"

"Knox wants every piece of dirt he can get his hands on. It looks like he's racing the JA Ranch for first place. Adair and Goodnight are staking claim to most of the good raw land near Palo Duro Canyon. They got the money to back it—paying fair price or more. Knox has money, but he's bought land all over the county and more out of it. The old KC was a good start, but he wants those like us to get out of his way. I hear he's up to Thornton now buying folks out. It seems you, me, and the Morgan place are the only ones stopping him from owning everything from here to Canyon Creek. It looks like we're a burr under his saddle," Kincaid said with a glint in his gray eyes and the flash of a sarcastic grin.

"Carl, I can't lose my place. I've invested darn near everything I've got into it. I was wonderin' if you'd join me in hirin' a few guards to watch our places until fall when we can sell the herds. I know Dale Morgan doesn't have a family to worry about and already has a couple of men working for him, but maybe he'll join in if he knows you and me is."

Kincaid removed his hat, displaying a smooth round sweat-shined head where hair used to flourish, and paused to ponder the suggestion. Virgil stayed silent, knowing he needed both Kincaid and Morgan to join him if his idea was going to work. The radiant heat choked out the fresh morning breeze. Flies and bees quickly became buzzing pests in the still air.

"As you know, I was here before Sam Coleman decided to sell out and move east. Before you arrived, we had a fine lawman in Canyon Creek by the name of Ben Chance. Rustlers killed Joel Thornton, and Ben joined up with a couple of gunslingers to track his killers. Although Ben was killed, one of the men was a federal marshal named Danner. Marshal Danner brought word of Chance's death back to Canyon Creek. In particular, the owner of the Sundown Hotel, Rachel Brennen. You see, Mrs. Brennen was a widow and sweet on Ben. Anyhow, the word is that Mrs. Brennen wrote a letter to Marshal Danner asking for help. It seems the business owners in town aren't too pleased with Knox building his hotel, store, and brothel at the end of town. Townsfolk say he's tarnishing the town. Could it be the suggestion of hiring a few gunhands has already been made? I think you, me, and Morgan need to take a ride into town and have a talk with Mrs. Brennen," Kincaid proposed.

"I'd heard about Thornton and Ben Chance's ride up to Six Shot. I didn't know all that, though. The girls haven't been to town in a while. Seems like a good time to pay a visit and see what Knox is up to."

"Very well. Let's ride over to Morgan's place. If I know Morgan, he'll be jumping to join us. One thing, Virgil, this business could get ugly. Make sure Madeleine knows what's at stake."

"And Anne?"

"Clay and I saw this coming. I've already had this talk with her. She can handle it," Kincaid advised.

"I better head back to the house and speak with Madeleine.

Shelley already wants to charge over to Knox's like a bull steer in heat, but Madeleine will need some convincing," Virgil stated flatly.

"All right. How about we see Morgan after you speak to Madeleine, then we'll meet for dinner at the Sundown in a few days. We can see Mrs. Brennen then."

"Yep. I'll let you know. Might be tomorrow or the next day," Virgil said, rising from his chair with a stroke of confidence he lacked when he arrived.

Kincaid stood with his hands on his hips and watched his neighbor ride away. *I don't know what kind of trouble you saw in the sugarcane fields, but I fear you're about to get into something you ain't ready for.*

CHAPTER 4

Sunday, 7 July 1878

ROBERTSON FAMILY – ROBERTSON RANCH

The sun settled behind the western horizon, stripping what limited light dusk had to offer into the black darkness of night. The crescent moon provided little more than the dim outline of the Robertson house. Virgil brought the wagon to a halt next to the front porch, where Shelley jumped down and took the reins from her father. Madeleine carefully stepped down from the wagon, then helped her two young daughters to the ground before they clamored up the steps and into the house. Virgil lifted a large basket of supplies off the back of the wagon and followed his wife and young daughters into the house. He set the basket down next to the table and lit the large candle in the middle of the kitchen table. The candle's soft light spread a warm glow throughout the kitchen. Madeleine began to unload the basket of baked goods Anne Kincaid gave her after their supper at the Kincaid ranch. Virgil slid his boots off and lit the stove.

"Coffee?" Madeleine asked in between filling the cupboard.

"Please," Virgil answered in a low voice.

Shelley stepped through the front door and stamped her boots on the frayed braided rug for such business. She removed her boots and placed them neatly next to the door before hanging her gun belt on a nail next to the front window. She then joined her parents in the kitchen.

"Shelley, do you have to hang that gun right next to the window?" her mother asked.

"Don't worry, Mother, I'll take it to my room before I go to bed," Shelley said. "What are we going to do now, Dad?" Shelley asked before taking a seat across the table from her father.

"Yes, dear, I'd like to know too," Madeleine added while setting three cups of hot coffee on the table, then taking a seat next to her husband.

Virgil stayed silent for a few moments, rubbing his weathered hand across the smooth surface of the table. Virgil took a sip of hot black coffee and set the cup down in front of him.

"This tastes especially good tonight," he announced with a slight grin.

Madeleine gently placed her hand on her husband's arm. "We're in danger, aren't we?" she asked.

Virgil let out a long sigh and looked at his wife. "I'm afraid so, especially if Marshal Danner doesn't come."

"If that bastard Knox or his men—"

"Michelle Denise Robertson! I've told you not to speak like that in this house!" her mother demanded.

"Your mother's right, Shelley. That kind of talk won't help us."

"Maybe not, but—"

"I don't know what we can do if Knox's men come here. There's only the two of us, and you know I'm not very good with a gun," Virgil interrupted his impetuous daughter. "That's why I want to hire a man or two."

"But we'll have to use our entire savings for that," Madeleine interjected.

"Look, Maddie, if we don't protect our herd until the fall,

then there won't be any money left anyway. Defending the ranch is a do-or-die situation," Virgil announced, loudly rapping his knuckles on the table.

"Virgil, I know selling the farm back home and coming here was mostly my idea, but I think we should just sell everything to Mr. Knox and go back to Louisiana," Madeleine suggested.

"What? Go back to growing sugar cane?"

"I believe that's the smartest and certainly the safest thing to do," Madeleine said.

"Well, I can't argue with it being the safest thing to do. I'm just a farmer trying his hand at cattle raising, but I've never turned tail and ran when things got rough," Virgil declared before taking another sip of his coffee.

Crack! A bullet shattered the kitchen window, then splintered the wall across the room. Madeleine screamed as Virgil slapped his hand down onto the burning candle, extinguishing its flame and light. Shelley jumped from her chair and bolted to the front window, grabbing her Colt Lightning from its holster before disappearing through the doorway.

"Shelley! No!" her father yelled, following her onto the porch where he saw her crouching at the corner of the house, gun in hand. He hurried to her side and peeked around the corner. The moonlight lit the landscape just enough to see the shadows of two men on horseback fading into the distance.

"Sons a bitches," Shelley mumbled loud enough for her father to hear.

Virgil patted his daughter on the shoulder when a flash of pain shot through his right hand. He realized he had burned his palm, trying to douse the candlelight. "Ouch," Virgil yelled, snapping his hand back toward his chest.

"What is it? Are you hit?" Shelley asked, looking up at her father.

"No, no. I just burned my hand on that damn candle, is all," Virgil answered, shaking his hand rapidly. "Let's get back into the house."

Virgil closed the thick wooden front door and dropped the cross timber into its steel brackets while Shelley pulled the kitchen window curtains closed, covering the broken window. Virgil found Madeleine on the bedroom floor, clutching a young daughter under each arm. "It's all right. Y'all can come out now. They're gone."

"Could you see who it was?" Madeleine asked.

"I reckon we don't have to. I'm sure it was two of Knox's men. Just trying to scare us is all."

"They did more than that, Virgil. That does it. I want you to see Knox in the morning and tell him we'll sell. I'm not risking the lives of my family for this Texas dirt!"

"I'm sorry, dear, but I'm not letting him or anyone else get away with shooting at my family. No. Tomorrow morning I'm going into town and hiring a gunfighter," Virgil stated.

"But Virgil!" Madeleine shouted.

"No. I've made up my mind. I'm not giving up my land. Not like this!"

Madeleine's face darkened with a deep frown. She slammed her fists into her hips. She looked at her husband, then Shelley, who had tucked her pistol inside the front of her trousers and was standing stoic with her arms folded defiantly across her chest.

"Fine! I'll sleep with my babies tonight!" Madeleine said.

The matriarch of the Robertson family then clutched her young daughters by their shoulders and guided them back into their bedroom before slamming the door shut.

Virgil looked at Shelley. "That didn't go very well, did it?"

Shelley just smiled and slowly shook her head no.

Virgil nodded in agreement with his gunslinging daughter, then headed for his bedroom. "Put the candle out before you turn in, please," Virgil asked without a glance or response.

CHAPTER 5

Sunday, 7 July 1878

LUXTON DANNER – ATOKA

The booming explosion of the shotgun blast rang like stampeding cattle hooves inside the saloon. Danner dove behind the bar, landing on shards of broken whiskey bottles. The razor-sharp edges sliced into the palms of his massive hands. Prone on his stomach, his face just above the wet roughhewn floor planks, the stench of cheap whiskey and warm beer stung his nostrils nearly as badly as the booze seeping into his shredded palms. *Crack! Crack! Crack!* Bullets blew up the front of the bar, one piercing the thick wood and puncturing a beer barrel behind his boots. He pushed himself to his knees and crawled toward the far end of his wooden barricade pulling both Schofield Russian .45s with bloody hands.

"No way outta here, Marshal! It looks like we're the boss now!" Milt Longwood boasted from across the vacated saloon.

"I told you, Longwood, I ain't a marshal anymore!" Danner shouted, trying to convince the horse-thief fugitive.

"Once a marshal, always a marshal. Just another name for a bounty hunter far as I'm concerned, Danner!"

Boom! Another shotgun blast obliterated a shelf above Danner, raining splintered wood down on his hat-less head. The shotgun's blast reverberated everywhere, including inside his ears, preventing him from gauging his adversary's location. Milt Longwood was a well-known horse and cattle thief who had managed to elude the US Marshals for the past two years. His slippery escapes from detection had earned him a fashionable reputation among the villains seeking refuge from justice in the Indian Territory. Danner had no idea who the louse with Longwood was, but if he was hanging with Milt Longwood, he was probably a wanted man himself. Danner listened hard as the ringing of the shotgun dissipated inside his ears. He could hear boot soles grinding against the dirty floor across the room to his left. The swinging doors dangled from rusted hinges after everybody ran out at the sound of Longwood's first wild shot.

Usually, being outnumbered two to one didn't put a crimp in Danner's confidence, but this arrangement had him at a disadvantage. Danner wished he had listened to the voice in his head two hours earlier that told him to ride on and leave the hellhole town of Atoka behind him. All he wanted was a beer and maybe a card game if one looked inviting.

The Choctaw Indians had settled the town of Atoka a decade or so before the Civil War. It had grown steadily after the Battle of Middle Boggy Depot in 1864 and the arrival of the Missouri-Kansas-Texas railway in 1872. Because of its location deep inside the Indian Territory, it remained a lawless frontier town and haven for fugitives on the run from the law, including Longwood and his jackass partner.

"Look, Longwood, I don't have a badge anymore. I can't arrest you two. Why don't you both just move on? No hard feelings!" Danner offered, gaining some time to decide his next move.

"No chance, Marshal! No need for us to move along! You're the one in a mess here, not us!"

Crack! Crack! Boom! Bullets and buckshot popped all

around Danner. He slid back away from the end of the bar. Scattered glass fragments pierced his knees.

Wait until he fires that damn shotgun again. He'll have to break it open to reload. Danner pulled back on the hammers of his pistols.

Boom! The second blast from the big bore shook the old saloon's walls.

Danner bolted up and fired both pistols in the direction of the last shot. His .45s exploded into the tabletop Longwood's jackass partner used as a feeble shield. Two bullets penetrated the rustic wood and sent Longwood's partner onto his back, shotgun falling harmlessly to his side. *Crack!* Longwood's shot missed, smashing more glasses behind Danner's head. *Crack! Crack! Crack!* Danner fired at the fugitive who'd misjudged the protection the narrow ceiling pole provided. One bullet ripped Longwood's right shoulder and another his left, causing him to drop his gun and stumble backward. Danner stepped toward the wounded horse thief with both pistols cocked and ready.

"You wouldn't shoot an unarmed wounded man, would ya, Marshal?" Longwood whined, both arms hanging at his sides.

"Why not? You'd shoot me double-quick if you had the chance. Besides, last I heard, you were wanted dead or alive, and I don't have to please Judge Parker anymore," Danner said, taking another step toward the cowering fugitive.

Longwood dropped to his knees. "I can't raise my hands," he said in pain.

Danner heard the doors of the saloon slowly open and the sound of footsteps behind him. He kept his steel blue-eyed glare on his attacker and didn't flinch.

"You're a lucky man today, Longwood. I'd just a soon kill you and collect the bounty, then wait for a marshal to come through. But, I figure I'll wait for a marshal," Danner announced as much for the people behind him as for Longwood. He lowered the hammers on his pistols and slid each into its holster before picking up Longwood's Colt from the floor. Danner turned and saw a dozen or so men standing near the door and bar, including the proprietor surveying the damage to his establishment.

"Who's gonna pay for all this?" the owner asked, looking at Danner.

"Well, since he drew and fired on me first, I reckon he should," Danner suggested, looking back at Longwood. "I figure he and his dead buddy over there have some rustling money in their pockets. It's up to you," Danner said.

"I need a doctor!" Longwood groaned.

"Ain't no doctor here," the saloon owner declared. "The ladies down the street will patch ya up for a price," he added, to the laughter of the rest of the men, who started to head back to the tables they occupied before the ruckus began.

"Anybody know who that one is?" Danner asked, pointing to the dead shotgun shooter.

Several men walked over to look, all shaking their heads no.

"When was the last marshal through here?" Danner asked aloud.

"Oh, about a week ago or so," the saloon owner answered. "We usually see a couple every few days," he added, rummaging through the pockets of the dead shotgun shooter.

Danner looked back at the crippled Longwood, leaving two swelling circles of blood on either side of his slumped body.

"You killed me," Longwood mumbled before his eyes rolled back in his head, and he fell forward in a thud.

Danner stepped over to the dead horse thief and grabbed a fist full of collar. He dragged Longwood over to his deceased partner, where Danner grasped another fist full of shirt collar.

He then lifted both corpses and hauled each out of the saloon, only the tips of their boots dragging across the floor.

CHAPTER 6

Tuesday, 9 July 1878

LUXTON DANNER – ATOKA

T he wary dealer glared at the big unshaven gunslinger across the table. His huge left hand covered most of the five cards he held. He peered over his hand and held up two fingers. The dealer peeled off two new cards and tossed both onto the table before moving on to the next man, who snapped down two cards, indicating he also wanted a double. After a glance, the dealer slid two cards his way. The next player flipped a five-dollar bill onto the pile in the middle of the table. The big gunslinger slid a twenty toward the money, triggering two of the four men to fold their hands amid mumbled cursing. After matching the bet, the dealer raised twenty. The gunslinger pushed two twenties across the table. The dealer smiled and laid down three jacks. The crowd of men who'd sensed big money on the table let out a collective breath and gazed at the tall stranger. Without expression, the gunslinger laid down three kings and carefully watched as the dealer's smile faded to a frown. The men erupted into cross comments and conversations.

"That's five in a row, mister," the dealer loudly exclaimed.

The saloon fell quiet as the gunslinger gathered the money from the middle of the table with his left hand, his right dropping down out of sight.

"Take it easy, Slade, you dealt that one," a bystander reminded the disgruntled loser.

"Maybe, but I say that's damn lucky," Slade announced, leaning forward in his chair, glaring at the stranger with narrow eyes above a crooked frown.

The gang of men huddled around the table stepped back when the sharp sound of the saloon's swinging doors broke the tension. Slade's eyes darted toward the doors and met a US Marshal's badge pinned to the man's vest.

"Come on, Slade, we'll buy ya a drink," another man offered.

"I reckon today's just your day, mister," Slade mumbled before slowly sliding back from the table and joining the men at the bar.

The marshal watched the gang make their way to the bar, sans the tall gunslinger who remained seated at the table. The marshal joined him, taking a chair that faced the bar and its restless patrons.

"I see you're still making friends the same way, Lux," Hank Laughlin wisecracked through a wide grin.

"Good to see you too, Hank. What the hell brings you back here so quickly? Couldn't Upham give you a couple of days before sending you out again?" Danner asked the deputy marshal.

"I'd say I got here just in time."

"You saved that jackass's life anyway," Danner added with a head nod toward Slade.

"I feel better already." Laughlin chuckled, reaching into his vest pocket and withdrawing the envelope with Danner's name neatly written on it. I'm back this quick to give you this," Laughlin explained, handing the piece of mail to Danner.

Danner gazed at the envelope for a long moment, then slid it into his vest pocket.

"Not going to open it and tell me what it's all about?" Laughlin asked, leaning forward.

"Nope."

"You mean I give up at least two days of glorious sleep in a real bed to bring this out to you double-quick, and I don't get to know what it's all about," Laughlin said with a laugh.

"Nope. Let's get out of here before ol' Slade gets drunk and decides to get himself killed," Danner stated as he took what seemed like forever to elevate his six-foot, six-inch frame from its chair before heading for the door.

Danner and Laughlin stepped out into the late afternoon oppressive heat beating down on the former Choctaw camp turned settlement.

Atoka was one of the few established towns inside the Indian Territory due to its proximity to Fort Smith. Because of its location, Atoka—and nearby Red Oak—had regular visits from US Deputy Marshals heading into and returning from the territory, and a reliable supply line. Getting its start as a store along the old Butterfield Overland Mail route, the town of Atoka grew steadily until several nearby Civil War battles stunted its progress. Despite a series of setbacks, the settlement hung on and eventually grew into one of the more viable towns in the territory.

After stepping out of the saloon, Danner veered off to his left and strolled across the street to greet the two guards riding with Laughlin. Danner approached with an extended right hand. Both men's faces broke into broad smiles.

"Jerry, Sam, good to see you both," Danner exclaimed, shaking each guard's hand. Both men had accompanied Danner on many a mission and were two of the more reliable guards Fort Smith had to offer. "No cook on this trip?" Danner asked Laughlin as he joined the trio.

"Nope, Sam here is doing double duty," Laughlin advised.

"Hope you're getting double pay," Danner said, followed by a loud laugh.

Sam smiled and shook his head no. "Nobody said nothing about double pay," Sam said through a laugh.

"Well, how about I buy y'all an early supper then," Danner offered, looking at Laughlin for approval.

Laughlin nodded toward the mobile jail cell. "Leave the wagon here, fellas. This will probably be the last good meal we get for a while!" Laughlin shouted to the delight of all four men.

A young freckle-faced boy wearing a crisp white apron and toothy smile met Danner and his company as they sat down. "Coffee, beer, whiskey?" the young boy asked.

"Four beers, young man, and what's that I smell?" Danner asked, referring to the pleasing aroma billowing from the kitchen.

"That'd be Ma's fried chicken, sir."

"We'll take four chicken dinners when they're ready."

"Yes, sir!" the boy exclaimed before rushing back through the kitchen doors.

A few moments later, the boy rushed through the kitchen door with four mugs of beer set atop a wooden tray. Putting a beer in front of each man, the boy looked to Danner. "Ma says it'll be a few minutes as she's just gettin' started with the chicken."

"Very good, young man. Tell your ma, as good as that chicken smells, we'll wait as long as we have to," Danner offered, his three guests nodding in agreement.

"Yes, sir!" The boy spun on his heels and ran back into the kitchen.

The hotel patrons' festive mood was shattered by shouting out in the street. Laughlin peered through the front window and saw the cause of the commotion standing on the boardwalk in front of the saloon. "Lux." Laughlin nodded toward the window.

Danner followed the marshal's gaze out the window to the saloon across the street. Slade, the man who lost to Danner at cards, looked up and down the road, shouting and pushing away men who were failing to convince him to go back into the saloon. Danner rose from his chair. "You stay here. This will only take a minute."

Laughlin stood with Danner. "I can't let you go out there and kill him without trying to stop ya, Lux," Laughlin mumbled.

"I ain't going to kill 'em, Hank, unless I have to," Danner assured the deputy marshal. Danner stepped out of the hotel and proceeded to walk straight toward the drunk ruffian. The men trying to pull Slade back into the saloon saw Danner and quickly backed away from the obnoxious card player, who also saw the reason for their retreat.

"You cheatin' son of a bitch! I want my money back!" Slade shouted at Danner, who kept his stride straight toward the lout without speaking a word. Slade stumbled off the boardwalk onto the packed dirt street and squared his shoulders to Danner, who kept his quick pace, closing on the would-be gunfighter. "I told you, I want my money back, you bastard!" Slade shouted as he reached for his gun.

Danner lunged forward, his massive left hand covering Slade's gun. Without hesitation or breaking stride, a crashing blow into Slade's unsuspecting face from Danner's huge right fist sent the unconscious drunkard into a heap of humanity, pounding the dirt street surface in a cloud of dust. Danner reached down and withdrew the Colt from Slade's holster and rotated the cylinder, allowing the six bullets to fall harmlessly onto the dirt. He then stepped over to the trough in front of the saloon and dropped the pistol into the clear water. Danner looked at the crowd of men who'd gathered in front of the saloon to watch the show.

"I'll kill any man who tries to take that pistol out of the trough. Understand?" Danner asked aloud.

Nodding heads and whispers of "yes, sir" answered his question.

Danner nonchalantly turned and strolled back to the hotel where Laughlin waited on the front porch sporting a wide grin. "You might want to tell those jackasses to get out of town, Marshal," Danner said, stepping past Laughlin into the dining room, where plates of hot fried chicken sat in front of each guard and two empty chairs.

Hank Laughlin shook his head and casually headed for the saloon to follow through with his friend's suggestion. Laughlin took his seat at the table next to Danner.

Danner set his fork down and leaned back in his chair. He removed the envelope from his pocket and looked at Laughlin. "So, what's the story behind this?" Danner asked while holding up the envelope.

"Well, right after I got back to Fort Smith, Marshal Upham called for me and asked if I knew where you were. I told him I would see you here, so he asked me to head out again and deliver it. I figured you'd still be here sitting at a poker table, and it turns out I was right," Laughlin explained.

Danner stared at the writing on the front of the envelope. "Canyon Creek, huh?"

"Upham thought having the letter sent to his office was odd, but he figured it was personal. Any idea who it's from?" Laughlin asked.

"Nope," Danner lied before returning the envelope to his pocket.

CHAPTER 7

Wednesday, 10 July 1878

LUXTON DANNER – SAWYER

Danner leaned his elbows on the slick, polished surface of the bar and stared into his whiskey glass. For Danner, the raucous chatter and piano music faded into extraneous background noise. His thoughts drifted back to when he believed he had a purpose, a plan, a reason for his existence. He reflected on the last few months. An inner calm crept into his mind. He had surprised himself with the ease of his transition to a drifter. Time had moved on, and so had he. His thoughts quickly cleared when he felt the presence of a man behind him.

"Well, look who we have here! If I'm right, and I'm guessing I am, we have the famous US Deputy Marshal Luxton Danner right here in little ol' Sawyer!" the intruder shouted, bringing the chatter and piano music to a halt.

Danner said nothing, picking up his glass and finishing his drink in one long swallow before setting the empty glass back down in front of him. He didn't turn nor shift his weight. He rolled his eyes to the left, where the bartender stood stiff as an oak tree, staring at him.

"I heard this hero gunned down two fellas in Red River City last year! Was no fair gunfight, neither!" the intruder bellowed, making another crucial mistake by taking a step closer.

The crowd in the cantina remained deathly quiet but for the periodic nervous shuffle of leather boot soles against the bare wooden floor. Danner stared down into his empty glass, looking at the last drop of amber fluid pooling at the bottom. The smell of lousy whiskey penetrated the air around him.

"I ain't scared a no deputy marshal!" the intruder boomed.

Danner placed his massive hands on the bar's shiny surface and slowly pushed himself to a standing position, then lightning-quick, sunk the heel and spur of his right boot deep into the intruder's groin, cutting through trousers and flesh alike.

"Uuugh!" The intruder grasped his groin, doubled over, and collapsed to the floor, unable to speak. He gasped for breath, curling his knees up to his chest. A gurgling sound preceded an explosion of vomit from his mouth. Danner turned, reached down, and removed the intruder's gun from its leather wrap. Standing straight, Danner scanned each face in the room to ensure the man had no friends with him. Danner slowly rotated the pistol's cylinder, allowing each cartridge to fall helplessly to the floor. After the sixth bullet bounced on the wooden planks, Danner swung the gun toward the bartender behind him, keeping his eyes on the crowded cantina. The rotund bartender quickly retrieved the weapon from Danner's massive hand and tucked it on the shelf under the bar. The piercing sound of oil-starved swinging door hinges broke the silence. Tapping boot heels followed. Danner slowly looked over his right shoulder. A short, stout man with a round face and sheriff's badge pinned to his vest stood in the doorway with a double-barrel shotgun leveled at him.

"Trouble, Ethan?" the sheriff asked the stubby bartender.

"No, sir. Tommy there just started mouthing off at this

fellow who was mindin' his own business. Accused him of killin' a couple of gunhands up in Red River City last year."

"He shot?" the sheriff asked, looking down at Danner's victim.

"No, Harold, this gentleman didn't need to use a gun," one of the ladies at the end of the bar announced through a wide red lipstick-framed grin.

"What's wrong with him, then?" Hal Stanley, the town's lawman, asked, lowering the shotgun.

"Let's just say he won't be a customer for a while," the lady said, lifting her long blue satin dress as she stepped over the motionless Tommy Banks toward Danner.

"He's drunk again, Sheriff. Shooting off his mouth as he does," Ethan added.

Stanley looked at two men seated next to the front door. "Will you two take him over to the jail for me?"

Both nodded, then each grabbed an arm and drug the drunken varmint out of the cantina. The piano music slowly built up tempo, and the room filled again with noisy chatter. Stanley walked over to Danner.

"Sorry for the poor welcome to town, stranger. Can I buy you a drink?"

Danner nodded, then turned back toward the bar, pointing to the floor behind the bar. The bartender reached under the bar, removed Banks's pistol, and then set it in front of Stanley.

"Tommy's pistol," Ethan explained before pouring whiskey into Danner's empty glass.

Stanley stood close to Danner to speak quietly.

"Were you part of that shootout in Red River City like he claimed?"

Danner said nothing, just took a sip of whiskey.

"Look, if you were in Red River City, you would be either Marshal Luxton Danner or Wes Payne, the Ranger. Based on your size and what I've heard, I reckon you're Danner," Stanley continued.

"Your boy talks too much," Danner said, taking another drink.

"I know. Tommy's a better shot with his tongue than his pistol. He's one of the few troublemakers I have in this town, then only when he's drunk, which is most of the time," Stanley said. "Am I right?" Stanley asked.

"I'm Danner."

"Thought so. You lookin' for someone here in Sawyer?"

"Nope. I'm not a marshal anymore."

"Well, that changes things a bit. You lookin' for a job, perchance?"

"Nope. I already have one, and I don't plan on staying in town. Especially after this."

"Well, I could sure use a deputy, but I reckon I can't change your mind."

"Nope," Danner assured the sheriff. "I'm on my way up to Canyon Creek."

"Oh, I see. It happens I've got a friend up in Canyon Creek, near the Llano Estacada country. Small rancher. He owns a few hundred acres up there. He's trying to hold onto his place but has run into trouble with a big cattleman who's buying up every bit of land he can get his hands on. I hear he's tried to come to a peaceful agreement, but the other fellow threatened a saddle war if he doesn't back down," Stanley explained.

Danner stood silent, then finished his drink. A saddle war hadn't been in his plans, but then again, he didn't have much of a plan. The letter Laughlin gave him spoke of a land baron exerting his power. The sheriff's story had to be the reason for Rachel Brennen's request for his help. She said the folks in Canyon Creek were losing their land and businesses to a rancher named Knox. The sheriff's story made sense of Rachel's letter.

"What's the name of this friend of yours?" Danner asked.

"Virgil Robertson. He's got 400 or so acres he's looking to hold on to, along with a couple of other smaller outfits. I guess there's plenty for the taking, but this other fellow wants all of it."

"Know who the other rancher is?"

"Nope. I just heard the scuttlebutt. I guess the other fella likes hirin' outlaws to do his dirty work. Virgil ain't like that. He's a law-abiding man with a wife and three daughters. He wants to keep his land legal. I reckon he could use a man like yourself," Stanley said.

"Where is this ranch of his?"

"Right close to Canyon Creek."

"How do you know all about this?" Danner asked skeptically, canting his head to one side.

"A wagon train loaded down with supplies came through here about a month or so ago. It had men from up that way headin' back. They said the roads to Oneida were choked off with too many gunmen. So, they came this a way," Stanley explained.

"When was the last time you saw this friend of yours?"

"Oh, I was up that way about six months ago. I started for Fort Worth when I got a little side-tracked here."

"Side-tracked?" Danner asked with a raised eyebrow, looking at the badge.

"Well, I broke up a fight between a couple of fellers here, and they offered me a job."

"I thought the county elected sheriffs."

"Yes, sir, got voted in as the official sheriff not long after," Stanley proudly replied.

"You always carry that scatter gun?" Danner asked, nodding toward the double-barrel.

"Yep. Found it was more convincing than a six-shooter," Stanley said, laughing.

"Excuse me, Harold," the lady from the end of the bar interrupted Stanley, reaching under Danner's arm and squeezing his massive bicep tightly. "Is there anything I can do for you this evening, big man?" she asked Danner with a sinister smile he hadn't seen in a long time.

Danner looked down into clear brown eyes that could easily ignite a man's desires. "As much as I'd like to, ma'am, I believe I'll pass this evening," Danner said, returning the smile.

"Very well, cowboy, just know it won't cost ya anything," she said as she reluctantly released her grip and moved on into the crowd.

"Not what I'm used to seeing out here," Danner said, watching her walk away.

"No, sir. She's a fine lady."

"You had supper yet, Sheriff?"

"No sir, can't say that I have."

"If you show me the way to a good meal, I'll buy you supper."

"Well, follow me, Mr. Danner!" Stanley exclaimed. The two men pushed through the swinging doors and stepped onto the street.

"Sheriff! Sheriff!" A young man ran toward both men.

"That's one of the fellas that took Tommy down to the jail," Stanley announced. "What is it?"

"It's Tommy! He came around and was mighty mad! He knocked Jason and me down, then took Jason's gun! Said he was coming for him!" the man reported, pointing at Danner.

"Where is he now?" Stanley asked.

"Here he comes, Sheriff," Danner said, looking down the street, seeing a lone man staggering their way.

"All right. Show Mr. Danner over to the hotel for supper. I'll deal with Tommy."

"No, sir. I'll join you if you don't mind, Sheriff," Danner forcefully said as he pulled up his gun belt and squared his massive shoulders.

A moment later, the street flooded with onlookers. Danner stepped away from Stanley as he heard him pull back on the shotgun's hammers.

Banks staggered toward them, pistol dangling from his right hand, his left clutching his bloody groin. His tan trousers were red on both sides of the crotch. Sweat poured from Banks's face as he stumbled forward. "You son of a bitch! I'll kill you, you bastard!" Banks yelled before falling face first onto Main Street.

Stanley eased the hammers of his scattergun forward and glanced at Danner. "Appears ol' Tommy is hurt worse than I thought. Better get Doc to look at him," Stanley announced.

Danner said nothing. He just turned and headed for the hotel.

CHAPTER 8

Wednesday, 10 July 1878

WES PAYNE – OUTSIDE BUFFALO GAP

Snap! Zeb Boyce's whip found the broad leather harness strapped across the haunches of horse number four. *Crack! Crack! Crack!* Wes Payne fired left and right as fast as he could rack his Winchester. The coach's wheels banged against rocks and ruts, tossing its passengers in every direction. *Snap!* Zeb whipped the harness again. *Thump!* A bullet shattered the F in the Fargo name on the side of the coach's box. *Crack! Crack! Crack!* Wes continued his deluge of lead at the four bandits pursuing the red and gold coach. *Ping!* A bullet ricocheted off the metal strongbox, its leather straps holding on for dear life.

"How we doin'?" Zeb called over his shoulder to his shotgun rider. Wes was spread eagle on the top of the stagecoach, doing his best, slinging lead up the trail but failing to hit bandit flesh.

"I can't hit a damn thing at this speed! We have to slow down! Bring 'em closer!" Wes called to his Wells Fargo whip.

"Bring 'em closer? We have women in here!" a passenger called from inside the rumbling carriage.

"I know, Doc, but we can't outrun 'em!" Wes called to his traveler.

"Horses are startin' to let out, Wes!" Zeb called up.

Bullets smashed into the rear of the coach, sending a shower of splinters into the air. A woman screamed inside the coach. The door flew open, then banged against its latch, shooting sparks into the coach.

"Here we go, Wes!" Zeb called as he pulled back on the reins just enough to slow his tiring four-horse team.

Wes caught his balance and leaned into the strongbox. The bandits didn't react quickly enough to the slowing coach, just as planned. All four pushed closer.

Crack! Crack! Crack! Crack! Wes fired point-blank at the two lead riders, hitting flesh and bone and knocking both bandits off their charging mounts. A third bandit's horse tripped on a dead bandit's falling body sending horse and rider into a mass of horse and human flesh. The third bandit was down.

Crack! Crack! Wes's final two rounds thumped into the fourth bandit, who briefly slumped onto his saddle before sliding off into a cloud of trail dust.

"Whoa! Whoa! Bring 'em to a stop, Zeb!" Wes ordered his driver.

"Whoa!" Zeb called to his team, pulling back on the reins with all the strength he could muster from his fifty-nine-year-old body.

The team came to a methodical halt, shrouding the coach in a massive cloud of trail dust. Wes lay on his back and watched the clouds drift lazily through the sun-drenched air. He took a deep breath, then soaked a blue bandana with the soiled sweat from his face. He stared up into the clear blue sky, watching a single white cloud languish above.

Funny what a man notices at times like these.

"Everybody okay in there?" Zeb called into the coach as he

grabbed a handful of brake lever and swung down from the driver's box, his cracked leather boots pushing up two puffs of dust.

"I believe so, driver!" Doc Unger shouted.

"No! She's hurt!" another voice shrieked.

Zeb tried to open the coach door without success. It had jammed shut when it slammed closed during the fight. Zeb pulled hard to no avail. "Who's hurt?" Zeb asked, peering through an open window.

"Mrs. Chamberlain's been hit in the back of his shoulder. It looks like a bullet came through the back of the coach," Doc Unger reported.

Zeb pulled on the door again. Wes stepped forward and moved his senior driver to the side. Clutching the brass handle with both scarred hands, Wes propped his right boot against the steel brace and yanked the door open in one motion.

"It's good to be young and strong!" Zeb cackled.

"These coach raids keep up; I'll be young and dead!" Wes quipped. "Everybody out, please," Wes asked the disheveled group.

The passenger list included: Mrs. Ella Chamberlain en route to Fort Concho to join her husband, Calvin and Ruth Porter on their way to Buffalo Gap to open a new boarding house, Zane Brinkman, his destination and purpose unknown, and Doctor Mitchell Unger on his way to Fort Concho to join its hospital staff. Everyone exited the coach except for Doc Unger and his patient, Ella Chamberlain, whose steel-gray Victorian dress had turned dark maroon behind her right shoulder. To expose the bloody bullet puncture, Doc Unger cut the back of the once beautiful dress trimmed in white lace at the collar, wrists, and bottom edges.

"Take it easy, Mrs. Chamberlain, you'll be all right," Unger whispered to his patient, who, despite glistening with sweat and breathing rapidly, was remarkably calm.

"Can I be of assistance, doctor?" Ruth Porter asked.

"Driver, is it safe to remain here for a bit? I'd like to remove the bullet promptly," Unger asked.

"Yessiree, Doc! Wes is coming back from checkin' on them outlaws. Looks like he got all of 'em."

"I'll need my bag from the back. Can you please give it to Mrs. Porter?" Unger asked Zeb, who immediately retrieved the black leather case from the rear boot compartment. Zeb passed Mrs. Porter and set the bag inside the coach.

"Mrs. Chamberlain, I'm going to use a little chloroform to put you to sleep and remove the bullet. It's not deep. It's lodged against your shoulder blade bone. Understand?"

Mrs. Chamberlain responded with a nod of her head. Although a short, slight woman of twenty-nine with long brown curled hair and high cheekbones set beneath clear brown eyes wrapped in flawless skin, Ella Chamberlain was the veteran wife of a career soldier. She moved from fort to fort, back east, and now onto another western garrison. She was tougher than her lovely appearance indicated.

Unger pulled the cork from a brown glass bottle and poured just a touch of the clear fluid onto a crisp white handkerchief, then gently placed it over his patient's nose and mouth before moving her onto her stomach on the floor of the coach. Withdrawing a pair of bullet probes from his bag, Unger leaned over the wound and manipulated his fingers around the oblong wound, feeling the hard lump of lead against the shoulder blade. The intense heat inside the coach caused beads of sweat to fall from Unger's face onto Chamberlain's exposed back.

Mrs. Porter quickly dabbed Doc Unger's face, to his great relief. He smiled at his new assistant, grateful for her help.

Carefully, Unger spread the wound on either side with thumb and index finger and inserted the tips of the probe. As diagnosed, the bullet had not fractured the bone and thus was easily targeted. The ends of the probe found the lead intruder's edges. Unger gently squeezed the looped handles securing a firm grip on the lead invader. Carefully pulling back on the instrument, he withdrew the bullet and dropped it into the open hand of Mrs. Porter. After cleaning the wound, Unger closed the gap with a few sutures, then placed a clean white gauze bandage over the area.

"It'll be a few minutes before she wakes up. We should be able to continue after that," Unger informed Zeb, who'd been watching the process from a window.

"Yes, sir. Just let me know when, Doc!" Zeb shouted. "Won't take long to get to Buffalo Gap from here!"

CHAPTER 9

Wednesday, 10 July 1878

ZEB BOYCE – BUFFALO GAP

The late afternoon sun sank low on the western horizon, sending its blinding yellow rays into the men's faces as Zeb piloted the damaged Wells Fargo stagecoach through the open grassland east of Buffalo Gap with Wes at his side. "Good thing this trail is wide and flat since I can't see a damned thing with that blasted sun in my eyes! It's stingin' like a hoard of bees!" Zeb cursed.

"The horses won't stray off the path. I'm just glad we ain't bouncin' Mrs. Chamberlain around anymore. Coming through those rocks back there was mighty tough on her," Wes said.

"Not too good fer my backside, neither! Yasser, she's a tough lady," Zeb declared before sending a stream of brown tobacco juice onto the dusty trail. Zeb snapped the reins, keeping his whip tied to the driver's box. He held the team at an easy trot after running from the outlaws as they did. Buffalo Gap crept up from the horizon at the bottom of the sun as the weary occupants of the embattled coach skulked closer to their destination.

As the coach drew closer to town, Zeb saw Travis Butler, the operator of the Wells Fargo office in Buffalo Gap, pacing back and forth in front of the stage office, nervously checking his pocket watch. A tall, slender man with a pale protruding nose, clean-shaven face, and close-cut hair, he resembled what most people envisioned an undertaker looked like. Zeb figured the message he sent from the telegraph office in Belle Plain had confirmed they had departed on time this morning, but it was nearly six o'clock now, meaning he was over four hours late. At a distance of thirty-five miles, the trip should've only taken four hours or so, putting its arrival time around three at the latest. Zeb spat another stream of tobacco through grinning lips as he watched Butler's boot heels pound the wooden boardwalk with added authority for each step he took. Butler turned and peered down the eastern road. He shaded his eyes and leaned forward at the waist. Zeb figured at this distance that everything looked all right, although he was driving the team a little slower than usual.

"Wait till ol' Butler gets a look at this coach." Zeb chuckled to Wes, who nodded in agreement.

"He is a nervous sort of fellow, that's for sure," Wes replied, matching his partner's snicker. "If he starts fussing, I'm blaming this mess on you," Wes added with a grin.

As Zeb pulled the wagon onto the red dirt road leading to the stage office, Butler called over to the livery stable to assist the coach. A boy, busy mucking out stalls, quickly dropped his rake and rushed across the street, nearly getting run over by a passing carriage.

"Yes sir, Mr. Butler!" the anxious boy shouted, stumbling up the single step in front of the narrow building that proudly displayed a giant red and gold Wells Fargo sign above a pointed white gable.

A short moment later, Zeb pulled back on the leather straps. "Whoa! Whoa!" Zeb called down to the exhausted team, bringing the bright red coach to a halt in front of the boss. "Take it easy young fellow! You nearly got plum run over!" Zeb called down to the out-of-breath youngster. "Had some trouble, Travis!" Zeb shouted as he crawled down from his driver's box and quickly turned the brass handle of the coach door.

"What is it? What happened? Everybody okay?" Butler shouted.

Before Zeb could speak, Mrs. Porter rushed out of the coach, clutching the bottom of her prairie skirt in one hand and a carpetbag in the other.

"No! Everybody is not okay! Mrs. Chamberlain was shot!" the excited woman shouted back.

Butler looked up and saw the coach's obliterated "Fargo" name. "Oh hell. What happened, Zeb?"

"Got jumped by four bandits outside Lucas Valley Farm. Had a running gunfight for about three miles before ol' Wes could git 'em all."

Zane Brinkman stepped out of the coach and assisted Doc Unger with Mrs. Chamberlain, who weakly stepped down from the coach's doorway.

"Here, she can take a seat!" Butler directed the men toward a long wooden bench anchored to the boardwalk in front of the office.

"Travis, this here's Doc Unger. He took care of the lady out on the trail. That's another reason we were late."

"I'm Travis Butler, Wells Fargo. Glad to make your acquaintance, doctor. Thank heavens you were on the trip."

"Good afternoon, sir. Can you direct me to your town doctor, please?" Unger asked Butler.

"I'll show you the way, Doc," Wes announced from behind the group of passengers who'd gathered around Ella Chamberlain.

"Wes, would you be good enough to come back here after showing Mr. Unger and Mrs. Chamberlain to Doctor Jones's office? I'll need to enter a full report into the record," Butler asked.

Wes nodded, then scooped up Ella Chamberlain into his arms. "Excuse me, ma'am. This way, Doc," Wes said before heading down the street.

Ella Chamberlain wrapped her left arm around Wes's neck and laid her head on his inviting shoulder. Hours on the trail in a hot dirty coach and a bullet wound in her shoulder, Mrs. Chamberlain abandoned her efforts to remain a proper soldier's wife and surrendered to her exhaustion. Zeb watched Wes stroll down the street with the beautiful woman in his arms.

"I'll be right back, Travis!" Zeb hollered as he shuffled after his shotgun rider and wounded passenger.

"Zeb! Zeb! I need your report right away!" Travis Butler called to his jittery driver.

"I know! I know! I'll be right back. I just want to see how the lady's doin' is all!" Zeb shouted back over his shoulder, knowing the saloon was next to Doc Jones's office. Zeb quickly changed direction to his actual destination, much to the dismay of Butler, who threw up his arms in frustration. A dozen curious men met Zeb as he punched through the swinging doors and headed for the bar. "Whiskey!" Zeb called out, waving his hand up over his head.

"What happened? Did you run into trouble? That lady dead?" The questions hit Zeb like a boxer's flurry of punches.

"Hold on, boys! Hold on! Let me wash the dust out of my throat first!" Zeb shouted as he picked up the shot of whiskey on the bar in front of him. Zeb downed the drink and smiled. "Set up another!" he ordered, then turned to the pesky group who anxiously awaited all the rousing details. "Got jumped, boys. Wes took 'em all, but the lady took one in the shoulder.

I had a doctor on board who patched her up. Says she'll be all right," Zeb reported soaking in the attention. Zeb turned back to the bar and swallowed the second drink in one gulp while getting slaps of approval on his back from the boys in the bar.

CHAPTER 10

Wednesday, 10 July 1878

WES PAYNE – BUFFALO GAP

W es slowly climbed the hotel's steps, finding it more difficult than usual to reach the top. The pounding he took on top of the stagecoach made him feel like a half-dozen men had pistol-whipped him. Once in the hallway, he saw Annette Gentry stepping out of a room with a handful of linens. A white apron, soiled with stains from a long day's work, covered the front of her light blue dress. Her dark hair was pulled back from a weary face and tied with a white scarf. She jumped when she noticed Wes walking down the hallway toward her. Quickly, she released the knot in her kerchief, allowing her long hair to fall around her face. She clutched the linens with her left hand and quickly ran her fingers through her hair, pushing the brown locks forward to hide the sides of her face.

"Good evening, Annette. Can I help you with those sheets?"

"No, no, thank you, Wes, I'll manage just fine," she answered, attempting to step around her favorite guest.

Wes stopped and gently took hold of her arm, causing her to slow her pace just enough for him to brush back the hair on the left side of her face. As Wes suspected, a massive purple and yellow welt marred her otherwise lovely look from the temple to below her cheek. Dropping the linens, she pushed

Wes's hand away and pulled her hair forward over the ugly wound.

"Please, Wes, I'm fine. It's nothing. Really."

Wes bent down and picked up the linens, allowing her to retrieve them from his grasp. Annette turned her face away from him, leaned against the wall, and began to cry. Wes protectively wrapped his arms around Annette, drawing her into his body. Like a herd of raging buffalo, a potent fit of anger he never felt before detonated from deep within him. Once before, Wes told Amos Gentry what would happen if he ever struck Annette again. And he meant it. Releasing Annette, he turned and headed back to the staircase, his boot heels digging into the boards like hammers. Annette let herself fall to the floor, covering her tear-soaked face with tired hands. The sound of her crying consumed Wes as he descended the stairs in search of the man he had unequivocally warned months ago in this same hotel.

"Amos! Amos Gentry! Where the hell are you?" Wes shouted. He searched in the lobby, behind the big front desk, then in the dining room. He turned at the sound of footsteps behind him. Fury hindered his vision. All he could see was what stood directly in front of him—the apathetic excuse of a man who thought nothing of beating his wife.

"What are you yelling about, Payne?" Amos Gentry shouted through gritted teeth wrapped in a weak chin.

Wes stepped toward Gentry. "I told you what would happen if you ever hit her again, didn't I?" Wes muttered in a low even voice.

"Don't you worry about my wife and me. What goes on between us is our business, not yours, the marshal, or the Rangers! Do you hear me? Now you get your things and get out of my hotel, now! And don't ever talk to my wife again!"

Annette's footsteps popped on the stairs as she ran down. "No! Please, stop! Both of you!" she shouted as she reached the bottom step.

Annette's arrival caused Wes to glance away from Amos to her. He caught a glimpse of Amos Gentry drawing a derringer from his vest pocket. *Crack!* Gentry fired wildly, hitting Wes in his left arm. Instinctively, Wes drew and fired. Unlike his adversary, his aim was true, his .45 slug thumping the chest of Amos Gentry, knocking him backward through the glass window onto the porch. Wes watched Gentry's body crash through the window, shattering glass in all directions. He looked back to Annette, screaming, but Wes heard no sound. Everything moved in slow motion. He turned back to Amos Gentry, whose cut and bloodied body rolled slowly onto the porch planks. Shards of fractured glass fragments rained down without a sound. Wes looked down at his pistol, then slowly slid it back into its holster. The sound of muffled voices on the stairway drifted toward him. He looked back to the staircase and saw two men and a woman standing behind Annette, saying something he couldn't understand. Wes peered down at his arm, blood soaking his sleeve.

Annette rushed to Wes. He saw her lips moving, but Wes did not hear her words. Slowly, his ears began to work again. He heard Annette saying something about his arm. He looked down at his arm again and realized he was wounded. His left arm began to throb with pain, and the sleeve of his white bib shirt was red and soaked with blood. Annette ran to the kitchen. One of the men who had come down from his room went outside to check on Amos. Another man talked to Wes, but he paid no attention, replaying what had just happened in his mind.

Amos fired first. Hit me first. I had no choice.

Annette returned with a towel and began to wrap it around Wes's wound. His vision and hearing had returned. He had never experienced anything like that before. The bell on the front door rang. Wes turned and saw his friend, Buffalo Gap Sheriff, Dan Kirby, standing in the doorway. Kirby's face was dark, and he held a stern frown. He looked hard at Wes and Annette, then looked back at Amos Gentry lying outside. Kirby approached Wes and saw Annette's handy work of bandaging his left arm.

"What happened?" Kirby asked Wes.

Before Wes could respond, Annette spoke up. "Amos shot first, Sheriff! Amos did this. Annette pulled her hair back, displaying her badly mottled face. Wes became angry, but Amos shot him when Wes wasn't looking!" Annette cried.

"Did anyone else see it?" Kirby asked aloud, looking around at the crowd of people that had gathered inside the hotel lobby.

The two men and the woman who had heard the shots before running down the stairs all shook their heads no. "I did hear two shots, Sheriff," one of the men said, the woman nodding in agreement.

"I'll come over to your office and give you a statement," Wes said, grasping Annette's shoulders and moving her from between him and Kirby.

"You'll need to see the doc about that arm first," Kirby ordered. "Then come see me. Annette, I'll have Amos moved over to the undertaker's if that's all right with you."

Annette looked out the broken window at her husband and nodded approval. Kirby escorted Wes out of the hotel through a crowd gathered near the hotel entrance to gawk at the dead owner. Wes looked over his shoulder and saw Annette standing over her husband's body, hands covering her face. He suddenly felt a sense of emptiness. Wes felt guilty for defending her honor and his own life. For the first time in his life, he was uncomfortable with himself. *It doesn't matter how I feel. He had it coming.*

CHAPTER 11

Wednesday, 10 July 1878

WES PAYNE – BUFFALO GAP

Kirby pointed toward the doctor's building, then to the undertaker's shed near his office. Wes paid little attention to his wounded arm, walking toward the white-painted house Doc lived in and used as his office. Wes heard people talking but didn't listen to what they said. He barely felt his feet as he walked. It was like Wes floated along the river's surface. He saw the front door of Doc's place open and the physician, clad in a white shirt wrapped in a black vest, filled the doorway. Wes paused at the single step leading up to the doctor's entrance. He saw the doctor's mouth move, but he didn't hear any words. His mind raced like a runaway mustang. He saw Amos Gentry crash through the window, and then a squeezing hand wrapped around his right arm. He looked down to see Doc leading him into the house.

Once seated, Wes began to feel the painful thump in his left arm. Wes shook his head. *Damn it! Snap out of it!*

"What happened, Wes?"

"I took a bullet, Doc. I think it went through."

Doc retrieved a pair of scissors and cut away the sleeve exposing a large wound still bleeding profusely. A quick examination proved Wes was correct. The bullet, a giant caliber slug, had punctured the front of the arm just above the left elbow and subsequently exited the back of his arm, taking flesh with it. Doc swiftly tied knots into a long bandage then strategically wrapped the wound as tight as possible with each knot placed over the openings. He added a broad dressing over the knotted one, tying it off with all the strength a fifty-year-old man could muster.

"That should stop the bleeding. You need to lay down for a spell. You've lost a significant amount of blood," Doc ordered Wes, who obliged by stepping over to a cot before everything went dark.

Wes opened his eyes and saw Dan Kirby peering down at him. The doctor stood behind Kirby, smiling slightly beneath a bushy white mustache. "Doc says you're gonna live after all," Kirby quipped through a faint grin of his own.

"How long have I been out?" Wes asked, attempting to sit up before deciding against the urge.

"Oh, about thirty minutes is all, I reckon. Long enough for Doc to sew you up and walk over to get me," Kirby reported.

"Thirty minutes? I feel like I've been out for hours, and my head feels like it's going to explode any minute."

"That's on account of the blood loss," Doc chimed in. "That bullet did some serious damage, I fear."

Wes slowly bent his arm, bringing his hand up to his chest, then straightened it back out as best as he could. Pain fired through the arm in both directions like a blacksmith's red-hot iron rod piercing his elbow and shoulder at the same time. Wes bit off a scream with clenched teeth and a wince that caused tears to seep from his eyes. He paused and took a deep breath.

"Doc says you need to rest for a couple of hours before you come over to my office. I'd like a written statement from you. Something I can give the district judge when he gets here," Kirby explained.

"Is there trouble?" Wes asked.

"Naw, not really. There's a couple of folks chirping about it, but it seems pretty clear Amos pulled on you first," Kirby said.

"I was damn mad, Kirby, but I wouldn't have killed him. I wouldn't have done that to her," Wes said before slowly sitting up.

"I know. It helps you were a Ranger, and ol' Amos wasn't liked much by folks here, but he had been here for years, and, well, you just pass through now and then," Kirby surmised. "I'll see you down at my place in a couple of hours."

"No, not necessary, I'll go with you now," Wes advised, holding up a hand toward the doctor who was about to protest his decision. "If I need ya, I know where to find ya, Doc," Wes said, forcing a smile.

"At least let me put that arm in a sling before you go running off."

Donning a new white sling, Wes slowly followed Kirby down the street to his office. Along the way, a few bystanders stopped and glared at the wounded gunslinger, but none were brave enough to speak up. After all, the word had swept through town that Amos had shot first.

Wes carefully navigated the single step up to Kirby's office and tucked himself inside, taking his usual seat in the ladderback chair next to the sheriff's desk. Kirby slid paper and a worn fountain pen over to Wes.

"Just tell the judge what happened. Nothing fancy. I'll take a turn around the town while you finish," Kirby advised.

"Good thing I don't write fancy." Wes chuckled. "When will the judge be here?"

"He's due tomorrow, so you have all night to finish it." Kirby laughed as he stepped out of the office.

Wes had made it through school long enough to learn to

read and write but was no scholar. With limited use of his disfigured hands, he found writing more of a challenge. Despite his handicap, Wes scribbled down the events beginning with Annette's battered face and his deadly meeting with Amos Gentry. As he put words to paper, his emotions whirled like a twister on the plains. Anger replaced a feeling Wes didn't quite understand. He paused.

Danner is the smart one, went to college and all. He'd know what is happening to me. Guilt? Why the hell should I feel guilty? Damn fool drew on me. What was I supposed to do? I did what I had to do. I've never felt guilty before. I've never killed a man that didn't have it coming, and Amos had it coming. As much of a bastard as he was, he was still Annette's husband. That's the problem. I hurt the woman I . . .

Kirby pushed through the front door and extinguished Wes's thoughts. "How's it going, partner?" Kirby asked pleasantly, stepping around Wes and taking a seat behind his desk.

"All right. This damn hand slows me down. I'll finish in a couple of minutes."

Kirby took a deep breath, pushed his hat up onto his head, and leaned back in his chair. "Annette wants to see you," Kirby said flatly. "I don't know if that's a good idea right now or not," he added. "Word's got out that you called out Amos for beating Annette."

Wes signed his statement, then slid it across the desk to Kirby before standing up.

"I don't give a damn what kind of word's out. I'll see you later," Wes announced before stomping out of the sheriff's office.

Wes wandered over to the hotel, where a couple of men nailed boards over what had been the front window of the Bison Hotel. Wes stepped past the men into the hotel lobby, where Annette Gentry mopped Wes's blood off the lobby floor. Neither spoke a word. Annette stopped her chore upon seeing Wes close the front door. She stood rigid, clutching the mop handle tightly and biting her bottom lip.

"I'm sorry," Wes offered in a low voice.

Annette leaned forward, took Wes's scarred right hand in hers, and gently squeezed. "Please don't be sorry, Wes. You were right all along. Amos was a miserable man."

"I wasn't going to kill him. I wouldn't do that to you," Wes whispered.

Annette nodded her head. Her usually smooth face was flush and interrupted with lines of sorrow and fear. "I feel sad and relieved all at the same time. I know I shouldn't, but I do. I'm not afraid anymore."

"There's no reason you shouldn't feel relieved. The man had no right to beat you as he did. There's no excuse for that. Do you know if you'll stay here in Buffalo Gap?"

"I don't know. This town and hotel are all I have. I'll need to think about it, I guess. What about you?"

"I'll stay over at the sheriff's office until the district judge gets here, then I'll move on."

"Will I see you before you leave?" Annette asked, peering down at the floor as if she was afraid of the answer.

"No. I don't think that would be good right now. I'll head out after I talk to the judge."

"Will you come back?"

"I don't know. I don't think I should with the way I feel about you and all."

"How do you feel about me?" Annette asked, managing a faint smile that erased some of the sorrow from her face.

Wes squeezed her hand and returned the faint smile. He pulled Annette close and gazed into her eyes. "I believe you know," he said, then turned and walked toward the door, not pausing to look back.

Wes closed the door behind him. One of the men repairing the window stopped Wes. "We heard Amos shot first. It looked like he had it coming. I just thought you should know that," the man said, offering a hand which Wes obliged with a handshake and nod.

Wes returned to the sheriff's office, where Kirby was busy scribbling away on a piece of tattered paper like he was angry with it. Wes took his seat in the ladderback chair next to Kirby's desk and waited.

Kirby finished his thought and looked at Wes. "I'd like you to stay in town until the judge gets here. That going to be a problem?"

"Nope. I figured I'd stay in case he wanted to talk to me," Wes answered. "Any chance I can bunk here until then?"

"No problem. Probably a better idea than the hotel," Kirby responded with a chuckle he couldn't hold back.

"And you call yourself a friend," Wes jibed, then shook his head and managed a nefarious smirk.

CHAPTER 12

Wednesday, 10 July 1878

VIRGIL AND SHELLEY – ROBERTSON RANCH

L ater that evening, three hundred miles north of Buffalo Gap, Virgil closed the barn doors and turned out the lantern hanging on the post near the corral before walking over to the house's front porch. Shelley sat in a small rocking chair beneath a lantern with her Winchester propped against the wall. Her mother and younger sisters had already retired for the night while she and her father took one more look around the pastures, then finished bedding down the horses. After a long day's work in the hot sun, the night air felt good.

Virgil stepped onto the porch and settled into a chair next to his daughter. "I thought you'd already turned in," Virgil said before taking a deep breath and leaning back in his chair.

"I don't trust Knox enough to turn in before you've finished in the barn," Shelley answered. It's only been a few days since his men ran off half our cattle, and I wouldn't put it past him to try and kill you."

"No, I guess I don't either, but I hate to see you lose sleep over this mess."

"I don't sleep much these nights anyway."

"I'm afraid I don't either."

"Dad, do we have enough money to hire guards?"

"I don't know. We have some from the sale of those calves last month, but I've never hired gunmen before. I'm not sure what their pay would be."

"What do you plan on doing if we can't afford the help?"

"I haven't given that much thought. Before this trouble with Knox, I found myself liking this ranching life. It was a hell of a lot better than worrying about the crops back home getting enough rain or being wiped out by grubs, borers, or red rot," Virgil conceded. "Your mother and I had plenty of bad years when you were young."

"I remember."

A horse whinnied in the distance cutting short Shelley and Virgil's chat. Shelley quickly doused the lantern and grabbed her rifle, racking a round into the chamber. Virgil carefully leaned forward into the darkness, straining to hear. Shelley quietly stepped off the porch, careful not to give away her position. She kneeled in front of the steps and listened. The chirp of an occasional cricket penetrated the otherwise quiet night. Shelley looked up into the star-drenched sky and watched a lonely thick cloud creep over the moon, momentarily obscuring any light the moon might offer.

The hidden horse whinnied again. This time, Shelley located the direction of the sound. It came from the small pasture on the right side of the house. "Get down out of that chair, Dad," Shelley whispered.

Virgil slipped off the chair and kneeled on the porch, unsure of what to do. He wasn't armed, and he didn't want to risk opening the door to get his shotgun. Shelley slid to the corner of the porch and brought her rifle to her shoulder. The cloud slowly passed beyond the moon, bringing the pasture visible again in the dim light. The silhouette of a lone rider materialized just beyond Shelley's rifle sight.

"In front of the house! Don't shoot! I mean no harm!" the rider shouted.

Shelley looked around the rest of the pasture. She couldn't be sure, but the rider appeared to be alone.

"What do you want this time of night?" Virgil shouted.

"I have a message for Virgil Robertson!"

"Stop at the gate! Don't come any closer!" Shelley warned.

The rider stopped at the gate. Shelley and Virgil saw the rider now in the moonlight.

"Damned late to be sneaking up to deliver a message!" Virgil barked.

"We've been watching you. We know what time you call it a night!" the rider declared.

"Who's watching?" Virgil asked.

"Gilford Knox sent me. He says you folks need to reconsider his fair offer for your ranch. Sell your place and move on. There's no sense anyone getting hurt."

"Tell that coward, Knox, the next time he wants a message delivered, he needs to do it himself in the daylight!" Shelley snarled.

"Mr. Knox isn't going to like that."

"I don't give a damn what Knox likes! Now get off our land before I shoot you where you are!" Shelley added.

The rider reined his horse around and paused. "You've been warned!" the rider snapped before kicking his horse and thundering off into the abyss.

Shelley stood up and listened until the sound of the rider disappeared.

"Let's get into the house, Shelley," Virgil said, his voice weary.

Shelley and her father stepped into the house. Her mother stood in the middle of the darkened room.

"I heard everything, Virgil. What are we to do now?" Madeleine asked with a shivering voice.

"Virgil hugged his wife. We'll do what we said we'd do," Virgil softly answered.

"They haven't gotten around to killing women and children yet," Shelley coldly said before she locked the front door and dropped the cross timber into its iron brackets.

"This is just harassment to frighten us off our land," Virgil added.

"Well, Virgil Robertson, it's working," Madeleine announced. "If that US Marshal doesn't get here soon, I'm packing up and leaving for Louisiana."

"I understand. We'll talk further in the morning. Let's try and get some sleep," Virgil said before guiding his wife toward their room.

Shelley heard her parents' door close. She pulled a chair away from the table and took a seat, her Winchester by her side.

CHAPTER 13

Thursday, 11 July 1878

LUXTON DANNER – BUFFALO GAP

T he following morning, Danner's arrival in Buffalo Gap was met with dark gray clouds swirling through the sky, mixing with an occasional glimpse of bright blue. The cloud cover was just enough to shield the heated beams of the morning sun, delivering cool temperatures to the old buffalo crossing. The crisp dawn breeze was a welcome change from the relentless heat that had baked the Texas landscape for the last two months. Danner took in a deep breath of clean air and exhaled slowly. He guessed it was around five-thirty or so, meaning most of the townsfolk were probably still asleep, except for maybe the keeper at the livery stable. Danner reined Bullet toward the stable, which still had the low glow from an all-night burning oil lamp flickering off the keeper's front door. Danner stopped in front of the stable and stepped down from his saddle. Bullet nickered before dipping his nose into the water trough. Before Danner could knock, the door swung open.

"Good morning, sir. What can I do for you?" the man asked, wiping sleep from his eyes with one hand and holding a steaming cup of coffee with the other.

"Well, I may need to put up my horse a little later. I'm

looking for a fellow named Wes Payne. You know if he's in town?" Danner asked the somnolent man.

"Yes, sir. Mr. Payne's horse is still here. I think he's over at the sheriff's office. Don't know if the sheriff's up and about yet, though."

"Sheriff's office?" Danner asked, looking down the street for the lawman's building.

"Yes, sir. He killed the hotel owner, so he ain't staying there, I reckon," the man explained.

"Killed the hotel owner? You know what happened?" Danner asked, leaning toward the man with increased curiosity.

"I heard Amos—he was the hotel owner—drew on Mr. Payne and shot him in the arm, first. Mr. Payne killed him. The word is that Amos was beating his wife, and Mr. Payne found out about it. I don't know, but it's what I heard."

Danner leaned back. "Where's the sheriff's office?"

The man stepped out and pointed down the street. "The other end of town across from the store. Can't miss it."

"Thank you," Danner replied, then swung back up on Bullet, who'd finished his assault on the water trough and waited patiently.

Danner slowly rode down a quiet Main Street, taking note of the saloon, hotel, and store before swinging over to the sheriff's building. Danner stopped and tied Bullet to the hitching post and noticed the boarded-up, pock-marked front door. He smiled and shook his head before the sound of his big boots striking the floorboards snapped the silence of the morning. Danner raised his massive hand to knock on the door when he heard a voice from inside.

"Who's there? What's your business?"

"Name's Luxton Danner. Wes Payne told me to look you up if I wanted to contact him."

Danner heard the metal bar slide out of its brackets. The door cracked open just enough for Danner to see two eyes, the tip of a gun barrel, and the bursting aroma of fresh coffee.

"US Marshal Luxton Danner?" Kirby asked.

"Used to be. Just Danner now. You Dan Kirby?" Danner asked to put the lawman at ease.

Kirby opened the door and holstered his gun before stepping aside from the doorway.

"Come on in. I'm Dan Kirby, all right, Sheriff of Buffalo Gap," Kirby said before engaging in a handshake with the towering Danner. "Wes has spoken of you often. His description of you was somewhat inaccurate. You're a lot bigger than he said." Kirby chuckled. "You'll find Wes in one of the cells around the corner." Kirby directed Danner, who paused and gave Kirby a look that included a frown and narrowed eyes.

"No, no! He's not in custody! He's just sleeping here these days. I'm sure he'll tell you all about it." Kirby laughed.

"I'm not sure I'll tell him anything!" Wes shouted before stepping around the corner, flashing a broad grin. "Damn good to see you, Danner!" Wes said, vigorously shaking his friend's hand. "What brings you to Buffalo Gap before sunup on a Thursday morning?" Wes asked, waving Danner toward the ladderback chair next to Kirby's desk.

"I've got a pot of coffee on. You two want a cup?" Kirby asked, walking over to the wood stove in the corner.

"I'd be mighty obliged, and call me Danner."

"I could use a cup of your mud myself," Wes chimed in, pulling another ladderback over to Kirby's desk.

"Last I heard, you were riding guard for the cattle outfits," Wes offered.

"Yep. I've been keeping busy with that most of the time. I ran into Clint Wade over in Fort Worth a couple of weeks ago.

He'll be here in a few days," Danner said, leaning back in his chair and looking Wes straight in the eye.

"Oh?" Wes replied, leaning forward and resting his elbows on his legs. "What kind of a job?"

"I don't rightly know just yet. I received a letter from Rachel Brennen. It seems there's some trouble up in Canyon Creek. She asked me to come up there and see if I could lend a hand," Danner said, accepting a hot cup of coffee from Kirby.

"You heard of trouble up in Canyon Creek, Kirby?" Wes asked the sheriff.

Kirby shook his head and took a seat behind his desk to join the conversation. "Nope. Can't say I have."

Danner removed the tightly folded paper from his shirt pocket and handed it to Wes. Wes opened the letter and began to read aloud:

Marshal Danner. I'm sorry to bother you, as I'm certain you are busy with your duties, but you may be able to help us with a situation here in Canyon Creek. Since Ben's passing, we have not had a marshal in town, and the sheriff only comes about once a week to check in. While there haven't been many problems for the sheriff to address, some problems with a new ranch owner's men have been. After you left, Gilford Knox bought the KC Ranch from Mr. Coleman. The moment he took ownership of the KC Ranch, he began to buy up as much land as possible around the town. Once he bought all the land for sale, he forced other landowners to sell. He bought the mill, then built a store, lumberyard, and saloon, and is finishing a hotel with a brothel connected to it. He has offered to appoint a marshal, but the men in town have resisted so far. At first, there didn't seem to

be a problem, but two men were killed. If possible, could
you come to Canyon Creek? I have told Mr. Knox I would
not sell my hotel to him many times, but he keeps asking,
and I am now considering leaving.
Thank you. Rachel.

Wes folded the letter and handed it back to Danner.

"Sounds like a saddle war to me," Kirby said.

"That's what I thought," Danner added.

Wes nodded. "Yep."

"If this Knox is as tough as he sounds, he'll have a couple of dozen gunmen riding for him," Danner said in between sips of hot black coffee, returning the letter to his shirt pocket.

"How many men you have?" Kirby asked Danner.

Danner looked at Wes. "I'm hoping three," Danner answered with a grin.

Wes returned the grin and nodded. "You have three. I got nothing else to do," he said with a chuckle. "I'm not sure three will be enough though, partner."

"Probably not, but me, you, and Wade are it right now," Danner reported. Danner glanced at Kirby. "Anyone in town might be interested?"

Kirby thought for a moment, then shook his head. "Nobody I know that'd be good enough," he said, rubbing his whisker-filled chin.

"Well, I'm hoping once we get to Canyon Creek, there will be a few ready to join us," Danner said, standing up, his six-foot, six-inch frame nearly reaching the ceiling beams. "That hotel open yet?"

"Should be. The lady running it has been serving breakfast around six o'clock the last couple of days," Kirby advised.

"Yeah, the fella over at the livery said the owner was shot,"

Danner said, looking hard at Wes. "Care to join me for breakfast and tell me all about it?" Danner asked Wes.

Wes kept his seat and stared into the knotted planks on the floor. "Naw, I'll stay here and wait for the district judge. He's due later today," Wes answered without further explanation.

"Very well. I'll stop by a little later," Danner announced. "Thanks for the coffee," he said, pausing to shake Kirby's hand one more time before disappearing into the misty dawn morning.

CHAPTER 14

Thursday, 11 July 1878

HARRY ALEXANDER –
BUFFALO GAP

L ater that afternoon, District Judge Harry Alexander snapped the reins and pushed his two-horse buggy a little faster down the middle of Main Street. He had been thinking about the cigars sold at the Buffalo Gap General Store for the last two hours and had grown impatient. The judge took a quick peek at his silver pocket watch and smiled. He had managed to get to town by one o'clock. Having left Sweetwater just after daylight, he had made suitable time. It helped that the thick cloud cover had kept the sun shy of the customary upper nineties that pummeled Texas day after day this time of year. It had kept his horses fresh.

"Whoa!" Harry called to his team, clutching leather straps in each hand and leaning back on the padded bench, both hands tugging on the reins, bringing the carriage to a halt in front of Buffalo Gap's general store. After looping the tie around the whip handle, he jumped down into the powdery dirt and quickly made his way up the two steps and into the store.

"Good afternoon, Judge!" Ed Rogatzki chimed, looking up from his leather-bound ledger spread open on the front counter's gnarled wooden surface. "Good to see you back,"

Rogatzki added, already reaching into the tobacco cabinet for a half-dozen cigars he knew the district judge craved. He tightly wrapped the thick cigars in heavy brown paper, securing the package with a white string tied in a slip knot.

"You're a good man there, Ed!" the judge exclaimed, reaching into his vest pocket and removing two silver dollars which he snapped down on the counter.

"Anything else I can get for you, Judge?" Rogatzki asked, handing over the neat package.

"No sir, not right away. I've been craving one of these since I passed through Lewis Canyon," Judge Alexander announced, taking a deep sniff of his purchase. "I understand Sheriff Kirby is waiting for me, so I reckon I best make my way over there right quick," the judge added before turning on his boot heels and ringing the door's bell on his way out to his carriage.

The judge wasted no time separating a fat aromatic smoke from its five compadres and, after snapping a match on his boot heel, burning the business end into a small flame. Three deep puffs and a wide grin sent a cloud of thick purple smoke circling above his head as he snapped the reins and continued to the sheriff's office. One of the more popular fixtures in Buffalo Gap, Judge Alexander found the need to answer greetings from several townsfolk on his short ride. Grasping his black leather attaché from the back of the carriage, Judge Alexander greeted one more well-wisher on the boardwalk before entering Sheriff Dan Kirby's modest office.

"Good afternoon, Judge," Wes offered a greeting while standing and extending a hand which Judge Alexander accepted.

"Good afternoon, Mr. Payne. Sheriff Kirby about?" he asked, taking a glance around the room.

"No, sir. He's down at the livery stable. He heard somebody lost a horse last night."

"Oh?" the judge responded with raised eyebrows.

"Kirby wasn't sure it was stolen. A drunk fellow thought he left it there last night but couldn't remember." Wes chuckled.

Judge Alexander laughed, then took the liberty of relieving some water from a pitcher Kirby kept on the shelf behind his desk.

"Well, Mr. Payne, according to the telegram I received in Sweetwater, it's you I need to speak with," Judge Alexander said, sitting down in Kirby's chair and patting the ladderback next to the desk, encouraging Wes to take a seat. "Now, what's this business with Amos Gentry?" the judge asked, blowing a stream of purple smoke into the air above his head. "Kirby's message said it was self-defense," the judge added, turning his attention to Wes.

Wes explained what had happened, describing each detail as best as he could remember, ending with the visual aid of the white bandage on his left arm. The judge sat quietly puffing on his tobacco treasure and listening intently. Just as the judge was about to ask a question, the door swung open, and Kirby entered.

"Sorry for the delay, Judge. I had a little misunderstanding down at the livery stable," Kirby explained, shaking the judge's hand.

"Was the horse stolen?" the judge asked, rolling his cigar between long, bony fingers.

"No, sir. It seems ol' Clyde forgot he left it out at the farm." Kirby chuckled before taking several papers from the corner of a shelf and placing them on the desk in front of the judge. "Here is my report and the witness statements."

The judge held his question and read through the statements. Wes and Kirby remained silent, watching the judge nod and shake his head as he perused the documents. After several minutes, the judge slid the papers across the desk toward Kirby, then looked at the lawman.

"I see no reason to believe this was anything other than a poor decision on Amos's part. Knowing Mr. Payne's background as a trusted Texas Ranger and honest man, I consider this case closed. I appreciate you staying here in Buffalo Gap until I arrived, Mr. Payne. That further convinces me that you only did what you had to do. How's that arm of yours anyway?" the judge asked, relieving what tension there was hanging in the room.

"It's getting better each day. It caught me near the elbow. Having a little trouble bending the arm, but the doc says that'll come around."

"Very good. Well, that's that. Any other immediate business we need to address before I head over to the hotel and get cleaned up a bit?" the judge asked, standing, and preparing to leave before Kirby answered there was nothing that couldn't wait. "Glad to hear it. This town is getting bigger by the day. I reckon we'll see a bit more trouble as time passes," the judge said, pausing to shake each man's hand before disappearing through the boarded-up door and into the street.

CHAPTER 15

Thursday, 11 July 1878

LUXTON DANNER &
WES PAYNE – BUFFALO GAP

W ith the confidence that a fresh shave, haircut, and clean clothes brought, Danner descended the roughhewn staircase at the Bison Hotel, where he noticed the faint red stain on the floor in the lobby. Annette Gentry's valiant efforts to clean the evidence of Wes's bullet wound had slightly failed and left a crimson reminder of her husband's demise. Danner turned into the dining room and found a table next to the rear wall allowing the gunslinger to sit with his back to the wall and see the front door and entire room. He had the opportunity to meet Annette Gentry upon checking into the hotel and understood Wes's attraction to her. Wes had never directly spoken of his interest in her, but he didn't have to. After piecing together several conversations Danner had with Wes, he knew of his partner's fondness for Mrs. Annette Gentry of Buffalo Gap. Danner scanned the room of occupied tables and presumed it was somewhere near the six o'clock hour. Rarely needing to know the exact time and thus not owning a watch, Danner based his clock on the sun's position and people's actions. He found these observations were entirely accurate.

"Good evening, Mr. Danner. Will you be having coffee with

your dinner?" Annette Gentry asked through a bright smile that seemed somewhat forced.

"Yes, ma'am. That'll be fine, and please call me Lux or Danner."

Annette Gentry tapped her hands on her hips and looked at Danner. A lock of dark hair fell across her face, which she, in turn, blew back to its last place. "Well, Mr. Danner, seeing as I don't know you very well yet, I'm sure calling you Lux would be inappropriate, and just Danner seems a bit disrespectful. I'll have to think about this," Annette Gentry offered with a laugh. Danner smiled and nodded.

Danner shifted his weight and leaned back in his chair. "Okay, Mrs. Gentry, you decide and let me know, but you'll have to decide pretty quickly as I'll only be in town for a couple of days!" Danner exclaimed, enjoying the interaction with such a pretty woman.

"Very well. Can I bring you a steak and potato, Mr. Lux Danner?"

"Yes, ma'am, that'll be fine," Danner answered, chuckling.

Annette Gentry started to walk away, stopped suddenly, and looked back at Danner. "Will Wes be joining you for dinner?" she asked softly.

"I don't know. We didn't discuss it, but I believe Wes is still uncomfortable with the idea of coming over here right now."

Annette Gentry returned to Danner's table and leaned toward him. "When you see him, please tell him it's acceptable for him to return. Despite what the ladies in town say, I'm fine."

Danner said nothing, just nodded, and smiled again. He didn't know or care what the ladies in town were saying, but he could figure it out. Despite Judge Alexander's decision the day before, Annette Gentry's husband had been buried only recently, and here she was, going about her business as if nothing had happened. Yep. That's what the ladies in town probably had to say. Those ladies who didn't own a business or had been beaten by their husbands when they had the notion, wouldn't understand. Danner had no use for such gossip and was further reminded of the matters men dealt with when they decided to settle down in one place. Nope. That wasn't for him. He was content with the life he chose. He was no farmer, rancher, or miner and had only met one woman in his life who could have convinced him to settle down, and that was a long time ago.

Danner's thoughts were interrupted by the arrival of his meal and the appearance of Wes standing in the lobby, hat in hand, apparently uncertain whether he should enter the dining room or not. After watching Wes fumble with his hat and glance around the entrance for a moment, Danner stood and waited. It didn't take long for Wes to spot his towering fellow gunslinger at the back of the room. Danner nodded toward the empty chair across the table. Wes walked directly to the table, avoiding eye contact with anyone else in the room. He quickly sat down and exhaled.

"Something's gotten into me. I don't know what it is. I've never felt like this before," Wes said, looking at two scratches on the otherwise blemish-free table surface.

Danner slowly sat down and looked at his partner. One of the other ladies came from the kitchen and asked Wes if he wanted coffee and a steak. Danner answered yes on behalf of Wes, who nodded. Recognizing his partner's dilemma, Danner decided the time had come for him to share a dark secret from his past.

"I once felt like everyone in the room was looking at me," Danner began, poking his fork into his steak.

"Oh?"

Danner paused and gathered his thoughts. He had never spoken of this to anyone and wasn't sure he cared to now. "I was still in college studying the law back in Pennsylvania when I attended a murder trial. The defendant was a drifter who got drunk one night and raped and murdered a young woman returning home after visiting a friend whose children were ill. It was late, and she was walking alone because she didn't live far away," Danner explained, now staring at the two scratches in the tabletop that Wes had fixated on when he first sat down. "Someone heard a scream, so they searched the dark streets and nearby buildings. A while later, the men who'd heard the cry found her. She was dead, strangled. They caught the defendant running away from where they found her body. The defense lawyer argued there wasn't enough evidence to find his client guilty during the trial. The jury agreed and let him go. The people in the courtroom nearly started a riot. It seemed like everybody but the jury thought he was guilty. As he left the courtroom, he looked at me and laughed. I knew everyone in the room was staring at me," Danner admitted, still poking nervously at his steak with his fork.

"Why was everyone staring at you?" Wes asked, somewhat puzzled by the story.

Danner swallowed hard and looked Wes in the eye. "Because that young woman was my fiancée."

Wes leaned back in his chair but said nothing. The waitress set a plate of food and coffee in front of Wes, who didn't notice. He rubbed the back of his neck, searching for words that wouldn't come. He shook his head slowly. Danner broke the unseen tension.

"I decided right then I wasn't going to be a damned lawyer. It wasn't the honorable profession my father had claimed. The only real justice happened outside the courtroom by men who knew the truth. I quit college and headed west. Wound up in Fort Smith working for the marshal's office," Danner said, pushing his plate away and standing up, no longer hungry.

"What happened to him?" Wes asked, staring back at the prevalent scratches on the table.

Danner stood tall, resting his hands on each of his holstered Schofield pistols.

"After boasting about how he got away with murder at a saloon that night, they found him two days later hanging from a tree outside of town," Danner said, placing his massive right hand on Wes's shoulder. "Evil men deserve what they got coming to them, partner," Danner added before walking toward the front lobby.

Wes leaped from his chair, grabbing his hat in one motion before hurrying after Danner. He caught the big gunslinger at the front door. "They ever find out who hung 'em?" Wes asked, knowing the answer deep down.

"Nope," Danner answered before pushing through the door.

Wes followed Danner into the street. "Where you headin'?"

"Lost my appetite. I thought I'd go have a whiskey or two."

"Mind if I join you?" Wes asked, matching his partner stride for stride.

"Only if you're buying," Danner responded with a chuckle.

"I reckon I walked right into that one!"

"You did."

CHAPTER 16

Friday, 12 July 1878

LUXTON DANNER – BUFFALO GAP

The following morning, Danner woke to the sounds of metal pans banging around in the kitchen downstairs in the Bison Hotel. The pain shooting between his temples reminded him of the whiskey he drank as he rolled out of bed. The sun was already up and sending a steady beam of heated light through the lone window in his room. He looked around, instinctively checking on his gun belt hanging on the bedpost, a chair tucked up under the door handle, and one Schofield .45, still in its place under the pillow next to him, thankful one of his recurring nightmares hadn't interrupted his night. He slowly stood to the resonances of snaps in his knees and back. The tepid water from the washbasin felt perfect on his face. He peered into the small, tarnished mirror hanging over the washbowl. He studied the lines that framed his eyes and pushed out from the lightning bolt scar that traveled from above his nose to the middle of his forehead, compliments of the broken window he dove through months ago in Red River City. For a twenty-nine-year-old man, he looked like a man who'd seen too much and been through even more. Ten years had passed since he walked away from Franklin and Marshall

College and began his one-person crusade to serve justice where it didn't exist.

Figuring a good meal would erase his indiscretions from the previous night's visit to the saloon, he made his way down the narrow staircase to the dining room. Based on the sun, the number of tables already in use, and others waiting, he guessed it was already after eight o'clock. He was also pretty sure it was Wednesday, which meant Clint Wade's prospective arrival.

"Would you like a table, or are you just gonna stand there and think about breakfast?" Annette Gentry asked from behind Danner before stepping to his side with her hands firmly planted on her white apron-wrapped hips.

"I thought breakfast would be an exceptional idea this morning, ma'am," Danner answered, looking down at the petite hotel owner. "How are you today?"

"Doing better today. Thank you. Now follow me, and we'll clear that head of yours," she spouted through grinning lips painted bright red.

She led Danner to a table against the back wall, then headed toward the kitchen.

"How would you know about my head?" Danner asked before she took the third step.

She stopped and smiled. "Well, everybody in the hotel heard you come in last night. It was rather late." She giggled before spinning around and walking into the kitchen.

Yep. I can sure see why Wes likes her. Danner took his customary visual scan of the room.

Danner saw Wes walk through the hotel's front doors halfway through his bacon and eggs, followed by Clint Wade. Wade was a well-known gunslinger with a solid reputation as a top hand. The dark-haired, thirty-something former wagon train guide and cattle drive guard was slightly shorter than Wes and Danner but still topped six feet with thick shoulders, muscle-clad arms, and a dark weathered face that made his brown eyes seem almost black like the clothes he always wore. Danner stood and shook Wade's hand as the two men snaked through the tables while nodding toward the two empty chairs at Danner's table.

"Look who I found wandering around the street this morning," Wes said with a laugh.

"Good to see you, Wade. Care for some breakfast or coffee?" Danner asked, seeing one of the waitresses heading toward his table.

"Just coffee," Wade said to the waitress.

"Same for me, Mrs. Joyner," Wes chimed in.

"Mrs. Joyner?" Danner asked with raised eyebrows.

"She's been helping Annette for some time now," Wes answered with a shrug of his shoulders.

"So, where'd you find this tired ol' gunfighter?" Wes quickly asked Danner, relieved to change the subject.

"I was up in the territory in Atoka when I received the letter from the folks in Canyon Creek. A couple of days later, Wade showed up with a cattle drive heading to Kansas City. I told him about the letter and Canyon Creek. Asked if he'd like to tag along," Danner explained.

"And here I am," Wade added. "When Sam Coleman said he was selling the KC to this man, Knox, I let out with the Hartsfield cattle outfit heading north. We stopped off in Canyon Creek on the way. Nice town. I stayed at the Sundown Hotel that night. Met Mrs. Brennen. Kind of a woman that's hard to forget. When Danner told me she asked for help, I figured I'd have a look-see," Wade explained. "He told me to meet him here in Buffalo Gap, figuring you'd be interested also."

"It'll take about two weeks to get up to Canyon Creek. I haven't sent word that we're coming. I figured it best not to let this Knox know anyone in town had called for help," Danner advised.

"Excuse me," Wes said, pushing his chair back at the sight of Annette Gentry standing in the kitchen doorway. "I'll see you two over at Kirby's office a little later."

"She the wife of that fella Wes killed?" Wade asked.

"Yep," Danner replied without further explanation. "I figure we'll head out in the morning. You okay with that?" Danner asked.

"Sure enough," Wade answered.

"Good. I left a list of supplies with the owner over at the store. I'll let him know we'll be by early to pick them up," Danner advised setting money on the table. "I'll see ya later," Danner added before leaving Wade at the table.

Danner stepped out into the blazing heat and proceeded to the store. Things were beginning to come together. He was relieved Wade agreed to join him, and he was relatively sure Wes would come on board. That made three good guns. He didn't want to recruit an army, but he'd feel more comfortable with a few more men. He'd put the word out at a couple of forts but finding men for a gun job at the moment was difficult with so many charging up to Colorado to dig for silver. Danner stopped in front of the store. It didn't matter. He got the two best he knew. That was all he needed for now.

CHAPTER 17

Friday, 12 July 1878

LUXTON DANNER & BUFFALO SOLDIERS – BUFFALO GAP

A t seven o'clock in the evening, the dining room at the Bison Hotel was raucous, with every table filled. A wagon train heading to Colorado had stopped in Buffalo Gap, and the would-be miners were flush with excited talk of striking it rich. The sizzling sound of steak and chicken frying, along with the familiar clang of steel pots and glass dishes banging around, rang out from the kitchen doorway. Loud bouts of laughter interrupted the constant chatter that bounced off the walls like a gunshot echo. Annette Gentry and her ladies were fighting a losing battle, trying to keep up with the constant demands for food and drink. Dan Kirby had joined Danner, Wade, and Wes at the back-wall table for what had become a rousing supper. Danner had already failed in his attempt to recruit the two gunslingers riding guard for the miners. He couldn't match the money the prospectors were paying. He wasn't even sure the folks in Canyon Creek were willing to pay for their services at all, let alone how much. Danner and company didn't bother with conversation. They decided to finish supper and get out of the hotel quickly. Besides, Kirby was more interested in what was happening over at the saloon, figuring if there would be trouble, it'd come from there or the tent brothel set up behind it.

Annette Gentry appeared at Danner's side as the foursome sawed through their steaks.

"Sorry to bother you, Mr. Danner, but there are some men on horseback in front of the hotel asking for you."

Danner set his knife and fork down and pushed his chair back from the table. "Did they say what they wanted?"

"No. The men just said they were looking for you. They didn't want to come in." She then leaned toward Danner and whispered something into his ear. Danner nodded, then stood, holding up his hands, motioning for the others to keep their seats.

"Any trouble, Danner?" Kirby asked.

"No, no trouble. Finish your supper. I'll see you after," Danner said, handing Annette two new Morgan silver dollars for his meal.

Danner stepped out of the noisy hotel and silenced the boisterous roar by closing the front door behind him. Four men, all armed with a single sidearm and Henry rifle, sat sharply in their saddles shoulder to shoulder on the left side of the wide front porch. Danner noted each man wore faded US Cavalry trousers tucked inside worn government-issued boots. The sun was setting behind the men, providing Danner with more silhouettes than the details of their identity. An intentional maneuver on their part, Danner mused.

"You men looking for Luxton Danner?" Danner asked, remaining on the elevated porch to speak at their level.

"Yes, sir. We hear he's looking for men to ride up to the Canyon Creek territory," the man mounted on the horse to Danner's right stated.

"I'm Danner. I'm looking for men that are good with a gun. May need it once we get there."

The door to the hotel flew open, and the rumble of the

energetic crowd inside preceded three wannabe prospectors stumbling over each other onto the porch behind Danner. Upon seeing Danner and the four horsemen, they stopped and fell silent. After a few moments, Danner ordered them to be on their way with a wave of his hand. They proceeded directly to the saloon, where they fumbled their way through the swinging doors. Danner turned his attention back to the four men.

"I'm not sure what we're getting into, and I don't know what the pay will be," Danner clarified.

The four men looked at each other, each offering a shrug of the shoulders as a response. "A job's a job," the man doing the speaking answered.

Danner leaned forward, propping his boot up on the railing that separated him from the four men. "You men former army?"

"Yes, sir. Tenth US Cavalry out of Fort Concho," the apparent leader advised.

Danner nodded his head. "Buffalo Soldiers," Danner said flatly. "Thought so once I saw those trousers."

"Yes, sir. Under the command of Colonel Benjamin Grierson. We fought in the Red River War. Our last post was at Fort Concho, but we've been out for about two months now. We ain't sharecroppers and ain't diggin' fer treasure, so we thought we'd see if you'd hire us," the leader explained.

The door opened behind Danner, and the noise spilled out once again. This time, the three men coming through the door were Wes, Kirby, and Wade, who joined Danner at the rail.

"These fellas were Buffalo Soldiers in the Tenth Cavalry at Fort Concho. They're looking to join us," Danner announced. "I haven't gotten their names yet," Danner said, turning toward the men.

"I'm Johnny Jackson, this is Buster, Isaac, and Edwin," Jackson introduced each man who nodded after their name.

"This is Wes Payne, Clint Wade, and Dan Kirby, Sheriff of Buffalo Gap. If you're still interested, you'll be joining me, Wes, and Wade in the morning."

"We'll join you, as long as it's good with the other two," Jackson answered.

"It's good with all of us," Danner assured Jackson without asking or looking at Wes or Wade, both of whom nodded in approval. "I'll make arrangements for you here in town," Danner continued.

"That won't be necessary. We'll pitch camp outside of town. Catch up with you in the morning," Jackson said before spurring his horse around and leading his men down Main Street and out of town.

"You reckon they'll be all right?" Kirby asked.

"I fought with the US colored troops in the war. Some of the best damn soldiers and riders I ever saw," Danner said as he watched his four recruits fade in the distance.

"Yep," Wade agreed.

"Well, gentlemen, I'd like to hang around, but I've got a job to do, so I'll see y'all later," Kirby announced before heading down to the saloon to check in on the business.

"You two care to join me at Kirby's office for a drink? It'll be a hell of a lot quieter there than here or at the saloon," Wes said.

"Sounds good to me. I could use a little quiet," Danner said.

"I'll take my chances over at the saloon. I'll see y'all in the morning," Wade announced.

"This oughta be a really interesting journey." Wes chuckled as he and Danner made their way to the sheriff's office.

"Yep," Danner replied.

CHAPTER 18

Saturday, 13 July 1878

RACHEL BRENNEN – CANYON CREEK

U p in the Texas panhandle town of Canyon Creek, three big Studebaker freight wagons rumbled down the sun-drenched Main Street, churning up a cloud of dust the likes of a tornado ripping through town. Seeing the massive twister charging her way, Rachel abruptly stopped her broom and rushed inside the Sundown Hotel, closing its doors just before the cloud could infiltrate its lobby. Rachel's twelve-year-old daughter, Adeline, descended the oak steps, her silver-buckle shoe heels tapping each step with a loud snap. Rachel sighed and peered through the dusty haze to watch the men methodically unload another shipment of lumber across the street where Gilford Knox was building another hotel next to his new saloon. Larger and more elaborate than the Sundown, it seemed clear Knox's purpose was to put Rachel out of business just like the Robertsons and other small ranchers. What once had been open land and cattle pens was now the end of town—owned by the ambitious cattleman. The only old building left on the west end of Canyon Creek was the jail and marshal's office, once occupied proudly by the late Ben Chance Sr. Now it was nearly hidden by the enormous Knox

General Store that the powerful rancher was building across from his Grand X Hotel. The two-story bawdy house attached to the back of the hotel was already in use, with lewd women arriving weekly.

"What's wrong, Mommy?" Adeline asked her bewildered mother.

"Nothing, dear. Are all the empty rooms upstairs tidy?"

"Yes, ma'am. All finished," Adeline proudly declared through an ear-to-ear smile.

"Okay, go get some sugar bread in the kitchen, then." Rachel barely got the words out before Adeline raced out of the lobby. "Wash your hands first!" her mother shouted after the energetic girl.

Rachel glanced through the window. Lumber-carrying men were scurrying around in all directions like ants building their hill. She heard the constant grating of the saws and the rhythmic pounding of the hammers. The building looked finished from the outside. Rachel figured it wouldn't be long before she lost most of her single male customers. Knox had built his saloon right next to his hotel, and the men wouldn't need to stray far for female attention. Rachel was amazed at the swiftness of Knox's progress. In a few short months, he dramatically changed the town of Canyon Creek.

The tapping of heels on the Sundown's steps startled Rachel, causing her to drop the towel she had been unconsciously twisting in her hands. Betsy Tyler's bright smiling face immediately lifted Rachel's spirits. She opened the door to greet the town's boarding house proprietor and part-time schoolteacher.

"Hello, Betsy! Please come in!" Rachel exclaimed with a bit more energy than usual as she kneeled to retrieve the towel from the floor.

"I seemed to have startled you, dear. Something wrong?" Betsy asked her friend.

"No, not really. I was just watching the activity across the street, is all," Rachel replied with a loud exhale.

Betsy Tyler frowned and glanced over toward the construction. "I try not to think about that too much. I don't know why. When I see Mr. Knox, he's always cordial, but his men are quite the opposite."

"I've only spoken with Mr. Knox twice. When he offered to buy the Sundown, and again when he came in for supper. He was very charming on both occasions, but there's just something about the man I don't trust," Rachel admitted. "I heard he offered to buy your place also."

"Yes, he did. I think he offered to buy just about everything in town when he first got here. I believe he would like to rename the town, Knox," Betsy mumbled.

"Can I offer you some tea?" Rachel asked, walking toward the dining room.

"That would be wonderful. I just thought I'd come by for a visit if you weren't too busy."

"I've actually had some time to myself since I hired Mrs. Gibson, and Adeline has also been a big help," Rachel advised. "I'm afraid that when Mr. Knox opens his hotel, I may have to let Mrs. Gibson go. I don't know if I'll have enough business."

"We should be fine when the cattle drives come through."

"True," Rachel said, pouring hot tea into two white cups.

Betsy took a sip of tea, set the cup down, and leaned forward, resting her hands on the table. "Have you heard from Mr. Danner yet?" Betsy anxiously asked.

Rachel smiled as she carefully set her teacup onto its saucer.

"No."

"Maybe he's been out and hasn't been back to Fort Smith to receive your letter," Betsy speculated, her red lips curling up on each end.

"I don't know; it's been a month now. I don't know how the marshals work, but I think he should have gotten it by now." Rachel sighed.

The two women sat quietly for several minutes before Betsy spoke up. "Have others been asking?"

"Every day, someone comes by and asks. Mrs. Gibson asks every evening when she arrives. She says that the lumberyard is near empty since Mr. Knox bought the mill. None of the ranchers or farmers can get lumber now. The lumber is for Knox's businesses.

"Yes, Mrs. Loman told me business was excellent when Knox first arrived, but he'll soon open his store, and then who knows?" Betsy added.

"It seems like most of the new people coming into town are working for Mr. Knox in some way. Their first stop is at Mr. Johnson's office before they do anything."

"I saw Mr. and Mrs. Johnson arrive on the stage a couple of months ago. I see he's a lawyer," Betsy stated.

"Yes, he's handling all of Mr. Knox's land business, I guess. Mr. and Mrs. Johnson have been regular guests for supper. She's a lovely woman. Her name is Abigale."

The sound of the bell hanging on the front door interrupted the conversation. Albert Loman appeared in the doorway, hat in hand. "Pardon me, ladies, I don't mean to intrude Mrs. Brennen, but I was wondering if you've heard from Mr. Danner."

"No, nothing yet, I'm afraid," Rachel answered, standing to address her guest.

"I figured as much. I just heard that Clarence Parks sold out to Knox. He stopped at the store to get provisions. The whole family is letting out in a few days," Loman advised.

"Oh no!" Betsy gasped.

"That's not all. Frankie says he's thinking about accepting Knox's offer for his livery stable also," Loman said, slowly shaking his head.

"Is there anything that man doesn't want to own in this town?" Betsy exclaimed, standing to leave. "Thank you for the tea, dear. I'll come to see you soon," she added before stomping through the dining room, her steps echoing through the space.

"Good day, Miss Tyler," Loman said as Betsy passed him in the doorway. "She seems a might upset."

"Mr. Walsh has been calling on her regularly for a while now. There was talk of them getting married until Mr. Knox fired him from the lumber mill," Rachel explained.

Loman thought for a moment, then nodded his head. "I see, and Frankie gave him a job at the stables, but if Frankie sells out, Stoney will be out of another job," Loman thought aloud.

"I'm afraid so."

"Well, I hope you hear from Mr. Danner soon. I heard that Virgil Robertson's herd was run off the other night," Loman stated.

"Even if I do, I'm not sure what he can do. Mr. Knox hasn't broken the law as far as we know," Rachel said.

"Maybe, but since he arrived, he's gotten his way on just about everything. We're all sure that he's behind the harassment the ranchers and farmers are experiencing. We need someone to stop that, and those who remember him believe Mr. Danner is just the man to do that. Have a good day, Mrs. Brennen," Loman said before turning and leaving quickly.

True. Regardless, it would be good to see Danner return.

CHAPTER 19

Saturday, 13 July 1878

VIRGIL ROBERTSON, DALE MORGAN & CARL KINCAID – CANYON CREEK

V irgil Robertson navigated his buckboard toward the Sundown Hotel, followed by the Kincaids and the Morgans in their carriages. The three men, along with their wives and Virgil's daughter, Shelley, who refused to stay home, were eager to meet with the business owners in town and discuss the option of hiring gunmen to guard their properties. The men believed it was the only way to slow down Gilford Knox's relentless quest for land supremacy. The wives weren't sure, fearing for their husband's safety, and Shelley reckoned she was the only guard her father needed. After tethering their wagons behind the Sundown, Virgil led the entourage into the hotel dining room, where they claimed a large round table near the kitchen. Despite the six o'clock supper time, the dining room was only half full of regulars. The departure of a wagon train of miners the previous day and the relentless construction by Knox cut the Sundown's business nearly in half. Madeleine Robertson waved to Rachel, who greeted the table of friends with a bright smile.

"Good evening, everyone! I haven't seen you all here in quite some time!" Rachel gushed as she made her way around the table, pausing to hug each of the ladies. "Is everyone here for supper?"

"Yes, dear," Madeleine Robertson assured her friend.

"We were also wondering if you've heard back from Mr. Danner?" Carl Kincaid quickly asked.

Rachel's smile faded. "No, not yet. It doesn't appear that he's coming. I believe he would have responded by now." Rachel sighed, twisting the towel in her hands into a tight knot.

"Not necessarily. Fort Smith is a long way from here, and communication isn't all that dependable," Carl Kincaid offered in an optimistic tone of voice.

"Well, as you and Mr. Morgan know, it's been over a month now since almost everyone in town asked me to send the letter," Rachel responded. "Oh, excuse me," Rachel added, hurrying away at the sight of a couple of cowboys entering the room.

"That settles it then, gentlemen. I believe we need to move forward with our plan to hire guards." Virgil wasted no time with his suggestion.

"That's what we needed to do a month ago!" Shelley exclaimed, much to her mother's dismay.

"Shelley, these decisions don't come lightly, and it takes money to hire gunmen," Virgil reminded his daughter.

"I've talked to several of the farmers nearby. Most of them are on board with hiring guards, but they don't have the money, and some of their crops getting trampled in the middle of the night don't help," Morgan said.

"Any idea how much pay a hired gunman gets?" Virgil asked.

"At least two hundred a month. For a good one anyway," Kincaid answered.

"Two hundred a month!" Madeleine gasped. "How are we going to pay that?"

"Could we write a letter to the governor and ask him to send some Rangers?" Anne Kincaid asked the men.

"We've already discussed that. The governor doesn't have enough Rangers to send for trouble with small ranchers and a few farmers. There aren't that many Rangers, and from what I hear, they have their hands full with the Mexican banditos down along the Rio Grande. That's why we were hoping to get Marshal Danner here. We figured Knox would know better than to cause trouble with a US Marshal around. If he brings too much attention to the marshal's office in Fort Smith, the president might send troops," Carl Kincaid explained.

"Besides, we won't be selling our stock until October, and it's only July. Three months is a long time to pay for protection. I, for one, wouldn't mind having those military troops here for a while," Dale Morgan added.

Virgil observed his fellow ranchers ponder their decisions. Carl Kincaid and Dale Morgan said nothing further, each looking off into the far corners of the dining room, slightly nodding their heads intermittently. Suddenly, Kincaid glared at the archway in the front of the room. Virgil followed Kincaid's gaze and looked over his shoulder and saw Gilford Knox and three of his men speaking to Rachel, who was looking around the room in search of an available and appropriate table. Knox noticed the three ranchers and immediately started to make his way toward their table. Not a particularly big man in his late thirties, Gilford Knox was nevertheless intimidating with his neatly trimmed coal-black hair that framed a weathered stone-cold face equipped with a sharp jutting jaw. Always impeccably dressed in a tailored suit, bolo tie, and topped with a mist-gray Stetson, Knox appeared to always be ready for business. He rarely wore a gun, opting to have armed men with him wherever he went. Rumor was that his father had been an ambitious high-ranking official in Washington and thus accumulated significant wealth before, during, and after the war. Ambition and wealth passed on to his son, who was now determined to build his empire in Texas.

"Good evening, ladies, gentlemen," Knox greeted the group as he removed his hat. "Good to see all of you in town. Soon you'll have a large, well-stocked store and another restaurant to patronize," Knox added, forcing the best fake smile he could muster.

"Hello, Mr. Knox. Here for the best supper in town?" Kincaid asked, looking past him to Rachel, who'd followed the wealthy rancher to the table.

"Absolutely!" Knox answered, flashing a more sincere grin as he looked back toward Rachel and slightly bowed. Not to mention the prettiest lady in town," Knox added, bringing a tight, thin grin to Rachel's ruby-red lips, enriched by her blushing face.

Knox returned his attention to the table. "If I'm not mistaken, gentlemen, this appears to be a meeting, so I'll leave you to your business, which I hope includes considering my latest offers for your properties. Oh yes, I also heard about your misfortune the other night, Mr. Robertson. I was sorry to hear about that. Let me know if my men or I can assist," Knox offered before turning away from the table.

"We're not selling out to you!" Shelley bellowed.

Knox turned and glared at the boisterous cowgirl, who received a stern look and slap on the arm from her mother. Knox's eyes narrowed to nothing more than slits on his face. He neither frowned nor smirked. He remained silent for a moment, then quietly turned to Rachel. "Would you have a table available?" he asked the hostess, who waved toward a table at the opposite side of the room.

Virgil watched Knox settle in at his table with his men, who'd waited dutifully at the front of the room until their boss called them over to the table. Virgil and the others knew Knox's visit to their table was anything but social. He delivered his message all right. He had also made the ranchers' decision for them. Despite the cost, they'd have to meet force with force. It was either that, sell out, or lose everything and leave town.

The loud ringing of glass pierced the boisterous chatter in the room. Virgil looked back toward the sound to see Knox standing at his table, tapping his glass with his dinner knife. Knox's actions resulted in the desired response of silence.

"Pardon the interruption, ladies and gentlemen, but if you permit me a moment of your time, I'd like to make an announcement. For those of you who don't know me, I'm Gilford Knox. I operate Sam Coleman's former KC Ranch, now the Circle X, the Knox Saloon, hotel, store, and the newly purchased livery stable and corrals. With the imminent opening of my hotel and store and because Canyon Creek has no marshal or sheriff here, I've instructed three of my men to remain in town to protect my interests," Knox announced in a booming deep voice.

Virgil slowly glanced back at Kincaid and Morgan, who mirrored his frown but said nothing. The crowd erupted into chaotic banter, with clashing shouts of support and displeasure reverberating around the room. Knox held up his hands and stepped out from behind his table, then stepped to the center of the room. The jovial expression he displayed earlier had been replaced by a narrowed brow and sharp frown.

"Please! Please! Folks! Settle down for a moment!" Knox roared in a deep, commanding voice, forcing his frown into the best smile he could muster. "I'm not suggesting my men will be the law in this town. That's for y'all to decide, but with no town marshal and only sporadic visits from the sheriff, I feel it's necessary to protect my interests."

"From what, Knox? You practically own this town already!" a man shouted from a distant table to the roar of the crowd's approval.

"Now you own the livery stable?" another man shouted.

"I just finalized the deal with Mr. Garcia. I believe you'll see much-improved service there," Knox mordantly began before more shouts of anger doused his further attempts to speak.

Knox, recognizing his efforts to explain his position further would be futile, waved toward his three men and pointed toward the front door. Just as Knox was about to pass under the arch, Virgil stood. He knew what he was about to say was only a half-truth, but Knox wouldn't know that.

"We don't need your gunmen in town, Mr. Knox! We've sent a letter to Fort Smith requesting a US Deputy Marshal! He should be here in a few days!" Virgil shouted.

The room fell quiet again as Knox slowly turned back to glare into the room, fixating on Virgil. Clutching his Stetson with both hands, his eyebrows arched high into his forehead. He tilted his head back slightly.

"Well, I was not aware we had a US Marshal coming to Canyon Creek. That may change things, but until the marshal arrives, my men stay," Knox declared before quickly donning his Stetson and departing the hotel, realizing he had worn out his dinner welcome.

"I'm not sure you should have said that, Virgil," Kincaid softly stated.

"I know, Carl. Now I really hope Marshal Danner is on his way."

"I don't know how the rest of you feel, but Mr. Knox scares me. If Marshal Danner doesn't arrive soon, I'm taking my girls and going to Louisiana," Madeleine declared.

"I don't blame you, dear," Anne Kincaid answered.

"I don't either," Mrs. Morgan chimed in.

"We'll discuss it further at home," Virgil quietly told his wife, patting her on the arm in a futile attempt to reassure her.

CHAPTER 20

Thursday, 18 July 1878

DANNER, WES, WADE, AND THE TROOPERS – OUTSIDE TANABE

A five-day ride south of Canyon Creek, a colossal southern live-oak tree was jutting majestically upward from the arid craggy West Texas terrain. It was a welcome sight to Danner and his men. Its long-reaching leaf-packed wings would provide much-needed relief from the sun's fiery rampage. Five days out of Buffalo Gap, Danner and company hadn't seen much other than an endless vista of rain-starved landscape dotted with Indian hawthorn, sumac, buffalo grass, and desiccated tumbleweed that had once masqueraded as purple sage. Based on the sun's whereabouts in the unblemished blue sky, Danner figured the hottest part of the day was behind them. Still, the relief from the oak's shade would provide a respite for the sweat-soaked men and their equally drenched horses.

"How far did you say that Tanabe settlement is?" Danner asked Wes.

"I reckon it's still a couple of hours north of here," Wes answered.

"How about an hour or so of shade, then we move onto

Wes's town?" Danner asked Wade and the former soldiers trudging along a few horse lengths behind.

The four men all nodded in approval, not bothering to remove the bandanas that kept their mouths from drying further.

After Wes and Danner removed their saddles, Ringo, Bullet, and the other mounts snorted in relief. The horses' hides were glistening from head to hoof.

"We better give these mounts some rest. They're about worn out," Wes commented to the mumbling agreement of the other men.

Danner leaned back against the ridged scales of the big oak's skin and took a drink from his canteen. "Is there a hotel or boarding house in this town of yours?" he asked Wes.

"Well, I never said it was a town. It was more of a camp or settlement the last time I was there, about a year ago. It's an old Comancheros trading post that turned into a settlement after the Comanche were runoff," Wes explained. "It's next to an arroyo near the Brazos River. The Comanche named it Tanabe, which means sun. The post was still there, along with a few other buildings and barns. There was talk of some farming, but it's so damned dry out here I don't reckon that happened. Might be some ranching nearby."

"I was up that way driving a herd about six months ago. No hotel, but there's a saloon, cantina, and a brothel," Wade chimed in with a chuckle.

"See. There you go. Food, water, and a lady's attention. What else do you need?" Wes laughed.

Danner allowed a thin smile to crack his stoic face, hooked his thumbs onto his gun belt, and shook his head as the sound of the seven noble gunfighters' boisterous laughter scattered about, dying out in the lonesome distance.

"I'll keep watch if y'all want to grab a little shut-eye," Danner offered, taking a cue from Jackson and his trio of former soldiers who'd not waited for an invitation to stretch out with hats tipped low over their eyes.

Figuring there wasn't a man within ten miles of their camp, Danner leaned his Winchester against the tree's scaled trunk and pulled the Canyon Creek letter from his saddlebag. He had already read it three or four times, but he wanted to be sure he hadn't missed something. A particular word, possible tone, anything that would offer additional information. Convinced the greedy rancher the sheriff in Sawyer had told him about was the reason behind Rachel's request on behalf of Canyon Creek, and after rereading the message provided no additional clues, he returned it to his saddlebag and watched the heat waves flutter off the land's surface in the distance. *I'll send word of our impending arrival when we reach Oneida.*

———◆———

Three hours later, after the horses rested, the men continued their journey. As the bottom edge of the day's sun began to kiss the western horizon, the once-bustling trading post of Tanabe came into view. The arroyo to its east looked like it hadn't felt the massage of moving water since the winter rains. Several large cattle pens sat vacant to the west. The reflection of the Brazos looked inviting just beyond the trivial settlement, and the swirling dust clouds floating above indicated activity inside its borders.

"I sure hope that saloon is well stocked," Wade offered as he pulled up next to Danner and Wes while Jackson and company preferred to follow a few horse lengths behind.

"Wouldn't mind that myself," Wes added.

"Nor I," Danner agreed.

The weary riders crossed the imaginary border of Tanabe behind four lumber-packed freight wagons escorted by several armed guards who all stopped and carefully scrutinized Danner and his men. Knowing the guards' apprehensions, Danner nodded and waved at the six-armed escorts who returned the gesture before spurring their horses back toward the wagons.

"That lumber is worth its weight in gold out here," Wes said. "Must've taken 'em a couple of weeks to get it here," he added.

"I figure you're right about that since the railroad hasn't made it this far yet, and I'm guessing the closest mill is up in Oneida," Danner stated.

Danner scanned the various unprepossessing buildings, tents, and shacks. The lumber wagons stopped in front of a half-built, new lumber structure that might someday function as a hotel. The old trading post was the largest structure in town. Its dilapidated roof and cracked timber walls had seen better days. Still, the town seemed to be reasonably busy. A solid barrier of horseflesh tied to various posts and makeshift troughs shielded the saloon.

"It appears we have the answers to our questions. No hotel, but the saloon looks inviting," Danner announced, reigning Bullet toward the building displaying a bullet-riddled sign that read "Tanabe Saloon."

Danner dismounted but couldn't find a piece of rail or hitching post to tether Bullet.

"I'll take care of the horses," Wade announced.

Danner nodded, then stopped to inspect the sign. He noticed the S in the word saloon had been nearly obliterated by what he figured were the bullets of pistols held in the hands of too many drunken men. Wes pushed through the doors first when Danner realized Jackson wasn't behind him. Danner paused and looked back to see Jackson and the former Buffalo Soldiers still mounted shoulder to shoulder in front of the saloon.

"Come on in, men, I'll buy the first beer," Danner advised his four gunfighters.

The four men didn't move. Wade stood near, waiting to take their reins.

"Look, fellas, the color of a man's skin don't mean much out here, and if it does, we'll take care of that. I'm sure you all could use a beer like the rest of us."

Jackson looked at his three companions and nodded before stepping down from his saddle. Wade took the horses around to the back of the saloon. Danner walked through the swinging doors with Jackson and company close behind. Danner rested his hands on the grips of his pistols and quickly scanned the packed and spacious room. An assortment of weathered drifters, dirty cowboys, and other worn-out-looking stragglers, all immersed in a cloud of thick purple smoke. Most were armed, some not. Two bartenders were briskly keeping the demanding men furnished with libations. Two tables pushed into a back corner were surrounded by several unkempt women. A saloon guard armed with a sawed-off shotgun sat on a stool next to the bar. The guard began to stand up when Jackson and the other former Buffalo Soldiers walked in. Danner looked at the saloon guard and shook his head. The shotgun guard paused, then nodded and returned to his stool. Wes stood against a wall with seven mugs of beer already lined up on a shelf. Danner proceeded through the gaggle of men to Wes, who'd nearly finished his first mug.

"Step on up, boys," Wes called above the raucous crowd noise.

Jackson and the former troopers snatched up their mugs and emptied each in one long gulp, followed by canyon-size smiles.

"Ooh we, that's mighty good!" Jackson declared, his fellow troopers vigorously nodding in agreement.

Danner took a long swig of his brew and watched the front door for Wade, who promptly stepped into the rowdy saloon and spotted Danner, who stood nearly a head taller than most anybody else in the place. As Wade navigated his way through the maze of humanity, he was intercepted by two of the prostitutes, one taking each arm, attempting to direct him to their table in the back. Danner, Wes, and the soldiers all burst out with laughter when Wade's refusal of their wares was met with hostile unintelligible shouts of blatant insults and curt waves of their hands.

"It appears you're not their favorite right now, Wade," Wes shouted as he handed his fellow gunfighter his beer.

"Nope. I reckon not," Wade responded through a laugh.

Danner paused while the men finished their first drinks, then leaned into his group of gunslingers.

"We ought to be in Oneida the day after tomorrow. When we get there, I'll send a telegram to Canyon Creek that we're on the way. It's only a long day's ride from Oneida to Canyon Creek. We should get there quick. That sound all right to everyone?" Danner asked.

The unanimous nods of approval prompted Danner to turn toward the bar for round two.

CHAPTER 21

Friday, 19 July 1878

VIRGIL ROBERTSON & SHELLEY ROBERTSON – ROBERTSON RANCH

S till troubled by his ill-advised comment to Knox at the Sundown six days earlier, Virgil tapped his spurs on his horse's flanks, sending his mount into a gallop. The sun was dipping out of sight, and he wanted to get back home before dark. His meeting with Kincaid and Morgan had gone well enough, but they still hadn't had any takers on their offer to hire gunmen to go up against Knox and his gunslingers. No one in town was good enough with a gun, and the settlers making their way into Canyon Creek these days were farmers and merchants looking for land or just passing through to the silver mining towns further west. Knox had been quiet since the night at the Sundown Hotel when he learned about the letter to Fort Smith. Everyone feared Knox's silence was just a ploy. The trio of ranchers pontificated at the thought of Knox being dissuaded by the news of a pending visit by a US Marshal. Earlier in the day, there was a rumor that a cattle drive would be passing near Canyon Creek. Virgil and Kincaid had decided they'd pay a visit to the town and see if the tale was accurate.

They thought there might be a cowboy or two looking to make better money than pushing cows paid.

Virgil galloped around the house and headed for the barn. He readied his horse for the night, then stepped through the front door.

"You take those dirty boots off, Virgil Robertson!" Madeleine shouted from the kitchen as she set a hot cup of coffee on the table next to a couple of cake donuts that she and the younger girls had made earlier that evening.

"Thank you, dear. These cakes sure look tasty!" Virgil exclaimed, taking a seat at the table.

"You had supper at the Kincaid's?" Madeleine asked.

"Yes, ma'am."

"Anything new?" she asked, removing her white apron and taking a ladderback chair opposite her husband at the table.

"No, nothing. There's a rumor a cattle drive might be passing near us in the next day or two, but nobody in town knew for certain."

"The more I think about this, the more I don't like it, Virgil," Madeleine confessed. "There's been no trouble for nearly a week now. Maybe telling Knox about the letter was enough."

Virgil shook his head and swallowed his mouthful of cake. "No, no, no. Knox is just waiting to see if a marshal will show up. And since it's been a few days and no marshal, he probably knows it was a lie."

Madeleine let out a long sigh before reaching across the table and collecting the empty plate. Virgil's two youngest daughters rushed into the room looking for their cake which their mother had promised after their father had gotten his.

"Hello, Daddy!" the girls shouted in unison as they grabbed their cake and hurried out of the kitchen back to their room.

"Where's Shelley?" Virgil asked, looking around the house.

"She said she had something to do and left right before you got home."

"Did she take her horse? Say where she was going?" Virgil asked, now standing with the wrinkled expression of a worried father.

"I believe she did take her horse, but I don't know where she was going. I thought she was just going to check on the cows. You know how she likes to sit and watch them in the evening."

Virgil tossed his napkin onto the table and hurried to the door, where he slipped his boots on and quickly left the house. He walked out past the barn and looked down into the pasture where the cattle he managed to round up were lazily grazing. He strained to see through the gray dusk air—no sign of Shelley or her horse, near as he could tell. *Now, what's that girl up to now?* He shook his head and plunged his hands into his coverall pockets before returning to the house.

Oblivious to her father's actions at the house, Shelley gently rubbed her horse's nose to keep the mare as quiet as possible. A short ten-minute ride from the main house, she reached into her vest and removed a carrot that the mare quickly crunched away. She pulled her Winchester from its scabbard and sat down against a mesquite tree on the western edge of their north pasture. The tree's low-hanging branches provided excellent concealment. Since no marshal had come to town, she figured Knox knew her father had lied. That meant he'd try something. At least, that's what she believed. This time she'd be ready. She laid her rifle across her lap and removed a donut from a satchel that contained extra cartridges for the Winchester. She ate the treat and watched the moon slowly come into view. The three-quarter white orb would provide enough light to see any rustlers come onto the pasture.

About two hours into her mission, she checked the silver pocket watch her mother and father had given to her on her eighteenth birthday. It had come from somewhere back east, they had told her. She didn't need to know the exact time of the day for the most part, but tonight it would serve a purpose. She flipped it open and turned it toward the moonlight and saw it was nearly ten o'clock. Except for the lone lantern hanging from the front porch rafter that her father kept as a beacon for her return, the house was dark. *Good. That ought to invite Knox's men.* She moved her legs under her hips and took a kneeling position, leaning on her rifle. She saw the herd milling around on the far side of the fallow. She settled back and waited.

The wait lasted less than an hour. Shortly before eleven o'clock, Shelley noticed movement in the shadows along the northern edge of the pasture. It looked like two riders moving slowly over the crest of the hill. Shelley stood and set the barrel of her Winchester into the crotch of a mesquite branch. She peered through the sights. A bead of sweat trickled down from the top of her forehead along the edge of her nose. She ignored the heat-generated intrusion and kept her eyes on the riders. The two riders separated and took positions on the herd's flanks.

Not this time. She squeezed back on the trigger.

Crack! The shot hit its mark. The rider jerked back and fell off his horse. The startled herd shuffled about but made no move toward a stampede. Shelley racked another round into the chamber. She carefully aimed at the second rider who'd kicked his horse into a gallop around the backside of the herd. *Crack!* Her second shot missed but caused the rustler to lean low in the saddle. He charged around the pack and jumped off his horse where the first rider had fallen. Moving quickly, he lifted the limp man over his saddle, then mounted and bolted toward the north hill, the presumed dead rider's horse running close behind. Shelley watched the rustlers disappear over the hill. She racked another round into the chamber and watched. Shelley heard the snap of the house's front door slam shut. Looking back, she saw her father in the glow of the porch lantern, rifle in hand, scanning the pasture.

"Shelley!"

She could hear her father calling her in the distance. She stayed quiet and waited another couple of minutes before sliding her Winchester into its scabbard and hopping up into the saddle. She maneuvered her mare out of the thicket, then galloped back to the barn where her father stood waiting.

"Get in the house, girl!"

"But Dad!"

"Get in the house, now!" Her father shouted in a voice that sounded more like a grizzly bear than her father. She never heard him speak to her like that before.

Shelley dropped her mare's reins and quickly marched to the house where her mother waited inside the screen door. Shelley stepped inside and began to speak to her mother, whose raised hand stopped the words before they could be said. Shelley turned and stomped into her room, slamming the door behind her. She unbuckled her gun belt and let it fall to the floor, then threw herself face down onto her bed. Shelley squeezed her pillow with tight fists. She wasn't sorry. She had only done what no one else had the guts to do.

CHAPTER 22

Saturday, 20 July 1878

SHELLEY ROBERTSON – ROBERTSON RANCH

The following day, a rooster's call shook Shelley from a restless night. She spent more time awake than asleep, and at some point during the night, she managed to change into her nightshirt, leaving her clothes scattered about the floor. The bedroom door slowly opened, and she heard her mother's light steps across the rough wood.

"Michelle. Your father needs to speak with you right away," her mother said in a voice shaking with anxiety.

Shelley turned to see her mother's face strewn with lines of worry. "What is it?"

"There are two men here from Mr. Knox's ranch. They say one of their men was shot here last night. Your father told them he didn't know anything about that, but they're very insistent."

Shelley leaped from the sheets. "Damn right, one of their men was shot here last night! I'll tell them I did it, and if anyone comes back, I'll do it again!" Shelley exclaimed, reaching for her robe dangling from a hooked nail next to her bed.

"You'll do no such thing," Virgil Robertson told his daughter, stopping her with two firm hands grasping her shoulders. "I told them we knew nothing about a shooting last night. I told them we heard what may have been gunshots about midnight, but I saw nothing when I came out to look. I don't know if they believed me, but they're gone now. If anyone asks, you'll say the same. You understand, girl?"

"They were going to run off the rest of our herd! I just stopped them!" Shelley shouted, locking eyes with her father.

"Did you know that for sure?" Virgil asked. "That was Knox's foreman. He said Knox sent riders over to check on our herd last night. He said Knox sent men to Kincaid's and Morgan's also. Said Knox wanted to make sure the herds were left alone. I'm going to ride over to Kincaid's and see if he knows anything about it."

"I'll go with you—"

"You'll stay right here and do nothing! You understand me!" Virgil ordered through gritted teeth before spinning on his right boot heel and stomping out of the room.

The front door slammed closed. Shelley's head spun, making her feel dizzy and sick. She never gave her father a reason to speak to her as he did. Her mother brushed her long hair away from her face.

"Get washed up, dear. I'll have breakfast for you in a few minutes," Shelley's mother said in a low voice, not knowing what else to say.

Shelley said nothing, just nodded her head. She watched her mother leave the room through blurry eyes. *Was it a mistake?* She wasn't sure, but she didn't believe Knox had sent those men to do anything but run off the herd again. She waited until her mind stopped racing like a runaway mustang, then she washed and dressed and joined her sisters for a deathly quiet meal.

After breakfast, Shelley tended to the horses, saddled her mare, and headed for the pasture to check on the herd. She found the animals milling around the same area they had been the night before. Shelley swung down from the saddle and began searching the grass for blood. Shelley knew the rustler fell off his horse, but she wasn't confident her bullet hit its mark. After a twenty-minute scan of grass and churned soil, she found her evidence. The dark crimson stain about the size of her hat brim covered grass and dirt on the west side of the herd. She stood and looked toward the thicket she occupied last night.

Yep. I reckon this would be the right spot. Good. It looks like I didn't miss.

She stepped into the stirrup and swung back up into the saddle. She tapped her spurs and guided her mare toward the north side of the pasture. A small hill at the northern end of the Robertson ranch provided a natural barrier from the Kincaid property. Being on friendly terms, Virgil and Kincaid had opted against a fence that could maim or even kill a stray cow. That wasn't the case on the west side, which butted against the Knox ranch, but Virgil hadn't had the money to stretch wire along the Knox land. That left the Robertson land open and susceptible to easy rustling. Shelley gazed down toward the Kincaid place and saw a single rider approaching at a gallop. She recognized Clay Cox heading her way.

"Morning, Shelley," Cox greeted as he reined his horse to stop.

"Hello, Mr. Cox. What brings you this far?" Shelley asked, fearing the answer.

"I saw your father on the way. He told me about last night and this morning's visit from Knox's men. I thought I should tell you that Knox did send men to our place last night. I was with a calving cow when they showed up. Said that Knox wanted to make sure everything was all right with our herd.

They said Knox sent men to Morgan's also. We haven't checked with Morgan yet, but my guess is he also got a visit."

"Why all of a sudden is Knox so interested in the safety of our stock?" Shelley asked, shaking her head.

"That's what Kincaid and I were talking about last night."

"I'm telling you, those two weren't looking to protect our stock. Those sonsabitches were going to run our cattle off. I'm sure of it."

"Well, I believe you, and so would everyone in town, but Knox may make trouble for you. We heard their man wasn't dead, but Doc wasn't sure he'd make it."

"He's still alive?" Shelley gasped.

"Last I heard," Cox nodded. "If Knox figures out you shot him, I reckon he'll use that against your father to sell out."

Shelley looked off in the distance. Her head began to whirl again. She closed her eyes and clutched the saddle horn with both hands. "What have I done?" she whispered aloud.

Cox waited a moment before speaking. "You did what any of us would have done."

"Yeah, but you didn't shoot anyone last night!"

"They rode right to the bunkhouse area at our place. Didn't go anywhere near the herd," Cox explained.

Shelley paused and looked hard at Cox with narrowed eyes. "They came right to your bunkhouse?" she asked.

"Yep."

"What time did they show up?"

Cox took off his hat and wiped the sweat from his brow and thought a moment. "I reckon it was about one, one-thirty or so."

Shelley shifted in her saddle and sat up straight, the leather crunching beneath her. She pushed the soles of her boots into the stirrup bars. "How long do you figure it takes to ride from here to Knox's house?"

"About half an hour or so."

"And then from Knox's to your bunkhouse?" Shelley continued.

"Another half-hour or so, I reckon. Why?" Cox asked, now intrigued by the line of questioning.

"Knox's men rode in here about eleven-thirty. They rode double out of here a few minutes later. They had enough time to get back to Knox and tell him what happened, even riding double. Knox could have easily sent riders out to your place and Morgan's to make it look like he sent men out of the kindness of his heart. The decision to send riders to the other ranches was made after I shot that son of a bitch!" Shelley said. Any guilt she harbored over the last few hours drained from her conscience, prompting the welcoming feeling of liberation. She looked at Cox from atop a wide grin.

Cox nodded in approval but kept a lid on any elation that might surface. "Sounds like Knox, all right. You may still have to convince the sheriff, though. Let's go tell Kincaid and your father about this," Cox said, reining his horse around and tapping his spurs.

Shelley followed Cox's lead, anxious to tell her theory to her father, Kincaid, and anyone else who would listen.

CHAPTER 23

Saturday, 20 July 1878

LUXTON DANNER & GUNSLINGERS – EN ROUTE TO ONEIDA

While the Robertsons attempted to cover up Shelley's shooting, seventy-five miles south of the Robertson ranch, Danner stopped Bullet and dismounted. He figured the horses could use a rest after marching across West Texas's unforgiving landscape all morning. He looked straight up into the high noon sun, which had unleashed its midday onslaught of oppressively high temperatures. Vegetation and rock pushed the swells of heat up off their skins, distorting the backdrop of an otherwise tranquil scene of tans, browns, and muted yellows. The jagged spears of Palo Duro Canyon jutted upward to the east, introducing various shades of red and orange into the otherwise bland region. It'd been a while since Danner had been this far west. He had not missed it. The seven gunslingers took turns snapping dried-up twigs and crushing petrified rock beneath their boots as they marched on toward their uncertain future. Jackson quickly stepped in between Danner and Wes.

"Pardon me, but looks like we have company," Jackson announced to Wes and Wade, who'd joined Danner.

The three men glanced around.

"Over our right flank, sir," Jackson said without looking back.

Danner peered over his right shoulder. At the base of the canyon wall was a single line of riders keeping pace. Danner counted seven.

"Now, what'll you reckon they want?" Wes asked.

"Renegades lookin' for a supply train, stagecoach, or settlers heading into Oneida," Wade mumbled.

"They gotta see we don't have a supply wagon," Wes added.

"I count seven," Danner announced.

"No sir, nine. There's two more, further back behind us," Jackson announced.

"You want to try and outrun 'em?" Wes asked with a grin.

"Nope," Danner replied flatly. "Let's mount up. Jackson, move your men up ahead of the three of us. Single file. Wes, Wade, we'll spread out behind them. Jackson, when they come running, you four peel off, two right and two left. Get outside of them," Danner ordered.

"Yes, sir. Feel like I'm back in the cavalry." Jackson smiled before waving to the three former soldiers to mount up.

Once mounted, Wade reined left, taking the left flank with Wes in the middle and Danner on the right.

"That ought to cause a response!" Wes hollered to Danner, who glanced over his shoulder to see the renegades begin their charge.

"It did!" Danner called back. "Let's go!" Danner yelled, banging his spurs into Bullet's hide.

The seven gunslingers hurtled forward into a full sprint keeping their intervals as best they could. Danner looked back and saw the puff of smoke pop from their pursuers' guns. The sound of the gunfire quickly followed, echoing off the canyon walls.

Wait, wait, wait. "Now!" Danner yelled, reining Bullet around to his right.

Wes and Wade did the same, turning toward their attackers. Jackson and Buster veered right while Isaac and Edwin went wide left. *Crack! Crack! Crack!* Gunfire erupted in every direction. Wes looped his reins behind his neck and pulled both Colts, firing at will. Wade stood in the stirrups and fired. *Crack!*

A renegade went flying backward, his horse not missing a step. *Crack! Crack!* Danner's Schofields exploded. Two more renegades went limp in the saddle and then fell. Crack! Wes's shot rang true, punching a hole in the chest of another renegade whose boot hung up in the stirrup. His horse kept charging, dragging its rider's corpse, which was torn apart by the relentless terrain. Jackson and the soldiers looped around their fellow gunfighters and opened fire. *Crack! Crack! Crack! Crack!* The crossfire from the former Tenth Cavalry soldiers sent renegade bodies soaring in all directions. Three more went down, smashing into the rock-hard dirt. The last two renegades tried to flee, but Jackson and the soldiers had them cut off. *Crack! Crack! Crack!*

Jackson's aim hit the mark, bouncing another renegade off his saddle. Wade slowed his horse and took careful aim. Crack! The last renegade jerked sideways, then slid off his horse, crashing face first into a prickly pear cactus. Danner and company slowed their horses, keeping an eye on the fallen assailants, making sure they finished their business. Clouds of dust drifted away in the faint breeze. Complete silence replaced what had been a cannonading battle. Danner looked at Wes and Wade, who each waved and nodded. Danner checked Jackson, who also nodded. He noticed Edwin was busy tying a bandana around the top of his left arm. Danner spurred Bullet over to the former Buffalo Soldier.

Edwin looked to be in his middle thirties. He was a short, stout, muscular man with a round face and black hair punctuated with flecks of gray here and there. The years spent working the cotton fields of a large Mississippi plantation had produced bulging arms that his shirt sleeves could barely contain.

"You all right?" Danner asked, looking at the blood-soaked sleeve of his fellow gunfighter.

"Yes, sir. Be okay. Took one in the arm is all." Jackson joined Danner, and the rest of the men circled their wounded partner.

"If I had arms that thick, I'd have taken one too!" Wade remarked through a wide grin, drawing laughter from the rest of the men.

Danner looked around at the dead men. He saw five of their horses had stopped further up ahead and were scrounging for anything that looked edible.

"Let's see if we can corral their horses. I figure we ought to take 'em into town with us if we can," Danner suggested.

"Might be a few have a price on their head," Wes said.

"Sheriff ought to know," Wade added.

The nine dead renegades dangled from their horses an hour later under hastily tied ropes. Wade had managed to round up another renegade horse, easing the animals' load.

"I figure it'll take us about three hours to get to Oneida with this cargo in tow," Danner said, looking back at the single-file horse convoy they had assembled.

"Why the hell you reckon they charged us? It made no sense," Wes asked Danner, shaking his head.

Danner poked the tip of his boot into the stirrup and swung up into his saddle. "I've stopped asking myself those fool questions a while back," Danner replied.

"Oh. Who's the fool? The one who asks the fool question, or the one who answers it?" Wes cracked with a wry smirk.

Danner shook his head and smiled. "Let's get going!" he shouted to the troupe.

CHAPTER 24

Saturday, 20 July 1878

LUXTON DANNER & GUNSLINGERS – ONEIDA

T he folks of Oneida weren't immune to the sight of a dead man tied across his horse. The settlement, named by the Indians years earlier, had been an unofficial transportation hub for nomads heading west and cattle drives moving up to Kansas from the southern ranches. Its proximity to the Indian Territory and the lawlessness that permeated its boundaries also provided Oneida with its share of ruffians and outlaw bands fleeing the law. Regardless, the folks scurrying about the streets this evening had reason to pause when Danner reached the edge of town with his horse-carrying mortuary in tow. Swathed in dirt, sweat, and blood, the haggard men looked weathered from too many scorching days on the trail. The sight of them went from dreadful to gruesome. Their horses stepped in unison, each bobbing their heads, causing the dead bodies to shift on the saddles as if they sought comfort. The lifeless dangling arms and hands swayed back and forth, appearing to wave at the people who'd begun to crowd the boardwalks on either side of Main Street. Silence crushed the noise that a western town yields on a busy evening. The only sounds were those of women's gasps before they looked away. The men were stoic and stared in disbelief. A man stepped out of the Oneida General Store and stopped to count.

"One, two, three . . . nine. Nine dead men. What the hell?" he mumbled loud enough for those around him, including Danner and company, to hear as they slowly passed. Danner pulled back on the reins and stopped Bullet in the middle of the street. He looked around at the stunned audience. "Is there a sheriff or marshal in town?" Danner asked aloud.

A man pushed through the crowd that had gathered in front of the saloon. "Yes, sir. Sheriff's office is right down the street on the left next to the livery," the man announced, pointing to his right.

"Thanks," Danner replied, then tapped his spurs and continued toward the opposite end of town.

The macabre parade passed through Oneida and came to a stop in front of the livery stable. A man about forty, with a thick crop of dark hair framed in graying temples under a wide-brimmed black hat, stood on the boardwalk in front of the building. He wore a silver badge on the left side of his black leather vest. He looked at Danner and his men, then glanced over the six horses laden with dead bodies.

"Looks like y'all had a little trouble," the man stated flatly. "Y'all a posse or something?" he asked.

"Nope. No posse," Danner stated, staying in his saddle. "We're on our way up to Canyon Creek. We were ambushed a few miles south of town. We figured they were renegades watching the road," Danner added. "You the sheriff?"

"Name's Sam Baxter. Some folks call me the sheriff, but I'm only the town marshal. Potter County's on the map, but that's about it these days. No county government yet."

"You get any flyers here?" Danner asked.

"Sure do. The marshals and Rangers drop them off from

time to time," Baxter reported. "Let me have a look," the marshal added. Baxter paused at each horse and examined the dead faces. After looking at each man, he stepped back to Danner, nodding at Wes, Wade, and the former troopers.

"Well, sir, you rode into a nest of vipers all right. That there is the Haley gang. I recognize the two Haley brothers and Ned Simmons. I'll have to check the wanted posters for the others. You say they ambushed you?" Baxter asked, looking up at Danner, who'd remained seated in the saddle.

"Yep. They waited until we passed them near the canyon, then charged us from behind," Danner explained, more for the crowd that had gathered around the marshal's office than for Baxter.

Baxter looked at Danner and the gunslingers, then shook his head. "I damn sure see why they're all dead, and you're here," Baxter stated.

"We have an injured man. Is there a doctor in town?" Danner asked.

"Somebody go fetch Doc Powell!" Baxter called into the crowd. "Gentlemen, could you bring those horses around to the back of the livery? There's a corral back there. I'll plan to get those men buried. I'll need to file a report for the district judge," Baxter said, looking at Danner.

"Wes . . ."

"On it," Wes answered before Danner could finish.

Danner swung down from Bullet and tied him to the hitching post in front of the marshal's office. Bullet sunk his muzzle into the inviting water trough set beneath it. The crowd began to disburse and a young man wearing a crisp white shirt and dark brown trousers emerged, carrying a black bag. Baxter directed the young man to Edwin, whose tattered blood-stained shirt sleeve announced him as the wounded man.

"I didn't get your name, sir," Baxter said as Danner stepped up onto the boardwalk.

"Luxton Danner."

Baxter paused and looked up at the big gunslinger.

"Luxton Danner. The US Marshal?"

"Not anymore," Danner answered, then stepped past Baxter, ducking under the overhang and pushing through the marshal's front door.

Baxter followed Danner into his office and found the former lawman already looking through a stack of wanted posters that had been stacked neatly on the desk. Baxter already separated the two Haley brothers' flyers from the pile. Baxter walked around his desk and quietly took a seat. He watched Danner examine each poster. Ned Simmon's mug was placed on top of Haley's. Danner sifted through the remaining papers and paused, turning the flyer toward Baxter.

"That look like one of them to you?" Danner asked.

Baxter nodded immediately. "Yep. That's Saddle Tramp Thomas, all right. I put that one out myself. He stole a couple of horses from the Shadowland Ranch. The owner put up the two hundred dollars. I can pay you for that one. The others—"

"Not interested in waiting to collect on the others," Danner interrupted the marshal. "I could use the Thomas reward to pay my men, though."

Bennett unlocked a desk drawer and removed a small leather pouch. He untied the bag and dumped four fifty-dollar gold pieces onto his desk. "I'll need your signature on the poster," Baxter advised.

Danner signed his name and scooped up the gold pieces.

"It'd be awful good if you'd write out a statement as to what happened out there. I could pass it onto the judge," Baxter said, removing paper from another desk drawer.

Danner pulled a chair over to the desk from the corner of the room. He wrote in silence for several minutes, then pushed the paper across the worn desk's surface to Baxter.

"You know anything about a rancher named Knox up in Canyon Creek?" Danner asked, leaning back in the squeaky chair.

Baxter took Danner's statement and slipped it into the drawer. He took a deep breath and looked at Danner through narrowed eyes.

"Should've known you'd be interested in Gilford Knox when you said you were on your way to Canyon Creek. Knox hire you?"

"Nope. Not working for Knox."

Baxter's eyes widened, and he cracked a wide grin. He sat back in his chair and looked out the front window of his office. Danner let the silence weigh heavy in the room.

"Now I see what's happening. The town folk have been gettin' fed up with Knox for a while now. He's taken over the town and all the good land around it. I don't know Knox, but his men come to town for supplies now and again. Rough bunch they are. So, if yer not workin' for Knox, you must be goin' up against him."

Danner said nothing. He just shifted in his chair, the joints straining and creaking under his 245 pounds. Baxter turned to Danner and leaned his elbows on his desk.

"I've never met Gilford Knox, but I don't have to. I know his type. He has big money and power, and he pays many people to do his business. That includes gunmen, and from what I hear, he has three times as many as you." Baxter paused for a response that didn't come. He continued, "Now for y'all to take down the Haley boys and their brood, you must be damn good, but don't underestimate Knox. Chances are he knows you're coming, and he'll be ready."

Danner stood up and started for the door before stopping and turning back to Baxter.

"You said you put the paper out on Thomas?" Danner asked.

"That's right."

"And yet, when you looked at all of them out on the street, you didn't identify him. Just the Haleys and Simmons," Danner clarified.

Baxter's smile faded, and he began to put the wanted posters back into a neat pile on his desk, his hands shaking. "I guess I just missed him," Baxter weakly offered.

"And I'm guessing that you figured on waiting until we were gone, then pocketing that two hundred for yourself."

"Look, Mr. Danner. This job doesn't pay much. I can't afford a room at the hotel, so I sleep on a cot in the back here. It's not worth it," Baxter clamored.

"And just how much is a man's honesty worth, Baxter?" Danner asked before leaving the Oneida marshal's office.

Danner found Wes, Wade, and the former troopers down the street at the saloon.

"You figure on staying here tonight?" Wes asked in between sips of beer.

"Nope. Let's grab some supplies and ammunition, then head out," Danner advised.

"You already send word to Canyon Creek?" Wade asked.

"Nope. I thought better of it. Meet me over in front of the store in about thirty minutes," Danner ordered, then disappeared through the saloon's swinging doors.

CHAPTER 25

Saturday, 20 July 1878

ALBERT LOMAN – CANYON CREEK

U naware that Danner and the gunslingers were preparing to leave Oneida, only a day's ride away, Albert Loman busied himself counting tin cans of beans and onions along with sacks of flour sewn tight inside double canvas bags. The provisions had arrived earlier in the week, and he was just now recording the inventory in his ledger book. With the impending dinner hour quickly approaching, his wife had gone over to the Sundown Hotel to assist Rachel with the cooking. While his wife's absence led to him handling the inventory alone, he embraced the opportunity to plug along at his own casual pace. The bell nailed to the top of the front door rang, interrupting his mathematical equation. Emerging from the poorly lit storage room into the sun-drenched store put him at a visual disadvantage for a moment. After a quick eye rub and resetting of his spectacles upon the bridge of his somewhat elongated nose, the image of Sam Johnson came into clear view.

"Good evening, Mr. Johnson. How are you this evening?" Albert Loman greeted Gilford Knox's lawyer.

Sam Johnson, a short, stocky man of thirty-five with thinning hair and a perpetually happy face, had been Gilford

Knox's lawyer just short of three months. Knox hired him away from a good law firm in Austin with the promise of adventure and a wage he still hadn't completely comprehended. Johnson was a pleasant man taking care of Knox's unpleasant land and property business. Clad in a three-piece gray suit and bolo tie, Johnson was the best-dressed man in Canyon Creek and beyond.

"Good evening, Mr. Loman. Sorry to stop in so late, but I was wondering if you'd gotten around to unpacking those cigars you'd spoken of the other night at dinner?" Johnson asked, extending his right hand for a friendly shake.

"Oh, yes, I certainly have. How many would you like?" Loman asked, stepping behind the cabinet that contained the tobacco products in oak barrels with tight-fitting lids.

"I'll take a half-dozen, wrapped, please."

Loman selected six of the best-looking coronas in the case, then wrapped them in thick brown paper secured with a section of twine. After setting the package on the counter, Loman withdrew a small dark green bottle of fragrance from the top shelf and handed it to Johnson.

"How about a fragrance for Mrs. Johnson? This perfume came from St. Louis," Loman boasted. "I don't get this quality very often," Loman added to close the sale.

Johnson tipped the bottle and took a whiff. He nodded before his face exploded into a wide smile. "Very nice. I believe I will take a bottle for Mrs. Johnson. Thank you."

"Mrs. Loman has special paper for these," Loman announced before tearing a small piece of paper imprinted with colorful flowers from a roll behind the counter.

"How are things with Mr. Knox's land business?" Loman asked while folding sharp creases into the colorful paper to cover the bottle.

Sam Johnson's happy face turned dark with a frown and lowered eyes. Loman noticed the change in demeanor but said nothing. He was probing for information more than he was interested in Knox's success. Many people around town had privately wondered how such a pleasant man coped with the broken dreams of ranchers and farmers.

"I fear that I may have made a mistake in accepting Mr. Knox's generous offer. The business hasn't been what he told me. Many of the transactions have involved people who appear to have little choice in the matters. Some have been angry, while others have been notably distressed. Mr. Knox is an ambitious man, and he demands swift action. I'm sorry to say that my visit here this evening is not purely personal."

"Oh?" Loman asked as he put the finishing touch on the bow he tied in the fragrance package twine.

"No, sir. Mr. Knox instructed me to meet with you and inquire again if you'd be interested in selling your store. He's upped the offer by one thousand dollars."

"Why does Knox want my store so badly? He's about to open his store that will be twice the size of mine."

"Mr. Knox says your place would make a good apothecary. He's already contacting chemists to gauge interest in moving to Canyon Creek."

"I see. Well, I certainly wouldn't be opposed to a chemist coming to Canyon Creek, but you'll have to tell Mr. Knox that I am not interested in selling at any price," Loman proclaimed, handing Johnson his packages.

"Very well. I'll inform Mr. Knox of your decision. Thank you for the cigars and fragrance. Have a good evening, Mr. Loman," Johnson offered before hurrying out the door.

Loman quickly entered the purchases into the ledger book under Sam Johnson's account, then hurried to the front door where he flipped the "Open" sign around to "Closed" and locked the door behind him. He hurried across the dusty street, pausing for a carriage to pass before skipping up the steps of the Sundown. Loman wanted to report his conversation with Sam Johnson to his wife, Rachel, and Miss Tyler from the boarding house, who also helped with dinner time at the hotel restaurant. He figured he'd then hustle over to the Creekbed Saloon and share his information with Dakota Jones.

Loman entered the busy restaurant, where the sound of chatter vibrated throughout the room. Pots, pans, dishes, and glasses tinged and banged around in the kitchen. He saw Rachel speaking to four people he didn't recognize at a table near the back of the room. His wife rushed from the kitchen. She dashed and darted around people and tables, balancing plates of food like a circus performer. Loman made his way through the maze of occupied tables to the kitchen door and waited. Rachel saw him and excused herself from her guests.

"Is something wrong, Albert?" Rachel asked with a twinge of concern.

"No, nothing wrong. I just had an interesting talk with Mr. Johnson. Knox offered to purchase my store again. He upped the offer a thousand dollars and wants to turn it into an apothecary. Knox is already looking to bring a chemist here," Loman said, nearly out of breath. He felt like an old lady gossiping after church on Sunday, but he didn't care. He relished knowing something everyone else didn't.

Delores Loman came bustling through the crowd.

"What are you doing here, Albert?" she called, pushing past her husband without waiting for an answer.

"I'll tell Delores all about it later. Tell her I'll be over at the Creekbed. I'll tell Dakota what's happening," Loman told Rachel, who nodded and hurried into the kitchen.

Loman rushed out of the hotel and headed for the Creekbed Saloon. He knew there'd be plenty of interest there since all the old-timers from Canyon Creek still went to Dakota's instead of Knox's new place. Loman passed in front of Knox's lumberyard, where Knox's two guards watched the excited store owner run around town. After Loman passed, one man mounted his horse and galloped out of town, heading for the Circle X to report on his actions. These days, nothing happened in Canyon Creek that didn't get reported to Gilford Knox.

CHAPTER 26

Saturday, 20 July 1878

LUXTON DANNER – CANYON CREEK

The moonlight lit up Canyon Creek like a glowing oil lamp, delivering blurry shadows across the town. Danner held up Bullet near the edge of town and looked over at Wade. The only man in the outfit who cared to carry a watch slipped it out of his vest and popped it open. Turning it toward the moon's beam, he leaned in close to the timepiece and strained his eyes.

"Half past nine," Wade reported before snapping the metal watch cover back into place and returning it to his vest pocket.

"Too late for the hotel?" Wes asked.

"I don't think so. We'll head there first," Danner stated.

"We'll pitch camp out here," Jackson advised, then turned his horse and tapped his spurs, his three former troopers close behind.

Danner looked over his shoulder and watched the four gunslingers head for a clump of trees not far off. "I figure they're more comfortable out there," Danner said aloud before nudging Bullet forward.

The trio quietly rode into town from the east, passing the stage office and livery stable, then the boarding house and tin shop before coming to a stop in front of the Sundown Hotel. Two burning oil lamps illuminated the front porch, and the front desk had a large candle burning brightly atop its polished surface. The three men dismounted and tethered their horses to the hitching post. Wes and Wade took seats in the rocking chairs positioned on each side of the wide front window. Danner stopped at the front door and looked at his partners.

"We'll wait here while you announce our arrival," Wes said through a wide grin.

Danner shook his head, then carefully opened the door, sounding the bell hanging from the inside door handle. Danner stepped forward just close enough to the flame of the burning candle so he could be recognized. A moment passed before he heard shuffling in the room behind the office. Danner fixed his sights on the dark opening to the back room. He watched as a figure appeared in the shadows, first as unidentifiable lines moving in the dark, then the outline of a woman slowly took shape.

Rachel Brennen emerged from the darkened room and stepped into the outer ring of candlelight. Her auburn hair was pushed up on her head and tied with a white ribbon. She wore a tan robe over what appeared to be a white nightgown underneath. Her bare feet whisked lightly across the wooden floor as she approached the big oak desk. Danner removed his hat and stood erect as though at military attention. Rachel looked at the man standing back from the desk. After a moment, she recognized the giant gunslinger and let out a scream of joy before throwing up her hands and running around the desk. Without hesitation, she slammed into Danner, wrapping her arms around the big man and squeezing as hard as she could. Danner pushed aside his tough façade and returned the hug, allowing a woman's touch to penetrate his emotional armor.

"I'm sorry to disturb you at this hour."

"Don't you apologize, Luxton Danner!" Rachel exclaimed, looking up at the big man with tear-filled green eyes. "I'd given up hope that you would come," she cried before stepping back and wiping tears from her face. She tried to straighten her robe and felt her hair. "I must look just awful!" she said, her voice wavering a bit.

Danner smiled. "You look just fine, ma'am."

"Ma'am! Oh, that settles it! I must look just terrible! Don't you ever call me ma'am again! You hear me!" She laughed. "I have so much to tell you, but I don't know where to begin!"

"Well, let's start with rooms for myself and two others that are with me," Danner suggested as Wes and Wade pushed through the front door, hats in hand. "This is Wes Payne and Clint Wade," Danner introduced his partners, each nodding to Rachel.

"Welcome to Canyon Creek, gentlemen," I have rooms for each of you," Rachel reported, hurrying around the desk and pulling keys from the cabinet. "I can't believe you're here!" Rachel gushed again, clutching the top of her robe closed with one hand while writing the room numbers into the open ledger book with the other. "I have a corral behind the hotel. You can put your horses there until tomorrow."

"We'll take care of the horses," Wes informed Danner. "I'll bring in your saddlebags and bedroll," Wes added with a grin before he and Wade left the lobby and disappeared onto the street.

Rachel finished writing in the book and handed Danner his key. Rachel slipped her soft hand around his leathery paw as he took the key. "Can I get you and your men some coffee? Are you hungry? I have some food leftover from tonight's dinner."

"That won't be necessary. We just need to get cleaned up and sleep," Danner assured his hostess.

"I'm so happy there's three of you," Rachel said, her smile fading for the first time since she recognized Danner.

"There's seven of us. There are four more men camped outside of town." Rachel began to speak, but Danner shook his head and held up his hand. "They'd rather camp out there," Danner explained.

"All right. Well, I'll put a pot of coffee on, get dressed, and put some food out for you and your men in case they're hungry," Rachel said.

"You can tell me everything in the morning if you'd like," Danner offered.

"Oh no! I couldn't sleep a wink now! Would you mind?" she asked.

"Not at all. We'll get cleaned up and meet you in the dining room in a bit. That sound all right?"

Rachel nodded and set two keys down on the desk before disappearing into the back room. Wes and Wade returned with their gear. Danner snatched up the keys and headed up the polished oak staircase, his boot heels sounding like claps of thunder in the otherwise quiet hotel. Danner told Wes and Wade about the offer of coffee and food, each nodding in approval. Thirty minutes later, the three gunslingers, washed and clad in clean clothes, took seats around a table laden with hot coffee, biscuits, and cold fried chicken. The front door opened and closed, the bell alerting Rachel and her guests. A man dressed in a black suit and gambler's hat peered into the dining room. He removed his hat and stopped at the archway.

"Good evening, gentlemen," the man said before turning and ascending the staircase.

Danner listened to the man's footsteps travel down the hall where they paused to open a door, then disappeared into a room.

"Kinda early for a gambler to call it a night," Wade stated.

"Must've been a loser tonight," Wes added with a chuckle.

Danner saw Rachel enter the dining room from the kitchen. She had brushed her hair, which now flowed over her shoulders, and had applied some makeup and red lipstick. Her green dress reached just below her knees and was fastened tightly around her waist with a wide black belt. The three men stood. Rachel arrived with the scent of a pleasant perfume none of them could identify.

"Please, gentlemen, sit," Rachel insisted before accepting a chair Danner had pulled away from the table for her. Once Rachel was seated, Danner removed the letter she wrote to him from his pocket and opened it before setting it on the table. Danner looked at Wes and Wade, then at Rachel.

"Now, tell us what this is all about," Danner said, tapping the letter.

Rachel started from the beginning, telling of Sam Coleman's decision to break up the KC Ranch, selling small sections to Robertson, Kincaid, and Morgan before selling the rest to Gilford Knox. She reported Knox's land and business purchases and the harassment methods to get the small ranchers and farmers to sell. Once Knox had bought the lumber mill, he started building his saloon, hotel, and store since he owned all the lumber passing through the mill. Rachel also advised Danner and his company about Knox's multiple offers to purchase her hotel and Loman's store. Finally, Rachel warned the men of the guards Knox had left in town to protect his properties. Rachel said that everyone in town figured the guards were there to spy on them more than protect Knox's businesses.

"I agree. Knox knows nobody is going to mess with his businesses. You said this Virgil Robertson told Knox about your letter to me?" Danner asked.

"Yes, about a week or so ago, Knox came in here after he bought the livery stable and told everyone he was leaving those men in town. That's when Mr. Robertson told him we'd sent a letter to Fort Smith asking for a US Marshal."

"Well, I guess this is as good a time as any to tell you I'm no longer a marshal," Danner admitted. "Wes is a former Texas Ranger, but that's in the past also."

"And I'm just a plain ol' gunfighter," Wade said with a crooked smile.

Rachel forced a smile, then looked at Danner. "Then, why . . ."

"I'm here because you sounded like you were in trouble," Danner explained. "And I convinced these two to come along," Danner added, waving toward Wes and Wade, who both nodded in between sips of coffee.

"What about the men camped outside town?" Rachel asked, a hint of concern in her otherwise songbird voice.

"I hired them. They're all former Buffalo Soldiers who rode with the cavalry. They're good fighting men, and just as important, I trust them. I'd heard about Knox and his money. I knew he'd have plenty of men on his payroll. I figured if he didn't listen to reason, we'd look to convince him to settle down differently," Danner said.

"I see. I know Mr. Robertson, Mr. Kincaid, and Mr. Morgan are all willing to hire men, so they may be willing to pay you, but I don't know about anyone else. We thought that if a US

Marshal came to town, that would keep Knox from harassing everyone," Rachel explained. "Now. I don't know what to think," Rachel added, lines of concern encroaching upon her otherwise serene face.

"You don't need to worry about that. We've talked about it. In the next day or two, we'll take a ride out to the Knox place and have a word with him. We'll see how he handles that," Danner advised.

"We're prepared to hang around town for a while, ma'am," Wes chimed in.

Rachel thanked each man, then stood to leave. She instructed the men to leave everything on the table. She would clean it up in the morning.

"Everyone will be happy to hear about your arrival," Rachel said, rubbing her hand on Danner's sleeve before leaving the room.

"Especially Mr. Danner," Wade mumbled through a grin.

"Yep," Wes added with a laugh.

"You two settle down," Danner said, unable to prevent a grin from cracking his otherwise stoic face.

"Looks like the big lug's got himself a girl," Wade said to Wes as the men pushed back from the table.

"Now he just has to make sure he doesn't get himself killed." Wes laughed.

"If you two don't watch yourselves, Knox will be the least of your trouble!" Danner growled before stepping out of the dining room, through the front door, and into the street.

Thin layers of clouds had muted the moon's glow, casting a pall over Canyon Creek's Main Street. Danner looked around and took a deep breath. A lot had changed since his last visit to this town. Would Canyon Creek be his final destination?

CHAPTER 27

Sunday, 21 July 1878

VIRGIL ROBERTSON & FAMILY – ROBERTSON RANCH

T he morning after Danner and the gunslingers' arrival, Virgil paused on the porch and looked into the house through a dust-filled screen door. Madeleine Robertson set a bowl of steaming biscuits on the table along with a cup of honey. The bacon frying on the stove cracked and popped in the pan. Virgil pushed through the front door and stomped his boots on the braided rug just inside the threshold. He washed his hands and sat down at the table. Madeleine set a plate of bacon in front of him. His two youngest daughters ran into the kitchen, chirping at each other about their Sunday dresses. Virgil leaned back in his chair and looked at his family. The sight brought a glint of a smile to his lips.

"Where's Shelley?" Madeleine asked her husband while scooping scrambled eggs onto a glossy white platter with a broad wooden spoon.

"She'll be here momentarily. She's tending to her horse," Virgil reported.

"Well, she better not take too long, or she'll be late for church."

Virgil took a long sip of coffee, then pushed his eggs around on his plate for a moment. "I told her she was excused from church this morning," Virgil announced with a wince, knowing he was in for an argument.

Madeleine stopped abruptly and spun around to face Virgil. "And why would you do that?" she spouted, jamming her fists into each apron-clad hip.

Virgil swallowed his eggs and set his fork on the table. "She's had a couple of difficult days, and when she asked, I thought it would be good for her to have some time to herself, is all," he answered, his voice firm.

"I wanna stay home too!" Virgil's youngest daughter shouted.

"Me too! I want time to myself!" his middle daughter added.

Before Virgil could respond, Madeleine ended any thought of not accompanying their parents to service this morning. Both girls slammed their forks onto the table and crossed their arms in protest. Virgil laughed, then continued eating breakfast.

As the family finished their meal, Shelley quietly stepped into the house and pulled off her dusty boots at the door. Already covered in a layer of sweat and dust, she looked like a ranch hand instead of the family's eldest daughter. A dirty barn and chicken coop were no places for a young woman, but her father needed her to help run the ranch. Shelley smiled and walked past her mother to the washbasin, where she did her best to make herself presentable for breakfast before joining the rest of the family at the table.

"Let me warm those eggs," Madeleine told her daughter as she began to rise from her chair.

"No, ma'am. That's not necessary. They'll be fine," Shelley insisted, wiping her hand with her napkin.

"Let me see your hands," Shelley's mother demanded.

Shelley slipped both hands under the table. "They're fine, mother, really."

"Are you hurt?" Virgil asked Shelley as he pulled her left hand from under the table to discover it seeping blood.

"Oh my!" Madeleine exclaimed, quickly jumping up from her chair and reaching for a wet cloth.

Virgil turned over Shelley's hands, palms upward. Both palms had bright red blisters, and her left had a deep laceration from the thumb to the little finger.

"What happened?" her father asked.

"Nothing. I moved that roll of wire away from the barn door and slipped. I'll be fine." Shelley tried to convince her mother, who'd returned to the table with two clean white wet cloths.

"That settles it! Virgil Robertson, you'll not waste a nickel on any gunmen! You use whatever money we must to hire a ranch hand! You hear me?" Madeleine ordered her husband.

Anytime his wife called him by his first and last name, he knew there'd be no argument. Besides, they recovered most of the cattle, and the garden was producing well this year. He knew he asked a lot of his eldest daughter, and she exceeded his needs thus far. But now, she shot a man in the pasture, and his worry had peaked.

"I'm fine, really, it's nothing."

"You'll need to go into Canyon Creek and see Doctor Carson for that hand," Virgil stated flatly. "I'll get the wagon. Madeleine, I'll let you and the girls off at the church, then take Shelley into town. Hopefully, we'll catch Doc before he leaves for church."

Virgil hitched the horses to the wagon and brought them around to the house where Madeleine had everyone waiting. Shelley had changed clothes and had white bandages wrapped around each hand. After the ladies settled in, Virgil snapped the reins and headed toward town.

The Canyon Creek church was a small white building with a tall narrow steeple topped with a large cross about a quarter-mile south of town. The townsfolk decided to build their place of worship near the edge of the creek, where clean water flowed lazily by an open area rich with grass, thistle, and sage scattered around sizable live-oak trees. The expanse around the church provided an ideal place for Sunday service and the litany of events that accompanied houses of worship. The banks of Canyon Creek were the favored choice for barbecue picnics and other social gatherings.

Virgil brought the wagon up to the side door of the church, where Madeleine and the girls joined several other folks who were feverishly gossiping about the arrival of Danner and the gunslingers. Before Virgil could get his team started, several men accosted him and informed the harried rancher of Danner and the men. After hearing the news, Virgil closed his eyes and bowed his head.

"Gentlemen, our prayers may have been answered after all. I had all but given up hope that help would come." Virgil took a deep breath to settle his excitement, then looked to the heavens. "Thank you," he added. After exchanging pleasantries with his neighbors, Virgil quickly headed for Doc Carson's office.

"This changes things, Shelley. With Marshal Danner here, I'll be able to hire a hand to help us around the ranch."

"I don't think that's necessary," Shelley said.

"You heard your mother. There will be no further discussion about it. I'll put out a word this morning that I'm looking for someone."

Shelley frowned and rolled her shoulders forward, lowering

her head. She wasn't happy about the decision, but deep down, she knew it would be good to have more help around the ranch. And despite her objections, her hands hurt something awful, her left palm throbbing with pain.

Virgil stopped the wagon in front of Doc Carson's house, quickly tied the reins to the brake lever, and jumped down. He helped Shelley down and knocked on the screen door.

Dr. Andrew Carson, an average-size man of forty-four with black hair streaked with sprouts of gray, had been a surgeon's assistant in the war. After a successful medical practice back east, he decided there were enough doctors in the big eastern cities and not nearly enough west of the Mississippi River. After convincing his wife he needed to follow his calling west, he ended up in Fort Worth for a while, then pushed further into the Wild West, finally landing in Canyon Creek, where he found a home. The soft-spoken physician was highly respected and trusted. Answering the door in his Sunday best dark suit, white shirt, and black tie, Doc Carson saw the concern on Virgil's face.

"What is it, Virgil?" Carson asked in his usual soothing tone.

"Shelley here opened up her hand on a roll of barbed wire. Could you look before you head off to service?"

"Certainly. Come inside Shelley, and let's have a look," Carson said, opening the screen door for his patient. Carson removed the bandages from Shelley's hands and examined the deep gash on her left palm. "That'll need a few stitches, young lady," he advised. Carson selected some equipment from a shelf, then looked at Shelley. "Chloroform?" he asked.

"I won't need any. Go ahead," Shelley firmly informed Carson.

"I thought you'd say that." Carson chuckled.

Shelley smiled at the confirmation of her tough-girl reputation.

"I'll be back in a bit, Doc," Virgil announced, then stepped out of the office. He knew most everyone would be down at the church, but he figured Dakota Jones would be cleaning up his saloon. Virgil found the saloon keeper busy washing the sticky beer and whiskey spills that had littered the bar and floor from the previous night's sloppy drunkards. Virgil knew Jones was the man to tell of his decision to hire a ranch hand. Now that Danner and his men were in town, Virgil felt he could use the money he set aside for a gunman to hire a wrangler instead.

CHAPTER 28

Sunday, 21 July 1878

GILFORD KNOX – CIRCLE X RANCH

Dark clouds replaced the afternoon sun, bringing the relief of cooler temperatures as they swirled across the sky. The wind had picked up, occasionally turning a dust devil or two. Having no time for church service or the social gathering that followed, Gilford Knox was busy at his desk looking over the most recent reports of cattle sales and beef prices in Kansas City. Even though the railroad companies had pushed the dollar to the brink with their over-zealous expansion efforts, the beef prices were steady. Of greater interest was the value of horses. The demand for horses was at or near the gold rush level. The miners in Colorado and Nevada were wearing out horses faster than they could replace them. Knox reached into the bottom right drawer of his polished oak desk and withdrew his horse count figures. According to his foreman's latest report, he had 293 healthy mature heads available for sale. Twenty-two young ones and seventeen colts filled out the herd. Knox paused and considered his options. A good horse was going for about fifty to sixty dollars in Texas. He figured the miners would pay double that. It looked like he needed a drive up to Colorado. The sound of boots pounding on the wooden porch interrupted his thoughts.

"Sorry to bother you, Mr. Knox, but one of the boys from town is riding in fast," one of the main-house guards informed the rancher.

"Very well. Send him in right away," Knox ordered, resuming his attention to his stock reports.

Gilford Knox was an intelligent, disciplined man. His father was a colonel in the Union army who went on to a successful political career in Washington after the war. Having graduated from West Point in 1862, Gilford Knox was eventually promoted to first lieutenant and assigned to his father's New York Heavy Artillery Sixth Regiment. Organized under Colonel William H. Morris in 1862, the Sixth saw action in the Siege at Petersburg, the Battle of Cedar Creek, and the Battle of Cold Harbor, among others. He retained his military presence and expected the men who worked for him to adhere to specific reverent protocols when in his presence.

A few minutes later, Knox's trail boss, along with one of his spies from Canyon Creek, stood at attention in front of the rancher's massive oak desk. Knox pushed his reports to the side, leaned back in his big leather chair, and lit a fat cigar he plucked from a well-oiled mahogany box on his desk.

"What is it?"

"Looks like we have company in town, Mr. Knox."

"Oh? What kind of company?" Knox asked with raised eyebrows and a faint smirk.

"Three men came into town last night. They went right to the Sundown Hotel. We didn't get a good look at them then, but we saw them this morning in the restaurant. Look like gunslingers, all right. One's a big fellow. He's huge and wears two guns. The second also wore two guns. I recognized the third, Clint Wade. He hires out his gun to the highest bidder.

Usually rides guard for cattle drives and supply trains," the spy reported.

"Get any names for the other two?" Knox asked, leaning forward, elbows propped on the desk, his square jaw resting atop his right fist.

"Yes, sir. We heard the names Luxton Danner and Wes Payne."

Knox settled back into his plush leather chair and looked at his trail boss, who was nodding. "Why does that name Danner sound familiar?"

"Danner's a US Marshal out of Fort Smith. He and that Payne, who I think is a Texas Ranger, were the ones that killed that gang up in Six Shot a year or so back," the trail boss answered.

Knox spun his chair and gazed out the big window in his office, taking a deep drag on his cigar, then sending a thick blue cloud of smoke above his head. "That's right. Sam Coleman told me about that. He was up there at the time."

As Knox gazed out the window, the distant sky was cracked in half by a crooked flash of white lightning. A few moments later, thunder clapped on the dark horizon. Knox remained silent for a moment while his men remained at attention. Thunder rolled closer to the Circle X, and lightning lit up the now gloomy sky. Knox looked at his men. "Round up a couple more men. Two of the better guns we have and bring them here right away," Knox ordered his trail boss, who spun and disappeared immediately. Knox waved at his spy to take one of the six chairs positioned in a semi-circle to the left of the rancher's desk. Knox turned back to watch the performance Mother Nature orchestrated in the distance. A few minutes later, Knox's trail boss returned with two men.

Knox pointed to the chairs. "Have a seat," Knox ordered, then stood and slowly walked around his desk, puffing nervously on his cigar before leaning back against the front of the desk to address his men. "Well, it appears the good folks of Canyon Creek have shown their hand. Apparently, we have a US Marshal and a Texas Ranger in our midst. What interests me is the fact they have a hired gun with them. Now, why would a hired gun be tagging along with the law?" Knox stated more than asked. "Something's not right," Knox told himself aloud, now chewing on the soggy end of his stogie. "Before we—"

The front door flew open, and another Knox man hurried into the office. "Mr. Knox, two riders coming. Don't know who they are."

Knox stepped out of his office into the large front foyer, then opened the heavy wooden double doors leading to the expansive covered porch that wrapped around the entire main house. Knox stood in the doorway while lightning fractured the black sky behind the silhouettes of the two riders who passed under the high iron arch that announced the Circle X Ranch. Knox's men stood behind him and watched the strangers' arrival. The two strangers stopped their horses halfway between the archway and the house, one rider keeping two horse lengths behind the other. Both men wore two pistols.

"That big fella in front is the marshal from town," Knox's spy whispered into his boss's ear.

Knox nodded, then stepped out onto the porch's top step, his four men splitting up with two moving to Knox's right, the other two to his left. Lightning flashed again behind the strangers and booming thunder followed as if the strangers had brought the ruckus with them.

"Good evening, gentlemen. Step down off those horses and

come inside." Knox mustered the invitation in the best friendly manner he could manage.

"No need. Not staying long enough for that," the big stranger announced.

"Well, whom do I have the pleasure of speaking with then?" Knox asked, a hint of annoyance in his voice.

"Name's Luxton Danner. This here is Wes Payne. We're looking for Gilford Knox. I assume that's you?"

"I'm Knox. What can I do for you, Mr. Danner?" Knox asked, now curious about the bold visit.

"Well, for one thing, you can call off your riflemen that are up on your roof," Danner said, looking up above Knox's head.

Knox turned and looked up to see three rifle barrels protruding beyond the roofline. "Put those guns away! And get down here now!" Knox ordered, irritated with the unnecessary display of force. "Sorry for the unwelcome display. My men are always prepared though, Mr. Danner."

Danner and Wes watched the three men jump down from the eaves and join the others on the porch. Danner and Wes moved up closer to Knox. Thunder banged overhead, rattling the lanterns dangling from the overhang of the house.

"The folks in town seem to feel that you're trying to take over Canyon Creek and buy all the property around it. They've asked us to deliver the message that they like the town the way it is, and nobody else is interested in selling out to you."

Knox took a long drag on his cigar, then took it from his mouth and looked at the burning business end. "Well, some folks just don't understand the ways of progress, Marshal. Canyon Creek can grow and prosper with the right leadership. I'm just trying to put Canyon Creek on the map, is all," Knox said through a thin grin.

"First, I never said I was a marshal. Second, the people here aren't interested in your leadership or your empire, especially the way you force it upon them," Danner stated, shifting in his saddle. "The rancher here before you knew how to treat the folks in town. He was well-liked and respected. That doesn't appear to be the case with you and your men," Danner added, scrutinizing the men behind Knox.

"I'm sorry to hear that. I am. But neither I nor any of my men have done anything inappropriate or illegal. All my business in and outside of Canyon Creek is reviewed and handled by my lawyer, Sam Johnson. Now, I'm still new to Canyon Creek, but maybe after I'm here for a while, the folks will come around to my way of thinking and see the benefits of progress," Knox offered. "Mr. Danner, you can go back and tell whoever hired you that their message was delivered. I have a business to tend to, so I'll bid you good evening," Knox added, tucking the cigar back into the side of his mouth.

Knox watched Danner and Wes slowly back their horses under the iron arch while they kept their eyes on his men. Once clear of the entrance, Danner and Wes reined their horses around and galloped into the lightning-fractured abyss. "Men, I think it's time to take care of business the way my father would have. I've tried a nice way. Now it's time to do it my way. I need two men to pay a visit to the Robertsons' barn tonight," Knox growled before stomping into the house.

CHAPTER 29

Sunday, 21 July 1878

LUXTON DANNER – CANYON CREEK

T hunder rolled, then exploded like cannon fire overhead as Danner and Wes walked out of the livery stable. They knew that Knox now owned the livery, but he had not put any of his men in charge of it yet, keeping Stoney Walsh for the time being. Danner remembered Walsh from his visit to the sawmill last year and knew that Walsh was no admirer of Gilford Knox. Therefore, both he and Wes trusted Walsh. Lightning lit up the ebony sky, and thunder pounded the town. Danner looked up at the coal-black canopy hanging over Canyon Creek.

"Don't seem like there's any rain coming," Danner said.

"Nope. I've seen it do this for hours and never rain," Wes advised.

Both men climbed the steps to the Sundown. As Danner opened the door, a clap of thunder shook the building and rattled the glass windows. "Sounds like April of sixty-five," Danner said, stepping into the lobby.

"April, sixty-five?" Wes asked.

"Fort Blakely, Alabama. The cannon fire shook the ground so damned bad we had trouble staying on our feet. That was the battle we got separated from our unit. That's when I ran into Chance at that creek," Danner reminisced.

"Welcome back, you two!" Rachel called as she sashayed out of the dining room, her bright yellow dress swaying from side to side. She paused to hug both men, then moved around behind the desk. "What did Mr. Knox have to say?"

"Sure, down to business right away. No coffee, drink, dinner, nothing!" Wes clamored, unable to withhold his laughter.

"Just like a woman. Uses us like a trusted mop," Danner chimed in.

Wade's steps on the wooden staircase echoed down to the lobby as he joined the others. "What's all this?" Wade asked through a wide grin.

"Oh, it seems these two gentlemen think I treat them like a mop."

Wade looked at his fellow gunslingers and nodded. "Seems about right." He laughed. "Probably get more work done with the mop."

Danner and Wes looked at each other. "That's it. Let's find Mrs. Carson. She'll take care of us," Danner boldly announced before ducking under the archway that led into the dining room, which remained busy with several customers finishing their supper.

"I believe I'll join you, sir!" Wes loudly proclaimed before following Danner into the dining room.

Danner and Wes took their usual table at the back of the room. Mrs. Carson quickly brought over two mugs and a coffeepot. After filling the mugs with steaming coffee, she confirmed that both men would have a steak and potato for supper. Wes took a sip of coffee and smiled.

"Mrs. Rachel Brennen looked especially pretty this evening.

I noticed she wasn't wearing her apron. I reckon that was just for you, pal," Wes goaded his partner.

Danner looked across the room and watched Rachel talking with two other women. "If I'm not mistaken, former Ranger Payne, you were the first to receive a hug from Mrs. Rachel Brennen this evening."

Wes followed Danner's gaze and saw Rachel across the room. Her long auburn hair appeared to melt over her shoulders, and her yellow Cordelia pioneer dress was stunning. Wes smiled and looked back at Danner. "So, I was indeed."

Wade pulled up a chair and sat down, blocking Danner's view of Rachel. "How'd it go?"

Danner drained his mug and set it in the middle of the table. "Hard to know. Knox didn't say much. We talked about progress and putting Canyon Creek on the map. Said his lawyer handled everything he did legally. One thing's for certain, he doesn't take any chances. He had four men on the porch and three more on the roof with rifles when we arrived. He also knew about our arrival in town. He called me Marshal. I figure one of his men from town rode out and reported on us before we got there," Danner said.

"Seems his spies haven't gotten the word that you're not a marshal and I'm not a Ranger anymore," Wes added.

"Well, they know who I am. I recognized one of the gunhands this morning. I don't know from where, but I could tell he knew me by the look on his face."

"You remember what he looked like?" Wes asked.

"About as tall as me and needed a shave. Wore a brown leather vest with some round silver buttons."

Danner thought back to the men with Knox. He pictured each man in his mind and remembered that on his left, one of the men behind Knox wore a brown leather vest with round silver conchos on the front. Danner nodded. "Yep. There was a man on the porch wearing a vest with silver conchos."

"Probably him, then."

"If Knox is as smart as we believe, and I think he is, he'll figure out that you're with us and we're not the law anymore," Danner suggested.

"He'll also know about us up in Six Shot. Coleman probably told him about that when he sold the ranch to him," Wes said.

"The next move is his then," Danner said, offering his mug to Mrs. Carson, who had returned with another full coffeepot.

"He'll probably send a couple more men into town to keep an eye on us. We'd do well to meet with those ranchers Rachel told us about out at their places," Wes added.

"Agreed. We'll do that tomorrow," Danner announced.

"Anyone seen Jackson and the troopers lately?" Wes asked.

"They're over at the Creekbed Saloon. I told Dakota Jones they were camped outside of town, and he practically ordered me to send them into the Creekbed. It seems Jones was with an infantry unit that rode with the Tenth a time or two," Danner explained.

"Well, gentlemen, I've already had supper, so I think I'll go over and join Jackson and the boys for a drink or two," Wade announced before leaving the table.

Danner watched Wade leave. "You think he's as good as we've heard?" Danner asked Wes.

"Yep. I've been around a couple of times after he's taken care of business. I wouldn't want to go against him."

Danner nodded. "I'm not sure what Knox will do, but one thing's for certain after today's visit. He'll not back down. He wants to build an empire out here, and he's not going to stop just because we came to town."

"Nope," Wes simply answered as Mrs. Carson arrived with steaks and potatoes.

Lightning flashed, then another cannonade of thunder exploded, shaking the Sundown to the rafters.

CHAPTER 30

Sunday, 21 July 1878

SHELLEY ROBERTSON – ROBERTSON RANCH

T hunder continued to explode high above the Robertson ranch, rattling dishes in the kitchen. Shock waves raced through the house like a stampede of wild mustangs. Shelley jerked awake, instinctively reaching for her gun belt loosely hanging from the bedpost. A blinding white flash of lightning followed a thunderous blast, lighting the entire bedroom for a moment. Shelley sat up and listened. Another barrage of thunder rolled across the sky. She heard the muted footsteps of her sisters scurrying around in the next room. She waited until the sound of squeaking springs confirmed both sisters had returned to their rustic bed. Shelley quietly slid off her paillasse and stepped to the window. Lightning lit up the sky, giving her a brief view of the barn and tack shed. Satisfied everything looked undisturbed, she returned to bed. Now awake, she sat against the wall and listened to the storm.

Clang! The sound of an iron skillet banging against the stovetop shook Shelley awake. She had fallen asleep with her back against the wall and knees tucked under her chin. Shelley's back hurt since she had fallen off her horse. Her feet were numb. She stretched her legs and stood, turning from side to side in a mildly successful attempt to flush the pain from her cramped body. Dawn hadn't entirely made an appearance, yet, when her mother opened her door and announced breakfast was ten minutes from being served. Shelley quickly washed up and dressed before joining her family at the kitchen table. Her two younger sisters now helped their mother in the kitchen. Shelley took her seat at the table when her father burst through the front door and rushed into the house. Shelley turned and saw an agonizing grimace on her father's face.

"What is it, Dad? What's wrong?"

Virgil Robertson pounded his hands on the kitchen table and stared into his empty coffee mug.

"Both of our horses are dead in the barn." Virgil forced the words through clenched teeth.

Shelley jumped up from her chair and ran out of the house, jumping over the porch steps, her boot heels slamming into the dirt. She ran into the barn and crashed against the stall gate. Both horses lay motionless in the mud and hay. Shelley harnessed her thoughts. Her legs weakened. She fell to her knees next to the crumpled body of her trusted companion.

Her father purchased the flaxen chestnut mare for her just after they arrived in Canyon Creek. Francisco Garcia told her flaxen chestnut horses were rare, especially hers, due to the gold-like appearance of the tail and mane. Shelley's thoughts slowed enough for her to focus on the horse she knew as "Flaxen."

Virgil stepped into the barn and stood next to Shelley.

"Did you hear anything last night?" Virgil asked.

"No. The storm was loud. I looked out here during the night but didn't see anything," Shelley muttered, reaching up to the top rail of the gate and pulling herself up. "They look strange."

Virgil reached down and picked up a grain bucket.

"They were poisoned," Virgil said flatly, showing Shelley the remnants inside the bucket.

"Poisoned!"

"They were fed hemlock."

"That son of a bitch, Knox!" Shelley screamed, pounding her fist on the split-rail gate. "He did this. He had to!"

"I'm sure you're right, Shelley, but we can't prove anything."

"I don't need any proof! I know it was him and his men."

"I'm going to head over to the Kincaid's and borrow or buy a horse from Carl," Virgil announced.

"No, Dad. I'll go. You stay here. I'll get there faster."

Shelley skipped breakfast against her mother's wishes, strapped on her gun belt, and started for the Kincaid ranch. She figured it would take an hour or two to get to the Kincaid house on foot, and she wanted to get there as early as possible. It was already hot and humid despite being only eight o'clock in the morning. Besides, with any luck, she'd run into Clay Cox close to their property.

Shelley's thoughts collided with each other, a new one forcing the last one aside. She felt responsible for killing her horse and helpless to do anything about it. She wanted to gallop over to Knox's ranch and shoot him between the eyes, but she knew she'd never get close enough to do the job. He had a stable full of gunmen, and she was alone. Her head felt like a mule had kicked her. The pain throbbed with every angry step, and the heat was rapidly draining her energy.

After an hour of stomping across the rough pasture, Shelley heard a horse nicker in the distance. She stopped and looked toward the sound. Two riders sat still on their horses on top of a high rise on her left. She strained to see if it was Clay and Mr. Kincaid but couldn't make out who they were. She slowly walked, watching the two riders, who were now riding toward her at a gallop. The open range didn't provide any cover. She drew her Colt Lightning and crouched low to the ground.

As the two riders drew near, she recognized Clay Cox on the lead horse with Mr. Kincaid close behind. She let out a deep breath, stood, and holstered her gun. Cox brought his horse to a halt and dismounted in one motion.

"Shelley. What are you doing way out here on foot?" Cox asked.

"I was coming to see you and Mr. Kincaid. They killed our horses."

"Killed your horses?" Carl Kincaid repeated from atop his horse.

"Who killed your horses?" Cox asked, offering his canteen to Shelley.

Shelley took a long swig of water, then handed the canteen back to Cox.

"Thank you. Both of our horses were poisoned last night. We didn't see anyone, but I know it was Knox."

"Poisoned? Do you know how?" Cox asked.

"Dad said it was hemlock. He found some in their grain buckets," Shelley said. "I was coming to borrow or buy a horse from you, Mr. Kincaid."

"Certainly. We'll get you back to our place and set you up with a couple of good mounts. Clay . . ." Kincaid said, nodding toward his foreman's horse.

"Come, Shelley. Jump up. I'll take you back to the ranch," Cox said, pointing to his horse.

Shelley slipped her boot into the stirrup and swung up behind the saddle's seat, giving Cox room to follow. Cox reined his horse around and settled in behind Kincaid, who already started back to his ranch house.

"I sure was happy to see you, Clay!"

"I'm glad we were out this way. We were looking for strays after we came up about twenty head short on our count this morning."

"You think they were stolen?"

"Don't know for sure, but it looks that way because we didn't find any away from the main herd."

"I'm sure it's Knox's men."

"Maybe, but Knox isn't the only problem out here. There are plenty of other rustlers this close to the territory border," Cox reminded his jaded neighbor.

"I reckon so, but I don't believe Knox would let any other rustlers near our herds right now."

"Probably not. After getting your horses, I'll get you a saddle, and then I'll ride back with you. I want to take a close look at your dead animals."

"Thank you."

CHAPTER 31

Sunday, July 21, 1878

VIRGIL ROBERTSON – ROBERTSON RANCH

Virgil sat quietly at the kitchen table, pushing the last bite of a buttermilk biscuit around on his plate. Madeleine and the girls were out behind the house, tending to the laundry. Virgil's mind slipped back to memories of his sugar cane farm in Louisiana. The worries he had back then were nothing compared to what he was facing in Texas. Rain and insect infestations were no match for stolen cattle, shootings, and poisoned horses. Madeleine had already voiced her acceptance of selling the ranch and leaving Texas. He figured if the family moved back to Louisiana, they would do it without Shelley. She was a grown woman now with the spirit of a wild stallion. Virgil grinned at the thought of his oldest daughter.

"Virgil!" Madeleine's voice shook him back to reality.

Virgil snatched his shotgun from its place above the door and stepped out onto the porch. Madeleine and the girls were looking past the tack shed.

"Three men are coming," Madeleine announced, pointing toward three riders galloping across the small pasture next to the house.

Virgil recognized the impeccably dressed Gilford Knox

leading the way. "Go back to your chores girls, it'll be all right," Virgil ordered, nodding to Madeleine.

Madeleine and the girls hurried away. Gilford Knox and his two men brought their horses to a halt at the front door, where Virgil waited.

"You always welcome your visitors with a shotgun, Virgil?" Knox asked.

"Just lately. Did you come to see if your hemlock did the trick last night? What do you want?"

"That's what I like best about a man—getting right to the point. I don't know anything about hemlock, but I believe you know what I want, Virgil. I want your spread here. The whole thing. House, barn, sheds, stock, everything. As you already know, I'm willing to pay top dollar."

"And as you know, I'm not inclined to sell, so you and your men can ride on."

Knox's faint grin collapsed into the look of a booted viper. His jaw jutted out, and both eyes narrowed into slits. He lowered his voice and leaned forward in his saddle.

"You listen to me. I'm tired of sodbusters like you getting in my way. You're nothing more than a cane farmer impeding my plans. You have no business running cattle in Texas. If you know what's good for you, you'll pack up your little family and get your stubborn ass back to Louisiana, where you belong," Knox snarled.

Virgil's grip on his shotgun tightened. His mouth was cotton dry, and his hands seeped with sweat. He did his best to hide his fear. He knew better than to raise the barrel of his shotgun, knowing Knox's men would kill him before he fired a shot. The voice inside his head screamed sell, but his heart shouted no. He gathered the courage to speak.

"I have every right to be here, Knox. I bought this land

legally, and now you think you're just going to come in here and force me to sell. Well, I'm not selling to you or anyone else!" Virgil declared in the best defiant voice he could muster.

Knox leaned back in his saddle and stared intently at Virgil. "Your right to be here ended when that trigger-happy daughter of yours shot my wrangler in cold blood. Now, since you're not smart enough to figure it out, I'll tell you plain and simple. Either you sell to me, or I'll swear out a warrant and put your daughter in prison for the next twenty years. And don't think those gunslingers in town can save you or anyone else. I have them outnumbered five to one. You understand?"

Virgil's chest felt hollow. The thought of Shelley going to prison turned him numb from head to toe. He set his shotgun on a chair next to him. He looked at Knox, whose deathly stare didn't waver. Virgil slowly nodded his head.

"That won't be necessary. I'll do what needs to be done. Who shall I talk to about this?"

"I'll send word to Sam Johnson in town. See him. He'll handle everything. I'm glad you've come to your senses, Virgil. Now, instead of top dollar, you'll get whatever I'm willing to pay. I wouldn't want any other misfortune coming to you and your family," Knox said before turning his horse and riding away, engulfing Virgil in a thick cloud of dust.

Virgil stood motionless, watching the red Texas dust swirl around him like a silent tornado. Madeleine and the girls stepped around the corner of the house.

"You girls go inside and have some bread and honey," Madeleine ordered her daughters, who didn't hesitate to hurry past their father into the house.

Virgil looked down to where his wife stood at the bottom of the steps.

"I'll be going into town to sell the ranch," Virgil muttered.

"I know. I heard everything. You didn't have a choice, dear. Besides, we'll be happier back home in Louisiana," she offered in a soft, soothing voice before climbing the steps and taking her husband's hand in hers.

Virgil and Madeleine stepped into the house and brushed the dust off themselves. Madeleine lit the stove to heat a pot of coffee while Virgil opened the lockbox containing the deed to the ranch. He unfolded the document and read over it briefly, then joined Madeleine at the table.

"I'll leave as soon as Shelley returns with the horse," Virgil announced. "I haven't felt like this since the winter of seventy-three. That was the year we lost the cane crop. Remember?"

"I remember. This time we'll have the money from the sale of this ranch," Madeleine said.

"Sure. You heard Knox. He'll pay what he wants. Not what it's worth."

"It will be enough for us to get back to Lafayette."

"I don't want to go back there. We could join my brother over in east Texas," Virgil suggested.

Madeleine didn't respond. Instead, she retrieved the coffeepot from the stove and poured two cups full, then returned to the table.

"We could buy some land near his farm and start a new life there. He invited us to join him a couple of times."

"Yes, I know," Madeleine answered, looking past Virgil to the front window. "Here comes Shelley, and Clay Cox."

CHAPTER 32

Monday, 22 July 1878

LUXTON DANNER – CANYON CREEK

The previous night's lightning storm gave way to a bright sunny morning accompanied by a stiff wind that pushed large, white, cottonlike clouds across an otherwise spotless blue sky. Canyon Creek was aflutter with activity. The sound of pounding hammers and grinding saw blades bled through the walls of Knox's new hotel while men worked feverishly mounting the gaudy sign on the façade of the Knox General Store. A steady stream of wagons filled the streets, and people moved about their day in every direction. Danner, Wes, and Wade stood on the porch of the Sundown Hotel and took in the sights and sounds of the bustling Texas town. Danner shook his head and exhaled.

"This sure isn't what I remember from the last time I was here."

"Nor me," Wade chimed in. "I came through a few months back with a drive, and this was nothing more than a good stopping point."

"Rachel told me this morning that Knox said he planned on building a bank next. Said this could be the Saint Louis of the west," Danner remarked.

"That's a helluva dream! Doesn't he know there ain't nothing out here but coyotes, rattlesnakes, and armadillos," Wes said while laughing.

"Looks like you were right last night, Wes. In addition to those two spies over at Knox's saloon, there's a couple more in front of his lawyer's office," Danner stated.

Wes and Wade glanced down the boardwalk to Sam Johnson's office. Two of the men with Knox at the time of Danner and Wes's visit yesterday were standing around looking uncomfortable. When both men realized they were being watched, they looked away, pushed on their gun belts, and leaned against the building. Danner checked the sun's position. "Looks about ten o'clock. Let's stop by the troopers' camp and bring them with us out to the ranches," Danner said before stepping down and heading to the livery stable.

Wes and Wade paused for a moment. Wade checked his pocket watch and confirmed the time read one minute to ten. Both men shook their heads.

"How the hell does he do that?" Wade asked, knowing Wes had no answer.

"I don't know. I think Danner's part Indian." Wes chuckled, then followed Danner to get the horses.

"Good morning, Mr. Danner," Stoney Walsh greeted the gunslingers. "I need to let y'all know I'm no longer needed here after today," Walsh informed Danner, Wes, and Wade while they saddled their horses.

"Oh? Knox fire you?" Danner asked.

"Yep. For the second time. First the lumber mill, now here. I knew he'd have his men take over once he finished the deal."

"What are you going to do now?" Wes asked.

"I figure I'll see if Miss Tyler wants to sell the boarding

house. If she does, then we'll be on our way. We're sort of engaged, you know," Walsh reported.

Danner paused and stood silent for a time. "I don't believe we'll be keeping our horses here after today. Rachel could use a hand with her corral over behind the Sundown. We'll be keeping our horses over there. Don't say anything to Miss Tyler just yet. Let me talk with Rachel. I think Knox could use a little competition."

Walsh's somber expression quickly changed. He smiled and clapped his hands. "Yes sir! I'll wait to hear from you before I do anything!" Walsh gushed, vigorously shaking Danner's hand.

"Can you tell us how to get to the Morgan ranch?" Danner asked Walsh, who nodded and promptly provided directions.

The three gunslingers swung up into their leather saddles, tapped their spurs, and headed west out of town for Jackson and the troopers' camp, three abreast. Danner tipped his hat as they passed Knox's men in front of Sam Johnson's office, triggering chuckles from Wes and Wade, who drew his gun, spun it on his trigger finger, then holstered it in one smooth motion.

"You reckon Rachel can afford to hire Walsh just to take care of our horses?" Wes asked with a wry grin.

"The way I see it. That corral she has back there is plenty big enough to add a few stalls and turn it into a stable. That'll make it easy for anyone with a horse staying at the hotel. Besides, it'll provoke Knox. That's all that matters," Danner said flatly.

After a brief stop at the troopers' camp, the seven men headed southwest toward the Morgan spread. The group rode in silence for a bit before slowing their horses. Danner moved Bullet next to Jackson. "How'd things go last night at the Creekbed?"

"Real good. Had a few drinks and played some cards for the first time in a long while," Jackson reported with a grin.

"Dakota Jones give you credit?" Danner asked, reaching into his vest and pulling out the leather sack containing the four fifty-dollar gold pieces he collected in Oneida.

"Yes, sir. Said you gave him the word. Thank ya for that!" Jackson exclaimed.

"Here you go. There's one for each of you. Call it an advance," Danner said, handing the sack of coins to Jackson, who heard the tinkling sound of money inside.

"Yes, sir. Thank you, sir!" Jackson said, tucking the money inside his shirt.

Danner smiled. "You bet! And don't call me sir!"

"Yes, sir! I mean no, sir!" Jackson laughed.

A short ride later, the Morgan ranch came into view. A good-sized spread with a big main house, an assortment of sheds, and what looked to be a modest bunkhouse next to a barn and corral. Vast green pasture surrounded the tall white house with several small groups of cattle grazing in fenced-off sections. A wide creek meandered through as far as the eye could see.

"I can see why this fella doesn't want to sell," Wade said as the men made their way through an opening in the fence to the front of the house.

"Damn nice place," Wes agreed.

Dale Morgan and Carl Kincaid had occupied rocking chairs on the front porch for the better part of an hour, waiting for Danner and company. The men stepped down from the porch and greeted the gunslingers.

Morgan stepped forward as Danner and his men stepped

down from their saddles. "Good morning, I'm Dale Morgan. This here is Carl Kincaid."

Danner extended his hand to Morgan, who accepted the offer. "I'm Luxton Danner, this is Wes Payne, Clint Wade, Johnny Jackson, Isaac, Buster, and Edwin." Danner rattled off the names as though he had been riding with the men for years.

"Welcome, gentlemen. You can tie your horses around on the side and come on into the house."

Once inside, Morgan directed everyone to a massive oval table made of sturdy hardwood capable of seating twelve. The Morgan circled M brand was burned into the center of the polished surface. "I believe this will do."

"It appears you were expecting us," Danner acknowledged.

"Yes, Marshal. A friend of mine rode out early this morning and said he had heard you were coming," Morgan admitted. "I sent word to Carl right away. Virgil Robertson won't be joining us, though. He's the other rancher who helped convince Mrs. Brennen to write you, Marshal Danner. He decided to hire a hand to help him with his ranch instead of putting up money for you and your men, and he is currently preoccupied with a little trouble regarding his daughter."

"Took us by surprise. Virgil's been hit the hardest. His herd's been scattered a couple of times. He's lost cattle both times. My foreman is over at his place now. We found out this morning his horses were poisoned last night," Kincaid added.

"Well, now he's got more trouble. His daughter shot one of Knox's men the other night. She figured he was a rustler and shot him before he started running off the herd. Virgil said Knox threatened to file charges on his daughter unless he sells his place to him," Morgan explained.

"His daughter?" Wes asked.

"Believe me, his daughter can handle a gun and ride better than most men," Morgan added.

"She kill him?" Wade asked.

"We ain't heard," Morgan answered.

"Sounds like we could use her." Danner chuckled.

"Don't let her hear you say that. She'd join you quicker than a rattler can sink its fangs into your hide!" Morgan exclaimed to the laughter of everyone at the table.

"We're not here to talk about money right now. And I'm no longer a US Marshal. What we need to know is how committed the three of you and any of the other nearby farmers and ranchers are," Danner said.

Morgan and Kincaid exchanged looks of concern about Danner's announcement. "I believe I can speak for the three of us who border Knox's land. We are committed to keeping our land and letting Knox know he can't just do anything he wants without consequences. I've heard that Knox has bought land extending up to Thornton," Morgan stated, with Kincaid nodding in agreement.

"We know Virgil feels the same way, but I don't know if this shooting by his daughter will change his mind," Kincaid said.

Danner glanced at Wes, who met his look. "Knox has bought land up by Thornton?"

"Yep. I heard Knox offered to buy out a couple of ranchers and farmers up there," Morgan advised.

"It appears Knox has more money than I thought," Danner said.

"He has plenty and the men to prove it," Kincaid said.

"Are there just the seven of you?" Morgan asked.

"That's it for now," Danner answered.

"I've only got a couple of cattle hands here. Probably not what you'd need," Morgan advised.

"Nor me, I'm afraid, except for my foreman Clay. I'm sure he'll join you," Kincaid added.

"He will," Morgan agreed.

"All right. We'll let you know. For now, let's see what Knox's next move is. That'll determine what our response will be," Danner said, standing to leave.

"Thank you for coming, Mr. Danner. We thought that having a US Marshal come to town would be enough to convince Knox to back off. Now, I'm not sure where we stand," Morgan admitted.

"You leave that to us." Wes beat Danner to the words.

CHAPTER 33

Monday, 22 July 1878

LUXTON DANNER – SUNDOWN HOTEL – CANYON CREEK

D anner finished washing up and peered into the mirror at his bare chest and face. Courtesy of Jared Barry's office window, the scar on his forehead was no longer a jagged purple line. The color had faded some, but the skin had mended into a serrated strip of flesh that looked like one of the lightning bolts from the previous night's storm. He noted the scars on each shoulder, one from an outlaw's knife on the right, the other from a Confederate soldier's bayonet. Other than the shotgun pellets that prostitute from Six Shot fired into the back of his legs, his muscular body was in surprisingly good condition. *Not bad for such a big-ass target.*

The gentle rap of knuckles on his door interrupted his thoughts. He drew a Schofield from its holster, then stepped to the side of the door. "Who is it?"

"It's me. Can I speak to you for a moment?" Rachel's soft voice sounded crystal clear and dangerously inviting.

Danner holstered his pistol and pulled the chair from under the knob before slowly opening the door. Rachel's eyes widened when she saw Danner's shirtless body.

"I'm sorry! I'll wait until you finish dressing," she stuttered.

Danner opened the door and stepped back. "Come in."

Rachel quickly looked left and right down the hallway before she stepped inside. "I'm very sorry to bother you like this, but it's about Mr. Walsh." Rachel kept her eyes on the floor, clutching her apron with both hands.

Danner reached down and took her hands in his.

Rachel slowly allowed her eyes to move upward, taking in every inch of the giant gunslinger until she met his steel-gray gaze. "Oh my," she whispered before collapsing back into the chair Danner used to barricade the door.

Danner smiled, then stepped back and took a seat on the edge of the bed.

"First, there's no need to be uncomfortable. Second, I apologize about Stoney Walsh. I meant to speak with you about him before he came over here," Danner said.

Rachel tried to gather her thoughts. She felt faint. *What if someone found me here?* She closed her eyes and took a deep breath. Danner reached past her and pulled open a drawer where he removed a clean shirt. He quickly slid his massive arms into the sleeves and fumbled with the buttons.

"I thought it would be good for business if you had a small livery behind the hotel, and Walsh was ready to pack up and leave town. Don't worry about paying him. I'll take care of that."

"Oh, no!" Rachel exclaimed, finding the energy to stand and protest. "That's not necessary," she said, catching herself by grabbing the door handle.

"It is, when I'm the one that hired him. Just call it a partnership for the moment. I'll have him build a couple of covered stalls and stock them with whatever he needs. You already have three paying customers," Danner informed her.

"But I'll—"

"Be happy about adding to your business," Danner finished her statement.

"Luxton Danner, what am I going to do with you?" Rachel asked, putting both hands on her hips.

Danner tucked his shirt inside his pants and threw his gun belt over his shoulder before opening the door.

"After you, ma'am," he said with a nod toward the hallway.

As Rachel and Danner stepped out of his room, they met Wes coming down the hall from the staircase. Rachel gasped.

"Not a word out of you, Payne!" Danner boomed.

Wes smiled, stepped aside, and removed his hat. "I don't know what you're talking about, Mr. Danner," he managed to say before breaking into raucous laughter.

Rachel blushed and slapped Wes on the arm as she hurried past him. She stopped at the top of the staircase and looked back at the two men. "You're both incorrigible!" she said, then rushed down the stairs.

"Incorrigible?" Wes repeated, looking at Danner.

"Means bad, unacceptable," Danner clarified.

"Oh, she has a point." Wes chuckled.

"I'm going over to the Creekbed Saloon. Care to join me?"

"Might as well, since we're both incorrigible."

Danner pushed through the Creekbed Saloon's swinging doors and checked the room from corner to corner. The half-empty watering hole lacked the energy card games and music generated. Danner and Wes joined Wade at the bar.

"Good evening, fellas," Wade greeted his comrades. "What'll y'all have?"

"I'll have a whiskey," Danner told Dakota Jones.

"Same for me," Wes added.

Jones brought a bottle of his best, along with two glasses,

and set them in front of Danner and Wes. He pulled the cork and filled each glass to the rim.

"The first one's on me, fellas," the saloon owner declared.

"Sure you can afford it?" Danner asked, taking another look around the room.

"For you three, I can. Business ain't been too good since Knox's place opened," Jones admitted. "All of his men go there, and he has girls."

"Can't you get girls?" Wes asked.

"Aw, I had a couple for a while, but once Knox brought in those, that was that."

"Not a bad setup. Knox pays his men, then they come into town and spend their money at his places. Knox gets the money right back," Danner mused.

"You're right. I never thought about that," Jones said, scratching his head. Jones filled the three empty glasses again and set the bottle down.

The sound of boots pounding on the boardwalk outside the Creekbed rattled the doors. The doors flew inward, smashing against the walls. Four men piled in, knocking the dust off their clothes and stomping their boots on the hollow floor. Danner, Wes, and Wade didn't flinch, just kept their attention on their drinks. Jones watched the men stumble over to a table.

"Whiskey!" one of the men shouted, falling into a chair.

Jones pulled a bottle and four glasses from the shelf behind him and walked over to the table. The man who yelled for whiskey snatched the bottle from Jones's hand before he could set it down.

"You got any women here?" another man yelled as if Jones was on the opposite side of the room.

"No, sir. You have to go down the street for that," Jones said.

"We were just there! They threw us out! One of them

prostitutes squealed. Said we were drunk!" another of the men barked, spilling more whiskey on the table than he put in the glasses.

"Maybe they were right. Maybe y'all take it easy," Jones suggested.

The man who poured whiskey all over the table stood up, drew his pistol, cocked it, and pointed it at Jones's face.

"We'll decide when we'll take it easy! Understand jackass?"

"Yes, sir, no need to get angry," Jones stammered, backing away from the pistol's gaping barrel.

After Jones stepped out of the way, the four drunkards saw Danner, Wes, and Wade standing at the bar facing them.

"Well, well, what do we have here? The three amigos?" the man who pointed the pistol at Jones bellowed. "I don't like the looks on yer faces, amigos."

The drunkards looked at each other and laughed. Three of them began to push away from the table. The fourth put both hands on the table and said nothing. The few others in the Creekbed Saloon shuffled out of the way as several of the men standing along the back wall waited for the fight.

"Stand up, and we'll kill you," Danner said bluntly.

"Is that so?" the pistol pointer slurred.

The three started to stand and reached for their guns. *Crack! Crack! Crack!* Danner, Wes, and Wade drew and fired before any of the three cleared leather. The three fell back, with two flipping over their chairs, the third spinning around onto the table before sliding onto the floor. The pungent odor of gunpowder billowed into the room. The fourth drunkard sat utterly still in his chair and said nothing. Danner, Wes, and Wade held their guns on the fourth man. A group of men gathered around the swinging doors and outside the Creekbed's front window. Wes stepped forward.

"Get up. Real slow. Don't think about touching that gun," Wes ordered.

The man stood, gripping the table to steady himself.

"Jones, you know who has the keys to the jail?" Wes asked without taking his eyes off the fourth man.

"I think Doc Carson has them."

"Go get them and bring them down to the jail right away," Wes ordered.

"Yes, sir!" Jones said before sprinting out of the saloon.

"You, step around that table."

Wes stepped behind the man and took his gun. He handed it to Danner before grabbing a fistful of shirt collar and pushing the man through the swinging doors out onto the boardwalk. The crowd separated, allowing Wes and his prisoner to pass. Danner told Wade to stay behind and then followed Wes out onto the street, where both men walked their prisoner down to the abandoned jail.

Doc Carson hurried from his office with Dakota Jones close behind. "Here are the keys," Doc Carson announced, handing the ring to Danner, who inserted the key into the rusty lock.

After a couple of turns, the rusty bolt clicked open. Danner pushed the door inward. The rusted hinges yelped like a wounded coyote. Wes moved the prisoner through a plethora of cobwebs to the dingy cell in the back. Danner performed the same lock-and-key ritual on the cell door before pushing it open. Wes threw the prisoner onto the wooden cot, then locked the cell door.

"You'll sit there until you sober up," Wes informed the man, who remained mute.

Wes joined Danner, Carson, and Jones in the small office area.

"What are you doing? We're not the law here," Danner reminded his partner.

Wes looked around the office and nodded. "It looks like I'm the law here now," Wes announced. "I'm not going to just hang around town and wait for something like this to happen again."

"Doc?" Danner looked at the physician.

"I'll take care of everything. I'll talk to those in town who matter the most. We've wanted a marshal since Ben Chance died. It looks like we've found our man," Carson said with a grin.

Carson and Jones hastily left the jail on their mission. Danner looked around the filthy office.

"You sure about this, Wes? Being the law isn't what we came here for," Danner stated the obvious.

"That son of a bitch sticking a gun in Jones's face got under my skin, I guess," Wes offered. "I don't know. Maybe I just feel better when I'm wearing a badge."

Danner took a second look around the office he once occupied in Ben Chance's stead.

"This is a hell of an office you keep, Marshal," Danner said as both men erupted in laughter.

CHAPTER 34

Monday, 22 July 1878

LUXTON DANNER – CREEKBED SALOON

Danner followed Dakota Jones back to the Creekbed Saloon. The somber crowd returned to the saloon and were boisterously talking over each other about the gunfight. The three dead men remained on the floor near the table they'd briefly occupied. Crimson blood splattered across the tabletop where one of the gunfighters spun and fell before sliding to the floor in a heap. Wanting to seize the opportunity to sell some liquor, Jones rushed behind the bar and offered up whiskey in honor of the gunslingers that had come to town. The men roared and crowded around the bar bouncing money on its sticky surface. Danner joined Wade, who was on one knee next to the dead men looking for anything that might tell who they were.

"Anything?" Danner asked.

"Nope," Wade answered, rising from his kneeling position.

"That one over at the jail can tell us," Danner said.

"There anyone in this town that buries dead men?" Wade asked.

"There used to be an undertaker," Danner recalled. "I'll go see if I can find him."

"Excuse me, gentlemen, can I be of service?" A slender man dressed in black, asked from the doorway.

"Hello, Bart! Got three for ya!" Jones called from behind the bar.

"Yes, sir. We don't know who that is yet, but there are three here," Danner advised.

"Very good, Marshal Danner. I will see that they are taken care of," offered Bart Steen, Canyon Creek's longtime undertaker.

Danner paused and looked hard at Steen. "Have we met?" Danner asked.

"Why yes, Marshal Danner. I'm Bartholomew Steen. I remember you from your time here with Marshal Chance," Steen explained. "Please, call me Bart."

"That's right, Bart. Now I remember you, although I'm not a marshal anymore," Danner corrected the undertaker.

"Very well. I'll have the dead men's things over at my place behind the jail when you're ready," Steen advised before pushing the swinging doors out of his way and leaving the saloon.

The gunfight caused quite an uproar, with men and a few women stopping in front of the Creekbed Saloon to take a look. Two saturnine seekers stood next to the bar, then quickly left when Danner noticed them. They were Knox men checking on Danner and the company's handy work.

"No doubt Knox will have a full report on this soon. Two of his men just hustled out of here," Danner informed Wade.

"Good. Now Knox will know who he's dealing with," Wade responded.

The rumble of a wagon came to a stop outside the Creekbed. Steen and another man pushed their way through the crowd.

The man with Steen grabbed a dead man by the boots and dragged him out the door without a word. Danner and Wade stood by while the undertaker loaded the three corpses onto his wagon. Jones stopped Danner and Wade before they could head for the door.

"Thanks for the business, fellas," Jones mumbled in a low voice.

Danner slapped Jones on the back, then stepped out onto the boardwalk. He scanned right and left before stepping out into the street. He noted Knox's men were still out in front of Knox's saloon, but the two that had been watching from the lawyer's office were gone. Danner's long strides quickly brought him to the front door of the Sundown Hotel where Rachel was waiting, arms tightly folded across the top of her white apron.

"Uh oh. It looks like you're in trouble, Mr. Danner." Wade chuckled as he hurried up the Sundown's steps right behind the big gunslinger.

Danner had barely cracked open the door when Rachel's fusillade of prattle hit him like a shotgun spray.

"What do you think you're doing, trying to get yourself killed? What happened over there? Are you hurt? Did Wes or Clint get hurt? What's this I hear about Wes being the new marshal? I don't know what to think!"

The questions came like rapid fire from a Winchester. Danner stopped and said nothing, looking down at the shivering woman. Wade kept moving right on into the dining room that was half empty due to the gunfight across the street.

Tears began to flood Rachel's green eyes.

"Do you have any whiskey in the kitchen?" Danner calmly asked.

"What?"

"Do you have any whiskey in the kitchen?" Danner calmly repeated.

Rachel fidgeted with her fingers and wiped her eyes with a corner of her apron. She tossed her hands above her head and let them fall against her hips in a loud smack. "Yes, I believe I do."

Danner put his arm around her shoulders and led her through the back office into the kitchen, where several ladies juggled pots and pans as they prepared the evening's dinner. The ladies stopped and gawked at Danner, who nodded as he placed Rachel in a chair in the corner. "Now, where would that whiskey be?" Danner asked aloud.

One of the ladies opened a cupboard door, removed a less-than-full bottle, and handed it to him. Before he could ask, another lady thrust a glass in front of him. Danner accepted, offered a smile, and then poured a touch of amber liquid and handed it to Rachel. Offering no argument, Rachel swallowed the drink in one gulp, then held out the glass for another, which Danner obliged. After the second swig, Rachel took a deep breath and looked at the big gunslinger. She paused and pictured him without his shirt. "Now that's better!" she exclaimed through a sideways grin directed at Danner.

Danner handed the bottle back to one of the ladies, said nothing, then walked into the dining room and took his customary seat at the back table where Wade had already camped out.

"Everything all right?" Wade asked.

"Is now," Danner reported, accepting a cup of coffee from a young woman he hadn't yet seen before at the hotel.

"What are we gonna do about Wes?" Wade asked, holding his hand up to decline the coffee.

"Nothing. If the town appoints Wes the new marshal, that

may give us an advantage," Danner suggested. "At least here in town."

Wade nodded. "Hadn't thought of that."

"Our decision about what needs to happen in town will be legal," Danner mused.

"And outside of town?" Wade asked.

"Same as it was when we got here," Danner said, shrugging his broad shoulders, keeping his eyes on the front door.

Stoney Walsh stepped into the dining room and quickly made his way to Danner and Wade.

"Hello, Stoney. How's the stable coming along?" Danner asked, pushing a chair away from the table with a big boot.

"Well, Mr. Danner, we seem to have a problem," Stoney Walsh reported, preferring to stand with his hat in hand.

"Oh? What kind of problem?" Danner asked.

"I went over to the lumberyard to purchase wood for the stalls as you instructed, but the fellow over there said he didn't have any lumber for sale. I saw two large stacks of fresh lumber in the back, but he said they weren't for sale when I asked. That it was only for Mr. Knox."

"I see. It's a little late now. We'll go over in the morning and have a word with whoever's in charge over there. Don't worry about it. We'll get the lumber we need," Danner assured his corral keeper.

"Yes, sir. The good news is we have a couple more horses," Walsh proudly informed Danner.

"Very good. Be sure to tell Rachel when you see her," Danner requested.

Walsh nodded, then left the room.

"Looks like the new marshal is coming to visit," Wade announced Wes's arrival, along with Doc Carson and Albert Loman.

"Pull up some chairs," Danner told the trio, who all took seats for the impromptu meeting.

"Well, Doc, has the town decided to settle for a worn-out Texas Ranger to be their next marshal?" Danner asked through a snarky grin.

"It appears so," Carson advised.

"It certainly does," Albert Loman agreed. "The vote was unanimous."

"Unanimous?" Danner asked.

"Well, with everyone we asked, that is!" Doc Carson laughed.

"We didn't bother to ask anyone over at the Knox Saloon, and the brothel don't get a vote," Loman admitted. "And his hotel and store aren't open yet, so . . ."

"This ought to light a fire under Knox," Wes chimed in.

"I'm counting on it. First, we take business away from Knox's stable. Now, we bring the law into town. I figure he wasn't counting on that."

"Nope. And wait until he finds out I'm deputizing Jackson and his troopers," Wes announced.

Danner looked at Loman, then Carson. Both nodded in approval. Danner leaned back and allowed a grin to crack his iron jaw.

CHAPTER 35

Tuesday, 23 July 1878

LUXTON DANNER – CANYON CREEK

T wo more big Studebaker wagons loaded down with freight rumbled past the Sundown Hotel. That made for a total of six Danner had counted while occupying a rocking chair on the Sundown's front porch. Like the previous four, these two stopped in front of Knox's new store. Danner propped his size-twelve, bull-hide boots up on the railing and leaned back in the rocker. The breakfast crowd had cleared out, and Rachel had Adeline sweeping up the floors. The late morning was surprisingly brisk, so Rachel propped the front door open, welcoming the fresh air into the hotel. With the door open, Danner heard the scrapes of the corn broom whisking across the wooden floor. The sound of a buckboard clanking along pulled Danner's attention away from Adeline's broom. Stoney Walsh pulled on the reins, bringing the old buckboard to a stop in front of Danner.

"I got this here wagon and helpers as you ordered, Mr. Danner," Walsh victoriously announced, remaining atop the bench seat. Two men sat on the wagon's back gate, legs hanging off at the knee.

"Let's go talk with the man over at the lumberyard," Danner

said, dropping his boot heels with a thud onto the wooden planks beneath him.

He didn't have far to go since the lumberyard was right across the street from the Sundown, which had become a recent point of annoyance with Rachel. Danner strode across the street while Walsh turned his wagon around and parked it in front of the yard. Walsh tied off the reins to the brake arm and jumped down, joining Danner at the wide opening of the yard. A tall, heavily bearded man, wearing a wide-brim tan hat pulled down low over his eyes and a large knife on his hip stepped out of the office near the gate.

"Help you two?" the man grunted more than spoke.

Danner ignored the big fellow and walked past him into the open yard where four hefty piles of lumber in various sizes were neatly stacked.

"Hey, you!" the man shouted, following Danner as quickly as his rotund gut would allow.

Danner stopped and fixed his eyes on one of the four lumber stacks. "How much for this full stack of lumber here?" Danner asked, pointing to a hefty stack on his right.

"That's not for sale!" the big man grunted.

Danner looked to the second stack. "How about that one?" Danner asked, nodding toward the pile of his choice.

"That one's not for sale either! None of them are!" the man growled.

Danner turned to the big man and noted he was of equal height, something Danner didn't see much. Danner's eyes narrowed into snake-like slits. He lowered his voice. "This is the Canyon Creek Lumberyard, isn't it?"

The man leaned toward Danner, putting his right hand on the handle of his knife. "I said it ain't for sale, jackass. Now why don't you and your three little bastards go on and git," the man snarled, sending darts of tobacco spit onto Danner's face.

Danner didn't flinch. He just stared straight through the man's bloodshot eyes. "If you don't take your hand off that knife, I'll put a bullet right through the top of your greasy head," Danner whispered as he pushed the tip of his Schofield .45 under the man's chin.

The fat man's bloodshot eyes opened into large rings of fear. He gulped at the touch of the gun barrel. Beads of sweat the size of raindrops began to pour down his ruddy face into his tobacco-soiled beard. He hadn't seen Danner draw his gun. The man released his grip on the knife and moved his hands away from his body like they were wings.

"That's better. Now, how much for the stack of lumber?" Danner kept his voice low like a wolf's growl.

"That's about two hundred, but—"

"We'll take it," Danner stopped the man. "Stoney, load up the wagon!"

Walsh and his two helpers quickly began loading the buckboard wagon. Danner kept the gun barrel pressed up under the man's jaw.

"Now, you and I are going into the office where I'll pay for the lumber, understand?" "Yes, sir, but Mr. Knox . . ."

"I don't give a damn about Mr. Knox. If he has a problem with me buying that wood, you tell him to come to see me. He knows where to find me. Understand?"

"Yes, sir."

Danner shoved the man toward the office and holstered his gun. Once inside the office, Danner handed the man two hundred dollars and demanded a bill of sale, which the man reluctantly scribbled out. Danner folded the paper and tucked it into his pocket, then looked out of the office to see Walsh snapping the reins on his team, sending the buckboard out of the yard. Danner followed the wagon and saw Wes standing next to the yawning lumberyard's gate.

"Been there the whole time?" Danner asked Canyon Creek's newly minted marshal.

"Long enough to see you buy lumber at the point of a gun." Wes chuckled.

"Just a little misunderstanding is all," Danner explained. "Everything worked out just fine," Danner added, walking past Wes and across the street back to the friendly embrace of the Sundown Hotel.

Wes followed Danner around to the back of the hotel, where Walsh and his men unloaded the lumber.

"Will that be enough to build what we talked about, Stoney?" Danner asked.

"Yes, sir. We'll get to it right away. It shouldn't take more than a few days," Stoney Walsh confidently declared.

"Very good. Let your men know they'll be paid for their work," Danner said, then headed back to the front of the hotel and the rocking chair he abandoned earlier.

Wes leaned against the railing that Danner used as a footrest and looked down at his lanky partner. "Mind if I ask you a personal question?" Wes prodded.

"Sure," Danner quipped, looking past Wes, keeping his eye on the lumberyard across the street.

"How are you paying Walsh and now his two buddies back there?"

"Walsh will get paid from the money Rachel takes in from keeping horses here. I've got the rest covered."

Wes said nothing, turning to look at the lumberyard. "You reckon that fella will cause trouble?" Wes asked.

"Not until Knox orders him to," Danner answered. "You know, hunting outlaws in the territory is a lot more profitable when you're not a US Marshal. You get to keep the rewards hanging on their heads. I was able to put together a rather good sum."

Wes nodded. "And I thought you were just riding guard for a couple of cattle outfits."

"Also did that a couple of times, and I managed to win more than lose at the poker table."

"Speaking of reward money, that dumbass I put in jail told me who those other three were. Doc Carson's been hanging on to the wanted posters that made it to town. Two of them had prices on their heads for being horse thieves. One hundred each. Soon as I collect, I'll split it with you and Wade," Wes advised.

"Give mine to Jackson and the troopers. Might be the only pay they get," Danner offered.

Danner checked Knox's saloon. Both of Knox's men were out front watching his every move. He glanced down to the lawyer's office and saw the lawyer talking to a man dressed like a farmer who appeared to be in a hurry to get into his wagon. The lawyer was shaking his head, but the farmer didn't seem to want to talk any longer, waving his hands at the lawyer. The farmer jumped into his wagon and sped off, leaving the well-dressed lawyer engulfed in a cloud of red dust.

"What do you make of that?" Danner asked Wes.

"I don't know. It looked like a little argument," Wes said.

"Looks like you're about to find out, Marshal. Here comes Knox's lawyer now."

Wes waited in the shade of the Sundown's porch for the lawyer to arrive.

"Good afternoon, gentlemen. I'm Sam Johnson, Gilford Knox's lawyer. I understand you're the new marshal?" Johnson asked, looking at Wes.

"That'd be correct. I'm Wes Payne, and this is Luxton Danner," Wes introduced himself and Danner. "What can I do for you, Mr. Johnson?"

"Well, I'd like to speak with you about a serious matter, but not out here in the open. I'm sure you know Knox's men are watching you, and now I've learned they're watching me as well."

"All right. Can you meet me at the jail in about fifteen minutes or so? Go around to the back door. I'll see you there," Wes suggested.

"That will be fine. Fifteen minutes, in the back. Thank you," Johnson said, then hurried back to his office.

"You best join in on this," Wes told Danner.

CHAPTER 36

Tuesday, 23 July 1878

WES PAYNE – CANYON CREEK

D anner and Wes walked down Main Street past Doc Carson's place a few minutes later, then came upon Sam Johnson's office where one of Knox's men had returned. Wes stopped directly in front of Johnson's office and stared at the guard.

"Don't you have anything better to do?"

"Uh, yes, sir," the guard mumbled, then hurried across the street to the Knox Saloon where he disappeared through the swinging doors.

"That wasn't very friendly, Marshal," Danner said through a thin grin.

"Not feeling very friendly right now, Mr. Danner," Wes responded with a chuckle before heading to the marshal's office and jail.

Wes cracked open the back door of the jail and watched.

"Did you recognize the fella that Johnson was talking to before he came down to see me?" Wes asked Danner.

"Nope. I figure it's one of the ranchers or farmers that Knox forced out," Danner said.

"Here he comes," Wes announced, opening the door and allowing Johnson to step inside quickly.

"Thank you for seeing me, gentlemen," Johnson said, taking a seat next to Wes's dilapidated desk.

"What's this all about?" Wes asked.

"Mr. Knox hired me a few months ago with the promise of great wealth and success. He offered me a great deal of money to come to Canyon Creek. Said I'd oversee the handling of all his legal business. He was correct about the amount of business and paid me well, but I'm no longer supportive of his dealings. I've seen too many people come into my office completely defeated and dismayed. Many people seemed to be nervous or in fear if they didn't follow through with the business with Mr. Knox. At first, I thought they were just uncomfortable dealing with a powerful man, but I began to suspect Mr. Knox was forcing them into the transactions. I recently spoke with Mrs. Brennen at the Sundown Hotel and learned that was the case. Now, this last deal is the final straw. This afternoon, Mr. Virgil Robertson came into my office and advised me that he decided to accept Mr. Knox's offer to buy his ranch. Mr. Knox had made numerous offers to Mr. Robertson, but he had been steadfast against selling. Suddenly, Mr. Robertson wanted the sale expedited. He refused to answer any of my questions regarding why he decided to sell, but I suspect Mr. Knox threatened him," Johnson offered, out of breath.

"Take a moment, Mr. Johnson. We're in no hurry here."

Johnson caught his breath and continued, "I heard about Mr. Robertson's daughter shooting one of Mr. Knox's men. I don't know much more than that, but I know Mr. Knox. I'm sure he threatened Mr. Robertson with his daughter's arrest unless he sold his ranch to him. I tried to talk Mr. Robertson out of it, even told him I'd investigate the matter, but he wouldn't listen, just told me to get the sale done right away. I'm not that kind of a lawyer, gentlemen. I'm an honest man. And now, Mr. Knox has his men standing outside my office watching my every move. I'm certain this will cost me my position, and frankly, I fear for my life now, but I no longer want to conduct that kind of business," Johnson declared. "Now, with a marshal in town, I thought you should know."

"Is there any way you can delay the Robertson sale?" Danner asked.

Johnson thought for a moment. "No, sir. Mr. Knox will expect me to deliver the deed to him this evening for his signature."

Danner nodded and thought for a moment. "If you can show Mr. Robertson signed the deed under duress, that would void the sale, correct?" Danner asked.

Sam Johnson smiled. "I've never heard a gunfighter talk like that."

"Danner went to college, Mr. Johnson. His father was a lawyer back in Charleston," Wes clarified.

"I apologize, Mr. Danner. I, of course, just assumed—"

"Never mind about that," Danner interrupted. "Are you willing to testify in front of the district judge that Knox forced Robertson to sign that deed?"

Johnson lowered his gaze to the worn floorboards of the marshal's office. He remained silent for several long moments.

"You're concerned that once Knox finds out about this, he'll kill you," Danner said bluntly, leaning back against the wall opposite Johnson's seat next to the desk. Johnson didn't speak, just nodded.

"It's not only me. I have a wife. She would also be in danger," Johnson muttered. "I couldn't forgive myself for bringing her here just to have something happen to her."

Wes and Danner exchanged glances, then Wes got up from his seat behind the desk. He walked around the desk and stood beside Danner, facing Johnson.

"Where are you staying?" Wes asked the overwhelmed barrister.

"That's just it. We live in a small house on the Knox ranch."

"Here's what you do. You take the deed out to Knox for his signature like any other business transaction. Then, tomorrow, have your wife come into town with you. We'll set you up at the Sundown Hotel, where she will be protected. Knox's men won't get to her there. You'll need to trust us on that," Danner insisted.

Johnson nodded enthusiastically. "I can do that," he assured the gunslingers. "My wife enjoys having breakfast at the Sundown anyway. Mr. Knox won't suspect anything about that."

"Good. I'll be in the dining room when you arrive. I'll have Rachel, Mrs. Brennen, prepare a room for you next to mine. Does that sound good to you, Wes?" Danner asked the marshal.

"As good a plan as any," Wes said with a smile. "Don't worry. Danner and I haven't lost a witness yet." Wes smiled, shaking Johnson's hand as he rose from his chair. "You best get back to your office before Knox's spies get suspicious," he instructed Johnson, who nodded and hurried out the back door.

Danner looked at Wes with arms crossed over his massive chest. "I wasn't aware we had ever guarded a witness," Danner said.

"Well, he doesn't know that," Wes offered with a straight face.

Danner held his grim look for a moment, then burst out in laughter. He shook his head and looked around the office.

"Are you going to clean this place up, Marshal?" Danner asked, kicking an empty can into a corner. "It's a real dump."

"I thought it was coming along just fine," Wes answered, scanning the room.

"Oh sure, if you're raising hogs." Danner chuckled before ducking under the top of the front door of the office and heading back to the Sundown to tell Rachel about Johnson's arrival.

CHAPTER 37

Wednesday, 24 July 1878

JOHNNY JACKSON – BUFFALO SOLDIERS CAMP – OUTSIDE CANYON CREEK

An armadillo scurried under a patch of dried thistle at the sound of a nigh coyote's call. A predawn whisk of wind swept over Johnny Jackson as he trundled out of his bedroll and stretched his aching body. Sleeping on the ground was beginning to take its toll on the former master sergeant. His joints felt like rusted hinges, and his back snapped like twigs under a horse's hoof. The fifty-dollar gold piece Danner gave him burned a hole in his pocket. The thought of paying for a room at the boarding house had crept into his mind like a tune he couldn't shake. He pushed a few cracked mesquite branches into the cold fire pit. The parched wood quickly ignited, and soon the comfort of a morning fire would embrace the former trooper's camp. As the minutes passed, the gray dawn was swept away by the burning embers of the daybreak sun. Jackson's comrades began to stir, performing the same ritual he acted out a few minutes earlier. Jackson emptied a little water from his canteen onto his face and rubbed vigorously. After wiping his face with the cleanest of his soiled bandanas, he saw three riders approaching from the west.

"Looks like we gettin' some company this mornin', fellas," Jackson announced as he casually stepped over to his gear and checked his Henry rifle, ensuring a cartridge was in the chamber. Isaac, Buster, and Edwin strapped on their gun belts, cautious not to make any sudden movements that would appear hostile. The three riders, all armed, rode side by side at a canter pace. Jackson kept his eyes on the approaching men.

"Spread out a little, fellas," Jackson ordered his troopers. "Just in case."

The three riders pulled up about five horse lengths from where Jackson stood.

"Good morning, fellas. Don't have any coffee on yet," Jackson greeted the men, whose somber expressions indicated this would be an unfriendly visit.

One of the men, older than the other two, dressed in a long brown canvas duster and wide-brimmed black hat, moved forward from the others. "What the hell are you four doing here?" the man spewed.

Jackson looked around their site and turned back to the man. "We've been here a few days now. Just set up camp is all," Jackson explained in a friendly tone.

"This here's private property. Gilford Knox owns it. You're trespassing on Circle X land," the man growled. "You need to pack up and git!"

"Well, now, we didn't know this was private land. Don't see much a nuthin' all around, 'cept for the town a ways yonder," Jackson stated, waving his hand toward Canyon Creek off in the distance.

"Well, now you know. We'll give y'all five minutes to get out. Mr. Knox don't need your kind around squattin' on his land," the man declared, faking a grin. The other two chuckled under their hats.

"I reckon we'd need more than five minutes, but we'll be on our way right quick," Jackson responded, shifting toward his Henry rifle.

"You get any closer to the rifle, and I'll just kill all of ya, and that'll be the end of it," the man threatened.

"I guess we best be gettin' a move on then, boys," Jackson told his troopers, who'd already begun to load their gear onto their horses.

The three Knox riders spread out, taking positions around Jackson and the troopers as they hustled to break camp and get mounted. Before leaving, Jackson looked at the Knox rider who'd been giving the orders.

"Now, you said this was Knox land?" Jackson asked.

"That's right."

"And who might you be?"

"Not that you need to know, but the name's Carter," the man said. "Now git!"

"Yes, sir!" Jackson called, then banged his spurs and galloped toward town with his three troopers in tow.

Isaac rode up next to Jackson after putting distance between themselves and the hostile evictors. "I don't much like being ordered about like that anymore," Isaac said.

"Nor me, but I reckon that's not the last we'll see of Mr. Carter. Our time will come," Jackson assured his partner. "The truth is, I was gettin' tired of sleepin' out on the dirt anyhow."

Jackson and the troopers rode up to the Sundown Hotel, where Danner occupied his favorite rocking chair, boots propped up on the top rail.

"Good morning, fellas. Finally decided to accept the offer of a fine breakfast?" Danner asked the men.

Jackson dismounted and handed his reins to Isaac, who led the others around the corner to tether the horses to a hitching post. Jackson climbed the steps and accepted Danner's handshake.

"No, sir. We was tossed out of our camp by three fellas, claimed they was workin' for Knox. Said we was trespassin' on Knox land. Gave us five minutes to get out or else," Jackson explained, cracking his dark face with a bright smile.

"Or else what?" Danner asked, dropping his boots to the floor and standing.

"There was some talk about killin'."

Danner's weathered face turned crimson with rage. He grabbed both handles of his pistols and pulled up his gun belt.

"No reason to get riled, sir," Jackson offered. "Fella said his name was Carter. We'll meet again," Jackson assured his angry boss.

Danner said nothing, just nodded, looking west toward the Knox ranch. He rested his hand on Jackson's shoulder and squeezed as Isaac, Buster, and Edwin returned from picketing their horses.

"Gentlemen, the owner keeps a table for us in the back against the wall. Breakfast is on me this morning," Danner announced before opening the front door and waving the four ex-troopers inside. Danner led the group through the sparse crowd to his table in the back and took his customary seat, back against the wall. The dining room was nearly empty due to the early hour. Seeing Danner leading the men, Rachel quickly called into the kitchen for five mugs and a pot of coffee before hurrying to Danner's table. She heard of the former Buffalo Soldiers riding with Danner and Wes but hadn't seen them until now.

"Good morning, gentlemen, I'm Rachel Brennen, the owner of this hotel. I have coffee coming for everyone. Will that be all right?" she asked, looking into the faces of the four men.

"Yes, ma'am, that'd be mighty fine. I'm Johnny Jackson. This here is Isaac, Buster, and Edwin," Jackson announced. "And that cookin' smells mighty fine!" he added with a wide grin.

"I'll have bacon, eggs, and biscuits for you right away if that's to your liking?"

"Yes, ma'am!" the four men answered in unison.

"If it wouldn't be too much, I'd also like a plate this morning, ma'am," Danner said.

"Rachel giggled and tossed her auburn hair aside, then lightly slapped Danner across the shoulder with her fingertips before spinning around and gliding to the kitchen.

"Oh, boy! Mr. Danner done got himself a girl!" Jackson blurted in between bursts of laughter from the rest of the troopers.

Danner fought back a grin and shook his head. Wade joined the boisterous group as Rachel and another lady arrived with coffee, biscuits, and honey. Wes came in and saw the troopers had joined Danner and Wade.

"Good to see you fellas again," Wes said, shaking Jackson's hand as he was the only one who didn't have his hands full of biscuits and honey. "What brought you into town this early?" Wes asked Jackson.

"We was ordered out of our camp by three of Knox's men. Said we was on Knox land, so here we are."

Wes looked at Danner, who shrugged a shoulder and took a sip of coffee.

"I didn't think Knox's property came that close to town," Wes said.

"I'm thinkin' Knox owns just about everything around here, and if he don't, he thinks he does," Jackson said before eating half a biscuit in one bite. "I'm lookin' forward to meetin' this Knox," Jackson said after gulping his food.

"We all look forward to meeting up again with Mr. Knox," Wes assured Jackson. "And, since you're all here, I've got an offer for y'all," Wes announced.

CHAPTER 38

Wednesday, 24 July 1878

SHELLEY ROBERTSON – ROBERTSON RANCH & CANYON CREEK

S helley rushed into the house and found her parents seated at the kitchen table. Her mother's trembling hands and solemn expression were definitive evidence of her sadness. Her father's frown and slumped shoulders alarmed Shelley. Her heart raced, and her breath grew short.

"What is it? What's wrong?"

"Please sit down, Shelley," her father asked.

Shelley reluctantly took a seat opposite her father.

"I sold the ranch to Knox yesterday," Virgil Robertson managed in a weak voice.

"No! Why?"

"I had no choice. Knox came here two days ago when you brought the horses back from Mr. Kincaid's. He threatened to have you arrested for attempted murder unless I agreed to accept his offer for the ranch. If I sold, he would forget about the shooting."

"No."

"We have three days to pack the wagons and leave," Virgil

added. "I purchased another wagon yesterday. That should be enough to carry our things."

"What about the herd?" Shelley asked.

"Knox demanded the herd be included in the sale."

Shelley quickly stood, knocking her chair back into the corner. She began pacing the floor, her boot heels pounding on the battered wood with every step. Her head swirled with thoughts that overran each other. She stopped the rustling of her father's herd, but now they'd lost the ranch.

"Knox paid us enough. It will be all right. We can take the money and find another town to settle in," Virgil offered to calm his eldest daughter.

"Oh? Another town? And what if we run into another Knox? Men like him are everywhere! What about fighting for what we have here? I thought Mr. Danner and Mr. Payne were going to help everyone!"

"Those men can't just come here and make everything right. Besides, the thought of you facing arrest and a trial was too much for your mother and me," Virgil said.

"No! I can't let this happen!"

"It's already done. I had no choice."

"There's always a choice! Fighting back is a choice!" Shelley shouted before stomping out of the house.

Shelley grabbed her gun belt from the saddle horn and strapped it on. She checked her Colt Lightning, then hurdled up into the saddle and spurred the horse before her father could chase after her. She pushed the horse into a full gallop. The reins pulled at the sutures that strained to keep her wire-gashed hand from tearing open. She had covered the wounded palm with a tight glove in a failed attempt to dull the pain. She couldn't fight back the tears that cut a watery path down each sunbaked cheek. She rode through the north pasture, up the hill, and over. She didn't know where she was going, but it didn't matter. Knox defeated her without her being allowed to fight. She hated Knox even more for what he had done to her family. All because of her. She reined Mr. Kincaid's horse left into a thicket of brush and stopped. She jumped off without bothering to use a stirrup. She let herself fall to the ground and buried her face in her wounded hands.

I can't let this happen. I just can't.

She took time to calm herself then sat back against a massive live-oak tree she found herself beneath. She thought through the list of who could help her. The Morgans and Kincaids couldn't help. Clay Cox might want to, but what could he do alone? She had no real friends, having distanced herself from the other young women in and around town. She liked and respected Rachel Brennen at the Sundown, but enough was enough. That's it. She had to go to town and see Danner and Payne. She hadn't met them but had heard all about their arrival.

Maybe they can help? It was worth a try.

CHAPTER 39

Wednesday, 24 July 1878

KNOX'S BORDELLO – CANYON CREEK

The crushing blow of his fist against her thigh sounded like a gunshot. Her broken front tooth sliced her bottom lip as she plummeted off the bed, her head banging against the floor in a raucous thud. He grabbed her bare shoulders and pushed her back onto the soiled sheets. He swung wildly at her swollen face, his leathered hand slashing her left eye. She thrust her hands into his face in a desperate attempt to defend herself. He reached down around her throat and squeezed off her breath.

"I told you I wasn't done with you, yet!" he snarled before a lightning bolt of pain shot through his skull.

He crashed against the bedpost and stagged backward. His vision returned in time to see the grain of the lumber collide with his forehead, sending him spinning against the wall. He shook his head and saw a woman in a red satin dress raising a club high over her head, ready to strike another blow. He lunged forward, pounding both fists into the Madam's chest, catapulting her across the room onto a dressing chair. The Madam gasped for air; the breath knocked from her lungs.

"Get out," the Madam managed to moan.

He reached up and pulled his holster off the hook before hastily shedding his clothes but for the grimy union suit. He drew his gun and pointed it at the weeping girl curled up on the bed.

"Don't you dare," the Madam warned. "Mr. Knox won't stand for that!" the Madam added.

"Damn woman didn't give me my money's worth!" he yelled.

"You hurt me," the bloodied girl groaned.

He grinned and leaned over the girl. "Ain't my fault I'm too big for ya," he sneered.

"Mr. Knox is going to hear about this. It's not the first time we had trouble with you!" the Madam said.

He grabbed the Madam by her hair and thrust the barrel of his gun under her chin.

"You say one word of this, and I'll come back and kill both of you. Knox doesn't give a damn about women like you. He pays you to keep us happy, and I ain't happy. Understand?"

His sour whiskey breath burned the Madam's eyes. "I understand."

"That goes for all of ya!" he shouted at several girls gathered at the door, watching in horror.

He pulled on his clothes, then stormed out of the room, pushing girls aside as he stomped down the hallway.

"One of you go get the doctor!" the Madam ordered the group at the door before examining the girl's wounds.

The Madam soaked a towel in the washbasin and wiped the blood from the girl's eyes and mouth. The girl's severed bottom lip framed a gap where a tooth had been. Her left eye was swollen shut, and large dark welts permeated her outer thighs and legs.

"That bastard isn't going to get away with this. I don't

care if he's a Knox man or not. I'll tell the new marshal what happened," the Madam assured her wounded scarlet.

With assistance, the girl dressed and lay back on the bed. She stared at the ceiling, wishing she had stayed in Oneida and ignored the promise of nice clothes, fine jewelry, and money. A few minutes later, the Madam escorted Wes into the room, followed by several other girls.

"This is Marshal Payne, dear. I told him what happened. The doctor will be here soon."

The girl looked at Wes through a blurred eye and nodded.

"Show the marshal your legs, dear. It's all right."

The girl pulled the sheet back, exposing her bruised legs.

"He's slapped us girls around before, Marshal," one of the other girls reported.

Wes nodded. "Any of you know who he is and where he went?"

"He's one of Knox's men. I don't remember what he calls himself, but I'm sure you'll find him over at Knox's saloon. You can't miss him. He's the one with the goose egg on his forehead, thanks to my club," the Madam declared.

Wes looked at the two-foot piece of smooth hickory at the foot of the bed and smiled.

"That'll do the job," Wes said.

Wes looked back at the girl and nodded. "I'll let him know he can't get away with this," Wes said before heading to Knox's saloon.

CHAPTER 40

Wednesday 24, July 1878

SHELLEY ROBERTSON – CANYON CREEK

S helley rode down Canyon Creek's Main Street, busy with endless lines of wagons, carriages, and men on horseback. Hammers and saws were polluting the air with the sound of progress. She stopped at the Sundown Hotel and quickly went inside, where she found Rachel speaking to a man and woman about leaving their wagon behind the hotel in one of the newly constructed stalls.

"Hello, Shelley. What are you doing here this afternoon?" Rachel asked the young cowgirl.

"I'm sorry to bother you, but I just found out my father sold our ranch to Knox, and I need some help!" Shelley yelled loud enough to startle the man that just finished speaking to Rachel. He peered at her from the bottom of the staircase.

Rachel quickly wrapped her arm around Shelley and escorted her past the man into the dining room, where she guided her to a table near the kitchen door.

"Wait here, dear. I'll be back in a few moments," Rachel advised, then disappeared into the kitchen.

Shelley removed her hat, tossed it on the chair next to her, and looked around the quiet room. Families occupied two other tables. Shelley saw the man from the staircase walking toward her, his hat in hand.

"Excuse me, miss. Would you be Virgil Robertson's daughter?"

"Why do you need to know that?" Shelley asked, a warning in her voice as she placed her hand over the Colt Lightning she wore on her right hip.

"I'm sorry. I'm Sam Johnson. I was Mr. Knox's lawyer. I spoke to Mr. Robertson yesterday and handled his ranch sale."

"I got nothing to say to you! You're lucky I don't shoot you where you stand."

"I understand your displeasure, but I'd like you to know that because of Mr. Knox's treatment of your father, I am no longer in his employ," Johnson explained. "My wife and I are now hiding from Mr. Knox and his men here at this hotel."

"Sit down," Shelley ordered the attorney. "No longer in his employ, means you quit, right?"

"Yes. I tried to help your father yesterday, but he wouldn't speak to me. I even offered to investigate the shooting that I assume you were involved in?" Johnson asked.

"I'm sorry. I'm Shelley Robertson. I shot the son of a bitch that was going to run our herd off again."

"I knew of the incident and Mr. Knox's arrangement to force your father into the sale. I am not in favor of that type of business, so I notified the new town marshal, and we—"

"New town marshal?"

"Yes, Mr. Payne has been named marshal."

"He's one of the men that came into town with Mr. Danner, isn't he?"

"Yes, I understand he used to be a Texas Ranger."

"I need to see him right away!" Shelley exclaimed, grabbing

her hat and hurrying toward the lobby. As Shelley turned the corner near the staircase, she ran straight into Danner. Danner didn't move, but Shelley bounced back and landed on her backside. Danner calmly looked down at the tousled cowgirl.

"Shelley Robertson, I presume?" Danner asked, holding his hand out to help Shelley back on her feet.

Shelley straightened her gun belt while Danner retrieved her hat from the floor. She looked up at the towering gunslinger and gasped.

"Oh my!" she exclaimed before allowing the glint of a smile to cross her lips.

"I'm Luxton Danner. Is something wrong?"

"No," Shelley quickly answered. "I was just looking for Marshal Payne, and well . . ."

"You found me instead," Danner said with a wide grin. "Care to join me at my table?" Danner asked, pointing to his customary table where Sam Johnson stood in the back of the restaurant.

After Sam Johnson excused himself, Shelley told Danner about Knox's threats and her father's decision to sell their ranch.

"I came to ask Mrs. Brennen for help. We heard you and Mr. Payne were going to try and stop Knox from taking everyone's land."

"Mr. Johnson told us about your father selling the ranch. We'll do what we can, Miss Robertson, but now, I'm not certain what that means. I suggest your family stays in town for a bit and see how this plays out," Danner advised. "Let's go find Marshal Payne, and we'll talk more about this," Danner said, escorting Shelley out of the Sundown and onto the street.

Danner glanced up and down the street, then started for the marshal's office when a man ran up to him and Shelley.

"Mr. Danner, Marshal Payne's over at the Knox Saloon fightin' with a big fella!" the man exclaimed.

"How bad is it?"

"Marshal looks pretty beat up!"

"Shelley, go get Rachel and find Doc Carson. It sounds like we'll need him," Danner said, then ran toward Knox's saloon.

CHAPTER 41

Wednesday, 24 July 1878

WES PAYNE – CREEKBED SALOON

Wes crashed into a table and flipped over a chair, thumping his head on the wall. His mouth filled with blood that tasted like he was sucking on a piece of rusted iron. His heart pounded inside his ears, and his jaw was numb. He shook his head and jumped to his feet just before his attacker blindly threw another right cross toward his jaw. Wes ducked, and the attacker's fist crunched against the window frame. Wes heard knuckles snapping like twigs. Wes twisted his body and turned into the attacker's gut with the force of a charging bull. He sank his fist deep into the attacker's rib cage, cracking bone, and forcing out whatever breath the attacker had left inside his lungs. Desperately gasping for air, the attacker stumbled backward a couple of clumsy steps, digging his spurs into the floorboards, giving Wes the opening he needed. Wes balled his scarred right hand into a rock-like orb and reared back. With every ounce of energy he had left, he fired his fist square into the attacker's face, crushing his nose and knocking teeth into the back of his attacker's throat. The attacker's face exploded, sending blood, teeth, and snot into the air as his head rocked backward, bouncing off his shoulder blades. His eyes rolled back into his head, and he collapsed into a bloody disheveled heap at Wes's boot tips.

Wes spun around with both fists and teeth clenched to defend against anyone else stupid enough to charge him. No one dared accept the challenge. The rest of Knox's men kept still and silent, watching in awe as Canyon Creek's new marshal stood over their fellow cowhand who'd been foolish enough to contest Wes's authority. Blood flowed from Wes's forehead down into his right eye, blurring half his vision. He did his best to retrieve the breath his opponent knocked out of him. He knew he needed to get out of Knox's saloon as fast as he could. The sound of the saloon's doors broke the flash of silence. Wes glanced over and saw Danner step over the threshold.

Wes relaxed for a moment and stood up from his defensive crouch. He saw his monster of a partner standing in the doorway like a mountain. Danner said nothing. He looked at Wes.

"I need this one," Wes said, taking a step back from the unconscious combatant.

Danner stepped over and picked the man up by his gun belt, then turned and walked out of the saloon.

Wes followed Danner to the door, then turned around to face Knox's men. "Tell Knox there's a new boss in town, and if he doesn't like it, he can come see me anytime," he announced before disappearing onto the street.

Wes followed Danner over to the jail, where he collapsed into the chair behind his desk. Danner threw the prisoner into a cell and locked the door before returning to Wes and looking down at his wounded friend.

"I sent someone over to the Sundown Hotel to fetch Rachel and Doc Carson," Danner advised.

Wes wiped the blood from his mouth and head with his bandana, then tossed the crimson-stained cloth onto the desk.

"What the hell was that all about?" Danner asked.

Wes made his way to the washbasin and carefully rinsed his face and mouth. He slowly made his way back to his chair and sat down. Pulling a bottle of whiskey from the desk drawer, he took a swig straight from the bottle. The whiskey seeped into every gash inside his mouth, burning its way up into his nostrils. His eyes watered, and the cough that followed sent thunderous pain into his temples and through his left side, where he had taken a couple of heavy-fisted blows from his attacker.

"I don't know why the hell I do that. I know it's going to burn like hell," Wes said with a chuckle. Wes leaned back and looked up at Danner with his good left eye. His right eye was nearly swollen shut. "That son of a bitch in there beat up one of the girls pretty bad at Knox's brothel. The boss lady came over and told me about it. She says he's done that before, but she can't keep him out. I met with the girl. She was busted up pretty bad. It looked like he hit her a couple of times in the face. She was black and blue on her legs. I went over to Knox's saloon to get him. He put up a little argument. I wished I hadn't sent the troopers out to watch the roads. I could've used their help," Wes admitted.

"A little argument?" Danner repeated with a grin.

"Who'd you send to get Rachel and Doc?" Wes asked.

"Shelley Robertson. She's the daughter of that rancher Sam Johnson told us Knox threatened. It looks like Johnson was right about Knox threatening Robertson with charges against his daughter if he didn't sell out. She came over to the Sundown looking for Rachel's help and ran into Johnson. He told her about you, so she started to run out of the hotel to see you but ran into me first. She told me all about it. We were walking over here when a man told us you were in a fight in Knox's saloon. I told her to wait outside and came in myself," Danner explained.

The jail door flew open, and Rachel burst through like a stampeding longhorn steer. Doc Carson was on her heels, black bag in hand.

"Oh, dear! Are you all right?" Rachel gasped, looking at Wes through open fingers across her face, which failed to cover her view.

"Well . . ." Wes began.

"Step aside, Rachel, and let me have a look," Doc Carson insisted, gently pushing on Rachel's hip to move her out of his way. "Now, let me see what we're dealing with here," Doc Carson mumbled as he kneeled next to Wes's chair. Doc Carson gently pressed his fingertips into the flesh around Wes's jawline, orbital bones, and forehead. He squeezed his collarbone areas and felt around his neck. "This may hurt," Doc Carson proclaimed before placing his fingerprints on the bulbous right eye of his patient.

"It does." Wes exhaled, inadvertently jerking his head back away from Carson's paws.

"What you think, Doc? Will he live?" Danner asked in between chuckles.

"You just give me a moment to catch my breath, and I'll kick your—"

"You men! Never taking this foolish behavior seriously!" Rachel shouted.

"I'm just thankful you don't have any bullet holes for me to mend for a change!" Carson exclaimed with a grin.

"Can't get shot yet, Doc. Not before you introduce me to this beautiful young lady over there," Wes said, glancing at Shelley with his good eye.

Shelley had followed behind Rachel and Carson to the jail, where she quietly waited near the door while the medical examination and subsequent jocularity took place. Shelley stepped forward wearing a broad smile beneath her weathered cowgirl hat when recognized.

"I'm Michelle Robertson, Marshal. Everyone calls me Shelley."

"Well, Michelle, I don't think I've ever seen such a beautiful woman wearing britches and a gun belt before. I hope you ain't offended by my saying that," Wes said, cracking a grin that sent shocks of acute pain through his jaw up into his swollen right eye.

Wes watched Shelley's face blush a bright pink. He was no ladies' man, but he figured she wasn't used to men other than her father, referring to her as beautiful. Her eyes and smile softened. She stepped toward Wes and reached out to shake his hand. Wes obliged but replaced the shake by taking her hand between his aching fingers and thumb, then leaning forward; he kissed the back of her hand. Wes felt the shiver that shot up Shelley's arm like a sidewinder darting down its den. Wes grinned, sending a second round of sharp pain through his face and eye.

"All right, Romeo, how about I get to taking care of that mess you call a face," Doc Carson said.

Wes looked at Carson with his functioning left eye. "Who the hell is Romeo?" he asked, sparking laughter from everyone else in the room.

CHAPTER 42

Friday, 26 July 1878

LUXTON DANNER & SAM JOHNSON – SUNDOWN HOTEL

T wo quiet days passed except for the constant hum of hammer and saw bustle erupting from behind the Sundown Hotel. The racket slowed to an occasional bang and rip. Stoney Walsh and company had nearly finished the covered stalls of the new Sundown livery stable. The open windows of the trivial storage room behind Rachel Brennen's hotel brought the scent of fresh-cut lumber wafting into the hotel's silent kitchen. The time between lunch and dinner rendered the activity in the hotel to that of a church house. Danner sat alone in the dining room, nursing a tepid cup of coffee. Rachel finished cleaning up the lunch clutter and went to visit Miss Tyler at the boarding house. Despite the intense heat outside, the dining room was uncharacteristically pleasant, with both the front and side doors open, allowing what passed for a summer breeze in Texas to drift through. Boot and shoe heels tapping on the polished surface of the oak steps directed Danner's attention to the foot of the staircase, where Sam and Anna Johnson emerged with wrinkled brows and lines of anxiety draped across their faces.

"Good afternoon, Mr. Danner," Sam Johnson greeted the gunslinger.

"Care to join me?" Danner asked, waving toward the vacant chairs at his usual table in the back of the room.

The Johnsons each took a seat. A short, petite woman, Anna Johnson was dressed in a snug gray prairie skirt and white Victorian blouse with long raven black hair piled up in a series of intricate braids. The cascades of curls fell down the back of her neck. She offered a smile Danner saw was both obligatory and uncomfortable.

"Rachel get you taken care of upstairs?" Danner asked, not knowing the purpose of the Johnsons' visit.

"Oh, yes. It's quite comfortable," Anna Johnson assured.

"I sent a written announcement of my resignation and our subsequent move to Mr. Knox yesterday. I received his answer this morning," Sam Johnson advised, handing a letter to Danner.

Danner quickly read through the brief correspondence, then returned the document to the lawyer. "It doesn't seem threatening to me."

"No, sir, not at all. Quite professional. With the amount of money Mr. Knox offers, I'm sure it won't take too much time to find my replacement," Johnson admitted. "The purpose of our visit is to inform you that we've decided to go to Dallas. I have a standing offer from the Texas and Pacific Railway Company there."

"We appreciate your assistance and offer of protection here at the hotel, but we thought it best to leave," Anna Johnson added.

Danner nodded and took the last sip of cold coffee that had waited patiently at the bottom of the cup. "Sounds like a good opportunity. When do you plan on leaving?"

"We'll take the stage tomorrow," Johnson advised.

"Sorry to see you leave. Canyon Creek could use two more good people," Danner offered.

"Thank you for saying that," Anna Johnson said before she and her husband shook Danner's hand and left the dining room.

Danner remained in the dining room mulling over Knox's words in his answer to Sam Johnson. It was true, there were no outright threats made. Knox was too clever for that, but Danner didn't like the tone of the message. His thoughts were interrupted by Rachel's return. Her long auburn hair flowed over her shoulders like water cascading over a fall. Her light blue dress hugged her waist and hips while the skirt swayed graciously from side to side as she approached.

"Have you been sitting here alone all this time?" Rachel asked through smiling lips painted bright red.

"No. The Johnsons just left. They told me they're leaving for Dallas tomorrow on the stage."

"Oh, I'm sorry to hear that. I like Mrs. Johnson. Did they say why they're leaving?"

"Seems Johnson has a job with the railroad, but I figure they're afraid of what Knox might do," Danner answered.

Rachel's smile faded. "You don't think he'd harm them, do you?"

"I don't know what Knox would do. I don't know enough about him yet. He seems like the type to send a message to anyone else who has thoughts of leaving him, though," Danner surmised. "What's that fella's name that runs the stage office?" Danner asked.

"Elmer. Elmer Barton," Rachel answered.

"I think I'll go have a talk with him about tomorrow's stage passengers," Danner said, standing and adjusting his gun belt.

"Will you be back for dinner?"

"I don't figure I have any other place to be," Danner said with an assuring grin.

Rachel smiled and headed for the kitchen. Danner watched her until she disappeared through the doorway. He fought back the urge to follow her into the kitchen, take her in his arms, and kiss her.

I can't get involved.

◆———◆

A few minutes later, Danner found Elmer Barton behind the stage office plunging a rag into a bucket, then twisting the water out, leaving just enough to wash down the seats of the Randall stagecoach. After wiping the dust from the leather seats, Elmer Barton folded the rag and closed the door, wiping the ever-present red dust from the brass handle. He kneeled and checked the through braces to ensure they were tight and free of tears, not entirely confident that his driver would perform such an examination. While dangling under the carriage, the sound of boots crunching the gritty red dirt indicated a customer was approaching. Pushing himself up from under the carriage, he found himself looking straight up into Danner's daunting glare.

"Good afternoon, sir," Elmer offered weakly.

"Are you the stage manager?"

"Yes, sir. What can I do for you?" Elmer asked, quickly wiping the dirt from his hands with the damp rag.

"What time does the stage leave tomorrow?"

"We try to get her underway about ten o'clock or so. Will you be joining the group?" Elmer asked.

"Not exactly. What is the route?"

"Well, it will head east out of town following the road to

Stratford, then continue south to Cactus and then Oneida. Anyone going on from Oneida will have to take the Wells Fargo line either south or east," Elmer explained.

Danner thought for a moment. *If Knox were going to make a move, it'd be between Canyon Creek and Stratford.*

"Do you have a shotgun rider?"

"Yes, sir. Cletus, he's the driver, usually has a man with him for the long trips to Oneida. Is there trouble?" Elmer asked.

"I don't know. How many passengers do you have right now?"

Elmer pulled a small notebook from his pocket and flipped it open. "Looks like four right now. There's room for two more if you would like to join the ride."

"No, I won't be joining the group. Thank you for the information," Danner said, then turned and casually stepped over to the boarding house where Jackson and the troopers had landed after being evicted from their campsite by Knox's men.

Danner found Jackson and one of the troopers watching the activity on Main Street from the far end of the house's front porch. "Good afternoon. Come over to the Sundown right away. We need to talk," Danner informed the duo, who snapped to their feet and followed Danner to the hotel.

CHAPTER 43

Saturday, 27 July 1878

JOHNNY JACKSON – RANDALL STAGE OFFICE

letus Bradley pulled back on the reins, bringing the Randall stage to a halt in front of the office building. After pulling the brake arm tight, he jumped down and began checking the traces and hames on his six-horse team. The boot was already heavily loaded with luggage, giving Cletus an excellent reason to double-check the whippletree for cracks.

Johnny Jackson watched Cletus perform his pre-departure ritual from his perch on the bench in front of the office. Danner had told Jackson of Johnson's departure and the possibility of trouble from Knox, thus joining the stage as the shotgun passenger for the ride to Oneida. He welcomed the assignment, becoming restless, waiting around for something to happen. He and the former troopers weren't accustomed to being deputies and getting paid to hang around town in case of trouble.

The Johnsons arrived as the other two passengers were stepping into the coach. Jackson noted the Johnsons were traveling with two fancy-dressed ladies from Knox's bordello. The dresses were the style the fine ladies wore when he worked on the plantation. All the most refined ladies dressed that way back then. Jackson glanced over at Mrs. Johnson just in time to see a frown of disapproval flash across her face. Jackson dipped his head down to hide his chuckle of amusement from the proper lady Johnson.

"Mr. Jackson?" Cletus asked, looking across the team at Jackson.

"Yes, sir, that'd be me," Jackson responded with another chuckle at the wide-eyed look on Cletus's face.

"Well, sir, I'm Cletus. Yer my shotgun rider today? That right?" Cletus asked before making a small pool of mud between his boots with a stream of brown tobacco juice.

"It is," Jackson confirmed, stepping around the coach and crawling up the passenger side with his Henry rifle in hand.

Cletus mumbled something as he helped the Johnsons into the coach, much to the delight of Jackson, who broke out in loud laughter atop the driver's box. Cletus shut the door and turned the brass handle. He looked up at Jackson.

"What's so funny up there, mister?" Cletus quipped from under the brim of his floppy hat.

"Nothing! Nothing at all! I just reckon you'd never had a fella like me ride shotgun with you before! That's all!" Jackson shouted through his laughter.

"Oh hell, something like that, I suppose."

"Everything all right out here?" Elmer Barton asked after stepping out of the office, register in hand.

"Oh hell, everything is fine," Cletus groused.

"Very good then. Have a good trip," Barton called to the coach.

Cletus joined Jackson on the driver's box, released the brake, and snapped the reins. The six horses responded in unison, and the Randall coach was underway with its hodge-podge of occupants.

Traveling east to Stratford meant the morning sun lay straight ahead, burning into the eyes of Cletus and Jackson. Jackson kept his head down, occasionally scanning the terrain around the trail for any unwanted visitors. Cletus stayed quiet but for the occasional yip and call to his horse team as they charged ahead down the path to Stratford. The stage rocked back and forth like a wobbly rocking chair on an uneven floor. Jackson had his Henry secured in its scabbard next to him, with two bandoliers of ammunition draped over his shoulders and across his chest. Jackson noted the holstered gun on Cletus's hip but knew the old rein master was no gunfighter. He wasn't sure, but he figured Mr. Johnson wasn't armed and knew Mrs. Johnson would have nothing to do with a firearm. The two bordello ladies were a different matter. He guessed both had at least a derringer in their possession and most likely knew how to use it. That wouldn't constitute much help if trouble started.

"So, how come you joined this trip?" Cletus finally asked.

"Oh, just in case of trouble is all," Jackson answered.

"My regular shotgun rider would be just as good if trouble started. Must be something else," Cletus accurately surmised. "It got something to do with them Johnson folks?" Cletus asked with a wry grin.

"Yep, it do," Jackson admitted, nodding his head.

"I figured. Heard Johnson quit ol' Knox and his bad business."

"They did."

"Think ol' Knox will do something?" Cletus asked, rocking back and forth with the rhythm of the coach.

Jackson didn't answer, just shrugged his shoulders and smiled.

"I reckon you'd know I got Mr. Johnson's money in the strongbox under my bench," Cletus announced. "I reckon it's a fair amount," he added.

Jackson nodded, then scanned the area around the coach.

"This trail get narrow any place?"

"Yep. A couple of places. We go past a rise on the right. Then up ahead a little, then through a small box canyon about a half-hour later. I usually stop the team in the canyon since there's grass and water."

"All right," Jackson acknowledged with another nod of approval.

As the coach passed the ridge along the trail, Jackson kept a close watch on the rise. The course cut next to an elevation on the right just a few feet above Jackson's head. The ground dropped off into a shallow swale of cactus, thistle, and sage on the left. Jackson's focus sharpened as Cletus slowed the horses to navigate the narrow passage, which showed a bend to the right up ahead.

Damn good place for road agents. Jackson pulled on Cletus's right arm in a gesture to slow the horses down a bit more.

Cletus pulled back on the reins, bringing the team to a slow trot. Jackson leaned over and spoke into Cletus's ear.

"Stop," Jackson ordered.

Cletus quickly brought the coach to a stop just before the trail's bend. The coach door opened, and Sam Johnson leaned out to see Cletus holding up both hands, palms toward him. Johnson recognized the gesture and said nothing, sliding back into the coach and quietly closing the door. Jackson carefully pulled his Henry from its scabbard and cocked the hammer back, having levered a cartridge into the chamber when they left Canyon Creek. Jackson closed his eyes and listened. The slight late morning breeze gently whistled as it navigated the talus along the steep hill's escarpment. He heard the creaking of the leather harnesses and the low chatter of the passengers inside the coach. Then, a horse's faint snort in the distance interrupted the tranquility. He opened his eyes and looked at Cletus, who nodded emphatically. One of the team's horses nickered.

"Damn it, Rosie," Cletus mumbled under his breath, quietly scolding his lead horse.

Jackson scanned the ground scrub in the swale to the left. He spotted a narrow opening between a dead redbud tree and a cluster of thistle and broken rock. He pointed to the space. Cletus followed Jackson's finger and saw the opportunity. The trail sat up about three feet from the swale bottom, but he figured he could make it. He pulled the reins hard to the left and snapped the leather straps. At first, the horses resisted, but Cletus jerked and snapped the leather reins, forcing the team to step down into the dry furrow.

"Hang on," Cletus called to the passengers as the coach leaned to the left, causing the right wheels to briefly lift entirely off the ground while the horses traversed the slope.

"Hurry up! I hear 'em comin'!" Jackson shouted, turning to his right and putting the middle of the trail in his rifle sights.

Cletus nestled the coach next to the dead redbud and pulled his double-barreled shotgun from under the bench. Three riders appeared around the edge of the jagged rock hill, pistols in hand. *Crack! Crack! Crack!* Gunfire erupted from the three trail bandits as they charged the Randall stagecoach. Jackson calmly took a breath and squeezed the trigger of his Henry. *Crack!* A bandit flipped backward off his horse. The other two jumped from their mounts and fired again. *Crack! Crack!* Bullets hammered the coach's side, sending splintered wood in every direction. One of the women screamed. Jackson fired another shot into the ground the bandits were hiding behind. In between the gunfire, Jackson heard the sound of pounding hooves on the trail behind the bandits.

"Don't shoot!" Jackson called to Cletus, who'd leveled his double-barrel at the dusty trail.

The pounding hooves appeared with three former Buffalo Soldiers mounted atop the charging horses. *Crack! Crack! Crack! Crack!* The soldiers' aim was true, silencing the bandits' guns, ending the fight before it began. Jackson let out a sigh, then a hearty laugh. He waved at his partners as they checked on the three dead bandits.

"Well, I'll be a brown head cowbird!" Cletus cackled. "Them fellas with you?"

"Yep. I wasn't fer sure the fellas would be here, but I'm damn sure glad they were!" Jackson answered, slipping his Henry back into its scabbard.

Sam Johnson jumped out of the coach and joined Jackson and Cletus.

"Was it Knox's men?" Johnson asked, returning his Colt Dragoon pocket pistol to its hold inside his vest.

"Don't know yet. Let's go have a look," Jackson stated.

The three men joined the former soldiers near the trail's edge.

"I didn't expect to see you until we got to Stratford, but I'm mighty glad to see you three here!" Jackson declared, shaking each man's hand.

"We saw these three camped near the mouth of the box canyon up yonder last night. We figured we'd track 'em this morning, knowing you'd be along," Isaac explained. "They don't look like no big rancher guns, though," Isaac added, rolling one of the bandits over onto his back.

"You know any of 'em?" Jackson asked Cletus and Johnson. Cletus shook his head no.

"I can't say I saw all of Knox's men, but I saw most, and these three don't look like anything Knox used to hire, but now, I don't know for certain. They look pretty rough," Johnson said. "It's a good thing Anna and I are getting out of the territory."

"I reckon it is," Cletus agreed.

Jackson looked down the trail and saw the bandits' horses grazing along the swale. "Let's get their horses and bring 'em to Stratford. See if the sheriff knows anything about 'em," Jackson said. "Once we get them tied to their horses, we'll push the coach up onto the trail," Jackson advised Cletus, who nodded in approval.

"I'll get the team up to the edge. The horses need some help gettin' that coach up there," Cletus announced before he and Johnson headed back toward the dead redbud tree.

CHAPTER 44

Saturday, 27 July 1878

LUXTON DANNER &
WES PAYNE –
CANYON CREEK JAIL

T he sun's burnt-orange hue reflected off the windows that lined Canyon Creek's Main Street. The piano music from inside Knox's saloon drifted along the boardwalks, turning the town into a massive music box. Danner stepped out from behind the Sundown Hotel, where he inspected the carpentry skills of Stoney Walsh and his hired hands.

The livery stalls Walsh built exceeded Danner's expectations. The thick timber posts were tall and solid, complementing sturdy walls and a strong planked roof. Bullet and Ringo already occupied two of the ten stalls. Wade, Jackson, and the troopers' horses would fill five more, leaving three open to bring in money for Rachel. A feeling of gratification flowed over Danner like crisp mountain water plummeting downstream. He let the thought of him staying in Canyon Creek linger for a moment before he pushed it from his mind. Once Knox's hotel opened, he knew Rachel would have fewer paying guests. The money from the stable would help her along if he left town. Danner saw Wes rambling down the boardwalk on the opposite side of the street. He decided to join Canyon Creek's marshal and take a turn around the town.

"Good evening, Marshal," Danner said as he stepped up onto the boardwalk in front of Wes. "How's that eye coming along?"

"Just fine. I can finally see out of it again." Wes chuckled.

"That's good. Nobody wants a one-eyed marshal."

"Did you hear Knox may be coming into town tonight?"

"Nope. I figure it's about time, though."

"Should be interesting. I reckon Knox won't leave without stopping in to say hello," Wes said with a grin.

"Especially after you beat up his man and threw him in jail the other night."

"As I recall, it was you that threw him in jail, Mr. Danner," Wes retorted.

The two men found their way to the boarding house where Miss Tyler, a short woman with a large waist, round face, and short brown hair, dressed in a white blouse and gray prairie skirt, casually occupied one of her rocking chairs on the wide front porch. Her white apron was folded and lying across her lap.

"Good evening, ma'am," Wes greeted the house owner and unofficial schoolteacher with a tip of his hat.

"Good evening, Mr. Payne, Mr. Danner."

"Good to see you having time to rest on a nice evening," Wes managed, not knowing what else to say.

"Mr. Danner made it easy for me this evening. He sent most of my guests to Stratford last night."

"What does she mean by that?" Wes asked Danner.

"I wasn't sure what Knox might do with the Johnsons leaving on the stage this morning, so I sent Jackson with the stage and the troopers to Stratford in case there was trouble."

"Good idea," Wes said, nodding in approval.

"With those gentlemen gone, my other two guests decided to have supper over at the Sundown, so here I am."

"Very good. Have a good evening, ma'am," Wes offered with another tip of his hat.

Danner and Wes returned to the marshal's office, where Wes paused and held the door open, allowing Danner to duck under the frame and enter. Wes followed and sat down behind his desk. Danner pulled up the old ladderback and took a seat. The chair cracked and squeaked under his 245 pounds.

"One of these days, that damn chair is gonna crumble under you," Wes said, opening a desk drawer and removing a bottle of whiskey.

Wes poured whiskey into two glasses on his desk, then pushed in the cork and returned the bottle to the drawer. He pushed one glass toward Danner and took a sip from the second.

"How much longer are we gonna stay?" Wes asked.

Danner emptied his glass in one gulp and returned the glass to the desktop. He rubbed the whiskers on his jaw but didn't answer.

"Other than Knox blackmailing Robertson into selling his spread and Johnson quitting on him, nothing's happened. It's like Knox figures he'll just wait us out. He knows we aren't going to stick around forever. Wade is already restless. He back from Oneida yet?" Wes asked.

Danner kept silent, then shook his head no about Wade.

"Look, I know you're thinking hard about Rachel, and building that livery behind her place was awful nice of you, but I reckon you're not settling down in Canyon Creek anytime soon," Wes added.

Danner nodded and pointed to the marshal badge pinned

on Wes's vest. "And what about that?" Danner broke his silence and asked.

"Aw, I just did this because I got mad. There isn't even any talk about payin' me yet. I'll stick it out until we're ready to leave, then pass it on to someone else."

"Well, if Knox comes to see us tonight, maybe we'll get some answers," Danner suggested.

"Hello in the jail!" a man called out from the street.

Wes quickly cracked open the door and looked out. "What is it?"

"Dakota told me to let y'all know Knox and a bunch of his men are coming into town. Should be here right quick!"

"All right. Tell Dakota thanks for the word," Wes answered, then shut the door.

"You wanted answers. I reckon we're about to get a few," Wes said with a smile.

Danner stood up and stepped to the door carrying his feeble chair. "I think I'll have a seat out front and wait for our visitors."

"Sounds like a good idea. Think I'll join you," Wes added, snatching up a wooden stool he found in one of the jail cells, then followed Danner out of the office.

Dusk hadn't quite taken hold yet, but the sun was dropping fast behind the black horizon, so Wes decided to light the oil lamp hanging from a rusty wire hastily nailed to the edge of the roof in front of the jail. He took a seat on the opposite side of the door where Danner had taken up a position.

A few minutes into their wait, a group of riders appeared at the west end of town, filling Main Street from boardwalk to boardwalk. Despite the twilight limiting his vision, it was evident to Danner the riders were Knox and his men. At least fifteen or so thundered into town, churning up dust and dirt as they rode up to the Knox Saloon. Horses snorted and nickered as the riders dismounted in unison after their boss had set foot in front of the swinging doors. Attired in a dark suit, bolo tie, and customary Stetson, Knox paused beneath the burning lamps that lit the entrance to his tavern. Two men tended to the horses while the rest followed the wealthy rancher through the doors. Once Knox disappeared into the building, the piano music stopped.

"Seems our visitor has something to say," Danner muttered.

"How long you reckon before he comes down here?" Wes asked.

"Not long. Knox isn't here to mingle with his men."

As if Danner was a biblical profit, the piano started up again, and Knox stepped out of the saloon with four of his men. He snapped a quirt against his leg, then led his men to the jail, where Danner and Wes kept their seats when he arrived.

"Good evening, gentlemen," Knox offered.

Knox stood erect with shoulders square and head held high. His four guards stood two to each side just behind him.

"I hear you're the new marshal," Knox said, looking at the star on Wes's vest.

"That's right. What can I do for you?"

"Well, for one, you can stop harassing my men. But most importantly, you can stop impeding my progress," Knox stated in an inhospitable manner.

"Harassing your men? You mean your men who like to beat women?" Wes asked, shifting his weight on the stool.

"That's not the way I heard it."

"Well, that's the way it was."

"And, this business of talking my lawyer into quitting and leaving town in such a hurry," Knox added.

"No one needed to talk Mr. Johnson into quitting. It seems

he didn't take too kindly to the way you did your business."

"Well, I guess some men don't have the stomach for putting a town on the map," Knox said, clutching the braided leather quirt with both hands.

"And some men don't have the stomach for men like you who abuse their wealth and power," Danner said, standing up and looking down on the mighty rancher.

Knox paused and looked up at the monstrous gunslinger glaring down upon him. Knox met Danner's eyes in the glow of the oil lamp's flame.

"Don't think for a minute that anyone is going to stop me, including the two of you and your ex-Buffalo Soldiers," Knox declared. "I have twenty gunfighters, all professionals. Don't make me use them. Good evening, gentlemen," Knox said before turning away and pushing past his four guards, who all stood still, keeping their eyes on Wes and Danner until Knox was safely tucked back inside his saloon.

"I think you professionals can leave now," Danner retorted.

The four guards took several steps backward before heading back across the street one by one. Danner sat back down on the rickety ladderback and leaned against the wall.

"Looks like we know where he stands now," Danner announced.

CHAPTER 45

Sunday, 28 July 1878

SHELLEY ROBERTSON – ROBERTSON RANCH

Shelley carried a basket of clothes through the house to the waiting big freight wagon her father had bought the day he told her about the sale of the ranch. Four days had passed since she learned of the consequences of her actions when she pulled the trigger of her Winchester. Shelley had been numb for four days. The sliver of hope she had of saving the ranch faded after she visited town. Wes and Danner had told her they'd do what they could, but her father's decision made it difficult. She pushed the basket in between some furniture, then looked out over the pasture she spent so many beautiful days on. She couldn't remember a single wrong moment from watching the horses gallop to the cattle grazing until Knox showed up and started trouble. She knew she should have listened to her father, but Shelley still believed she had done nothing wrong. *When did defending our property become a crime?*

"Shelley?" her father's voice snapped her memories apart.

She turned to see her father, shoulders slumped forward and bent at the waist. He looked utterly defeated and lost on what once was his property. She met him next to the buckboard with a hug.

"I'm so sorry, Dad," she whispered into his ear.

"Don't be. Our leaving didn't happen just because you defended our land," Virgil assured his daughter. "Maybe this is for the best. It's been a tough go ever since we left Louisiana. I was a good cane farmer, but not much of a rancher."

"Nonsense!" Shelley exclaimed. "We made this ranch one of the best around. That's why Knox wanted it so bad."

"Knox wants everything around here," Virgil sighed. "That's just about everything in the house," Virgil added.

"Good, let's finish up and get to town then," Shelley said.

"I wanted to talk to you about that. I don't think we ought to go into town. I figured we'd just head south to Oneida, then decide what to do there," Virgil said.

"No, Dad! Marshal Payne and Mr. Danner said we should stay in Canyon Creek for a bit and see if we can get the ranch back!" Shelley pleaded.

"I know what they said, Shelley, but I've got to care for your mother and sisters. I can't just wait around hoping for two men we don't even know to solve our problems," Virgil insisted, shaking his head.

"I know we don't know them. But I've talked to people in town and seen why Mr. Danner and Marshal Payne have a reputation for making things right. They need help, and I'm going to join them."

"You'll do no such thing, young lady! I'll not have you risking your life over ranch land I've already sold. We can always start over someplace else! Knox paid me good money—"

"Knox gave you half of what this land is worth, and you know it!" Shelley shouted, slapping her hand over her mouth and stepping back.

"Don't you speak to your father like that, Michelle Robertson!" her mother shouted from the porch.

Tears filled Shelley's eyes but refused to tumble down her

cheeks. Anger flooded her body like water bursting through a dam.

"I'm sorry, Mother, but I can't just give up like this. You didn't give up when the tornado hit and never gave up when the droughts came. Now, we have two good men and a whole town on our side, and we're just going to run off like scared colts?"

Virgil stood silent for a long moment, then looked at his wife, who met his eyes with a glare of defiance, and hands propped on each hip. Shelley saw her mother's look and knew they'd be heading for Canyon Creek. Her mother had been the reason for their move to Texas, believing a better life was waiting for her family. Shelley covered her smile, not wanting her father to see her satisfaction.

"Very well. There's not enough money to buy a cane farm back home anyway. We'll go to town and stay for a few days," Virgil said, leaning against the buckboard.

"All right, then. Let's finish this business and get along!" Madeleine Robertson announced before disappearing back into the house.

Shelley headed to the barn to see if she left anything of value behind. She paused at the barn door. To the right of the frame were her initials MDR, carved into the rough wood. She remembered the day she etched those letters onto the barn with the new pocket knife her father gave her on her birthday. Both joy and sadness tussled inside her mind. She took a few steps back and looked at the big building she had helped her father construct.

I'll be back. And a faint smile crossed her lips. She returned to the house where her mother directed her sisters to the bench on the freight wagon where they'd ride next to their father for the quick trip into Canyon Creek. Shelley would drive the buckboard with her mother seated at her side and the two additional horses they'd kept, hitched to the back. The freight wagon was packed full of belongings piled high over the side rails. The buckboard burgeoned with their remaining possessions. The two wagons, cargo, and the four horses they bought from Mr. Kincaid represented everything they'd decided to keep. They left the rest for Knox.

The late afternoon sun sent ripples of heat up from the packed dirt surrounding the house. Shelley checked on the leather straps that tethered the horses to the buckboard, then climbed up and took a seat on the bench next to her mother, who seemed incredibly anxious to leave. Shelley said nothing. She reached under the seat, ensuring her Winchester was within grasp, adjusted her holster that housed her Colt, then pushed the brake lever forward and snapped the reins steering her two-horse team toward the red dirt road to Canyon Creek. Her father followed the same actions and reined his team behind the buckboard. The trip to town usually took less than an hour, but today's loaded-down wagons would extend the time. Regardless, they'd reach the Sundown Hotel with some daylight left.

Shelley tipped her hat back off her forehead and took a look around at the surrounding landscape. She made this ride plenty of times before but had never looked at the scenery this way. The countryside seemed to be more vibrant than she recalled. Bright purple blooms permeated the sage's pale green leaves, and the cholla trees were dark green and plentiful despite the hot summer's tight grip on rain. Even the dirt road looked like a swath of red paint along the brown- and green-framed trail. Shelley took a deep breath. No matter what happened with Knox and the ranch, she knew she wasn't leaving this place.

Snap! The loud, piercing sound of splitting wood accompanied by her sister's screams disrupted Shelley's thoughts. Shelley pulled on the reins and looked back over her shoulder. The freight wagon was askew. The left front wheel felly rim had broken in half, and her father had fallen onto the doubletree. Shelley jumped down and quickly rushed to her father's aid.

"I'm all right, I'm all right," her father assured her. "No wonder I got this thing so cheap. It's falling apart!" Virgil cried, pushing himself up from the cross-timber support just below the bench.

"Can you fix it, Dad?" Shelley asked, taking a closer look at the damaged wheel.

"I'll take a look. I have tools and some nails in the box under the seat. We'll have to lift the corner of the wagon, though. Not sure how we'll do that," Virgil said, removing his hat and scratching the top of his head.

Shelley looked around. She saw a group of mesquite trees clustered together beside the roadway. She darted over and began searching the ground. Various-sized branches were scattered about under the trees. *I need a big one.* "That'll do!" she yelled out loud. She picked up the end of the hefty branch and began to drag it to the wagon. Her father met her halfway and helped carry the tree limb over to the left front corner of the wagon. Virgil knew what his daughter had in mind for the five-foot-tall limb with a fork at the top.

"We'll tie a rope to the corner, then loop the rope over the fork and have one of the horses pull. That should work!" Shelley confidently announced.

Momentarily, the freight wagon was lifted just enough for Virgil to support the bed with other fallen tree branches and hastily repair the wheel. "That ought to hold it until we get to town."

Shelley slipped back onto the buckboard's bench and

snapped the reins, getting the Robertson wagon train back en route to Canyon Creek. The repair had taken hours, and the evening sun was beginning to sink beyond the horizon. The daylight Shelley had planned for was rapidly fading. They'd not get to town until after dark now.

Shelley kept the buckboard in the middle of the road as dusk shifted into night. They were close to town now, navigating one last turn in the road that led to Canyon Creek. Shelley found the turn quickly enough, and her father followed close behind. The moon rose and provided enough light to guide the way. Shelley saw the tops of the town's buildings come into view. She also saw a strange orange glow above the roofs. It looked like the sky was moving.

"What could that be?" her mother asked aloud, seeing the same strange glow.

It's a fire. "Something's on fire!" she called back to her father.

CHAPTER 46

Sunday, 28 July 1878

LUXTON DANNER – CANYON CREEK

D anner raced toward the back of the Sundown Hotel and ran smack into a wall of flames. Frantic horses snorted and squealed, running about inside the corral's fiery cage. Danner ripped the gate from its hinges freeing Bullet, Ringo, and the rest of the horses. The fresh lumber Danner forcibly bought from Knox's lumberyard was burning hot and quick. The flames' blazing tentacles reached deep into the sky while billowing murky gray smoke filled the air, engulfing the hotel. Wes and several of the town's men were bringing buckets of water to the blaze as quickly as they could, but the raw timber burned like petrified driftwood in a fire pit.

"Throw the water onto the back wall of the hotel! Keep it from burning down the hotel!" Danner yelled to Wes and Stoney Walsh as the two men arrived with overflowing buckets in each hand.

Both men nodded and emptied their buckets onto the hotel's back wall. Danner charged around to the front of the Sundown, where Madeleine Robertson and the women from the kitchen were promptly escorting guests out the front door. Danner pushed past Madeleine in the foyer and saw Rachel waving feverishly to unseen lodgers in the hallway at the top of the staircase. Adeline sat on the floor next to the front desk, clutching a doll and crying. Danner snatched Adeline up like a rag doll. He rushed out to the street, where Mrs. Carson took the girl and guided her to a crowd of onlookers. Shelley and Virgil joined several men who had established a line from the water troughs along the street to the rear of the Sundown, quickly passing buckets of splattering water to each other. Danner rushed back into the Sundown. Rachel started to dash down the stairs when the toe of her right brocade ankle boot caught the bottom of her prairie skirt. Rachel plunged forward, tumbling headfirst down the stairs. Danner lunged to the bottom step and caught Rachel before crashing onto the floor. Unconscious and bleeding from a nasty gash in her forehead, she lay limp in Danner's arms. Danner felt his hands trembling. His heart raced. He pulled Rachel to his chest and squeezed; her blood smeared across his cheek. Danner quickly carried her out of the hotel to Doc Carson's office, where Carson was busily tending to several injured firefighters.

Albert Loman found Danner in front of Carson's and grabbed the big gunslinger. "Marshal Payne's hurt! I don't know what's wrong, but he's over at the fire!" Loman reported.

Danner hurried past the front of the Sundown and noticed several men standing in front of Knox's saloon watching the rest of the town's men valiantly attempting to save the Sundown and its new livery stable. None of Knox's men moved to help. A couple of them leaned back against the wall, smiling. Danner continued around to the back of the hotel, where he found Wes slumped against the east wall of the Sundown clutching his right hand. A closer look confirmed Danner's alarm. Wes's right hand was curled into a grotesque claw and bent at the wrist. Wes was breathing heavily and sweating profusely while he fought through the excruciating pain Danner knew he was feeling.

"Can you get to your feet?" Danner shouted to his partner.

Wes shook his head no. "It'll pass," Wes managed to mutter between gritted teeth.

Danner rushed back to the fire and saw the men were making progress. The fire near the back of the hotel was extinguished, but the livery stable was burning out of control.

"We're running out of water!" Dakota Jones shouted to Danner. "The troughs on this side of the street are about empty!"

"Get it from the troughs in front of Knox's saloon and lumberyard!" Danner yelled, grabbing a full bucket and tossing its contents into a monstrous flame.

"That might be a problem, Danner! They ain't lookin' to help over there!" Jones proclaimed.

"Get a couple of men and follow me!" Danner shouted before emptying another bucket into the raging yellow and orange flames.

Danner hurried across the street with Jones and three other men, each clutching two empty buckets. Danner plunged his buckets into the trough in front of Knox's saloon.

"You ain't takin' water from that trough!" a man shouted at Danner.

Danner dropped his buckets and drew both pistols, cocking the hammer on each. He fanned the barrels across the faces of the men loitering on the saloon's boardwalk.

"I'll kill any man who gets in our way! Understand?" Danner ordered.

A man lunged forward, pulling his gun. Crack! Danner fired one shot, blowing a hole in the ill-advised gunfighter's chest, knocking him back against the saloon. The dead man slowly slid down to the boardwalk's planks, leaving a jagged trail of bright red blood on the wall behind him.

"Next?"

Knox's men glared at Danner, whose silhouetted figure against the raging fire behind him made him look more like a grizzly bear than a man.

"All of you sonsabitches get back into the saloon and don't show your faces out here until we're done!"

The men carefully pushed through the saloon doors and disappeared inside.

Danner looked back at Jones and the men. "Let's go!" he hollered, holstering his guns and clutching two full buckets of water before charging back across the street.

The rest of the men fighting the fire hurried across the street and began filling their buckets. Danner handed off his buckets to another man and checked on Wes, who was back on his feet and shaking his right hand vigorously. Danner pointed toward Knox's saloon.

"Make sure those bastards don't stop anyone from getting water. I had to kill one of them who went for his gun!"

Wes nodded, then disappeared into the crowd of people who'd gathered in the street to see the dead gunfighter and the fire.

Danner rushed to the front of the line and watched a section of the stable roof collapse into a burning pile of rubbish, destroying the hay ring in the process. Danner stood to the side, watching several men toss a continuous stream of water into the inferno. He checked the small storage room attached to the back of the hotel but did not see any visible damage. The fire was beginning to burn itself out, its hunger for fresh timber diminishing by the minute. The men slowed their efforts, dumping the last few buckets of water onto the smoldering wood and hay pile in the middle of the corral. The touch of a hand on his shoulder sent Danner spinning around. Clint Wade stood with Jackson, the troopers, and a stranger.

"What the hell happened here?" Wade asked his soot-covered leader.

"Our friend, Knox, sent a message," Danner stated unequivocally.

The men looked over the burned mess. "Look who we came across on the road into town," Wade said, swinging his thumb toward Jackson and the troopers.

"We?" Danner asked Wade.

Wade turned and waved to the stranger. He was a young-looking man not much shorter than Danner, with broad shoulders, carrying a single gun on his right hip.

"This here is JD Case. JD, this is Luxton Danner," Wade introduced the two men.

Case offered his right hand, which Danner slowly shook. "Glad to meet you, Marshal. Sorry we didn't get here sooner to help out," Case said flatly.

"We could have used it, and I'm not a marshal anymore," Danner answered, looking Case over carefully.

"Case here agreed to join us if we go up against Knox and his men," Wade announced.

"Oh? And why would you want to do that?" Danner asked with a raised brow.

"Let's just say I don't like Knox or his men and leave it at that for now," Case replied.

Danner nodded, then looked past Case to Jackson. "Everything go all right?" Danner asked.

"Yes, sir. We'll tell you all about it tomorrow," Jackson answered, then waved his troopers toward the boarding house.

"I'll make sure everything gets taken care of out here," Albert Loman assured Danner.

"I need to get back over to the Creekbed Saloon. A bunch of the men are already lookin' fer a drink!" Jones said.

"Put the first drinks on my bill," Danner ordered the saloon keeper, who nodded in approval.

"I need to get over to Doc Carson's and check on Rachel. She took a bad fall on the stairs when this all started," Danner informed Wade and Case.

"We'll see you later," Wade said before he and Case started for the Creekbed Saloon.

Danner watched Wade and Case cross the street.

JD Case? That name sounds familiar. Danner headed to Doc Carson's.

CHAPTER 47

Monday, 29 July 1878

WES PAYNE & GILFORD KNOX – CANYON CREEK

A brilliant ray of morning sunshine penetrated the office's front window where Sam Johnson had conducted Knox's dirty business. Wes reluctantly sat quiet and listened. Gilford Knox preached like a pulpit-pounding church minister on Sunday morning. Surrounded by several of Knox's men in the tight confines of Sam Johnson's former office, Wes sat against a wall and listened to Knox's demand for justice. The morning had barely reached half past eight o'clock when Wes was summoned to Knox's former lawyer's office to meet with the wealthy rancher about the killing of one of his men the night before during the fire.

"I demand you arrest this Luxton Danner immediately! He shot down one of my men in cold blood in front of twenty witnesses! I'm here to swear out a murder complaint!" Knox rattled on seemingly without taking a breath. His face gleamed dark red, and the veins in his neck looked like agitated serpents about to burst through his skin at any moment.

Six of Knox's men, tasked with the chore of spying on Wes, Danner, and the troopers, stood around their boss in the small room and nodded at every word Knox blurted out.

"If you're not going to do anything about this, then I will!"

Wes held up his hand and nodded. "Hold on for a moment, hold on."

Wes listened for another moment, then stood up and leaned over the desk Knox stood behind. "I was told your man went for his gun when Danner and others tried to get water from the trough to fight the fire. None of your men raised a hand to help," Wes retorted.

"I have twenty witnesses!"

"You don't have twenty witnesses! You've got a handful of your men who'll say whatever you pay them to!" Wes growled. "You find me one witness who's not on your payroll, and I'll listen then!" Wes demanded before quickly pushing through the door. He heard the office door swing open and slam against its frame. Wes spun around and covered his gun. Knox stood in the doorway.

"I'll take my complaint to the district judge in Oneida. I'll come back with two warrants! One for Danner and the other for you!" Knox shouted before stepping back inside the office.

Wes hurried past Doc Carson's place to the Sundown Hotel, where he cleared the porch steps in one leap, then slipped through the entrance into the lobby. Rachel was seated behind the front desk donning a bright white bandage on her forehead above her left eye. Dark bluish rings invaded her otherwise flawless complexion and framed her lovely green eyes. Wes stopped and smiled.

"How are you feeling this morning?" Wes asked, leaning against the front of the desk.

"I'm sure I feel better than I look! I feel like a raccoon with these black eyes!"

"Everyone make it back to their rooms?" Wes asked, his smile fading to a frown.

"Just the Robertsons. They came in late last night during the fire. The others all left. Mr. Kincaid and Clay Cox came in this morning. They heard about the fire and offered to help. They said there was talk of trouble around here today. Is there trouble?"

"It looks like Knox is going to Oneida to see the district judge. He wants to swear out a murder complaint against Danner," Wes admitted.

Rachel gasped, covered her mouth, and closed her bruised eyes. "Tell me that won't happen," she whispered, keeping her eyes closed as if to avoid seeing the answer.

"I don't know, Rachel. Knox has a bunch of witnesses."

"Yes, but Danner has witnesses also! I thought Dakota was there with other men."

"He was, and I'll get written statements from everyone I can. I think it will be all right, don't worry about that right now. Just take care of yourself. Where's Danner?"

"He's out back cleaning up. I think Mr. Kincaid and Clay are with him."

Wes hustled out of the hotel and walked around to the corral where Danner was talking to Kincaid and Cox. Stoney Walsh and the troopers were loading scorched wood onto a wagon. "Howdy, Mr. Kincaid, Clay. Talk to you a minute, Danner?"

Danner excused himself while Clay helped Stoney Walsh heave a charred timber onto a wagon. Danner stepped over to Wes.

"Knox wanted me to arrest you for murder this morning," Wes bluntly announced with a slight grin.

"Oh? And what did you tell him?"

"I told him he needed to find a witness that wasn't on his payroll," Wes said, allowing a chuckle to escape his lips. "Who else was with you and Dakota last night?"

"I don't know who they were. They looked like a couple of men I've seen around town. They're damn sure not Knox's men."

"All right. We have a couple of days. Knox said he was going to Oneida to fetch the district judge and swear out a complaint. I'll find out who was with you last night and get written statements. My guess is the judge will come back with Knox to see for himself. I'll be ready for that," Wes assured his partner.

"Let me know if I can assist in any way, Marshal," Carl Kincaid offered.

"Yes, sir. I sure will," Wes answered before Kincaid headed to the Sundown's dining room for breakfast.

"By the way, we found a broken barn lantern that smelled of kerosene behind the stable. I figured Knox's men started the fire. That lantern and none of them lifting a hand to help settles it," Danner announced.

"I'll head over to the Creekbed Saloon and find Dakota," Wes said.

"Hold on. You ever heard of a man named JD Case?" Danner asked Wes.

Wes stopped and peered at Danner. "John David Case?"

"I don't know. Wade came back with him last night. Said his name was JD Case. I thought the name sounded familiar."

"Young fellow? Nearly tall as you?"

"Yep."

"John David Case would be about twenty-one, twenty-two now. He's a gunhand who hates the railroad. Claimed some railroad agent murdered his father near San Antonio about five, six years back. The Rangers looked into Case killin' three railroad agents in Carrizo Springs back then. The sheriff down there witnessed it, so they called it justified. He's suspected in a few other killings at railroad camps. I don't know if he was charged with anything, though," Wes reported. "Why is he here with Wade?"

"I don't know. When I asked Case last night, he said he didn't like Knox. No reason why," Danner said. "I'll talk to Wade later. He might know more. By the way, Kincaid's foreman Clay Cox said he'd join us if we must go up against Knox."

"Good. We'll need him when, not if, we do," Wes said. "I'll see you later. I'll go find Dakota and see if we can keep you out of jail." Wes laughed.

Danner didn't share in the laugh. *You do that.*

CHAPTER 48

Tuesday, 30 July 1878

LUXTON DANNER & GUNSLINGERS – SUNDOWN HOTEL

The pounding of a half-dozen men's boots charging down the staircase of the Sundown hotel sounded like the thunder of a cattle herd stampeding down Main Street. Cowboys donning freshly shaved chins and neatly trimmed hair rushed into the dining room, filling scattered empty chairs. Seated at his customary table against the back wall with Wade and Case, Danner set his coffee cup down and looked over the spectacle created by men who'd been on the trail too long. Rachel and Mrs. Carson buzzed in and out of the kitchen like bees around their hive. The incessant sound of sizzling bacon and clanging plates radiated from the hotel's galley, along with the aroma of fresh-baked biscuits. Danner lifted his cup and tipped it back, draining the last of his bean brew. A sharp pain shot across the top of the knuckles on his right hand, a poignant reminder of last night's raucous bustle at both the Creekbed and Knox Saloons. The prior evening's arrival of the Swift ranch cattle drive turned Canyon Creek into a cesspool of unsavory behavior at Knox's bawdy house and the taverns for most of the night. Danner, Wade, and the troopers had joined Wes in doing their best to keep order, which meant busting a few jaws along the way. Before the night was over, the jail was overflowing with drunk cowhands.

"Think we'll get one of those ladies back here with more hot coffee sometime this morning?" Wade asked aloud.

Danner glanced around the room. "I don't know if they can make it fast enough," Danner quipped, keeping his gaze on Rachel, who was doing her best to dodge roaming hands and mordant offers of courtship.

Spinning out of the grasp of a cowhand who still appeared drunk from the night before, Rachel's green eyes met Danner's from across the room. She smiled, and sensing Danner needed her, she quickly dashed over to his table with enough coffee left in the pot to fill the three empty cups on the table.

"How did you know?" Danner asked with a faint grin.

"I'm a woman, aren't I?" Rachel laughed, then rushed into the kitchen.

"I know I'm new in town, but I'd say ol' Danner here has a girl," Case muttered before taking a drink.

Danner's grin faded. He looked at Case with narrowed eyes but said nothing.

"You'd be right, JD. The rest of us know it, but we're not sure he does." Wade chuckled.

Danner spotted Jackson standing in the archway. Jackson jerked his head, requesting Danner join him in the lobby. Wade saw Jackson and pushed his chair back. Danner stood and reached out with his sore right hand, palm down, motioning for Wade and Case to stay seated. Danner twisted and turned through the maze of tables and patrons and met Jackson in the quiet lobby near the front door.

"What is it?" Danner asked.

"I talked to the trail boss of this cattle outfit. He said they could use the boys and me on the rest of the drive. The boss offered all of us a job. I think we'll take it since there's not much happenin' around here," Jackson explained uncomfortably, shifting his weight from one foot to the other.

Danner rubbed his jaw. It was true Knox hadn't done much other than burn the Sundown's stable, and they had no proof of that. Now Knox was trying to use the law to eliminate Danner. There was no additional money to entice Jackson and the troopers to pass on a paying job. Danner nodded his head slightly, then looked at Jackson.

"I don't blame you and your men for wanting to take a paying job. I still think Knox will make a move, but I don't know when, where, or what. You and the boys satisfied with the bounty money you got from those three coach robbers?"

"Yes, sir. We each got fifty dollars when we brought them to Stratford," Jackson confirmed.

Danner extended his right hand. "It's been good riding with you and the troopers. Take care of yourselves," Danner said, shaking Jackson's hand.

"Same here, boss. I heard we'll be lettin' out sometime late this afternoon," Jackson stated, then turned and walked out the door.

Danner took a moment to look out the window at the busy street. Wagons, carriages, and a herd of cowboys on horseback traversed the street in both directions. Danner pulled his gun belt up and tucked his thumbs behind the buckle. *I don't recall this town ever being this busy.* He returned to his table.

"Wes ought to have let those drunks go by now. Let's take a walk down to the jail," Danner suggested to Wade and Case, who didn't waste the chance to escape the noisy bedlam of the dining room.

The three men stepped out into the bright morning daylight

and looked around. Knox opened his hotel and rented out the unfinished rooms since the Sundown had filled up as soon as the cowhands made their way into town yesterday. Both the Creekbed and Knox Saloons were bustling with business despite the early hour. The same was true for both stores. A seemingly endless line of cowboys was going in and out of both shops. Danner stepped up onto the wood-planked entrance of the jail and opened the door. He ducked under the frame and stepped inside, Wade and Case close behind. Wes was in the back, emptying a bucket of water onto the cell floor. The small room reeked of sour whiskey and vomit.

"How's the morning?" Danner asked, unable to hold back a wide grin.

"It's bad enough we had to fight those sonsabitches last night, and then they leave me this," Wes growled, waving at the filthy floor. "And I went to open the window, but it was nailed closed," Wes added, throwing the empty bucket into the corner of the cell.   "How are you fellas this morning?" Wes asked, seeing Wade and Case had joined Danner for a visit.

"We'll be doing a lot better when we get out of here," Wade said, waving at Case, who was already stepping toward the door. "We'll see y'all later," Wade added before fleeing the rancid office.

"Was it something I said?" Wes asked before breaking into raucous laughter.

"How about we talk outside?" Danner suggested.

"Sounds like a good plan."

The two men took their seats on the front porch, Danner in the rickety, old ladderback, and Wes on the equally unstable stool.

"What did you do with those drunks?" Danner asked.

Wes removed six silver dollars from his vest pocket and shook them in his hand. The coins jingled.

"The trail boss came by at first light wanting to bail them out. I told him it'd be a dollar per man. He paid up quick and ordered them all back to their camp," Wes announced. "I sure did appreciate you and the troopers' help last night. Things could have gotten out of hand pretty quickly. How's the hand?" Wes asked.

Danner reached out in front of himself and opened and closed his right hand twice. "It's howling at me a bit this morning, but it will be all right," Danner reported. "About the troopers . . . Jackson talked to me this morning. It seems that the trail boss offered all four of them a job, finishing the drive. Jackson said they all decided to take the offer since there wasn't much happening around here."

"That's too bad, but I don't blame them. I can't pay deputy wages right now. I wish they'd stay, though. They're good men," Wes answered.

"Yep," Danner agreed. "They're right about not much happening. I don't like all this waiting around. I wish Knox would make his move."

"He's already made a move."

"Oh?" Danner looked at Wes with raised eyebrows.

"Knox left yesterday afternoon for Oneida. He's going to fetch the district judge and bring him back here so he can swear out that complaint I told you about."

"Who told you that?"

"The bartender at Knox's saloon told me before this cattle outfit showed up and wreaked havoc. I know the judge down in Oneida. Name's Jeremiah Holt. I brought a couple of prisoners before him when I was a Ranger. He's a good, fair man, and he damn sure won't let Knox's money make his decisions for him," Wes declared. "Besides, I found a few more folks who were out in the street the night of the fire. They saw what happened, and more importantly, they were willing to testify and knew how to write. I got statements from all of them. Don't worry. I can match anything Knox shows the judge," Wes stated confidently.

"Not that I was distraught, but thanks," Danner offered.

CHAPTER 49

Tuesday, 30 July 1878

WES PAYNE – CANYON CREEK

Two more of Knox's freight wagons rumbled by the marshal's office, churning up a bulbous cloud of red dust that lazily hung in the hot, stagnant air. Wes paused and waved his hat back and forth in front of his face in a futile effort to clear the air. He watched the big Studebakers pull up in front of Knox's store. Each wagon had a driver and two guards armed with Winchesters and two bandoliers of ammunition draped over their shoulders. More men came out of the store and greeted the drivers before relieving the overloaded wagons of their cargo. Wes walked past the men who buzzed around the wagons like flies and stopped in front of the Sundown where Danner, Wade, and Case had taken refuge from the high noon sun. Tucked under the ample shade of the hotel's covered porch, the three gunslingers occupied Rachel's big wooden rocking chairs. Wes waved at the gunhands, then noticed two riders slowly approaching from the far end of town. Both were slumped over their saddle horns, their bodies rocking with each stride of their horse's gait. Wes waited a moment, seeing Stoney Walsh step out of Miss Tyler's boarding house and take a long look at the sagging riders. Walsh grabbed both horses' reins and began running toward Doc Carson's place.

"Trouble!" Wes called out to Danner, Wade, and Case, who quickly joined Wes in the street.

Wes heard Walsh yelling but couldn't decipher what he was saying. He ran forward and met Walsh, taking the reins to one of the horses. Both men were wounded, one of which looked terrible with dark red bloodstains on the front of his shirt.

"They look like—" Wes began.

"It's Carl Kincaid and his foreman Clay Cox! Cox looks hurt bad!" Walsh called out.

Wes stopped the horses in front of Doc Carson's place, where Danner led the physician out the front door. Carson feverishly waved for the men to get both riders down off their horses and get them inside his office.

"Knox's gunmen, it was Knox's gunmen," Kincaid mumbled to Wes, whom Danner joined, each looping an arm over their shoulders and helping Kincaid walk into Carson's office.

Wade and Case did the same for Cox, who couldn't walk under his own power.

"Put Carl in that chair and bring Clay into my examining room right away!"

Once on the table, Carson cut open Cox's blood-soaked bib shirt, exposing two bullet wounds. One on the upper left chest and the other lower on the left side. Both wounds were still seeping blood. Carson waved for Wade and Case to leave the room.

"What happened, Mr. Kincaid?" Wes asked the wounded rancher after Kincaid took a swig of water.

"We were out in the pasture checking on the herd when riders charged in and just started shooting. We saw the first few, but there were more to our right and left. We opened fire, but I got hit right away and knocked off my horse. I think

Clay got two or three of them before they got him. Is he alive?" Kincaid asked in between short rapid breaths.

"Yes, he's alive. Doc's taking care of him."

"Looks like he took two hits," Wade added.

"It's that son of a bitch, Knox! I'm sure it was his men! After Clay went down, they gathered around the herd and started toward the creek. Took the whole herd!" Kincaid shouted, wincing with every word.

"How many were there?" Wes asked.

"I don't know. Six, eight, ten, or so I guess. I didn't see them all. The bastards came at us from three directions."

"Can you show us where he's saying they went?" Wes asked Walsh.

"Sure can. It'd be down by the creek that borders his property and Virgil's," Walsh answered.

Wes stood up and looked at Danner.

"Let's go get 'em back," Wes stated.

The four gunslingers rushed out of Doc Carson's place right into Jackson and Edwin, both armed and mounted, ready to go.

"Danner told me y'all pulled out with the cattle outfit," Wes said.

"Ain't left yet. We was clearin' out of Miss Tyler's boardin' house when we saw those fellas ride in. We figured somethin' bad happened. We decided to stick around. Buster and Isaac let out though," Jackson advised.

"Maybe rustlers, but it could be Knox's men. We're goin' after 'em," Wes advised the former troopers.

"Looks like y'all are stuck with us then," Jackson said, Edwin nodding in agreement.

A few minutes later, the six gunfighters, led by Stoney

Walsh, thundered out of Canyon Creek toward the Kincaid ranch against an unknown number of shooters who'd probably see them coming long before they'd like. Wes considered his options. At full gallop, Walsh said it wouldn't take long to get to the creek bed on the southern edge of the Kincaid ranch. Walsh explained the creek divided the Kincaid place from the Robertson ranch, which Knox now owned. Wes figured by the time they found the herd; it'd be on Knox land.

Good. That'll make it look bad for Knox.

Walsh slowed his horse and held up his hand, bringing the group to a halt. Wes and Danner rode up next to Walsh, who was pointing ahead. "Just over that crest is a drop. It's sort of a shallow valley. Coldwater Creek splits it right down the middle. There's grass on both sides, then a hill on the other."

"If they know anything about cattle, they'll stop and water the herd before they continue," Wes speculated.

"There won't be any cover. They'll see us coming," Danner said.

"Let's spread out some and walk the horses in. Don't make it look like an attack," Danner suggested.

"That way, they won't know what our intentions are until we get closer," Wade added, having joined the brain trust.

"Good a plan as any. Walsh, you wait here," Wes ordered their guide.

"Let's go see if these gentlemen will listen to reason," Wes said, tapping his spurs on Ringo's sides. "Spread out some," Wes added as he reached the edge of the crest. Wes stopped and looked down onto the creek. As expected, Kincaid's herd milled around the stream. Wes counted the rustlers. Nine total that he could see. They were scattered about, forming a loose ring around the cattle.

"I count nine. All mounted," Danner said.

"Yep," replied Wes.

"Me too," Wade agreed.

"Well?" Wes said, then started down into the shallows of the grass-rich valley.

Danner stayed at Wes's side. Wade and Case took up the left flank while Jackson and Edwin spread out along the right. They kept their rifles in their sheaths, hoping to close the distance between them and their enemy before going to guns. Two of the rustlers spotted them and called out to the rest that surrounded the herd. Wes watched the rustlers maneuver their horses around the roaming cattle. Two rustlers pulled their rifles and rested the stocks on their hips; business ends up in the air and ready.

"Damn," Wes mumbled.

"At least we can see them all," Danner offered.

Danner and Wes stopped twenty-five yards from the closest rustler, who'd moved toward Wes and Danner. He was a short, thin man with a drooping mustache and long hair. He wore two pistols—one on his right hip, the other in a cross-draw on the front of his left side. The three rustlers who'd pulled their rifles moved their horses into the middle of the herd. Suitable for cover, bad if the cows decided to stampede, which they were sure to do once the shooting started.

"That takes care of those three," Danner uttered quietly to Wes.

"Afternoon!" Wes called out.

"What is it you want?" the short, thin rustler asked.

"Just curious is all. We heard a rancher named Kincaid had his herd stolen. Wondered if y'all know anything about that," Wes stated flatly, deciding to remain in the saddle.

Several of the rustlers laughed out loud. The short, thin rustler didn't join in on the jocularity. He just stared at Wes and Danner, then spit a brown stream of tobacco juice into the grass.

"Like I said. What do you want?" the rustler asked again, this time looking across the line of gunslingers in front of him.

"We're here to look at those brands. If they have the Kincaid "K" on 'em, we're taking them back," Wes said flatly.

The rustlers laughed again. Several of their horses snorted and bobbed their heads. Two more rustlers they hadn't seen joined the group on the right.

"Hear that, boys! These cows belong to us now. If you brought money, I reckon we could sell them to ya," the short rustler offered. "You bring money?"

"Nope," Wes answered.

"Then I reckon y'all ride on if you know what's good fer ya—"

Danner drew both Schofields. *Crack! Crack! Crack!* Danner's lead blew the little rustler off his horse before he could pull his gun. Jackson and Edwin charged forward on the right, then turned toward the herd that was scattering in every direction. The three rustlers who'd sought refuge inside the cattle flipped off their saddles into the pounding hooves of the spooked animals. Wade and Case charged in from the left, Case firing quickly. *Crack! Crack! Crack!* Two rustlers went down. A rustler on each end of the herd returned fire. The two rustlers on the right laid down a barrage of bullets at Jackson and Edwin.

Wes and Danner emptied their pistols at the two rustlers firing at the troopers. Bullets hit all around Jackson and Edwin, then Edwin flipped back off his horse, hurtling to the ground. On the other side, Wade methodically fired at the rustler on the left, killing him with a single shot. The remaining four rustlers spun their horses around and kicked them into a run heading up the back side of the valley. Wes watched them disappear over the far crest. The gunfire ceased. Cows were haphazardly running in every direction but remained inside the creek bed's wide swale. Danner and Wes saw the three trampled rustlers lying near the creek's bank. One was moving. Wes and Danner, joined by Wade and Case, slid off their saddles. Wes kneeled next to the trodden rustler. His arms and legs were broken and crushed. Blood flowed from the rustler's mouth and ears. He was mumbling incoherently.

"Who sent you to steal the herd? Who hired you? You work for Knox?" Wes rapidly demanded.

The rustler mumbled a bloody last word, then stopped.

"He's dead," Wes stated, standing.

Danner looked over to where Jackson was checking on Edwin. Wes and Danner hurried over to Jackson.

"Edwin's dead," Jackson solemnly reported.

"Damn it," Danner muttered, removing his hat.

"We'll take him back to town and have a proper burial," Wes offered.

"No, sir. I was his sergeant. I'll take care of him," Jackson stated before picking up his fallen trooper and carrying him away.

CHAPTER 50

Wednesday, 31 July 1878

SHELLEY ROBERTSON & FAMILY – SUNDOWN HOTEL

S helley walked into the Sundown Hotel's dining room and saw her parents and sisters seated at a far table having breakfast. Her attention quickly diverted to Danner, Wes, and Doc Carson, who occupied Danner's table in the back of the room. The dining room was calm compared to the boisterous, unruly bustle it had endured the previous day. The men with the Swift ranch were gone, so the customers were the regular townsfolk who spent most mornings enjoying Rachel Brennen's hospitality. Shelley heard her parents' conversation about leaving Canyon Creek last night, their voices escaping the confines of their room's walls. She already decided she wasn't going with them, but she knew her father would fiercely challenge her decision. Shelley already discussed her intentions with her saddened mother, who understood her daughter's brashness more than her father. Shelley slowly made her way to her family's table, where she claimed the one empty chair.

"Good morning, Shelley. Sleep all right last night?"

"Yes, Dad," Shelley lied.

"We had Mrs. Brennen bring a plate for you. It should still be warm."

"Thank you, but I'm not very hungry this morning."

"I'm sure you heard some of the discussion your mother and I had last night?" Virgil asked, setting his knife and fork on the table.

"Yes, I did."

"We've decided we're not returning to Louisiana. Instead, we are going to leave for Kilgore this afternoon," Virgil announced.

"Kilgore?" Shelley asked, somewhat confused.

"Yes. It's over near Louisiana. My brother has a good-sized farm there, and I understand the railroad has a station there now, allowing shipment for his crops. After seeing what happened to Mr. Kincaid and Clay, I've decided I don't want the ranch back. Mr. Knox can keep it and good riddance," Virgil huffed.

Shelley looked at her mother, who managed a slight smile beneath a pair of sad, dark eyes.

"I've decided I'm . . ." Shelley began.

"Virgil, Shelley will be staying here. She's already discussed this with me, and I support her wishes," Shelley's mother declared before Shelley could finish her announcement.

"I won't permit it! You're a member of this family, and you'll go where the family goes!" Virgil raised his voice, drawing attention from folks seated at nearby tables.

"You quiet down, Virgil Robertson. Shelley's a grown woman. She needs to make her own life, and if that means staying here, then so be it. I'll miss her as much as you, but it's time you realize she can't stay with us forever," Madeleine

Robertson professed, reaching across the table and squeezing Shelley's hand.

Virgil looked at his two young daughters, who sat quietly, then at his wife, and finally at Shelley. He nodded and looked off into the distance, past Shelley.

"I'm sorry, Dad," Shelley said quietly.

"No. Your mother's right. I knew this day would come. I'd just hoped I'd have a few more years with you," Virgil confessed. "You need to promise me one thing, though."

"I'll be careful, Dad," Shelley said with a smile she hoped would put her father at ease.

Virgil returned the smile and picked up his knife and fork. He began to push his food around on the plate. "I'll leave you some money to help you along."

"Thank you. I'll see you a bit later," Shelley said, then left her family's table behind.

Shelley hastily made her way to Danner's table, where Wade and Case had joined the others.

"May I join you?" Shelley asked the men.

All five men stood and collectively responded yes over each other. Doc Carson stepped back and waved for Shelley to take his chair.

"I've got to be on my way and check on my patients."

"Thank you. How's Mr. Kincaid and Clay?" Shelley asked before the doctor could leave.

"Kincaid is all right. A couple of flesh wounds. Clay, on the other hand, is a bit more serious. He lost a lot of blood. The next couple of days will be mighty important. If he makes it through those, I believe he'll recover. I won't know for certain until then. Good day, gentlemen."

Shelley turned her attention to Wes and the gunslingers.

"I heard you brought Mr. Kincaid's herd back to his ranch," she directed her comment toward Wes.

"Yes, ma'am. We rounded up most of them. They didn't get far, so it wasn't much trouble."

"Was it Knox's men?"

"We don't know for sure. Four got away, and none of the others could tell us," Wes said, looking around the table. "None of us recognized any of them, neither did Stoney Walsh," Wes added.

"Knox has been hiring so many men; it's hard to tell, I guess," Shelley said.

"Pardon me saying, but Rachel told me this morning your family was leaving town today. Why?" Danner asked.

"That's right, but I'm staying. My father decided to go to Kilgore and farm with my uncle. He says he doesn't want the ranch anymore, not after what happened to Mr. Kincaid and Clay. But I believe he wants to stay. He's just afraid for my mother and sisters."

"Are you staying?" Wes asked.

"Yes. It's my fault my family's leaving. I want Knox to pay for that."

The gunslingers took turns glancing at each other, then at Shelley.

"Miss Robertson," Danner began.

"Please call me Shelley."

"Shelley, we lost three men yesterday. One was killed, two others joined that cattle outfit, and you saw what happened to Clay. One day after he said he'd join us, he was ambushed. I'm not saying we couldn't use the help, but this is no place for women. Even one that rides and handles a gun like we heard you do," Danner stated.

"Don't think that just because I'm a woman, I can't handle myself. I understand the risk. If you don't want me to join you, then I'll do it alone," Shelley avowed, pushing back from the table.

"Whoa! Whoa! Ma'am. Take it easy!" Case said. "I'm new here. What do you mean it's your fault your family's leaving?"

"I shot one of Knox's men before he could run off our herd." Shelley repeated the story.

Case leaned back and tipped his hat to look at Shelley, standing next to him. "You shot a Knox rustler?" Case asked through a wide grin.

"That's right, and I'd do it again," Shelley blurted before turning on a boot heel and stomping away from the table.

"That's a damn pretty gunfighter." Case chuckled.

Danner hurried after Shelley and caught her by the shoulder before she escaped up the oak staircase. She turned and looked up at the big gunslinger. Her eyes were narrow and her lips pressed together. Her face had the look of determination Danner had seen in the mirror many times.

"What?" Shelley asked.

Danner released his grip and smiled. "I think I have a way for your father to get the ranch back. If it's all right with you, I'll talk to him and your mother. I'll see if I can persuade them to stay close to town for a while longer."

Shelley looked past Danner to her family and nodded her head in approval. "My father's not like you or Marshal Payne, but he's no coward. I believe he'll stay if you tell him to."

"Let's go talk with him now," Danner said, stepping aside for Shelley to lead the way.

Virgil saw Shelley and Danner walking toward his table and stood to greet his daughter and the gunslinger.

"Dad, Mr. Danner wants to talk to you and mother."

"Certainly, Mr. Danner. Please have a seat. Girls, go up to the room. Your mother and I will be there soon."

"I don't usually interfere with a family's business, but I've got a proposition for you. It won't take much of your time."

"Please, Dad," Shelley added.

"Of course, Mr. Danner. Please proceed," Madeleine requested with a pleasant smile.

"Shelley told me you're preparing to leave Canyon Creek. I would suggest you stay in town for a while longer. I have an idea that may allow you to reclaim your ranch," Danner said.

"I've already sold the ranch to Knox. How can you get it back?" Virgil asked, leaning forward in his chair.

"I understand you sold the ranch because of threats Knox made regarding the safety of your family and prosecuting Shelley."

"Yes, that's true, Mr. Danner."

"If we can prove that you sold the ranch under duress, the sale would be invalid, and you would retain possession," Danner explained.

"Duress? I don't know what that is."

"It's a word used in court. It means you only sold because you were forced and or threatened."

Virgil sat quietly for a few moments and looked at Madeleine. His wife nodded in approval of staying. Virgil looked at Shelley, whose broad grin provided her answer. Virgil nodded.

"My brother's farm can wait a while, I guess," Virgil announced.

Shelley jumped from her chair and wrapped her arms around her father's neck.

"Thank you, Dad!" she said. "And you, Mr. Danner. If those lips weren't two feet above mine right now, I would kiss you!"

Danner looked over his shoulder toward the kitchen and saw Rachel standing in the doorway. He looked back at Shelley and chuckled.

"It's best you don't. I might end up with a frying pan banging against my head," Danner quipped.

"I can guarantee that Luxton Danner!" Rachel shouted across the room, having heard his remark.

Rachel joined the gunslingers and the Robertsons in a loud laugh at Danner's expense.

CHAPTER 51

Wednesday, 31 July 1878

LUXTON DANNER & RACHEL BRENNEN – SUNDOWN HOTEL

anner wiped the sweat from the back of his neck, soaking his dark blue bandana. The late afternoon sun beat down like fire from the sky. He was about finished up with the removal of the charred remains of the Sundown's stable. Stoney Walsh repaired the corral with spare timber before his trip to Oneida. Wade and Case's horses had joined Bullet and Ringo under what remained of the roof. Danner had purchased stockpiled hay from a nearby rancher, and the fire hadn't damaged the grain barrel. Now, all Danner needed was for Walsh to succeed in his mission to buy lumber down in Oneida. Danner had decided, and more importantly, had the money to rebuild the stable and let Knox know he couldn't run him out of town as some of the others had been. Danner looped the barbed wire hoop over the corral post and heard the creak of the storage window's hinges. Rachel's lovely face filled the small frame and ignited a feeling he hadn't felt since his days in Lancaster.

"Hey, cowboy, can I tempt you with a tall glass of fresh lemonade?" Rachel asked in her customary songbird voice.

Danner leaned on the top rail of the gate. "If you pour a touch of whiskey in it, you can," he replied, allowing a broad smile to crack his indifferent expression.

"I believe I can accommodate you," she said, propping the window up with a slat of wood cut perfectly for the purpose.

Danner stepped into the dining room and sat against the back wall at his table. The cavernous space was empty except for Adeline, who was lazily scraping the tips of a corn broom across the surface of the wooden floor. Both the front and side doors were open in a futile attempt to keep the room comfortable. Danner sat down and tossed his hat onto the chair next to him.

"Hello, Mr. Danner!" Adeline shouted from across the room.

Rachel appeared from the kitchen carrying a silver tray with two tall glasses of lemonade in the middle. Danner noticed the lemonade in one of the glasses was darker than the other. Rachel set the tray on the table and smiled coyly.

"Guess which one is for you?" she asked, her skin flush with a pink glow.

Danner smiled and reached for the dark drink. "This appears to have whiskey or dirt added. Either way, I'll take this one."

Rachel sat next to Danner and ran her hand over his arm. "I was worried about you yesterday when you went after those men."

Danner stared at his drink. Rachel's touch was exhilarating. He liked it and thirsted for more but knew he couldn't succumb to her advances. Conflict churned inside his heart and mind. He couldn't let himself lead this wonderful woman down the path of regret. And regret would surely be the outcome. He was a gunfighter, nothing more. His way of life wouldn't allow room for a woman's love or companionship. He had his chance at those things years ago, and they were stolen from him by the wicked act of an evil man. Now his mission, his commitment, was to rid the land of as many evil men as he could. Danner felt uneasy. He shifted his weight, causing the wooden joints in his chair to groan. Rachel pulled her hand back and rested it with the other on her lap.

"I make you uncomfortable, don't I?" Rachel asked, faint lines of worry cupped each bruised eye.

Danner lifted his gaze from his glass to Rachel's green eyes. "You don't make me uncomfortable. I'm a gunfighter, Rachel. Like it or not, that's what I am. I can't let myself get involved. It would be dishonest to you and Adeline. Look what my being here has brought you. Your hotel could have burned to the ground, and you're still healing from a fall that could have been much worse. I've tried to be honest with you. If I've done anything to—"

"No, no. You've been a perfect gentleman, just like Ben was. He finally decided to settle down in one place, but he said he was too old to get involved. Now here you are, not too old, but not ready to settle in one place. I guess that's just my luck."

"Maybe I should move out of the hotel and get a room at Miss Tyler's."

"Luxton Danner! If you even try to leave this hotel, I'll have Shelley Robertson shoot you! And she'd do it!"

Both Danner and Rachel laughed.

"I believe she would," Danner agreed. "It was all I could do last night to keep her from charging after Knox by herself! All right, I'll keep my room."

Mrs. Carson walked into the dining room. Her tapping heels echoed off the walls. "Hello, dear. I thought I'd come by a little early and start getting supper ready."

"Oh my! It is getting late, isn't it?" Rachel said, standing to embrace her good friend and helper.

"Well, from what I can remember, time passes quickly in the company of a handsome man," Mrs. Carson cackled as she waltzed into the kitchen.

"I think I'll go down to the jail and see what our marshal is up to," Danner announced, plopping his hat on top of his head.

"You might also want to visit the barbershop," Rachel offered with a whimsical smile.

"I know, I know. Shave and a haircut."

"Just reminding you!" Rachel gushed before hurrying into the kitchen.

Danner stepped out into the street just in time to see another freight wagon pull up in front of Knox's store. The blast of red dust stung his eyes and left a muddy taste in his mouth.

Sure could use some damn rain. He marched down the boardwalk past Doc Carson's to Knox's store, then beyond to the marshal's office where he found Wes seated on his rickety stool, propped against the railing of the front porch watching Knox's men scurry around the wagon.

"Sure would like to know where Knox is gettin' all the money to bring wagon loads of goods in every day," Wes rhetorically said as Danner took a seat in the ladderback chair.

"Well, I hear his father's a rich man back in Washington," Danner flippantly answered.

"Maybe. But think about it. First, Knox builds that brothel back there, then a big hotel, saloon, and store. Plus, he's buying up all the land he can get his hands on around here. What's his old man do? Own a gold mine or something?" Wes muttered. "Walsh make it back from Oneida yet?"

"Nope. I don't know if he'll be back tonight or tomorrow. I figure it'll depend on if he finds lumber to buy," Danner said.

"Speaking of gold mines . . . ain't no business of mine, but you've been spending plenty over at the Sundown, partner," Wes said.

"Ya, I know. That's about to end, though. I had a good stash I'd saved from bounty money and riding guard, but it's about gone," Danner admitted. "The undertaker identify any of those rustlers we brought in?"

Wes nodded. "Seems a couple of Knox's ranch hands came in this morning and took a look. They claimed none were Knox riders, but the undertaker told me they were lying for sure. Said he could tell they were mad. Besides, how the hell they know what happened unless those that got away went right to Knox's ranch," Wes surmised. "Shelley went over there and checked it out. Said she didn't recognize them either. She's something else. Ain't she?"

Danner nodded. "She is at that. Seeing dead men don't seem to bother her none."

"I find looking at her is mighty pleasant. She's got spirit and fills out those britches awful nice," Wes said through a wide grin.

"And what about that girl back in Buffalo Gap?" Danner asked, keeping his eyes focused on the street activity.

Wes's grin faded. "I reckon I can't go back there after what happened," Wes somberly mumbled.

"I don't know. That son of a bitch Gentry beat his wife and shot you first. If you didn't kill him, somebody else would've," Danner assured his partner. "Looks like three riders coming in with the stage," Danner announced, looking down to the opposite end of the street.

Wes stood and walked into the street for a better look. He shaded his eyes from the evening sun. A tall thin man stepped out of the coach wearing a black vest over a white shirt, black trousers, and a black bowler hat. Another sharp-dressed man followed, sporting an impressive dark brown suit and a gray Stetson rancher's hat.

"Looks like Knox has returned," Danner announced.

"And Judge Jeremiah Holt is with him," Wes added.

CHAPTER 52

Thursday, 1 August 1878

WES PAYNE – CANYON CREEK JAIL

The whisks of the broom scratched across the cell block's marred wooden floor. Wes scraped up the last vomitus evidence of the drunken cowhands from the Swift cattle outfit. He found himself regretting his decision to take on the marshal's job. No man relished the chore of cleaning up another man's spew, and now he may be ordered to arrest his friend for murder. He paused and checked the pocket watch Rachel had given him when he became marshal. During last night's meeting at Miss Tyler's boarding house, Judge Holt said he'd pay Wes a visit in his office at eight o'clock sharp this morning. The judge was fifteen minutes away from that meeting which Wes had decided would be his last as Canyon Creek's marshal if Judge Holt decided to honor Knox's complaint and issue an arrest warrant for Danner. Wes felt he did all he could to show that Danner had acted in self-defense and hoped Holt would rule against the issuance of a warrant, but he couldn't be sure.

Nevertheless, Danner and Knox would be joining him and the judge in less than fifteen minutes, thus Wes's superfluous effort to clean the office. The clunk of heavy boot heels on the front boardwalk preceded the door swinging open, then closed. Wes stepped out from the cell to find Danner hanging his hat on one of several rusted nails protruding from the wall near the front door.

"Haven't seen this place this clean since you became marshal," Danner mused as he took a seat on the ladderback chair he customarily used on the porch.

Wes had arranged the small room with three chairs set as far apart as possible against the wall across from the desk where Judge Holt would preside over the meeting. The judge advised Wes that the meeting would be handled like a hearing with statements from the complainant, the accused, and the marshal. Wes had placed the stack of witness statements he gathered in Danner's defense on the desk for the judge's review. He heard the men approaching and stepped to the door, which he opened for the judge and Knox.

"Good morning, Marshal Payne," the judge greeted Wes with a firm handshake, then looked to Danner, who'd stood for the judge's arrival. "You must be Mr. Danner then," Judge Holt stated, repeating the firm handshake with Danner. "I believe you both know Mr. Knox, so we'll get right to business. Be seated gentlemen." The judge set his hat on the desk before taking a seat behind the small, ragged bureau.

The judge removed a document from his brown, hand-tooled leather satchel and set it in front of him.

"Now, Mr. Knox has already provided his knowledge of the incident—such as it is—since he was not present when the shooting occurred, but as the deceased was an employee of his, Mr. Knox exercised his right to submit a written complaint. That complaint is right here in front of me. Mr. Danner, can you read?"

"Yes, sir."

"Very good. I'll hand this to you and ask you to read through it. Take all the time you need."

Danner read the statement, which accurately described the shooting with two significant omissions. The fact that Knox's gunhand warned Danner of taking water from the trough, and him pulling his gun and lunging at Danner. Danner finished and handed the document back to the judge.

"I've already provided Marshal Payne with the opportunity to read the complaint last night upon my arrival. Therefore, we'll pass on that formality. Mr. Danner, do you have a response to this written statement?" the judge asked before leaning back in his chair.

"Yes, sir. The statement omits two important facts. The deceased would not allow myself or anyone else to take water from the trough in front of the Knox Saloon even though we were trying to put out a fire across the street. Also, the statement omits the fact that the deceased pulled his gun and lunged at me when we began to fill buckets with water," Danner explained.

"I have a dozen witnesses!" Knox began.

"Mr. Knox, I'm aware of the fact that you claim to have several witnesses. You inundated me with that fact during our trip from Oneida. I understand Marshal Payne also has several witnesses who have provided a written account of the incident and are willing to testify in court if necessary. I believe these are your witness statements, Marshal Payne?" Judge Holt asked, pointing to the stack of paper on the desk.

"Yes, sir. Seven townsfolk were fighting the fire behind the Sundown Hotel when the water supply ran out. Danner crossed the street to fetch water from the Knox Saloon trough, and that's when this happened," Wes quickly stated before Knox could stop him.

Judge Holt retrieved the statements, carefully read each one, and placed the finished documents face down on the desk.

Knox jumped up from his seat. "Judge, I don't care what those damn papers say! One of my men is dead, and he never cleared leather." Knox abruptly stopped speaking.

Wes and Danner glared at Knox but said nothing. The silence in the room was a loud endorsement of what Knox had let slip. Judge Holt lifted his gaze from the last statement and looked at Knox.

"Mr. Knox, I'm no gunfighter, but I've overseen many a murder trial. If your man didn't clear leather, then that implies he attempted to draw his gun," the judge stated. "And if he started to draw his gun and met a faster draw, that would be his problem and a justified shooting," the judge added. "Now your complaint here clearly states your man never even attempted to reach for his gun and was shot down by Mr. Danner in cold blood."

Knox stood rigid, his face flushing dark red. He squeezed his hat into a broken mess and glared at Danner with gritted teeth. His chest heaved from the angry breath caged inside of him.

"Would you care to amend your complaint?" Judge Holt asked slowly, standing up from his chair and looking at Knox eye to eye.

Knox exhaled in a loud rush of breath. "Never mind, Your Honor! You've made your decision! I withdraw my complaint!" Knox shouted, then dashed out of the office, the door slamming into the frame behind him.

Wes and Danner slowly stood. Judge Holt stepped around the desk and shook hands with Wes and Danner.

"Mr. Danner, I've heard a great deal about you in the last year or so, and I've known Wes since his early days as a Ranger. You and Wes have carved out quite the reputations for yourselves here in Texas. I must admit, when Mr. Knox came into my office and told me what happened and who was involved, I was somewhat skeptical. We've heard some unpleasant rumors down in Oneida about Mr. Knox and his methods. Would you two join me tonight for dinner and share what you know about what's going on here in Canyon Creek?"

"We'd be glad to, Your Honor."

CHAPTER 53

Thursday, 1 August 1878

LUXTON DANNER, JUDGE HOLT & WES PAYNE – SUNDOWN HOTEL

D anner plunged his massive hands into the clean water occupying his wash basin's ceramic bowl. Cupping his hands, he vigorously splashed the water over his clean-shaven chiseled face. After repeating the process twice more, he gazed through the murky water in the bowl. Its brown, tan, and blue swirls permeated the remnants of shave soap and whisker stubble that floated on the water's surface. He propped himself up over the basin, hands spread wide across the table's wooden surface. Beads of water fell from his face into the bowl's contents, forming small rings that slowly reached out toward the edges of the colorful bowl. He looked up into the flawed mirror and stared back at himself for a moment. He already admitted to himself that he was relieved with Judge Holt's observation skills and his ultimate decision. He also knew the prosecution's loss would provoke Gilford Knox to make an irrational decision, which would directly affect him and the men who chose to join him. His thoughts faded into the sound of the activity downstairs, meaning it was time to meet with Wes and Holt for dinner.

Danner stepped under the archway and into the Sundown's dining room. Rachel had saved his table for the meeting with the judge, who made his way around the room, shaking hands and greeting the townsfolk. Wes was flirting near the kitchen door with Shelley, whose smile and head tilt announced she enjoyed it. Danner's long strides allowed him to quickly close the distance between him and his back-wall table. He kept his eye on Shelley, who wore a dress for the first time in Danner's memory. Danner soaked in the sight of the purple dress that flowed from her shoulders to the top of a pair of brown Victorian laced boots. It was the first time he saw Shelley in anything other than britches, bib shirt, and gun belt.

Shelley glanced at Danner and immediately stepped over to his table. "Good evening, Mr. Danner. Coffee? We have beer tonight if you like," Shelley announced in a pleasant voice.

Danner ignored the offer for the moment. "You look beautiful this evening. Special occasion?"

Shelley's face emitted a peach-like glow that accentuated her hazel eyes. "Thank you kindly. It's called a Cordelia prairie dress. It's the only one I own. It was my Sunday church dress and boots."

"Much different from the riding pants and gun belt I'm used to seeing," Danner admitted with a wry grin.

"I can be a lady when I want to be, Mr. Danner. Besides, the horses are all taken care of, so Rachel asked me to watch the front desk this evening. I figured this would be more appropriate," Shelley stated, crossing her arms across her chest and displaying an exaggerated frown.

"Nobody will argue that!" Wes exclaimed, joining the conversation.

"How are your parents making out?" Danner asked.

"Very well. They decided to stay over at Miss Tyler's boarding house. It's a little easier there with my sisters. Thank you for convincing them to stay in town."

Danner waved his hand and shook his head. "It didn't take much convincing. Would you ask one of the ladies to bring me a beer?" Danner asked, then turned to greet Judge Holt, who'd pulled back a chair and extended his right hand, which Danner accepted for a shake.

"Make that two, young lady," Holt added, taking a seat.

Wes said nothing, just held up three fingers, which Shelley acknowledged before disappearing into the kitchen. Danner took his seat back against the wall and looked around the room one more time before directing his attention to the judge.

"Anything more from Knox after this morning?" Danner asked the judge.

"No, nothing. I did see a fellow—tough-looking type—arrive on the stage this afternoon. Gunfighter, I reckon. He was dressed all in black. He got off the stage and walked across the street to the livery stable, where he had a horse saddled and waiting. After talking to a couple of men there, he rode west out of town. That the direction of Knox's place?" Holt asked, leaning back in his chair.

"Yep," Danner confirmed.

"What did this fella look like, judge?" Wes asked.

"Oh, average size, I guess. Short hair, about your age, and had a goatee, I believe. Kind of came to a point right about here," Holt explained, pointing about two inches below the bottom of his chin. "Know who he is?"

"Not me," Wes stated.

"Me neither," Danner added.

Mrs. Carson arrived with three mugs of beer. "Is everyone having dinner?"

"Yes, ma'am, I know I am!" Holt said.

"Give us a few minutes before you bring everything out," Danner instructed Mrs. Carson.

Danner and Wes rehashed what they knew about Knox, the Robertsons, Kincaid, what Sam Johnson had told them, and the torching of the Sundown's stable.

"I'd heard the rumor Knox was forcing small ranchers and farmers off their land by nefarious means, but burning buildings here in town? That's a new one for me," Holt admitted. "Maybe I'll stick around town for a few days. If I recall, I don't have anything on the calendar until next Monday," Holt said, rubbing his chin and looking up at the ceiling.

"It'd be good to have you here for a bit, Judge," Wes chimed in.

Danner kept a constant eye on the activity in the room, checking on each new person who entered. While Wes was schmoozing with the judge, Danner noticed a young man step under the archway and stop. He removed his hat and looked around the room. Danner fixated on the man, believing he looked familiar, but couldn't decide from where or when. The young man stopped his gaze on Danner and began to approach the table. The young man wore a gun but didn't exude any sign of a threat.

"Looks like we're about to have company, gentlemen," Danner said, pushing his chair back against the wall and standing.

Wes turned to see the man walking toward them. "I'll be damned. That's Jake Rawlings!" Wes exclaimed.

Wes shook Jake's hand enthusiastically, then turned to Danner, who now recognized the kid who'd been with him and Wes when Ben Chance was killed.

"Hello, Marshal Danner!" Jake greeted the surprised gun-slinger.

"Hello, Jake. Good to see you!" Danner said with a robust handshake of his own. "Judge Holt, this is Jake Rawlings from up in Thornton."

"Glad to meet you, son. How is it you know these two desperados?" Judge Holt asked with a wry grin.

Danner pulled a chair away from the table for Jake, who accepted while answering the judge.

"Well, sir, Marshal Danner and Mr. Payne helped track down Mr. Thornton's killer up in Six Shot a year or so ago. I was with them until Mr. Chance was killed," Jake answered, his smile fading to a dark frown.

"Oh yes, I'm familiar with that story," Holt advised.

"How's Elizabeth?" Danner asked.

Jake shed his frown, and his face lit up again with a wide smile. "She's doing very well. We're married now."

"Oh!" both Danner and Wes simultaneously blurted.

Jake's face turned a sheepish red. "Yes. I finally convinced her to marry me about six months back. We've combined my parents' farm and her ranch. We've been slowly building up the herd again. We won't make a drive this year, but hopefully next unless . . ." Jake paused.

"Unless what?" Danner beat Wes to the question, both leaning forward in their chairs.

Jake looked at the three men at the table. "A rancher named Gilford Knox is trying to buy us out. He wants the ranch and the farm. Everything."

Danner and Wes leaned back in their chairs. Both grunted, then looked at each other, then the judge.

"What do you mean trying to buy you out, young man?" Holt asked.

"Well, he made us a pretty low offer. When my father and I told him we weren't selling, he told us we'd better reconsider if we knew what was good for us."

"He done anything to threaten you or your father?" Holt asked.

"No threats, just some harassment. Scattered our herd once, then trampled some of the crops," Jake said. "I rounded up our cows. As I said, we don't have that many, but ruining the crops cost us plenty. That's why I'm here. I heard Mr. Payne had become the marshal of Canyon Creek, and Marshal Danner was here to help, with some other men."

"I'm not a marshal anymore, Jake. Wes and I came here with a few other men at the request of this hotel's owner and a few other business folks," Danner clarified.

"I see. You don't have jurisdiction in Thornton then," Jake gloomily asked, nervously rubbing the surface of the table.

"Don't need jurisdiction, Jake. We're not here to arrest Knox or his men yet," Wes clarified.

"Jake, I hope you planned on staying in town tonight because you're not leaving until we hear everything about you and Elizabeth," Danner said as Mrs. Carson and Rachel arrived with three fried chicken dinners.

"We'll need one more," Danner announced to Rachel, who smiled and nodded before brushing her hand against Danner's arm as she returned to the kitchen.

CHAPTER 54

Friday, 2 August 1878

DALE MORGAN – CIRCLE M RANCH

The piercing sound of gunshots caused Dale Morgan to jolt awake. He spun out of bed and dashed toward the front door, tripping over the firewood carelessly left in front of the fireplace's hearth in the front room. He scrambled to the door and tossed aside the thick crossbeam timber that served as the door's lock. It banged against the wooden floor with a thud. He grabbed his Winchester from its rusted nail perch. He pushed through the screen onto the porch, a sliver of plank wood penetrating the underside of his right foot. The pain lessened at the shadowy scene occurring in the distance at the bottom of his pasture.

The crescent moon's hazy glow offered nothing more than a blurry view of mounted shooters sporadically firing into the air, causing his herd to scatter in every direction. Morgan heard the yawps and yips of the riders in between the muzzle flashes of their pistols and rifles. He saw the images of cattle charging blindly through the darkness. He racked his lever-action carbine but knew it would be useless to fire into the swirling black canvas. His rifle shots would just help the rustlers scatter his herd. He strained his eyes trying to see, but the darkness of the still, humid night was like blinders on a carriage horse. One of his steers thundered toward the corral, where it collided headfirst into the center split-rail post. The post snapped like a twig. The steer stumbled, then fell forward into a stunned pile of beef flesh. Morgan saw jutting shadows moving away from the pasture toward the west tree line. He couldn't make out how many. He just knew it was enough to send his cattle into the four corners of the night's gloomy abyss. Morgan slumped into a repined heap on the step.

"Are you all right?" a soft voice broke Morgan's sulk.

"Yes, dear, I'm fine. Might as well go back to bed," Morgan told his wife.

"What happened?"

"They ran off our herd."

"Who?"

"Can't say for certain, but I'm sure it's that bastard, Knox," Morgan said, pulling himself up and stepping back into the house. "It's all right. I'll round up what I can find after daylight," Morgan assured his wife. "Best you go back to bed."

"It's almost five o'clock. I'll make some coffee and get breakfast started. It'll be daylight soon."

Morgan hadn't sensed the time. He retrieved his watch from the bedroom and confirmed the time.

Time to get up anyway.

Morgan washed and dressed, then joined his wife at the kitchen table for a silent breakfast. Morgan pushed his hotcakes around his dish and stared into the black coffee pooled at the bottom of his heavy mug. Thoughts of his meetings with Kincaid and Robertson darted back and forth in his mind. The three ranchers' plan to defend their land and fight back against the powerful Knox hadn't materialized. Robertson sold out anyway, Kincaid and Cox got shot to hell, and now his stock was gone. Anger rumbled inside Morgan like a volcano ready to erupt. They had relied on Rachel Brennen's letter to a US Marshal, only to receive no marshal and no Ranger. Nothing but a few gunslingers that hadn't done much of anything to stop Knox. Morgan noticed the faint ray of sunlight creeping through the kitchen window bouncing off the shiny tin coffeepot resting on the stove.

"I'm going into town," Morgan announced.

"Town?"

"I need to round up a few men to help me recover the herd. There's nobody out here to help us anymore," Morgan reminded his wife. "I'll be quick about it and get back soon."

Morgan walked over to the corral where the charging steer had died from its collision with the rail post. Morgan was thankful he put his horses in the barn the night before and not left them in the corral. Otherwise, he'd be searching for spooked horses in addition to his scattered cows. He looked out over the pasture and saw two dozen cows and a couple of calves that hadn't fallen victim to the early morning ruckus.

Well, that's a start. He tapped his spurs and headed for the road to Canyon Creek.

Morgan slowed up his horse at the edge of town. Main Street was bustling with more freight wagons, buckboards, and mounted riders than he could count. People moved up and down the boardwalks on both sides of the dusty street. The Knox store was twice the size of Loman Mercantile, and the Knox Hotel was markedly more extensive than the Sundown. Morgan had heard the Knox store was open, but he couldn't believe the change in the town since he and his wife joined the Robertsons and the Kincaids at the Sundown three weeks earlier. Several men watched Morgan ride past Knox's saloon. A few more peered at him as he rode past the lumberyard.

Morgan stopped in front of the Creekbed Saloon and tied his horse to the hitching post. He paused and looked around. The rancher didn't recognize most of the people moving about at such an early morning hour. He pushed through the swinging doors of the saloon and found Dakota slapping a sloppy water-soaked rag across the bar top.

"Hello, Morgan, what brings you to town so early," Dakota asked the rancher.

"I'm lookin' to hire a few men," Morgan answered, leaning up against the dry end of the bar.

"Oh? What fer?" Dakota asked, dropping the dirty rag into a bucket of water behind the bar.

"My herd got run off last night. I need some help to round up what I can find."

His interest piqued, Dakota joined Morgan at the end of the bar. "Knox?" Dakota whispered as if to keep a secret despite nobody else in the room.

"I couldn't see any of them, but I figure it was his men."

"You need to see Danner," Dakota declared firmly.

"I don't need no damn lazy gunslinger, I need cowhands!"

"Lazy gunslinger? The hell you say? Danner, Payne, and his men ain't lazy. That's fer damn sure!"

"Really? What have they done for us since they got to town? Robertson sold out, Kincaid got shot—"

"You just hold on there, Morgan! It ain't Danner's fault Robertson sold out, or Kincaid and Cox got shot. And by the way, Danner convinced Robertson to stick around until this mess is over. They've done plenty here. Built a stable, fought a fire, got one of his men killed gettin' Kincaid's herd back. Now they're rebuilding the stable behind the Sundown. Danner killed one of Knox's gunmen, and Knox brought the judge from

Oneida and tried to charge him with murder. Don't come in here saying those fellas ain't done nothing!"

Morgan took his hat off and wiped a trail of sweat from his brow. "I didn't know about all that. I heard about the fire, but—"

"Let's go see Danner. He'll be at the Sundown with Marshal Payne this time of the morning," Dakota said, pulling his wet apron off and heading for the door.

Morgan followed Dakota into the dining room of the Sundown, where Dakota directed him to five men sitting at a crowded back table.

"Hello, fellas. Morgan had his herd run off last night," Dakota blurted before Morgan could say a word.

The five men looked at Morgan.

"You see who did it?" Wes asked.

"No sir, Marshal, it was early this morning. Not much of a moon, so it was dark. I couldn't see any of them, but I figured it was Knox's men. I'm the only one he hasn't harassed yet."

"Morgan came in lookin' to hire a few hands to round up his stock. I told him he should see you," Dakota said, looking directly at Danner.

Danner looked around the table, getting a nod from each man. "No need to hire any men. We'll give you a hand rounding up your herd," Danner advised before the five gunslingers stood and retrieved their hats.

"This here is Clint Wade, J. D. Case, and Johnny Jackson," Danner introduced everyone at the table. "We'll meet you out front in about fifteen minutes," Danner added before leading the men out of the dining room.

Morgan followed his new cowhands into the lobby, where Rachel wrote in her ledger book. "Good morning, Mr. Morgan. Nice to see you here," Rachel greeted the rancher with a broad smile, which quickly faded as she realized Danner and the men were all leaving at once.

"Is something wrong?" Rachel asked.

Morgan removed his hat. "Yes, ma'am. My herd got run off last night. These men are going to help me find them."

Rachel looked at Danner, her green eyes framed with thin lines of worry. "The last time, a man died," Rachel murmured.

"This is different," Danner said.

"Don't worry, ma'am, I'll make sure he comes back without a scratch," Case said with a grin.

Danner looked at Case with one eyebrow raised. "Oh?" Danner cracked to the delight of Morgan and the men. "Tell Jake Rawlings—"

"Tell me what?" Jake asked, thundering down the staircase steps into the crowded lobby.

"This here is Dale Morgan. We're heading out to find his herd that got run off last night. Care to join us?" Danner asked.

"I wouldn't miss it!"

"Neither would I!" Shelley exclaimed from the top of the staircase.

"Thanks, but—"

"Don't try and talk me out of it, Mr. Morgan!"

"Not exactly like old times," Wes said, looking at Danner.

"Nope."

CHAPTER 55

Friday, 2 August 1878

JD CASE & GUNSLINGERS – OUTSIDE MORGAN RANCH

J D Case reined his horse to the right and back to the left, then pushed him straight ahead, trotting behind a group of seven cows that had the Morgan ranch brand burned on their right hindquarter. Case wasn't the best cowhand in Texas, but he had been along on enough drives over the past five years that he was holding his own. Danner, Morgan, and the rest were scattered all across the north bank of the Canadian River, which was a hard ride south of the Morgan ranch. The river had supplied a barrier for most of the herd that headed south when the rustlers sent them into a frenzy.

Each man was looping around as many cows as they could, then driving them into a flat, open area about two hundred yards up from the river. Not knowing how many cattle Morgan had, Case couldn't tell how well they were doing in finding his herd. Case pushed his seven cows into the larger group, then returned to the river's edge, where a few more cows were milling around, looking as though they were waiting their turn. Case rode his horse straight down the river's bank in between the water's edge and the handful of cows bunched together at its watery bank. He looped behind the cattle and pushed them toward the group. Case counted another nine. That made fifty-nine head he managed to drive up from this section of the river.

Not bad for four hours. He reined his horse away from the group and rode over to Danner, who'd moved several cows into the cluster.

"How's it going?" Danner asked the young gunslinger.

"Good, I think. I was able to push fifty-nine up from the east end. How about you?"

"About the same, I figure. I didn't count exactly. Morgan, Jake, Wade, Shelley, and Jackson are bringing the main group up from the west. Here they come now," Danner said, pointing west to where a large herd was being pushed quickly by Morgan and his gunslingers turned cowboys. "Did you find any in the river?" Danner asked.

"One dead. It looked like it hit the river too fast and got caught up in the mud," Case reported.

"Yeah, I saw two more that did the same," Danner acknowledged. "Wes went back to town. Let's give them a hand. You take the right flank. I'll take the other," Danner added before spurring Bullet onward.

Case and Danner closed in on each side while Morgan and the others continued to push from the rear. Danner and Case joined the other three wranglers after moving the large group into the clearing.

"That about it for down here, Morgan?" Danner asked.

"Yes, sir! It looks like we picked up most of what came down this way! We found four drowned in the river, not bad considering."

"I found two dead," Danner advised.

"I found another," Case added.

"Well, seven's not good, but considering how many ran down this way, I reckon I'm lucky," Morgan said.

"How many more you reckon you lost?" Case asked.

Morgan looked over the recovered herd. "About two hundred or so."

"East of here is a thick scrub and tree line. Can't see them running into that," Case suggested.

"Nope. I agree. The rest probably went west toward Knox's land," Morgan speculated. "No sense headin' that way," Morgan added, taking his hat off and slapping it against his leg in frustration.

"I disagree. I say we go give Knox a visit and tell him we want your cows back," Case emphatically announced in a bold voice.

The six riders sat quietly in their saddles for a moment before Danner spoke up.

"You looking to get yourself killed today?" Danner asked with a touch of sarcasm in his voice.

"Nope. But Knox isn't coming to us in town. We'll have to go to his place at some point," Case declared.

"Well, I can't argue with that. Knox has shown himself. He's not going to rush the town with twenty gunmen and shoot the place up. He owns half the damn town already. Maybe more. He just needs to get rid of us. That may be why he sent for that gunfighter Judge Holt saw get off the stage," Danner offered.

"What gunfighter?" Case asked.

"Yeah, what gunfighter?" Wade chimed in.

"The judge said a man about my age, dressed all in black with short black hair and a black goatee that narrowed to a point on his chin, got off the stage yesterday. He had a horse waiting for him at the livery and then rode toward Knox's place out of town. Neither Wes nor I know who he is. Any thoughts?" Danner asked.

"Sounds like Ike Thurgum," Case confidently answered in the same bold voice.

"Ike Thurgum? I've heard the name but never saw him," Danner said, looking at Wade, who shook his head.

"I've also heard of him but never came across him," Wade added.

"I've seen him a couple of times. He calls himself the 'Undertaker.' That's why he dresses in black and wears that goatee. Word is he's one of the hired guns for the railroad bosses," Case explained.

"Which is how you know him," Danner said.

"What did ya mean by that?" Case asked, pulling back on his rein, causing his horse to snort in protest.

"Not that we can't use your help, but why exactly are you here in Canyon Creek anyway?" Danner finally asked the question that had been caged in his head like a wild mustang since Case's arrival.

"I'm here because of Knox. I may not know as much as y'all about him, but I know plenty."

"Like what exactly?" Danner prodded.

"His father is Horace Knox. He was a colonel or something in the Union army. During the war, Horace had connections with the railroad owners. After the war, he went to work for the railroad owners in Washington. That's where he got all his money. That's where Knox is getting his. How do you think he's been able to take over Canyon Creek and build without worrying about money? Those freight wagons that come and go non-stop are part of a supply train his father set up with the railroads. His old man is most likely paying those gunhands Knox hired. That's why he wants to build up Canyon Creek so badly. When the railroad gets out this far, he wants it to run right through his property. They won't build the rail near town unless it's worthy," Case reported.

"How do you know all of this?" Danner asked, leaning forward in his saddle.

"I've spent the last five years making the railroad my business. One of Horace Knox's land grabbers threatened my father five years ago. My father died, and we lost our farm. The railroad bought it for next to nothing. Since then, I've paid a few visits to some of the railroad's outlaws."

"Outlaws?" Wade asked.

"The gunmen that ride out ahead of the rail and force owners to sell their land for half of what it's worth. Or worse, take it in the name of progress like Knox," Case clarified. "When I heard about Knox buying up land near Canyon Creek, I decided to head this way. I met Wade in Oneida, and he let me tag along. That all right with you, Danner?"

Danner nodded in approval. "As I said, we can use your help. We need to get back to town. I believe you're right. We're going to have to pay Mr. Knox another visit. Morgan, you ready to move this herd back to your place?" Danner asked, spurring Bullet ahead without waiting for an answer.

CHAPTER 56

Friday, 2 August 1878

LUXTON DANNER – CANYON CREEK

Danner and his gunslingers rode into Canyon Creek, where the sounds and smells of early evening enveloped them like a firm embrace. Piano music pounded out of the Knox Saloon while the aroma of fresh-baked bread mixed with the tang of beef sizzling on skillets in the Sundown's kitchen. The riders guided their horses into the newly repaired corral behind the Sundown and tended to their horses. Before they emerged onto Main Street, Shelley and the five men set buckets of water and hay bales into the makeshift stalls.

"I don't know about the rest of you, but I could use a beer," Wade announced before dodging horse and wagon traffic while crossing the street to get to the Creekbed Saloon.

Jake headed for the Sundown and Shelley made her way to the boarding house while Danner, Case, and Jackson followed the jagged course behind Wade to the Creekbed where Dakota Jones poured beer into mugs lined up on the bar. Wade grabbed the first mug and slid down the bar rail allowing Danner, Case, and Jackson to follow.

"Thanks, Dakota!" Danner called across the bar top to the proprietor.

"Saw y'all comin' and figured you'd be needing to wash the dust out of yer throats!" Dakota called back through a wide grin.

Danner looked around the busy saloon. Several tables hosted poker games, and the rest of the bar was stacked shoulder to shoulder with cowboys and regulars.

"Looks like business is good this evening," Danner announced.

"Yes, sir. Lots of folks are in town today. A bunch came in to see Judge Holt. He has been talkin' to everyone about their dealin's with Knox," Dakota reported.

"Oh?" Danner asked.

Dakota leaned over the bar and looked around. "Seems ol' Judge Holt ain't too pleased with what he's hearing about Knox and his men. He talked to Kincaid and his foreman Cox about the shootin', and a few more said they sold out to Knox because they were scared. Also talked to Virgil Robertson over at Tyler's boarding house about him selling out to Knox," Dakota explained in a low voice so as not to draw added attention to his gossip.

"It sure would be good if the judge were on our side," Wade chimed in.

"I believe he already is. I just don't know what that means yet," Danner offered.

Danner looked past Wade and Case and saw Wes push through the double doors. "Right here, Wes!" Danner called out from the middle of the bar.

"Judge Holt wants to see all of us right away. He's waiting down at Betsy Tyler's boarding house," Wes announced.

"Did he say what he wants?" Danner asked.

"Nope. Just told me to come to see him when y'all got back from Morgan's place. You find his cows?" Wes asked.

"Most of them. A few were dead in the river, and the rest probably ran onto Knox's land," Danner reported.

"The judge has had me rounding up anyone who'd dealt with Knox over the past few months. I've been bringing them to the boarding house so the judge could talk to them."

"We miss anything else today?" Danner asked, swallowing the last of his beer before sliding the empty mug across the bar top to Dakota, who was neglecting his customers by eavesdropping on Wes's report.

"Looks like the Lomans are closing up their store and heading out," Wes advised.

"Why? They sell out to Knox?" Danner asked.

"Didn't sell to Knox, but Loman says his last two supply wagons never showed up, and Knox's store has taken most of his business anyway. Says he can't sell what he ain't got, so he and his wife are thinking about leaving town."

"Loman have any idea what happened to his wagons?" Wade asked.

Wes shook his head. "No, but Knox's wagons ain't having any trouble coming in," Wes said.

"Maybe we ought to ride out to Knox's place and see if those missing wagons are there?" Case suggested.

"Not a bad idea, except for Knox's twenty or so armed guards out there," Danner mused. "Besides, I figure Knox is too smart to keep stolen wagons at his place. He probably hid them close by but off his ranch," Danner added, rubbing his fingers across the barbed wire that passed for whiskers.

"Well, if I'm Knox, wanting to keep stolen wagons loaded with supplies close, but not too close, I'd put 'em on the old Robertson place. They had a good-sized barn out there," Wes suggested.

Danner nodded in agreement. "Let's talk with Shelley,"

Danner said before Wes grabbed his arm and stopped him from leaving.

"First, we'd better head over to the boarding house and see Judge Holt. Shelley's already over there," Wes advised.

"Let's go then."

As Danner led the men through town to Tyler's boarding house, he noticed the number of Knox's men keeping an eye on the town had increased. There were four in front of the Knox Saloon and more loitering around Knox's lumberyard, hotel, and store. Danner began to question his belief that Knox wouldn't attack the town. With so many of Knox's men already in town, it wouldn't be hard to make a move on the six of them. Stoney Walsh stood at the boarding house door and greeted Danner and the rest. Still dressed in his crisp black suit, white shirt, and silver clasp bolo tie, Judge Holt sat straight and firm in the chair at the head of a long narrow table Betsy Tyler used to serve her guests their three meals a day. Shelley and Virgil were seated with Holt. Several documents and a thick black leather-bound book sat on the table in front of the judge.

"Please have a seat, gentlemen. I shall not keep you long this evening," Judge Holt announced with a wave of his hand over the tabletop.

Once his guests were seated, Holt laid his hands on the documents in front of him. "I have here numerous written statements from Mr. Robertson and an array of people in and around Canyon Creek. These people have some level of complaint or distrust of one Gilford Knox. Many have reported force and threats toward them and their families if they did not follow Mr. Knox's wishes. There is also the possibility of theft connected to Mr. Knox and his men. I had heard rumblings of this behavior down in Oneida, but I had not expected this apparent level of abuse of power. I now fully understand the citizens' actions in contacting men of your abilities to challenge Mr. Knox's aggressive behavior. That said, I have investigated the possibility of deputizing each of you as officers of the court, but as there have been no formal charges brought against Mr. Knox or his men, I believe that is not an option at this time. Therefore, I have summoned Mr. Knox to meet with me tomorrow morning. I will confront him with these allegations and seek an explanation. Depending upon his response, I will decide if I will remain here in Canyon Creek for an extended stay or return to Oneida. Questions, anyone?"

"Judge, we have reason to believe Knox's men hid stolen supply wagons at the Robertson ranch. As you've heard, Knox used duress against Mr. Robertson to sell his land," Danner explained.

"Yes. Mr. Robertson explained his plight quite well, and Miss Robertson was quite forthcoming about the incident that led to her father's decision. Frankly, Mr. Danner, I agree with your assessment of the use of duress. Furthermore, Mr. Knox had no legal basis for filing charges against Miss Robertson. Only the man she allegedly shot would have that right. I've told Miss Robertson I would listen further to her case as soon as possible. Now, regarding these stolen wagons. I will authorize Marshal Payne to look for these wagons on the Robertson property. I might suggest you perform this service immediately. Give me a moment to write up your authorization."

CHAPTER 57

Friday, 2 August 1878

LUXTON DANNER & POSSE – EN ROUTE TO FORMER ROBERTSON RANCH

G hostly swirling clouds filled the vast sky draping a dark fractured canopy over the burnt-orange sun devoured by the hungry western horizon. After Danner ordered Jake to return to Thornton rather than join them, Wes, Jackson, Wade, and Case followed Shelley, keeping their horses at a steady gallop. Taking advantage of the cool air brought on by the threatening sky, they would reach Shelley's disputed home sooner than planned. Armed with written authorization to search the Robertson ranch for Loman's wagons and or supplies, Danner felt a sense of authority he had not experienced since his awkward separation from the US Marshal's office. He was surprised by the comfort the newfound, albeit temporary, legal power had brought him. He realized he missed carrying the badge of a lawman, though he didn't miss the responsibility that came with it. They had already passed the Morgan place and approached the Kincaid ranch when Shelley slowed her horse to a walk. Danner joined her at the head of the group.

"You see something I missed?" Danner asked Shelley, who

was blissfully back in her brown riding pants, tan bib shirt, and gun belt that carried her Colt Lightning.

"No. But if Knox has men guarding our old place, they'll be able to see us once we pass through this gulley."

"We'll split up and ride in from two directions," Danner said before bringing Bullet to a stop. "Wes . . . you, Wade, and Case ride up along that crest and circle around the house and barn. Jackson, Shelley, and I will head toward the Kincaid place, then ride in from there."

The two trios split, each making a wide arc in opposite directions around the pasture of the former Robertson ranch. Shelley provided accurate details of the house, barn, and tack building's positions, along with critical information of the surrounding trees and thickets that could cloak their arrival as long as possible. The posse moved into place without notice, aided by the onset of heavy cloud cover. The wind had picked up and was churning up grass, dirt, and brush that the recent stampeding cattle had uprooted. Shelley held onto her hat as she led Danner and Jackson through a dry creek bed on the north side of the pasture. Wes, Wade, and Case were out of sight now. Danner feared they would be spotted first and fired upon by trigger-happy guards. As if he was a biblical prophet, gunfire erupted beyond their view.

"Get back!" Danner ordered Shelley as he spurred Bullet past the lady gunfighter.

Jackson drew his pistol and followed Danner's charge up the side of the creek bed. *Crack! Crack! Crack!* The sound of rifle bullets cut through the wind. Danner saw two guards firing from the front porch of the house. Case, Wade, and Wes had split up and charged in on horseback, badly exposed on the open plain. *Ping!* A bullet zipped past Danner's head. Another rifle-armed guard emerged from the side of the house and was firing at him and Jackson. Danner drew a Schofield from his right holster and fired at his assailant. *Crack! Crack! Crack!* Jackson veered off to Danner's left to engage the two riflemen on the porch. Shelley grabbed her Winchester from its tattered leather scabbard and rolled off her horse, tumbling behind the scattered remnants of a fallen mesquite tree. Ping! Another bullet shot past Danner, this one closer than the last. *Crack!* A bullet struck the guard at the side of the house, knocking him backward and sending his rifle into the air. Danner glanced over to see Shelley racking the lever of her Winchester, ready to fire a second round. Danner followed Jackson toward the front of the house. Wade, Case, and Wes had jumped from their horses and were all pinned down, unable to advance toward the house or barn.

A rifleman on the porch fired at Jackson, who leaned down on the side of his charging horse, firing over his saddle. Danner had seen other cavalry troopers use the same tactic in battle. *Crack!* A bullet pounded the flesh of Jackson's horse near its front shoulder, causing the great steed to stumble headfirst into the ground. Jackson flew from his saddle, crashing into a spread of thistle and cactus. *Crack!* Danner fired another round, his bullet smashing into the face of the guard who had just felled Jackson. Danner charged at the other guard on the front porch. The guard racked his rifle's lever and squeezed the trigger. The hammer fell on an empty chamber.

Danner leaped from his saddle, crashing all six-foot, six-inches, two hundred forty-five pounds onto the helpless gunman. The force of Danner's body snapped bones and pounded the gunman's head against the wooden floor, knocking him out cold. Danner rolled over and came up with both Schofields cocked and ready. *Crack!* A bullet shattered the door frame above him, sending an explosion of splinters into Danner's face and neck. Danner dropped to the floor, brushing the wood fragments from his face with the back of his hand. *Crack! Crack!* Another guard fired from the barn door, shattering glass above Danner's head. Danner looked up and saw Wes and Case running to the back of the barn. *Crack!* The guard in the barn door grunted, then dropped to his knees and fell face first into the red dirt. Danner heard Shelley rack the lever of her Winchester on the opposite side of the house.

That's twice she's saved my hide.

Stomp! Danner rolled over onto his back and leveled his Schofield .45s square at Wade, who had jumped over the rail and landed behind him on the porch.

"Whoa! It's me!" Wade shouted, pointing his Colt over the rail back toward the barn. "Anyone in the house?" Wade asked.

"I don't know. Didn't get the chance to knock and say hello," Danner quipped, rolling back onto his chest and scanning the barn and adjacent tack building.

"Well, the hell with knocking!" Wade declared before putting the bottom of his right boot into the front door, sending it flying off its hinges.

Wade charged into the dwelling, Colt first, looking for any movement that needed to be stilled.

Danner kept his eyes on the barn and tack building. The gunfire ceased, and the whistling sound of the wind was all he could hear. He saw Wes and Case appear from opposite sides of the barn, moving carefully, with guns drawn and ready.

"Don't shoot! Don't shoot! I give up!" a guard called from inside the barn.

"Throw out your guns and come out with your hands up high!" Danner ordered, rocking back onto his knees, keeping the porch railing and post between him and the forthcoming prisoner.

Wes and Case paused at opposite corners of the barn doors, pistols ready.

A six-shooter plopped onto the dirt entrance to the barn doors with a thud. A man clad in a brown leather vest with a sunburnt pinch-front hat to match slowly stepped out from the shadow of the barn's dark tunnel, both hands held as high as he could muster.

"Keep walking!" Danner shouted, then stood with both Schofields pointed at the man's chest.

"Don't shoot!"

Wes scurried up behind the prisoner as Case ducked into the barn, covering his partner. Wes holstered his Colt, then ran his scarred hands over the defeated gunmen's clothes, searching for a hidden weapon. Nothing. Wes waved to Danner, who holstered his guns and stepped down from the porch. Case stepped out of the barn.

"All clear! No wagons in here!" Case announced.

"Go check on Jackson! See if he's alive!" Danner ordered.

Case dashed away toward Jackson's horse, which had stopped and stood by its incapacitated companion like a trusted sentinel. Shelley surfaced from her hiding place next to the house, keeping her Winchester trained on their captive. Wade walked through the doorless threshold and announced the house was empty. Danner stood directly in front of their captive and looked down on the man.

"I'd advise you to tell us what we want to know," Danner growled between gritted teeth.

"Yes, sir."

"We already know you work for Knox. What were you and these others doing here?"

The man looked around at everyone, then back to Danner. "Waiting for you."

"Waiting for us?"

"Knox knew you'd come out here eventually. Either to get this place back for her or to look for those wagons."

"Where are the wagons?"

"I don't know. I swear. A couple of men came yesterday and took both. They went toward Knox's ranch. That's all I know."

"Are those the wagons that belong to Mr. Loman?" Shelley asked, taking a step forward and jamming the barrel of her Winchester into the man's ribs.

"Yes, ma'am. I think so. I didn't take them, though. You have to believe me!" the man shouted. "I just needed a job, and Knox was payin' big money."

"Why is Knox payin' big money to the likes of you?" Danner asked.

The man hesitated and looked at the dirt down by his boots.

"Answer him!" Shelley yelled, prodding the man's ribcage again with the business end of her rifle.

"It's all about a land grab for the railroad!"

"You're damn right it is," Case muttered as he arrived with a wobbly Jackson, whose faded look and swaying body resembled a town drunk fighting to stay on his feet.

"You all right, Jackson?" Danner asked the big Buffalo Soldier.

"He'll be all right. Got his bell rung, I reckon. Good thing he landed on his head," Case quipped with a grin.

Danner looked back down on Knox's overpaid cowhand with narrowed eyes and a clenched jaw.

"You ain't gonna kill me," the man growled, leaning back against Wes, who stood firm.

"Kill you? Oh, no. You're going to deliver a message to that land-grabbing son of a bitch Knox for us. You tell your boss we put out the word, backed by Judge Holt, that they'll be no more sales of anything to Knox. We're going to start getting land back that Knox bought with threats, including this ranch. You got that?" Danner roared.

"Knox ain't gonna like that, mister," the man said defiantly, no longer in fear of being shot.

"You tell Knox that if he doesn't like that, come and see us. But if he does, tell him to bring better men than he left here because he's going to need them," Danner declared. "Now git!"

"What about my gun and horse?"

"I'll have your gun and horse at the marshal's office. You come and claim them anytime," Wes announced, bending down to retrieve the dusty pistol.

"Move," Danner demanded.

"Wait!" Shelley shouted. "What do you know about the thief I shot trying to scatter our herd?"

The man flashed a faint grin. "You barely nicked him."

The man turned and stumbled over his boots as he hurried off toward the Knox ranch. The six gunslingers watched as the former guard-turned-messenger scurried into the tree line, then disappeared into the gaping mouth of a yawning thicket.

"Son of a bitch!" Shelley mumbled.

"What?" Danner asked the disgruntled lady gunslinger.

"I can't believe I didn't kill him," she muttered, shaking her head over the top of slumped shoulders.

Danner cracked a grin and shook his head. "By the way, thanks for saving my hide a second time."

Shelley smiled and flipped her Winchester onto her shoulder. "You're welcome."

CHAPTER 58

Friday, 2 August 1878

LUXTON DANNER –
CANYON CREEK

Danner guided Bullet into his stall behind the Sundown hotel and slid off his saddle. His boots hit the ground with a heavy thud causing thin lines of red dust to creep up through the porous golden strands of scattered hay. Wade and Shelley followed his lead, putting up their horses in neatly mucked stalls at the end of the stable frame that Stoney Walsh had finished rebuilding. Danner removed his hat and ran his massive forearm across his sweat-soaked brow. He dipped his hand into Bullet's water bucket and splashed a palm full over his face. The cool water felt good against his sunbaked skin. He took a deep breath and set the bucket down in front of Bullet, who plunged his muzzle into the welcome tonic.

Danner sent Case with Jackson over to Doc Carson's, and Wes had stopped off at the marshal's office with Knox's cowhand's horse and gun. Danner scratched at his wire-like whiskers. He leaned against a bale of hay and inspected his shirt. It was soaked clean through. Wade walked past him, waving toward the other side of the street, indicating he was heading to the Creekbed Saloon. Danner nodded. He made it clear to Knox what their next move was. Now he figured they'd have to wait for Knox's response to his challenge. But how long and what response? Danner wished he knew.

"You look like you've been kicked into the river by a mule," Shelley said, sliding up next to Bullet.

Danner looked up and winced at the remark. He figured she was right. It had been a long day. Shelley smiled, took her hat off, and untied the knot that had bunched her long brown hair just above the nape of her neck. Her mane fell over her shoulders as she ran her slender fingers through it in the absence of a brush. He realized again how pretty she was. Despite the prairie winds and warring rays of the Texas sun, her skin was smooth and flawless. Her hazel eyes were large and clear. Her face was slim, her bare lips not requiring the customary red paint most women wore to enhance their look. Her neck glistened with a hint of moisture wrangling a horse caused.

"Danner!" Shelley called out.

"What? What is it?" Danner stammered.

"I asked what you thought Knox would do when he finds out what happened out there today," Shelley said, slipping her thumbs behind her belt buckle, shifting her weight, and widening her smile.

"I wish I knew. You know Knox better than I do. We've only been in town a couple of weeks, although it seems a lot longer than that."

"We knew him before y'all got here, but now, I don't know." Shelley shrugged. "It's starting to get late. I'm going to get cleaned up and get something to eat. Care to join me?"

"I'll be along in a few minutes. I need to get this saddle off Bullet and rub him down. I'll join you at our table in the back. Rachel keeps it for us."

"You mean she keeps it for you." Shelley laughed, then headed for the street.

Danner watched Shelley walk away. Despite wearing riding britches, a gun belt, and a man's bib shirt hanging off her shoulders, there was no denying she was a fine figure of a woman. Danner shook his head and released his saddle strap. He swung his saddle up onto the stall rail, then looked for a brush or cloth. All he could find was a torn piece of burlap.

"Sorry, pal, but I guess this will have to do," Danner said, rubbing Bullet's mane.

"Danner! Danner!" Shelley screamed from the street in front of the Sundown hotel.

Danner hurried around the side of the hotel and froze at the porch rail. Ike Thurgum stood in the middle of the street, facing Shelley at twenty paces. Thurgum's grin quickly faded when he saw Danner step away from the railing and meet him.

"Shelley, get inside!" Danner ordered.

"I can . . ." Shelley began.

"Now!" Danner growled like an angry grizzly.

Shelley walked toward the Sundown's wide porch, keeping her eyes on the black-clad gunfighter. Danner slowly moved further into the street and stopped, his right hand covering his Schofield.

"You take to gunning down women?" Danner barked, his fatigued body now energized with the bolt of an adrenaline surge. People flocked out of every nearby building door, including both saloons. Boot and shoe heels clamored on the boardwalks sending echoes up and down both sides of the street. Windows flew open, filled with anxious faces wanting to see the showdown. Wade and Case stepped out of the Creekbed. A half-dozen Knox men gathered in front of his saloon. Danner took two long strides toward Thurgum, who covered his gun with his right and raised his left hand toward his adversary.

"You're good right there, Danner!" Thurgum announced loud enough for the whole town to hear. "I ain't here for a fight, but I'll oblige ya, if need be."

Danner stood tall and said nothing. A couple of horses nickered in the distance cutting the silence like a knife. The wind whipped up a scarlet dust devil between the two gunfighters.

Knox stepped through the swinging doors of his saloon and joined Thurgum in the street.

"You and your men have until noon tomorrow to ride on!" Knox announced, keeping a steady eye on Danner's gun hand.

Danner's eyes narrowed. The giant gunslinger clenched his teeth and flexed the fingers on his right hand but remained deathly silent, ignoring Knox, staring straight into Ike Thurgum's eyes. A man's decision to draw flashed through his eyes before his hand ever moved. Danner watched like a cougar ready to pounce.

"Just ride on, and they'll be no trouble. You don't want any innocent people in this town to get hurt, do you? Ride on Danner. Noon tomorrow," Knox repeated, then began to step back before he slowly turned his back to Danner and took the reins of his horse from one of his men in front of the Knox Saloon. Thurgum stepped back to his horse.

Thurgum and Knox swung up into their saddles and galloped out of town without turning back to look at Danner. Danner stood still watching Knox and Thurgum fade into the murky dusk. Shouts and sighs bounded off the façades of Main Street's buildings. Wade, Case, and Shelley met Danner in the middle of the street where wagons, carriages, and men on horseback began moving again. Wes joined the four gunslingers in the street.

"Maybe we should get out of the middle of the street," Wes offered emphatically to his counterparts.

After a moment's pause, Danner turned and walked in silence to the Sundown, where he disappeared through the door. Men approached Wes and the others who stopped at the steps of the Sundown Hotel.

"I'll be damned! I ain't never seen anything like that!" one of the men yelled.

"Well, that didn't take long," Shelley exclaimed.

"What didn't take long?" Wes asked.

"Come inside. I reckon the big man will let you in on the secret," Shelley added before skipping up the steps into the hotel.

"What the hell does that mean?" Wade asked aloud.

"I don't know, but I reckon we have until noon tomorrow to figure it out," Case quipped before leading Wes and Wade into the Sundown Hotel.

CHAPTER 59

Friday, 2 August 1878

LUXTON DANNER & GUNSLINGERS – SUNDOWN HOTEL

anner's boots pounded the oak steps of the Sundown Hotel's staircase as though the polished wood had betrayed him. He looked up and found Wes, Wade, and Case waiting at the bottom step with Rachel and Shelley. Danner paused and looked at each of them with a stoic glare that meant business. He rested his hands on the grip of each Schofield pistol and listened. The dining room around the corner was booming, with the sound more familiar with that of a saloon. Men were talking over each other, trying to prove their opinion of what had transpired out on the street was gospel. Rachel stepped around the desk and stood next to Danner.

"Albert Loman is waiting for you in the dining room. After meeting with Judge Holt earlier today, he and his wife decided to stay."

"Ask him to meet us out here," Danner requested.

Rachel disappeared around the corner.

"How's everybody set on ammunition?" Danner asked.

"I only have what's on me," Wes announced.

"Same here," Wade admitted.

"I've got what's on my belt, plus one extra box," Case added.

"I also only have what's on my belt," Shelley chimed in.

"You're not in this fight!" Wes told the lady gunslinger.

"The hell I'm not! I'm the only one here that has lost anything! I'm in!" Shelley defiantly snarled, grabbing the handle of her Colt Lightning.

"I don't want—"

"She stays," Danner announced. "We need ammunition."

Rachel appeared with Loman.

"Do you have any ammunition at your store?" Danner asked.

"Yes, sir. I only have a few boxes. Follow me. I'll give you whatever I have left," Loman stated.

Everyone followed Loman out the front door of the Sundown except Danner, who was held back by the desperate grasp of Rachel.

"Please, Lux. Maybe it'd be best if you all left town. This mess isn't worth being killed over," Rachel begged, her green eyes filling with tears.

Danner looked at Rachel with an unsuccessful attempt to soften his piercing look. He reached around the diminutive woman's shoulders and gently squeezed as though he feared breaking her.

"Having a woman care if I get shot or killed isn't fair to her or me. That's why I try to keep my distance, Rachel."

"Well, it's too late, Luxton Danner. Far too late."

He said nothing more before leaving the hotel.

Danner stepped into Loman's store. "Wes, check in on Jackson. See if he can join us," he ordered his partner, who quickly darted out of the store. "Everyone carrying .45s?"

"My Lightning is a .38," Shelley verified.

"I only have three boxes of .45s and no .38s," Loman advised.

"Don't matter. Shelley, I want you to cover the rest of us with your Winchester. Only use your Lightning if you have to," Danner stated.

Wes returned with Jackson. "He says he's good to join us."

"That right, Jackson?" Danner asked.

Jackson nodded slowly. "Head hurts like hell, but I can shoot."

"All right, that makes six," Danner said.

"Seven," Stoney Walsh announced as he busted through the door like a wild boar.

"This is no place for an amateur," Danner told Walsh coldly.

"After everything you've done for me, I'm not hiding in the boarding house hoping y'all defend our town. Besides, I may not be a gunfighter, but I'm no amateur."

"All right. That'll give us a rifle at each end of town," Danner said.

"What are you thinking?" Wes asked.

Danner pulled a bullet from his belt and grabbed a sheet of paper Loman had on top of the counter. Danner drew a quick sketch of the town.

"Now, I still don't think Knox will send every man he has into town tomorrow to flush us out. This town is his, regardless of how he got it. His ranch is west of town, so I believe most of his men will come in that way, but if he knows anything about tactics, he'll have a couple of men also ride in from the east. Knox owns most of the west side of town except for the marshal's office and undertaker's place. Shelley, I want you inside the undertaker's with your rifle. You can see the entire end of town from there. Walsh, you take a position inside the stage office at the other end. We don't want a fight inside of town. Wes, Jackson, and I will stop Knox's men before coming into town from the west. Wade, you and Case stop anyone coming in from the east. If Knox doesn't have anyone over there, hightail it down to us as quickly as you can, but don't come down Main Street. Knox will still have men at his saloon and store. Don't ride into an ambush," Danner warned.

The small bell Loman had nailed to his front door dinged, interrupting Danner's briefing. All eyes turned to see Judge Holt, still dressed in his stately black suit, carefully closing the door behind him. He turned to Canyon Creek's champions.

"I'm sorry to interrupt what I'm certain is an effective yet dangerous plan to meet Gilford Knox's most recent challenge."

"Can we help you, Judge?" Danner asked.

"No, sir, but I believe I can help all of you if you humor me for a few minutes."

"Yes, sir, of course," Danner answered.

"I have an alternative plan, a legal plan to propose. I have a meeting with Gilford Knox scheduled for tomorrow morning at ten o'clock. I plan to confront him with the information I've obtained from various townsfolk regarding his land appropriation. In light of the events that occurred out at Miss Robertson's former homestead, and the admission of the theft of Mr. Loman's supply wagons by Knox's man, and the foolishness that occurred out in the street less than an hour ago, I anticipate Mr. Knox will not appear for our meeting. I believe I have enough evidence to issue an arrest warrant for Knox when that occurs. I will have that warrant ready at ten o'clock. In the absence of the sheriff, I will authorize Marshal Payne and anyone who accompanies him to arrest Knox and return him to the Canyon Creek jail," Judge Holt proclaimed. "This way, whatever actions Marshal Payne and this group take will be legal," Judge Holt added with a sardonic grin.

"Well, Knox did say we needed to be out of town by noon. He didn't say where." Wes chuckled.

Everyone nodded in agreement.

"In that case, this meeting is over. And since we're free to remain here in town tonight, I could use a drink," Danner muttered.

"Me too," Wade said.

"Sounds good," Case added.

"I believe I'll pass," Shelley chimed in.

"And me," Jackson said, rubbing his head.

"I'll see you all later," Wes announced, waving at Walsh to follow him.

"Thanks for the use of the store and the ammunition, Mr. Loman. I figure we'll still need it when we ride out to Knox's ranch tomorrow," Danner said.

CHAPTER 60

Friday, 2 August 1878

GILFORD KNOX – CIRCLE X RANCH

Knox slammed the whiskey bottle onto his desk with a force that shattered the glass, sending knife-like shards and whiskey splashing in every direction. He pounded both fists on the sodden desk surface. Thurgum stood next to the big desk sipping his drink.

"Son of a bitch! Those bastards aren't going anywhere! They can't! They've committed to fighting me, and they can't back down now!"

"Men like them can't back down," Thurgum calmly stated.

Knox looked up at his hired gunslinger. "No, you can't," Knox mumbled.

"I want every man you can spare when you go into town tomorrow. Tell them I'll double their pay! Kill every one of those bastards, including that Robertson bitch! I should've killed her weeks ago! That's what I get for being soft! Well, no more! I don't give a damn what I have to do. That damned railroad is going right through my land even if I have to kill everyone against me to do it!"

"Take it easy, Mr. Knox. We'll take care of the business at hand. If it were up to me, we'd ride in there tonight and burn down everything you don't own," Thurgum casually remarked.

Knox took a deep breath and gathered his composure. He stepped over to his bar and poured another drink from a fresh bottle of whiskey. He slammed down the glass and poured another before pushing the stopper back into the bottle.

"As much as I'd like to do just that, I can't. Judge Holt's presence complicates things. Besides, I need to build up the town, not burn it down. My father was very explicit about that. He wants Canyon Creek to be as big as Oneida when he brings the railroad bosses here."

"Okay, but I'd—"

"You just do what I pay you to do and leave the rest to me. Understand?"

"Yes, sir," Thurgum answered. "So how you want this handled then?"

"They'll know we'll have men enter town from the west. Send a few men around town and go in from the east. They keep their horses in the corral behind the Sundown. Send a couple of men there to kill their horses. They'll have to fight on foot then. Now that I think of it, burn the Sundown Hotel. I won't need it anyway. Keep the fight near there," Knox ordered.

"What about the woman who owns that place?"

Knox paused and looked at Thurgum but said nothing. "I'll come into town about one o'clock. That should give you enough time to settle this."

"Just make sure your gun's loaded. I don't know what you'll be met with," Thurgum offered.

"Don't worry about my gun. You just do what I'm paying you for, and then you can move on."

"What about the judge?" Thurgum finally asked.

"You make damn sure nothing happens to Holt. A district judge gets killed, and we'll have every lawman in the territory on our asses. I'll deal with him afterward," Knox said. "Send a rider into town tonight and have him pass the word of the plan to our men," Knox added before waving Thurgum out of his office.

Knox snatched the map and carried it to the table before rolling it out and taking another look. Based on the information his father had sent, there was no way around the Robertson, Kincaid, and Morgan ranches, as well as the Rawlings place further north near Thornton. The rail coming up from Austin would bypass Palo Duro Canyon on the east, then veer west toward Oneida and Canyon Creek before connecting to the westward rail line. His father would ensure the locations. It was his job to provide the land.

And that's precisely what I'm going to do.

CHAPTER 61

Saturday, 3 August 1878

LUXTON DANNER – SUNDOWN HOTEL

D anner leaned against the ridged slats of the Sundown's porch railing, watching the sun gently pull itself up from behind the horizon like a prairie dog cautiously peeking out of its sunken den. Its golden rays stretched across Canyon Creek like a translucent blanket offering the comforting promise of a new day. An armadillo traversed Main Street, battling the ruts and clumps of red dirt the horse's hooves had kicked up the night before. Danner surprised himself with the three hours of sleep he managed after saying good night to a weary Rachel and hell-bent-for-leather Shelley in the Hotel's dining room. Both women were firm in their styles. Rachel, as the tough businesswoman and mother, and Shelley, as an equal woman and a gunslinger. He just hoped the gunslinger didn't get her killed. Danner heard a door slam to his left. He peered down to see the big doors at Knox's livery stable swinging open.

If Knox goes to prison, who the hell will run his businesses?

The front door of the Sundown opened behind him. A pair of silky hands glided over his shoulders and began to massage his bulging muscles.

"Good morning, Rachel," Danner said without having to look to see who owned the hands that were sending waves of solace down each side of his body.

"Good morning, cowboy," she whispered into his ear. "How long have you been out here?"

"Since well before sunup," he answered, allowing himself to accept the full attention of her manipulating fingers.

"Can I get you breakfast?"

"Just coffee this morning, please."

"Just coffee it is then," Rachel said, detaching her enchanted hands from his shoulders.

A righteous man sure could get used to that. He headed for his hot cup of coffee.

A beam of sunshine caught the side of the silver coffeepot Rachel held as she emerged from the kitchen, adding a florid glow to her sleek auburn hair. Danner found himself at peace with himself as he usually did before a fight. His air of confidence in himself and the men, and in this case woman he surrounded himself with, provided a sense of reassurance.

"Here you go, sir, hot coffee as requested," Rachel said louder than necessary since they were the only two people in the place at the early hour.

"You all right?"

"Not at all," she replied with a broad smile and nod of her head before whirling around and disappearing through the kitchen doorway.

Danner stared into his coffee cup while the aroma of bacon, eggs, and bread intensified with each passing minute. His focus on the sizzling frying pans was broken by the front door bursting open, followed by thundering footsteps from the hoard of townsfolk rumbling into the dining room.

Danner finished the last of his coffee, then wound through

the suddenly crowded room to the lobby, then out the front door. The street was busy now, with people hustling up and down both sides of the road. Danner noticed two of Knox's men standing in front of the Knox Hotel and two more sitting on the hitching post in front of the saloon.

Only four.

He hoped for a couple more in town, meaning less out at the Knox ranch. Everyone agreed to leave town at different times that morning so as not to draw attention. Everyone except Walsh would meet outside of town where Jackson and the other Buffalo Soldiers had camped when they first arrived. Wes deputized Walsh and ordered him to remain in town to watch things. No sense getting Betsy Tyler's future husband killed this morning. Wes's last-ditch effort to convince Shelley to stay behind failed before it began, mainly due to Danner's approval that she join the posse. The only real laugh the night before followed Wes's threat to punch Danner because he wouldn't back him regarding Shelley. Danner cracked a smile at the thought of Wes's outburst. He strolled down to the boarding house where Jackson was convalescing, and Judge Holt watching the seconds tick by on his pocket watch.

"Ten o'clock can't arrive soon enough!" Judge Holt exclaimed when Danner entered the front room of the boarding house.

The judge was seated at the head of the table, an arrest warrant awaiting his signature lay flat on the polished surface in front of him. Jackson sat in an oversized stuffed chair in the corner of the room, his legs fully extended out and crossed at the ankles.

"What are you going to do if Knox shows up?" Danner asked through a forced grin.

The judge stopped and thought a moment before scratching

his head and chuckling aloud. "I guess I haven't thought about that!"

Danner turned his attention to Jackson. "You look comfortable there, Jackson!"

"No sense in gettin' riled up over nuthin'," Jackson offered.

Betsy Tyler entered the room with a plate full of hot biscuits and honey, which she set down in front of the judge. She turned to Danner and sighed.

"Thank you for keeping Stoney here in town, Mr. Danner."

"It was Marshal Payne's decision, ma'am. I just went along with it," Danner clarified before quickly removing his hat.

"Thank you anyway," Betsy repeated before hurrying back to the kitchen.

"Help yourselves, gentlemen," Judge Holt offered, waving his hand over the steaming biscuits.

"No thanks, Judge. I'm not hungry," Danner advised.

"Speak fer yerself, boss!" Jackson quipped, leaning over and snatching two of the hot biscuits.

"It's almost nine, Judge?" Danner asked.

"Two minutes after."

"You better swallow those biscuits, Jackson. Time for you to head out to the campsite. Wade and Case should already be there. Shelley and I will follow after you, then Wes will join us after Judge Holt gives him the warrant."

"I'll tell Marshal Payne the same thing. Bring him back alive if you can," Judge Holt instructed Danner.

"That'll be up to him, Judge," Danner said before following Jackson out of the room.

"I'll follow a few minutes behind you. I'll walk back to the Sundown and let Knox's men see me before I slip out the back door," Danner informed Jackson.

"Yes, sir. On my way."

Danner walked slowly across the street and down the boardwalk to the Sundown, where he stood and waited a moment, ensuring Knox's men saw him. He climbed up the three steps to the porch and looked to see Jackson riding out.

Danner saw Adeline sitting on the stool behind the big front desk. She could barely see over the top.

"Good morning, Mr. Danner," she managed to say before spinning around in a circle and giggling.

"What are you doing at the desk?"

"Mommy said for me to say good morning to everyone that comes in," Adeline announced.

"I'll be sure to tell her you're doing an outstanding job, and she should pay you extra," Danner said with a nod.

Danner hurried up to his room. He took his rifle and the Colt Peacemaker he carried for a third gun from under the mattress. Danner opened the small drawer in the bed table and checked to ensure his note for Rachel was still there. It was resting on top of the three hundred dollars he left for her in case he didn't return. He wanted to leave more but building and rebuilding the stable out back and paying Walsh had cost him about everything he had. No matter, Knox and his men may eliminate his need for money anyway. He closed the drawer and locked the door behind him. He left the key on the hook behind the desk.

CHAPTER 62

Saturday, 3 August 1878

LUXTON DANNER & GROUP – OUTSIDE CANYON CREEK

anner untied Bullet from the tangled twigs of the Texas sage he used to keep his mount from straying off. There was plenty of dried bunchgrass for the horses to graze on while Judge Holt's posse waited for Wes and the warrant. Finally, after what seemed like hours, Wes appeared galloping toward the impatient band of quasi-lawmen.

"Mount up!" Danner ordered, looking over his shoulder at his approaching partner.

Wes reined Ringo to a stop. "Knox didn't show. The judge waited until a quarter past before he signed the warrant and instructed me to bring Knox back alive, if possible," Wes reported. "We're all officers of his court, whatever that means. Let's go."

Wes followed Danner's lead and rejoined his partner at the end of the group, which was riding in tight formation side by side. Next to Danner was Jackson, then Shelley, Wade, and Case. They rode in silence for a time before Jackson broke the hush.

"I just want you all to know that I ain't never been treated so good by folks in all my life. All you, and Miss Tyler and Mr.

Walsh been mighty fine to me. The colored boys back at the fort wouldn't believe me. Even the white soldiers in the cavalry didn't treat me this good 'cept when I was savin' their asses! Then I'm their best friend!" Jackson exclaimed to the rousing laughter of the posse. "'Cept for Colonel Grierson, he was always good to the Buffalo Soldiers. He's a good man. You all like Colonel Grierson, 'cept for you, Missy," Jackson said, looking at Shelley with a wide grin.

"You don't need to explain, Jackson. Out here, a man is judged by how hard he works or who he backs with his gun. You're among friends, and that's all that matters today," Danner stated.

"And about today. What exactly is the plan once we get to Knox's place? We're gettin' close," Wade asked.

"Wes and I have been there. Out in front of the main house anyway. There's not much in the way of cover. We'll spread out a bit, then honor Judge Holt's wishes and announce we have a warrant for Knox. If the shootin' starts, everyone scatter and find cover as quickly as you can. The only other option I can think of is to wait until dark and try to sneak in, but by then, Knox's men in town may return, and we'll have more guns to deal with."

"Not much of a plan," Case remarked.

"We're all listening if you have a better one," Wes offered.

"Nope. Just as soon start shooting. I think better when I'm shootin'," Case declared.

"I believe you do," Shelley mumbled. "Knox's men will see us comin' once we clear the rise up ahead."

"Spread out once we clear the top. Since Wes is the only real lawman here, I figure he ought to lead us in," Danner quipped, looking at Wes with a grin.

"Thanks," Wes retorted with a smirk.

"You're welcome," Danner answered to the delight of the rest.

———◆———

Forty-five minutes later, Wes pushed Ringo a few horse lengths ahead of the group, which spread out as they cleared the top of the rise. Knox's main house and outbuildings came into view. A white split-rail fence, divided in half by a wide-open gate framed in a tall archway with "Circle X" cut out at the top, ringed the front pasture. The house was broad, with a large front porch wrapped all around. On the right appeared to be a large tack building, and to the left a big barn, with a smaller one just beyond. The split-rail fence surrounded the entire house, with the only easy way in being the front gate. Danner saw two men sitting in chairs on the porch and another milling around the big barn. A long narrow building with several doors leading to a boardwalk sat behind the tack building. That was likely the bunkhouse for the cowhands. Danner kicked Bullet up to Wes.

"I only count four men in view. The rest will come from the bunkhouse behind the tack building on the right," Danner suggested.

"You and I will ride straight to the front door of the main house. Let's have the rest head for the bunkhouse. Maybe we can get there fast enough to pin most of them inside," Wes said.

"Right," Danner agreed, then slowed to join the other four. "Wes and I will head straight for the main house. You four charge to the bunkhouse behind the tack building on the right. Knox's guards will probably be in there or the house. The rest of the cowhands should be out in the pastures this time of the morning. Try to get to the bunkhouse before too many guards can get out. Questions?" Danner asked.

"Nope," Wade replied.

"Sounds good," Case added.

Wes and his team spurred up to a gallop as they approached the main gate, the man near the barn and the one at the tack building hustled toward the house's porch where the two guards there stood and adjusted their gun belts. One guard opened the front door and called inside. Two more men, armed with rifles, ran out of the big barn.

"That's six!" Danner shouted to Wes, who guided Ringo under the Circle X sign and into the fenced pasture.

Danner followed close behind Wes. Wade, Case, Shelley, and Jackson penetrated the fence line and veered off to the right heading for the tack building and bunkhouse. The two guards on the left racked their Winchesters and leveled them at Danner and Wes. All four guards in front of the house drew their pistols. No one fired a shot. Wes reined Ringo to a stop in front of Knox's house. Danner stopped behind Wes on his left side. Wade, Case, Shelley, and Jackson drew their guns. Several men who ran out of the bunkhouse stopped, looking square into the ends of four gun barrels. All six of Judge Holt's group members stayed mounted, taking advantage of their opponents on foot.

"Gilford Knox!" Wes shouted. "Gilford Knox!"

The big wooden front door slowly opened. Sharply dressed in a dark gray suit and mist-gray hat, Gilford Knox calmly stepped through the front door. His suit coat covered his gun. He moved to the edge of the porch near the top of the steps and frowned. Two guards stood ready on each side.

"Just who the hell you think you are riding in here without an invite?" Knox snarled.

"Gilford Knox, I've been sent by Judge Jeremiah Holt with a warrant for your arrest!" Wes announced.

Knox's guards laughed. Knox stood rigid and said nothing. The muscles on his jaws twitched as he gritted his teeth. The powerful rancher looked toward his bunkhouse and saw Shelley poised in the saddle, Winchester in hand. He looked back to Wes, then Danner.

"I see you have a girl riding in your posse. That tells me there aren't any more of you. Suppose I don't care to be arrested today? What are you going to do? Shoot your way out of here?"

"I told Judge Holt we'd bring you in alive if we could, but that'd be up to you," Wes stated.

"Bold words from a man who's outnumbered and outgunned. Wouldn't you say?" Knox bellowed. "Now. Here's what's going to happen. I'm going back inside the house, and you all will get off my land. Whether that's alive or dead is your decision," Knox declared. "Men, these sonsabitches are trespassing. Get them off my property," Knox ordered before he turned toward the open front door.

"You heard him! Git!" one of the guards shouted, raising his pistol at Wes.

"That's far enough, Knox!" Wes called.

Crack! A bullet ripped through Ringo's neck, sending the stallion crashing to the ground. Wes drew his Colt as he was falling from his saddle. Danner drew both Schofields and fired at the two guards armed with Winchesters. Both riflemen spun and fell to the ground.

Crack! Crack! Crack! Gunfire erupted from every direction. Wes slammed into the dirt, firing his Colt. Another guard on the porch rocked back and fell. *Crack!* A bullet smashed into Danner's right shin, hitting the bone, and sending painful fire up his leg. He turned Bullet and kicked his spurs as he fired back at three guards on the porch. *Crack! Crack! Crack!* Two porch guards jerked and fell. Case charged past the front of the porch, firing both pistols. Danner turned and galloped past Wes, who ducked behind his fallen horse's body.

"Get Knox!" Danner yelled at Wes as he headed for the bunkhouse.

Boom! The sound of a shotgun blast echoed off the tack building. Danner saw Shelley, Wade, and Jackson scatter. The guards at the bunkhouse ducked back inside. *Boom!* Another blast from a shotgun pushed through a window of the bunkhouse. Wade, Shelley, and Jackson fired into the bunkhouse windows. A man ran out of the bunkhouse, firing his pistol. *Crack!* A bullet from Wade's Colt felled the fighter. Bullets blew up the corner of the tack building, raining shards of splintered wood down on Wade. Another guard fired from the bunkhouse doorway. Jackson recognized him as the man who ordered him and the troopers out of their camp. Jackson leveled his Henry rifle and fired. Crack! The man named Carter spun and collapsed in a bloody heap.

"I said we'd meet again, Mr. Carter," Jackson muttered through a crooked grin.

"Help Wes!" Danner called to Shelley as he charged past her.

Shelley reined her horse to the left and dug her spurs into her horse's hide. She galloped toward Wes, who was pinned down behind Ringo. Wes was still taking fire from the last guard on the porch and another inside the house. Bullets kicked up clods of dirt all around Wes. He reached over Ringo and fired blindly at the house. Shelley pulled hard on the reins and stopped her horse. She leveled her Winchester and fired. *Crack!* Her bullet hit its mark, sending the guard at the front door rolling down the steps, a crimson blood trail marking the path.

Danner slid off Bullet, his boots crashing onto the boardwalk in front of the bunkhouse. His right leg buckled under him, causing him to collapse onto his right side. Another man charged out of the bunkhouse door and pointed his pistol at Danner. *Crack! Crack!* Jackson's two shots dropped Danner's assailant in the doorway. Suddenly, the shooting stopped. Clouds of gunpowder dissipated into the morning breeze. The stubborn smell of hot lead remained.

"Don't anybody come out of the bunkhouse!" Wade shouted from his position next to the tack building.

Danner scrambled to his feet and limped back to the front of the house as fast as he could. Wes and Shelley crouched down on either side of the open front doorway. Danner crawled over the railing and fell onto the wooden planks with a thud. He crept under a window and slid up behind Shelley.

"Sorry I'm late," Danner winced with each word.

"At least you're not dead," Shelley muttered flatly.

"Your guards are dead, Knox! Come out with your hands up! It's the only way!" Wes shouted through the open door.

"You want me, come and get me! The rest of my men heard the shots. They'll be comin' in from the pastures double-quick!" Knox yelled back.

"He's right about that," Wes muttered to Shelley and Danner.

"Well," Shelley said before she leaped up and rushed through the door.

"Wait!" Wes hollered.

Crack! Crack! A shrill scream preceded a loud thump.

"No!" Danner busted through the doorway, firing both Schofields.

Wes followed on his partner's heels. Shelley hit the floor, then spun toward the bar clutching her Lightning with a two-handed grip. Danner took cover on the right. Wes did the same on the left. Shelley's chest heaved in quick gasps of breath. Blood oozed from her right side and neck. She bit her lip so hard it began to bleed.

"Now, look what you've done. You got your girl shot," Ike Thurgum muttered in between laughs. "You didn't think I was just going to let you two come in here and take my boss, did you?"

Danner couldn't see inside the room. It looked like Knox's office. Danner shook his head at Wes, who returned the gesture, indicating he couldn't see Thurgum or Knox. Danner looked over at Shelley, who nodded. He raised his .45 Schofield to his face and pulled back the hammer. He nodded at Wes. Suddenly, Danner leaned around the thick oak molding and fired. *Crack! Crack!* Chunks of oak wood exploded as Thurgum's bullets shattered the frame next to Danner.

Crack! Crack! Wes charged in and fired. Shelley slid out from behind the bar and fired, both bullets punching holes in Ike Thurgum's chest. The man dressed in black dropped his gun and sunk to his knees, then collapsed in a pool of blood. Knox reached for a gun on his desk but stopped at the sight of Wes's two Colts.

"You're under arrest, Knox," Wes ordered.

"The hell I am!" Knox shouted, pulling a gun from under his vest.

Crack! Crack! Knox and Wes exchanged fire, both men diving to the floor. Crack! Knox fired at Danner, shattering the glass door of his office bar. Danner spun and fired back, destroying Knox's cigar ashtray. Danner tossed Shelley over his shoulder and turned toward the archway. *Crack! Crack!* Knox crouched behind his splintered desk and fired at Wes. *Crack!* Shelley fired at Knox from Danner's shoulder. The bullet hit Knox's left arm, spinning him back to the floor. Wes pounced over the desk, crashing onto Knox before Knox retrieved his pistol. A devastating blow from Wes's scarred right hand crushed Knox's face, ending the fight.

Dragging Knox by his shirt collar, Wes followed Danner and Shelley out the front door where Case stood guard.

Knox came to as Wes dragged him down the steps. Blood from Knox's broken nose flowed into his mouth, causing him to cough and spit.

"You got a horse?" Wes asked Knox.

"In the barn."

"Case." Danner nodded toward the barn.

Wes looked down at Ringo. His once white mane was soaked red with blood. His companion was dead.

"Damn it! You better bring two," Wes muttered, carefully removing the saddle from his stallion's back.

"Take Shelley's horse. She'll ride with me."

CHAPTER 63

Saturday, 3 August 1878

LUXTON DANNER & SHELLEY ROBERTSON – DOC CARSON'S OFFICE

Danner spurred Bullet past Wes and Jackson, who stopped at the jail to tuck the bloodied Knox into his iron-barred holding pen. Wade and Case shielded Danner, keeping their guns trained on Knox's men who remained in town. Danner stopped in front of Doc Carson's, then swung his gunshot-damaged right leg over Bullet's head despite having his arms full of a bloody Shelley Robertson. He softened his landing the best he could by bending his knees to absorb the shock, then thundered through the front door in two strides, ignoring the pangs of pain shocking his right leg. Wade and Case dismounted and stood guard in front of Carson's place.

"Doc!" Danner called a moment before the town physician popped his head around the corner of his examining room screen.

"My God! What has happened now?" Carson exclaimed, grabbing his spectacles from his reading table and taking a closer look at Shelley's neck and side. "Bring her to the back and get that shirt off."

Danner gently laid Shelley on the table, then froze.

Get her shirt off?

Emily Carson rushed into the room. "Out!" she ordered, rescuing Danner from his quandary.

Danner stepped away, then stumbled to one knee, his right leg collapsing beneath him. Doc Carson paused, then rushed to his new patient.

"Are you wounded?" Carson asked, seeing the bloody tear just above Danner's boot top. "What is it?" Carson asked.

"Nothing, Doc, take care of her. I'll see you later," Danner said, pushing himself up from the floor.

"The hell you will! You sit in that chair and don't move until I can look at that!" Carson ordered, pointing to one of the three chairs in his waiting room.

Knowing that Shelley was in good hands, Danner sat, as his leg began to pound out every beat of his heart inside the burning wound. He reached down and felt around the opening. He slid his fingers to the back of his calf, where he found a larger hole than in the front.

Good. Went through.

Blood slowly seeped from the gaping cavities. His right foot felt wet. He pressed on his shinbone and felt around. The bullet had hit the outside of the bone and punched through the back. A burning pain shot up his leg like a wagoner's whip. He leaned back in the chair, stretched out, and closed his eyes. Rachel rushed into the room, the door crashing against the wall. Her eyes locked onto Danner's bloody limb. She dropped to her knees and examined the gnarly mess.

"What happened?"

Danner looked into her bright green eyes. He knew the rest of Rachel was there somewhere in the blurry background, but those green eyes were clear as dawn's early light.

"Took a bullet through the leg. It's all right. I'll be fine once Doc patches it up."

"Let me get this boot off," Rachel said, cupping the dirty boot heel with gentle hands.

"No, I can wait for Doc."

"Nonsense! He's a little busy at the moment. You keep quiet and hold onto that chair!"

Danner took a deep breath, wrapped his hands around each wooden arm, and then nodded. Rachel tugged on the heel, trying to pull the boot off and not move it simultaneously. Danner exhaled.

"Just pull as hard as you can," Danner ordered, pressing his chin into his chest.

Rachel grabbed the boot and yanked as hard as she could.

"Aaaahhhhh!" Danner groaned, his eyes squeezed shut.

Rachel fell backward and gasped. Danner's sock was soaked blood-red. She looked inside his boot and saw a puddle of blood at the bottom. She stood and gathered herself.

"This will need to be washed, as will that sock. You bled into the boot. It's filled with blood," Rachel reported coolly.

"What? No tears?" Danner asked, cracking a faint grin.

"I don't have any left for you, Luxton Danner!" she hollered at the big gunslinger.

Emily Carson stepped into the room. "I thought I heard you, dear," she greeted Rachel before looking down at Danner's leg. "Oh my!" She sighed, shaking her head, and propping her hands on her hips.

"How's Shelley?" Danner asked.

"She'll be all right. According to the good doctor, one bullet cracked her collarbone, and the other missed her ribs and passed through her side. He removed the bullet near her neck and is dressing the wounds now," Emily Carson reported. "Then we'll have a look at you!"

"Send him in here!" Doc Carson called from the other room.

"You heard him, mister, let's go," the doctor's wife and nurse ordered Danner.

Danner carefully pushed himself up from his chair, then limped into the examining room, which was a tad too small for two patients. Carson directed him to a chair in the corner, then propped his wounded leg up on a wooden stool.

"Went all the way through, Doc."

"So, it did. It just grazed the bone. You're a lucky man, Mr. Danner. Had it shattered that bone, you would have lost that part of your leg," Carson advised. "This shouldn't take too long."

Thirty minutes later, Danner pushed his freshly bandaged leg into a wet, albeit clean, boot and then limped out the door with Rachel's assistance. People scurried all about town. Men were running down the street toward the jail. Danner stopped a man trying to rush past him.

"What's happening?" Danner asked.

"There's gonna be trouble. Knox's men have surrounded the jail and want him out!" The man shouted, pulling away from Danner's clutches.

"Damn! You get back to the Sundown and stay there until this is over," Danner ordered Rachel, who knew better than to argue.

Danner paused in front of the Sundown and checked his pistols. He replaced the empty cartridges with new lead, then slid the Schofields into their holsters. He then limped to the jail, where five Knox men lined up in front of Wes, blocking the door to his office. Wade, Case, and Jackson stood behind Wes, covering their guns. He limped up behind the five jail busters without them noticing—a bad mistake on their part.

"Judge Holt will be here in a moment. He'll decide what will happen to your boss," Wes informed Knox's men.

"We ain't waitin' fer no judge! Let him out right now or else!" one of the men shouted.

"That's right!" another added.

Danner drew both .45s and cocked the hammers, causing the five men to spin around and start to reach for their guns.

"Or else what?" Danner asked in a low clear voice.

"Mr. Knox ain't done—"

"If it were up to me, Knox would already be dead, and so would all of you sons a bitches. Now, unless you want to give the undertaker more business, get the hell out of here, and don't come anywhere near this jail."

"We don't take orders from you, mister!" one of Knox's men decried.

Danner stepped forward toward the five men. "Anyone comes near this jail without an invitation, and I'll kill 'em personally, then put a bullet in Knox," Danner muttered. "Now git!"

The five men hesitated, then followed orders and pushed their way through the crowd of people gathered, looking for a gunfight. Wes stepped into the street, where he and Danner watched Knox's men disappear into their boss's saloon.

"You reckon they'll heed your warning?" Wes asked.

"Nope," Danner answered, then limped into the marshal's office.

CHAPTER 64

Saturday, 3 August 1878

LUXTON DANNER & GUNSLINGERS – CANYON CREEK

Wes closed the shutter that covered one of the two small windows in the front of his office. He set the cross timber into its iron mounts, then repeated the process on the other window opposite the front door. Danner sat next to the desk he used to prop up his bullet-riddled leg.

"Are you bleeding on my desk?" Wes snapped a grin at his partner.

Danner didn't move or look at his leg. He swallowed the last drop of whiskey and set the small glass on the corner of the desk. "Hadn't bothered to look," Danner answered.

Jackson occupied a spot around the wall corner that separated Knox's holding cell from the office. Jackson's new assignment was simple. Watch the back door and the prisoner. For his task, he was armed with a sawed-off, double-barrel, twelve-gauge shotgun, courtesy of JD Case.

"You know, Mr. Payne, if I pull both triggers on this scattergun, I'll blow the whole back wall out of this tiny jail," Jackson mused.

"That's the idea," Wes answered, taking a seat behind his tattered desk.

"Mighty nice of Judge Holt to go fetch a US Marshal from Oneida," Danner said.

"Sure was. I reckon the judge won't be back till the day after tomorrow, though," Wes added.

"We should've just taken Knox to Oneida ourselves," Danner mumbled, thumbing through the dozen or so wanted posters Wes had accumulated.

"Holt thought it was just asking for more trouble," Wes answered.

"Don't matter if the trouble was out on the road or here in town. At least out on the road, nobody here would be in danger," Danner offered.

"Well, if there's gonna be trouble, we won't have to wait long. Sun's going down out there, and Knox's men from his ranch have had plenty of time to get here," Wes said.

"Agreed," Danner nodded.

"Payne! Danner! It's us!" Wade called out from in front of the jail.

Wes lifted the cross beam and cracked the door just enough to see Wade and Case. He swung the door open and stepped aside, letting the gunslingers enter. Wes closed the door and replaced the beam.

"Tight quarters in here," Wade commented, pulling up the wooden stool Wes usually perched on out front.

"And hot as hell," Case added.

"It'll cool down in another hour or so," Wes assured his troops.

"What's happening out there?" Danner asked.

"All kinds of commotion over at Knox's saloon. The place

is crawling with cowhands who want to be the ones to spring Knox. We talked to Dakota over at the Creekbed. He said he doesn't know what, but there's talk of something happening tonight. They know Holt left for Oneida to get the US Marshal, so they don't want to wait till he gets back," Wade reported.

"Payne!" Knox shouted from his cell in the back.

Wes stepped around Jackson and looked at Knox, standing at the cell door clutching the bars in each hand. A snarky smile crossed his lips.

"What is it, Knox?"

"There's no reason to let this get out of hand. There's no reason for anyone else to get killed. Just let me go, and you all can leave town peacefully. No one will agree to testify against me anyway. You're wasting your time. I'll deal with Holt and the marshal when they return."

Wes said nothing. He returned to his desk and took a seat. He poured two fingers of whiskey into Danner's glass and pushed the cork back into the bottle. Payne swallowed the drink and pushed the bottle into the middle of the desk next to Danner's blood-stained boot.

"Help yourselves."

Wade picked up the bottle, pulled the cork, and took a swig before offering it to Case, who waved his hand and shook his head no. Wade returned the bottle to the desk and looked at Wes and Danner.

"You know, if they rush this jail, we're in trouble. I like the walls for cover, but they could burn us out pretty easy," Wade said.

"I don't think they'll risk killing their boss by burning this jail," Danner surmised. "I agree that all of us shouldn't be bottled up in here if the shootin' starts."

"This damn place does feel like a coffin," Case said.

"Now I know how those boys in the Alamo felt," Wade added with a chuckle.

Wes peeked out through a narrow slot between two boards he had nailed over the window next to his desk. "Dark out there. Must be after nine."

"Wade, maybe you and Case would be better off out there. You could slip out the back and find positions that could cover us in here," Wes suggested, looking at Danner.

Danner nodded in agreement. "I'll stay inside," Danner said, pointing at his bullet-punctured leg.

"Marshal Payne! Marshal Payne! It's Doc Carson!"

Case and Wade drew their guns and rushed to each front window. Wes blew out the lamp burning in the corner of the room. Danner's wounded leg slammed into the floorboards before he moved out of the middle of the room. Wes paused, letting the men get ready.

"Jackson, you keep where you are. Both barrels if somebody tries to come through that back door!" Wes ordered.

"Yes, sir!" Jackson called cocking back both hammers.

Wes quietly slipped the cross beam off its iron brackets and cracked the door open. He did not light the oil lamp hanging from the awning, so all he could see was the shadowy outline of a man standing in the street in front of the jail.

"Doc?"

"It's me. They've snatched Shelley! Let me in!"

"Come in!" Wes called, opening the door just enough for the physician to squeeze in.

"I'm sorry, gentlemen, but there were too many for me to keep 'em out."

"What happened, Doc?" Danner asked.

"Emily and I were changing Shelley's bandages when

several men rushed in and grabbed us. They said they were taking Shelley and for us not to try and stop them. They pushed us into a corner and kept guns on us while two men grabbed Shelley. She tried to resist, but she was too weak. Then they ran out."

"Knox's men?" Wes asked, knowing the answer.

"I don't know. I believe so because they took Shelley into Knox's saloon," Carson said, wiping sweat from his face with a white handkerchief he pulled from his vest pocket.

Wes looked at Danner. "Hostage."

"Looks like," Wes agreed.

"Doc, are you up to going over to Knox's saloon and finding out what they want?" Danner asked.

"Sure, I—"

"Payne! Danner! This is Erwin Colbert! We got your girl!" Knox's foreman shouted from the street.

"What do you want?" Wes answered.

"Simple. You give us Knox; we give you the girl!"

Damn it! "This is Danner! I'll come out unarmed. You can have me for the girl!"

"No deal, Danner! Knox for the girl! You got twenty minutes!" Colbert declared, then retreated to the Knox Saloon.

"He's gone," Case advised, having watched through a crack between the shutter and frame of the window he guarded.

Danner ran his fingers over the cactus thorns growing out of his square jaw. Everyone remained quiet for a moment before Danner spoke.

"Wade, you think you and Case can sneak out the back and circle around to the back of Knox's? They have a back door. I'm sure they have guards, but if they don't see you coming . . ."

"No problem," Wade answered.

"All right. Jackson will stay here and watch Knox. Wes, it

looks like you and I go through the front door unless you have a better idea," Danner stated.

"Nope. We'll keep them occupied while you two get in the back and find Shelley before they can harm her," Wes said, looking at Wade and Case.

Wes walked over to his desk and opened a drawer. He removed his third Colt, rotating the cylinder to ensure it had six loaded cartridges. He handed the pistol to Wade.

"When you get to Shelley, give her this. She may be able to help once the shootin' starts," Wes quipped with a grin.

"Doc, check inside Knox's saloon. See how many men he has in there and get back here as quick as you can," Danner ordered.

Carson slipped out the front door and vanished into the night. Case watched from his spot at the window.

Danner stepped around the wall and glared at a smiling Knox, who decided to sit on his bed and keep quiet.

"If they break in here, you give them Knox. Don't get yourself killed over this son of a bitch. Got that?" Danner ordered the former 'Buffalo Soldier' sergeant.

"Yes, sir," Jackson answered.

"Here comes Doc," Case announced, opening the door.

"They have men outside and inside. They wouldn't let me in, but I insisted on checking to make sure Shelley's bandages were all right. They let me in to look fast, then pushed me out. It looked like eight or ten inside and a few more outside."

"Let's go then," Danner said.

Jackson let Wade and Case out the back, then locked the door and set the crossbeam in place.

"Lock the door after us," Wes told Jackson, who nodded and followed the two gunslingers to the front door.

After they disappeared into the darkness, Jackson barred

the front door and turned off the gas lamp Wes had lit after Carson first arrived. Jackson felt his way to the chair in front of the jail cell and waited. He could hear Knox breathing but couldn't see the man responsible for what was about to happen.

CHAPTER 65

Saturday, 3 August 1878

LUXTON DANNER & WES PAYNE – KNOX SALOON

D anner and Wes stopped in front of the jail and looked around. The sky was chock full of clouds that hindered the moon's ability to light up the night. The sheer blackness of the night ate up the light from the burning lamps in front of the buildings. Danner saw three men standing guard on the boardwalk in front of Knox's saloon. They looked relaxed and indifferent to their assignment, more worried about rolling and lighting their cigarettes than an approaching threat.

"How do you want to handle this, partner?" Wes whispered to Danner.

"I figure we'll walk up and tell those jackasses that our man is bringing Knox, but we want to make sure Shelley is unharmed. Once we see that she is all right, we'll signal our man to come ahead with Knox. Then—"

"Got it," Wes answered.

The two gunslingers walked across the street and approached Knox's saloon.

"Hey, y'all in the saloon!" Wes shouted before he and Danner emerged from their cloak of darkness.

The three guards drew their guns and stared into the night's black wall. "Who's there?"

"It's Marshal Payne. I have Danner with me!"

"Step into the light and show yourselves!"

"Don't shoot! Our man is bringing Knox!" Wes shouted, then stepped into the glow of the oil lamps hanging in front of the saloon.

"We want to see the girl first," Danner said.

"Toss those guns before you come closer," a guard ordered.

Danner and Wes each grasped the grip of their guns with two fingers and gently pulled them from their holsters. Danner laid his on the step in front of the boardwalk with the grips toward the swinging doors. Wes did the same.

"You can see her through this window," a guard said, pointing to the big window on the right side of the doors.

Danner and Wes stepped up in between the guards and looked inside. Shelley was seated near the door at the back of the room. A single guard stood over her.

"Now!" Danner called as he rocked his right elbow back, smashing into the face of one guard.

Wes's right fist broke teeth, bone, and cartilage as it collided with another guard's face. Danner's massive right fist split the third guard's nose in half, sending the man's eyes rolling back in his head before he fell to the boardwalk with an enormous thud. Wes reached for the grips of his guns, tossing one of Danner's Schofields to him as he spun around to face the doors. Wes fired a shot into the overhang then dove under the doors, sliding into the saloon on his belly. *Boom!* The back door exploded off its hinges, crashing into Shelley's guard and knocking him to the floor. Wade and Case charged in, guns ready. *Crack! Crack! Crack!* Gunfire erupted. Bullets smashed into the swinging doors above Wes, blowing each off its hinges into the street. Shattering glass preceded Danner, who crashed through the big front window, firing both Schofields. Danner saw the bartender duck behind the bar as he rolled over, firing into the smoke-filled room. Wes spun around and fired. *Crack!* A Knox man went down in a heap. *Crack! Crack!* Wade's .45s found their mark knocking two men off their feet. Case pulled the extra Colt out of Wade's waistband and tossed it to Shelley before he rushed past, firing his pistol. Wes jumped to his feet and fired point-blank at another Knox man. *Crack!* The .45 hit the man in the gut, causing him to bend and fall face first onto the floor. *Crack! Crack!* Bullets splintered tables and chairs. Danner fell behind a table. Bullets exploded into the wood, one going through and zipping past his head. Danner lurched over the table and fired. *Crack!* Another Knox man stumbled and fell backward. *Boom!* A blast from a shotgun echoed off the walls. A dozen steel fireballs hit Wade in the back, catapulting him into the back wall of the saloon. *Crack!* A bullet from Shelley's Colt blew a hole in the bartender's head, knocking him into shelves of whiskey bottles and beer mugs. *Crack!* A bullet pierced Case's thigh, spinning him to the floor. He fired a wild shot into the ceiling before crashing into a whiskey barrel. *Crack!* Danner fired, punching a hole in another one of Knox's gunfighters. The last two of Knox's men dropped their guns and threw their hands up.

"I give up!" each man yelled as loud as they could.

The shooting ceased. The pungent odor of hot lead and gunpowder packed the room. Case propped himself up and tied a bandana around his leg. Danner stepped over to where Wade lay face down, his back a bloody mess. Danner leaned down just in case. Wade was dead.

"Danner?" Wes asked from across the room.

Danner stood and shook his head. He looked at Shelley, sitting on the floor, blood oozing through the white sling Doc Carson had secured over her left shoulder.

"You hit?" Danner asked the lady gunfighter.

She shook her head no. Footsteps hammered the boardwalk in front of the saloon. Wes spun with both guns ready.

"Don't shoot, Marshal! We're just seein' what happened!" a man shouted.

Doc Carson pushed past the blowhard and stepped into the saloon. He looked around. Dead men strewn in pools of splattered blood littered the floor. He looked at Wes, Danner, Case, and then Shelley. He saw Shelley was bleeding again from her wounded shoulder. He glanced back at Case, who used the bar to pull himself up onto his feet—another bloody leg.

"Weren't there four of you?" Carson asked.

"Wade is dead, Doc. He's over there in the corner," Danner reported grimly.

"Let me through, get out of the way!" Stoney Walsh ordered the spectators before bursting into the room.

"Everything all right at the Sundown?" Danner asked Canyon Creek's Deputy Marshal.

"Yes, sir. I stayed with Mrs. Brennen and her daughter like you ordered."

"Thanks," Danner said.

"Marshal, we got these three out here for ya," Albert Loman called into the saloon through the glassless window frame courtesy of Danner's plunge through it.

Bart Steen, the undertaker, poked his head through the empty window frame. "You need me, Marshal?"

"Yes, sir, Mr. Steen. There's six here and another behind the bar."

The man who had been guarding the back door when it knocked him senseless began to groan and move. Case bent down and took his gun from its holster.

"Looks like we got three prisoners here," Case said.

"Yep, and three more outside," Wes answered. "I'll get them over to the jail so they can visit their boss," Wes said.

"Wait," Danner demanded. He grabbed the two men who had surrendered inside the bar and threw each against the wall. "Who the hell are these men?" he demanded, waving his hand around the room.

"Every man here was a gunhand that Knox hired. Us and the ones you killed out at the ranch. The cowhands working Knox's cattle stayed out at the ranch. They didn't want any part of this," one of the prisoners explained.

"You mean wranglers weren't getting paid for this," Danner corrected the man.

"Right."

"There any more?" Danner asked.

"None that I know of."

Danner looked over at Doc Carson and Stoney Walsh. "Looks like you got your town back then. At least until Knox goes to trial."

CHAPTER 66

Thursday, 5 September 1878

LUXTON DANNER & WITNESSES – EN ROUTE TO CANYON CREEK

L ow-slung dark clouds churned above, reminiscent of a nest of cottonmouth snakes bubbling on the surface of a stagnant pond. Thunder rolled overhead and boomed in the distance. The ominous sky promised a forthcoming deluge, seemingly unsure of when it'd finally unleash its stormy ballast. The Randall stage twisted along the circuitous road, the hooves of its six-horse team plowing up its red dirt surface. The coach left a trail more redolent of a hoard of armadillos scrounging for food than a means of transport for the five witnesses returning from a three-day court trial in Oneida. Virgil Robertson and another Canyon Creek rancher whom Gilford Knox had browbeaten into selling his ranch accompanied Danner, Wes, and Shelley. A sixth witness, Johnny Jackson, opted to join a cattle outfit heading north, choosing to say his goodbyes in Oneida. The five passengers sat silently rocking with the dancing sway of the coach.

"Canyon Creek straight ahead!" Cletus Bradley called down through the dust-shrouded open windows. "And none too soon by the looks of those thunder-bangers up there!" Cletus chortled.

"How's that shoulder and side holding up?" Danner asked Shelley, whose constant wincing didn't elude the perceptive gunslinger.

"I thought it was good until this coach found every rut and hole in the road."

"From what we heard at the trial, someday we'll all be able to ride in the comfort of a rail car," Wes quipped.

Boisterous laughter from the group punctuated by a clap of thunder overhead followed Wes's remark.

"Too bad Knox won't own any of the land the railroad will travel through," Shelley chimed in.

"Not unless it takes another ten years to build," Wes added.

The stage turned to the right giving the passengers a late afternoon scenic view of Palo Duro Canyon's northern edge. Fiery reds and oranges fused with purple and brown hues along the crater's walls painted a glorious picture. A jagged bolt of white lightning shot down into the canyon's gaping jaws. Thunder exploded and shook the coach.

"There won't be any rail cutting through that," Danner mused.

An hour later, the coach came to a halt in front of Canyon Creek's stage office, where Elmer Barton opened the door for the weary passengers. They filed out through the coach's narrow entrance into the onset of large raindrops splattering into the dirt and splashing the wood-planked boardwalk.

"Might want to get indoors before the rain gets bad! I'll get your luggage over to the Sundown and boarding house right quick!" Barton assured his passengers, who didn't hesitate to heed the stage master's proposal.

The group quickly crossed Main Street, then hurried past the new tin shop and into the welcoming doors of the Sundown Hotel. Rachel skipped around the desk and offered hugs to everyone, holding Danner a bit longer.

"I've hot coffee and tea if everyone would like some."

Danner, Wes, and Shelley accepted. Virgil gently hugged his daughter, then announced he needed to return to the boarding house and inform Madeleine of the court proceedings. Virgil thanked Wes and Danner, shaking each gunslinger's hand before leaving the hotel. The other rancher followed Virgil's lead, thanking Wes, Danner, and Shelley before announcing he was anxious to get back to his family and share the good news that Judge Holt had ordered the return of his land. The trio took their seats in the back of the dining room where Danner had spent most of his stay in town. Rachel quickly arrived with a silver tray of coffee for Danner and Wes and tea for Shelley and herself. She set the tray down in the middle of the table and pulled up a chair next to Shelley.

"Rachel, is JD Case still in town?" Danner asked.

"I'm afraid not," JD said his hip healed enough, so he left town a couple of days ago," Rachel reported.

"Did he say where he was heading?" Wes beat Danner to the question.

"He said something about San Antonio, but I'm not sure."

"Well, I guess that's that," Danner muttered.

"Before you all tell me about the trial, there is a man here to see you, Shelley," Rachel announced.

"Oh? Did he say who he is?"

"He signed the register Arlo Wheeler, but that's all I know. He didn't say what his business was. He arrived yesterday from Stratford. He's here in Room #1," Rachel explained.

"What'd he look like?" Wes asked, glancing at Danner.

"Very well dressed in a brown suit and hat. He also spoke very well," Rachel answered. "Now tell me what happened in Oneida!"

Wes and Shelley looked at Danner, who set his cup of coffee down.

"Despite a couple of his men lying on the stand, Knox was found guilty of three counts of swindling mortgaged land, accessory to the theft of Loman's wagons, and the abduction of Shelley. He was fined for keeping a brothel and accessory to unlawful assembly. Judge Holt sentenced him to ten years in prison and five thousand dollars in fines. Shelley got her family's ranch back, so did the other rancher that went with us," Danner reported. "Judge Holt said there wasn't enough evidence to convict him of rustling or burning the livery stable."

"What about all the land he owns around here?" Rachel asked.

"He keeps the land he bought legally, including the Coleman place, unless he sells. He claimed his father would send someone to manage his property," Danner advised.

Emily Carson and two other ladies came into the room.

"We should start getting dinner ready," Emily reminded Rachel, who nodded in approval.

"What are you going to do now, Lux?" Rachel asked, her gaze focused on the table's polished surface.

Before Danner could answer, the man looking for Shelley came down the stairs and entered the dining room. He approached the only occupied table in the room and looked at Shelley.

"Miss Michelle Robertson, I presume?"

"Yes, sir."

"I'm Arlo Wheeler. I'm a detective with the Pinkerton

Detective Agency. May I have a word with you?" he asked, removing his hat.

"Sure," Shelley answered. "This is Luxton Danner, Wes Payne and I understand you've already met Rachel," Shelley added.

"Good afternoon, everyone."

Wes, Danner, and Rachel stood to leave. Shelley held up her hand. "Please stay," she said.

"I'd better get into the kitchen. I'll see you later, dear," Rachel said to Shelley before excusing herself and disappearing through the kitchen door.

"I need to check on Deputy Walsh down at the jail," Wes insisted before quickly leaving the room.

"Please stay," Shelley asked Danner before he could formulate an excuse.

"Is it all right with you, Mr. Wheeler?" Danner asked.

"Certainly," Wheeler advised, taking a seat next to Shelley.

"I'll get right to business. Are you familiar with the Pinkerton Agency, Miss Robertson?" Wheeler asked, propping his elbows on the table, and leaning forward.

"Not really. Y'all work for the railroads or something?"

"Well, not just the railroad companies, although they appear to be our primary employers now. Alan Pinkerton started the agency many years ago to help law enforcement officers hunt down outlaws and such. The United States Department of Justice now employs us to investigate federal crimes. Mr. Pinkerton believes that the agency needs good people, including women like yourself. That is why I'm here in Canyon Creek. You see, news of the events from last month and the trial in Oneida travel faster than you might expect. I was in Oneida and attended the first day of Mr. Knox's trial. I was impressed with your abilities on the stand. I immediately came here and asked about you around town. You appear to be quite respected by those who know you, especially Mrs. Brennen," Wheeler explained.

"Rachel said she didn't know why you were here looking for me."

"Yes. Don't blame Mrs. Brennen for that. I requested that she not reveal my intentions until I could speak with you," Wheeler admitted. "I would like to offer you a job with the agency, and I do hope you'll consider it."

"Me? A Pinkerton Detective?" Shelley asked with a chuckle, looking over at Danner.

"If I may offer an opinion?" Danner asked with a pause.

"By all means, Mr. Danner, your opinion would be most welcome."

"I don't think you'd find a better woman for the job. She's smart, tough, and can handle a pistol when she needs to. I think you should consider the offer, Miss Robertson," Danner added with a smile before excusing himself and heading for the kitchen and another difficult talk with Rachel.

CHAPTER 67

Sunday, 8 September 1878

LUXTON DANNER, RACHEL BRENNEN, WES PAYNE & SHELLEY ROBERTSON – SUNDOWN HOTEL

Danner thrashed his razor in the water, turning his washbowl into a soapy mess. He dried his face and looked in the mirror. Since the Knox Saloon shootout, his self-examination had become an all too frequent practice these last few weeks. He looked closely at the lines around his eyes and the scar in the middle of his forehead. He knew he wasn't getting any younger, but he had not been able to convince himself to settle down in Canyon Creek or anywhere else, for that matter. His decision had initially brought a tear to Rachel's eyes, but she had time to allow his choice to sink in. He stepped over to the window he opened an hour earlier and peered out into a dull, cloudy morning. The impending storm from two days ago had never materialized, but the low-hanging gray clouds continued to loiter above. They had brought a preferred cool gentle breeze over the oppressive heat of the Texas sun this time of year. He dressed in a clean dark blue bib shirt he had purchased from Loman's store, part of the supplies recovered from Loman's two stolen wagons found on Knox's ranch. He strapped on his gun belt and looked at the bulging saddlebags hanging from the bedpost. Leaving Canyon Creek today wasn't going to be as easy as he had thought.

Danner descended the Sundown's oak staircase with his saddlebags slung over his shoulder and rifle in hand. He looked for Rachel at the desk when he reached the bottom but found it vacant. He stepped around the corner and glanced into the dining room. Rachel, Wes, Shelley, and Stoney Walsh were already seated at his customary table against the back wall. Their quiet conversation stopped when he entered the room. He set his rifle and saddlebags down and joined the group.

"I didn't realize I was so late this morning," Danner said, taking his seat.

"You're not late. It's not even seven o'clock yet," Rachel advised with a smile Danner hadn't anticipated.

Danner looked around the table. "It seems everyone knows something I don't," Danner offered before leaning back in his chair and reaching for the coffeepot. "Did something happen after we parted last night?" he asked, filling his cup with hot black coffee.

"The mail came in on the late stage last night. Mr. Barton brought this over to me early this morning," Wes announced, handing an opened envelope containing a letter to his partner.

Danner paused and examined the envelope. It was from Richard B. Hubbard, Governor of Texas, addressed to Wes Payne and Luxton Danner, care of Canyon Creek, Texas. Danner scrunched his brow and narrowed his eyes, then looked around the table a second time before removing the neatly folded paper from the envelope. He unfolded the document and began to read, then stopped. He looked at Wes.

"You've already read this, I assume?"

"I did. I've only told everyone who it was from, not what it says. I thought it best if you read it out loud. There are a few words in there I don't know," Wes said, grinning.

Danner brought his attention back to the letter. He read it aloud:

Dear Mr. Payne and Mr. Danner,

Your actions along our state's northern border, specifically the towns of Range, Red River City, and Canyon Creek, were brought to my attention. After discussions with Texas Rangers and the United States Marshal's Office, I believe the two of you may be just what Texas requires regarding our current crisis with Mexico along our southern border. Therefore, I request your presence at the capitol building here in Austin as soon as possible. Mind you, this is not an order, as I have no authority to force your acceptance, but a formal request for assistance in the best interests of Texas and the United States. Please provide your response through any means available as soon as you are able."

Sincerely,
Richard B. Hubbard, Governor
State of Texas

"What the hell is going on along the Mexican border?" Danner asked aloud.

"No idea, partner, but it sounds mighty interesting," Wes answered with a chuckle.

"Sounds dangerous to me." Rachel sighed.

"Sounds exciting to me. I wish I could go with you!" Shelley added.

Return to Canyon Creek

"Oh?" Danner responded.

"Since my father hired a couple of men to help him run his ranch, I decided to accept Mr. Wheeler's offer to join the Pinkertons," Shelley announced.

"Oh my!" Rachel exclaimed.

"Congratulations, kid!" Wes offered.

Danner smiled and nodded his head in approval. "They'll do well to have you," he added.

"Will you still leave today?" Rachel asked.

Danner looked at Wes and nodded. "I figure we shouldn't keep the governor waiting," he said.

"Nope. I reckon not!" Wes agreed. "Walsh here has already agreed to stay on as marshal until the town finds somebody permanent. He's already ordered the girls out of Knox's bordello," Wes reported with a laugh.

"I told 'em they could do their business someplace else, but not in town," Walsh announced with pride.

"Any word on Knox's other businesses in town?" Walsh asked.

"Albert Loman said he talked to the man running Knox's store. Now that Knox is gone, there's no more supply train, so he said he would sell what he had to Loman and leave town. The hotel never did open, and his saloon will close up with Knox's men all but gone. I hadn't heard about the mill, livery, or lumberyard," Wes reported.

"Can I bring you breakfast before y'all leave?" Rachel asked.

"I don't care what he says," Wes declared, nodding toward Danner. I'd be mighty obliged, Rachel," Wes added.

"Me too," Shelley added.

Danner smiled and nodded.

Halfway through their bacon, eggs, and biscuits, Carl Kincaid, Clay Cox, and Dale Morgan walked into the dining room with a group of townsfolk and proceeded directly to the gunslingers' table.

"Sorry to intrude, but we couldn't let you all leave without thanking you for everything you did," Kincaid announced.

"That's for sure. We would've lost our town for certain," Morgan chimed in.

"Good to see you back up and around Clay," Shelley said, carefully hugging her former neighbor.

"Damned glad myself," Cox answered with a grin. "I heard you're a Pinkerton detective."

"Yep. Looks that way," Shelley affirmed.

"It won't be the same around here without you," Kincaid said to Shelley, with Morgan and Cox both nodding in agreement.

"Well, we'll be on our way, just had to pay our respects," Kincaid announced before the three men turned and quickly departed.

"I sure hope they can keep their town once Knox's old man gets here," Wes muttered.

After breakfast, Wes followed Walsh back to the jail to collect his gear. Shelley met with Wheeler to schedule their departure, and Danner found himself in the kitchen immersed in an embrace with Rachel that'd make a bear proud.

"No tears and no goodbyes," Danner told the beautiful hotel owner.

"No. Just until we meet again as we agreed," Rachel said softly, her face buried in Danner's new blue shirt. "You be careful doing whatever the governor wants and take care of that leg."

Danner said nothing, just leaned down and allowed Rachel's soft, warm kiss to penetrate his lips. He paused and smiled. A smile Rachel knew was genuine. He then gathered up his rifle and saddlebags and walked out of the Sundown into Canyon

Creek's bustling Main Street. He strapped his bags to Bullet, then slid his left boot into the stirrup and swung his damaged right leg up over the saddle. Wes was mounted and riding toward him from the jail.

"How's that new horse?" Danner asked.

"He's young but shows a lot of spirit. I sure do miss Ringo, though."

The two gunslingers tapped their spurs and headed down the street past the Creekbed, where Dakota smiled and flashed a wave. They rode past Betsy Tyler's boarding house where she and Stoney Walsh did the same, and then finally the stage office where Cletus Bradley was cussing while preparing for the departure of the Randall stage. They rode out of town without looking back, knowing no good would come of that.

"How long you figure it'll take us to get to Austin?" Danner asked after thirty or so minutes of silence.

"Oh, I reckon it'll be about ten days. We can catch a train part of the way," Wes surmised. "We can send a wire once we get to Oneida. Don't want to keep Governor Hubbard guessing," Wes added.

"Nope. Sure don't. The best interests of Texas and the United States are at stake!" Danner quipped.

"We better get goin' then!" Wes laughed, prodding his new horse into a gallop.

I figure we better. Danner snapped Bullet into a gallop down the long road into the unknown.

ACKNOWLEDGMENTS

Thanking the people and organizations that have helped me throughout my storytelling adventures ...

To my wife, Elizabeth, who continues to support and inspire me, offering important feedback throughout the creative process.

To my daughter and biggest fan, Rachel, who has elevated my public relations and marketing footprint in the industry.

To Janet Fix, whose literary production and editing expertise have guided me toward a new path in my writing voyage, and to everyone affiliated with her publishing company, *thewordverve*, for their expert participation in the creation of this book.

To Christine Baker, to whom this book is dedicated. I would not be where I am today without her encouragement and confidence in my abilities.

To my family, friends, and supporters who continue to motivate me.

And, of course, to the ever-expanding membership in the John Layne posse.

ABOUT THE AUTHOR

John Layne is an international, award-winning Historical Western and Contemporary Mystery Fiction author, screen-writer, and actor. A screenplay adaptation of his second novel, *Red River Reunion*, is currently under consideration for production. He is a member of The Authors Guild, Western Writers of America, Writers League of Texas, Wyoming Writers Inc., and the Oklahoma Writers Federation.

Stay current with news about John's books, movies, and events at **www.johnlaynefiction.com** as well as these sites:

Instagram:
https://www.instagram.com/johnlayne.entertainment

Facebook:
https://www.facebook.com/johnlaynefictionbooks

IMDb:
https://www.imdb.com/name/nm13445965/

BOOKS BY JOHN LAYNE

John Garrison Mysteries

A Rude Reception, book 1

Luxton Danner Western Series

Gunslingers: A Story of the Old West, book 1
Red River Reunion, book 2
Return to Canyon Creek, book 3

www.ingramcontent.com/pod-product-compliance
Lightning Source LLC
Chambersburg PA
CBHW021227190726
48289CB00005B/1206